"Now may I speak to you of my feelings?"

"Oh yes ... please!" she said softly.

He groaned and snatched her up into his arms and kissed her firmly, as though his feelings, too long held in check, had broken through like a dam bursting.

"Hester, my darling, please say that you love me; I have waited so long to hear it."

"Oh, I do love you, I do. But I must protest you have not waited so long. We met barely two weeks ago...."

Other Fawcett Books
by Norma Lee Clark:

KITTY QUINN

THE TYNEDALE DAUGHTERS

HESTER

by

Norma Lee Clark

FAWCETT CREST • NEW YORK

To Connie Clausen

A Fawcett Crest Book

Published by Ballantine Books

Copyright © 1978 by Norma Lee Clark

ISBN 0-449-21143-6

Manufactured in the United States of America

First Fawcett Crest Edition: November 1978
First Ballantine Books Edition: August 1986

I

MISS HESTER WYCKHAM crossed the drawing room and gave the bell pull a firm, no-nonsense tug. She then turned to her brother-in-law, Lord Geoffrey Hallam.

"Geoffrey, I wish you will stop pacing about and hemming and hawing and tell me what is wrong."

"Wha . . . wha . . .? Pooh, nonsense, H-h-hester. Nothing wrong in the world. 'Pon my soul, you mistake me."

"Ah, you may be right. But my remembrance is that when you are perturbed you stammer just the least bit. And you have definitely stammered several times. Now, stop being such a ninnyhammer and tell me. Is it Julie? Is she . . . ?"

The drawing room door opened to admit the solemn-faced butler of the Wyckham household. He placed a tray quietly on a side table, then, with a bow, withdrew.

"Damned spooky fellow, that. Does he ever speak?"

Hester laughed and crossed to the table to pour a glass of madeira for Geoffrey.

"Don't try to change the subject, sir. Here, take your wine and sit down and tell me all."

"I really don't know what you're on about, Hester. There's nothing to tell. I mean to say . . . well, actually, the thing is . . . "

"There, you see? You're at it again . . . hemming and hawing. Out with it!"

"Dash it all, H-h-hester, I merely came to extend Julie's invitation. She thought you might like to come down and stay with us for a spell. Poor child gets lonely sometimes. Lovely neighbors and all that, and plenty of routs and evening parties and such like, but . . . "

"Why, Geoffrey, I should like it of all things. It seems an age since I've had a good long coze with Julie. But I must protest, sir, at hearing her called a 'poor child.' She may be delicate-looking, but she's four and twenty now and an old married lady of five years. And, since I know your income is even greater than Papa's, not to speak of her own money, neither can she be called poor."

"Well, the thing is, you see, she's not been quite the thing lately. Says there's nothing wrong, but seems mopish to me. Thought it might cheer her up to have someone to go about with."

Hester gave him a shrewd look. "So it was your idea and not Julie's?"

"Not a bit of it! No sooner told her I might be coming

this way on my way back from London than she was all in a taking that I must bring you back with me. Will you come?"

"I must speak to Papa, of course, but you may depend on it; he will be happy to have me gone for a while. He says I'm too bossy by half. He's deep into his Roman history. All note-taking, I doubt he'll ever get into the writing of it. But it keeps him busy, so I mustn't complain."

"Capital! Have your abigail pack your boxes and we'll be off first crack tomorrow. Like to get home before dinner. Promised Julie I'd do it."

When Hester climbed into her bed that night it was with the comfortable feeling that everything was in hand for an early departure. Moreton, her personal maid, delighted with the prospect of a trip, had spent the afternoon packing the cases. All were now ready to be carried downstairs in the morning. Hester had conferred with the cook and the housekeeper on domestic problems that might arise during the next few weeks. Both ladies being highly competent, Hester felt no qualms about leaving her father to their ministrations.

But in spite of this virtuous feeling of much work well done, a niggling uneasiness persisted in making itself felt. She explored it delicately. It was not Papa nor the house. Nor could it be her wardrobe. For in spite of her forthright, practical attitude in dealing with the world, Hester followed the fashions eagerly. Not being hampered by any lack of funds, she was possessed of all she could want in the way of gowns and bonnets for every occasion.

She felt that what she called her "plainness" was less

apparent when clothed in gowns featuring cut and fabric rather than ruffles and furbelows. In this she was right, for her taste could not be faulted. But in the matter of her appearance, she was definitely not plain. All compliments from family or friends upon her looks were dealt with brusquely and forgotten immediately. This blindness on her part was the result of growing up in the shadow of a quite startlingly beautiful older sister.

Her earliest memory of Julie had been one of awe, not only because she was the elder but also for her fairy-like loveliness. Julie had always seemed a figment of the imagination with her delicate, tiny figure and silver-gilt hair. Enormous blue eyes and a sensitive, gentle disposition complemented the rest. Though she was five years younger than Julie. Hester had quickly out-stripped her in size, and from early childhood had adopted the protective attitude usually associated with an older sister.

Hester was not unusually tall, and was willow-slim, but compared to Julie she seemed sturdy. This impression came mostly from Hester's calm, practical good sense, and her ability to handle most situations with a minimum of fuss. The early death of their mother had left Hester more or less in charge of the household, the place which would normally have gone to Julie. But though Julie was seventeen and Hester but twelve at the time, it was to Hester that everyone, including her Papa, had turned for decisions and comfort. Her strength had supported Julie through her paroxysms of grief over her mother's death, and two years later through the flutterings of tears and joy occasioned by several infatuations and finally by the steady love she discovered for her dear Geoffrey—as unlikely a candidate as could be found. He was well-favored enough, but large and burly, and almost inarticulate. Since most of Julie's flirts had been rather pale and poetic-looking, her choice of Geoffrey had come as something of a shock to her family. But it had turned out to be a most sincere attachment, Julie evidently finding a secure refuge in being anchored to his solidity. The astonishment of her family was as nothing, however, compared to his own. And after five years his astonishment and adoration remained. He treated her as a rare piece of porcelain, denied her nothing, and altogether doted on her.

Reviewing her wardrobe—to be sure she had included suitable clothing for whatever entertainments Julie might have in store for her—had brought her thoughts to Julie herself. And again she experienced that small uneasiness. Could it be something with Julie? Surely it was Geoffrey's unspoken uneasiness that had set off her own. Now, what could he be worried about? She could not imagine Julie's behaving in any way that was not proper, and certainly, although very sensitive, she was not given to displays of temper or moping. But "mopish," Geoffrey had said. But then Geoffrey, unused to expressing himself aloud, sometimes meant something quite other than the words he used. Ah well, she would soon see Julie for herself and no doubt could easily sort things out. On this optimistic note she fell asleep.

Her first glimpse of Julie the next day, as the carriage rolled to a stop before the gracious portico of Geoffrey's family home, certainly belied the term

Geoffrey had applied to her. She flew out the door and down the steps, in a flurry of pale blue muslin, trailing a Norwich silk shawl, with what seemed a river of honey-colored spaniels barking at her heels. The flaxen curls haloing her face seemed almost white in the bright June sunshine, and again, as always, Hester gasped with wonder. But she was given no time for thought. Julie launched herself into Hester's arms, laughing and talking excitedly, while the dogs leaped upon both of them, barking wildly and tangling themselves in the fringes of Julie's shawl.

"Oh, Hester, dearest sister, how I have longed to see you. What absolute ages it has been! Why do you not come more often? I've ever so many things to tell you and you're just in time for the Litheys' party next week. Oh, it's going to be such fun to see their eyes pop when I introduce my baby sister."

She paused to take a breath. Hester had to laugh at this tumbled speech as she hugged her sister and marveled at the happiness shining in her blue eyes.

"Now, poppet, still as flyaway as ever," she said, and taking charge as usual she firmly ordered the dogs to be quiet. Recognizing authority when they heard it, they immediately backed away and sat down, grinning up at her with their tongues lolling out, perfectly willing to rest for a moment and await the next scene.

"Now, Julie, let me look at you. Really, my love, you haven't changed at all. Still tangled curls and ribbands coming untied and losing your shawl. And I saw you not above three months ago in London. Surely you cannot think I'm such a goose as to come barging down upon you before you had quite settled in here?"

Julie, till recently, had spent most of her married

life in London with her husband during the season, and at their house in Bath during the summer. Though Geoffrey had brought her on brief visits to his country estates, he had never till now actually wanted to live in the country. Raised by a guardian most of his life, and kept immured in the country safely out of that gentleman's hair, Geoffrey had fled to the city as soon as he had come into his estate. Julie had been content to be there also. But several seasons of being quite the most popular and beautiful young wife in London seemed finally to have palled. When she had suggested to Geoffrey that they try country life he had agreed immediately. Though he had loathed it before, he felt quite sure that anywhere with Julie would be wonderful. And now he had discovered quite a love for the country, riding around his estates, conferring with his tenants, and entertaining and being entertained by his neighbors.

"If I may make so bold, could not I be greeted by my wife?" Geoffrey interrupted.

"Oh, Geoffrey, my love, please forgive me," and Julie flung herself into his arms just as enthusiastically. "You understand, dearest husband, how I have longed to see Hester. Indeed, I quite forgot myself with happiness. We're going to have such fine times, you know, now that Hester's here. Such a romp, Geoffrey! You know that Hester and I get along quite famously."

"Yes, yes, little one. But take her inside, take her inside. Let us not all stand around in the drive. I'm off to the stables to see Barnaby about the new mare. I will join you later."

Linking arms with Hester, Julie half pulled her up the steps, talking excitedly the while. Moreton was

taken in hand by the housekeeper and Julie's personal
maid, who fussed over her and helped direct the footman about the luggage.

Julie led Hester through the large oval reception
hall and threw open the drawing room doors, then
spun around, flinging her arms around Hester again in
a fierce hug.

"Oh, Hester, I *am* so happy to have you here. And
your gown! Exquisite, my love, did you design it yourself? Never tell me that Miss Bumbry did it."

Hester laughed. "No, no, of course not. I took it
from a French design—with a few alterations, of
course. But Miss Bumbry executed it quite well, I
think." Then looking around, "This room is lovely,
Julie. You've made it quite your own, I see. It must
have cost the earth!"

"Yes, I believe it did," said Julie proudly. "Geoffrey
never tells me those things. About money and such.
But I don't believe he minds, you know. He has lots."

Hester's mouth twitched with a suppressed smile.
"Yes, he has. And I'm sure he would deny you nothing."

Julie blue eyes glowed. "Oh, he quite spoils me.
Everything . . ." She broke off abruptly and the glow
dimmed.

"Yes, little one. Go on."

Julie, who had turned away indecisively, now turned
back and, only a trifle forced, smiled gaily again.

"Nothing, only silliness. Come, dear one, let me
show you my lovely home. And oh, your room, Hester.
I've made it so beautiful for you. Let me show you
some of these rooms, and then we'll go up."

Hester, nothing loath, rose. "I'm sure I must look

all to pieces. I hope I'll have time for a bath before dinner."

"Of course, you will. I've had the water heating this last hour. Come along now."

Accompanied by the three spaniels, they went through the beautiful dining room, large enough to serve thirty people, through the smaller breakfast room with french windows overlooking a broad sweep of terrace and a rose garden below, frothing with blossoms. There were several salons, Julie's morning room, Geoffrey's library, and a ballroom, dim and shrouded.

When finally they reached Hester's room, she was more than ready for her bath. As Julie swept ahead of her and flung open the door, Hester stopped and gasped involuntarily. The room, filled with sunlight and warm, scented June air, was a vision in yellow and white, dominated by the huge, canopied bed, swagged in sheer white gauze and fluffy with ruffles. The priceless Chinese carpet was delicately figured in white, pale yellow, and gold, with traces here and there of blue. Near the windows a golden chaise invited one to linger and drink in the view out the long windows, whose sheer draperies billowed in the gentle breeze.

"Oh, Julie! Thank you!" Hester turned and hugged Julie to her and kissed her.

"You're welcome, my darling sister, in every way. Now, I see Moreton has all ready for you, so I'll slip away and leave you to rest. No need to be too grand for dinner tonight. Just a small party. Friends of Geoffrey's. You'll like them all enormously." And with that she threw a kiss and skipped away.

Moreton advanced upon Hester and began to divest her of her traveling dress. "Now, my lady, you're to have your bath and put on your wrapper and lie yourself down on your bed. All is ready, and I've laid out your blue Indian mull for dinner. Just the thing for a small party, I think."

Hester submitted gratefully to Moreton's services and, later, soothed by the warm, scented water of her bath and drowsily content on the soft bed, she allowed her mind to wander lazily over the events of the past hours. Julie's radiance and the look on Geoffrey's face as he watched her, the lovely home Julie had made from the neglected, old-fashioned country mansion, and, inevitably, though she had been pushing the thought away, to the tiny slip on Julie's part in the drawing room. "Everything . . ." and then the full stop. What had she been going to say? The tone of her voice seemed to imply a "but" after that single word. Everything but . . . what? What could Julie possibly want that she didn't have? She obviously had all the material things, and certainly the extravagant adoration of her large, bumbling husband, just as she obviously still adored him. Her mind nagged at the problem gently, like a tongue probing a sore tooth, but with no answer forthcoming. Ah well, she thought, I will soon know. Julie's simplicity and innocence made it impossible for her to hide anything. There was never any duplicity in Julie, all feelings being quite obvious on her expressive face and trustingly confided to those she loved.

II

THOUGH HESTER appeared to be staring straight into her own eyes as she sat at her dressing table, she actually did not see her own face in the mirror. Practically the only time she allowed herself the luxury of an idle mind was when Moreton brushed her hair, as she was now doing.

Had she actually been looking at her own face, she would have noticed that she was uncommonly pretty tonight. Her eyes, a much deeper blue than Julie's, were clear and sparkling and were matched perfectly by the dark blue of the Indian mull. Her complexion was as flawless as Julie's. Her eyes refocused as Moreton, having brushed Hester's hair till it shone, began to arrange it in the fashion that suited Hester best— pulled sleekly back and set in a waterfall of curls. Only Moreton seemed able to make Hester's hair behave in this way, for it was as uncompromisingly straight as Julie's was curly, and a satiny brown in contrast to Julie's silver-gilt.

As Moreton finished by tucking a tiny bunch of blue forget-me-nots into each side of the waterfall and stood back to survey her handiwork, Hester exclaimed appreciatively, "Oh, well done, Moreton, I like it exceedingly. You are so clever."

"You do look ravishing, my lady, if I do say it."

"Why, Moreton! *Ravishing*? Coming it much too strong, my girl. You know I'm never taken in by your nonsense."

"Not nonsense in the least. You know perfectly well by now, Miss Hester, that I'm a plain-spoken woman. I say only what is there for all to see."

"Well, and I thank you, dear Moreton, if not for clear sight, at least for loyalty. Now if you said Julie was ravishing I might agree."

"Well, and so she is in her own way. Quite different, of course, and I won't deny that she is uncommonly pretty, but you are . . . are . . ."

"Commonly pretty?" teased Hester.

"Certainly not . . . that is . . . now, Miss Hester, you're getting me all flustered the way you twist my words. You're certainly not common looking . . . nor pretty neither . . . you're . . ."

"An antidote?"

"Miss Hester! What a thing to say. As if I would want to be lady's maid to an antidote. I took you straight out of the schoolroom and I've never had cause to be less than proud. Now, you can stop trying to send me up, my lady, and stand up and let me pull your skirt straight. The dinner bell has gone already, and you don't want to be late."

"Oh, my goodness, quickly Moreton, hand me my fan and reticule . . . and please don't feel you must wait up for me. You must be tired after the trip," she called as she rushed out the door and down the hall.

She stopped as she reached the top of the stairs to catch her breath, and descended the wide sweep into the hall with as much dignity as she could muster. The butler watched her progress with an approving eye, and turning to the drawing room door flung it open for her and announced, "Miss Wyckham," in ringing tones. Hester blushed as every head turned to her. Julie floated across the room and took her hands.

"Oh, my dear, you look lovely. Now do come meet everyone. They are all agog to be presented to you."

So saying, Julie led her forward proudly to a formidable looking lady seated by the fire. "Lady Breckinridge, allow me to present my dear little sister, Miss Wyckham, to you."

Lady Breckinridge raised her lorgnette and gazed at Hester unnervingly for a long moment. Hester could hardly blame her for her look of disbelief. To be presented as Julie's "little" sister had this effect on people. And well it might, since Julie was a least a head shorter than Hester, and certainly looked the younger.

" 'Struth, Julie, my dear, I think you would be better advised to introduce her as your 'younger' sister, though even that . . . well, never mind. Pleasure, I'm sure, Miss Wyckham, we're very happy to welcome you to Littlecomb. I do hope you will be making a long stay. There are many happy events planned for the next few weeks."

"Thank you, Lady Breckinridge, you're very kind."

Hester was then introduced to a bewildering array
of extremely pleasant people. There was Lord Breckinridge, a wispy, red-faced gentleman, who blew out
his mustaches and made several incomprehensible,
though definitely approving, noises. Then the Honorable Susan Breckinridge, who unfortunately combined
the plain features of her father with the stoutness of
her mother.

There was the charming Lithey family. Mother and
father, both pleasant and fashionably dressed, and their
three pretty daughters, all giggling and madcap-
looking, and obviously the delight of their fond parents.
However, they were prettily behaved girls and welcomed Hester charmingly, rhapsodizing over her gown
and hair style and fan.

"Oh, Caro, only see—the clever way the train is cut
to fall so beautifully."

"Your hair, Miss Wyckham, enchanting . . . we
can never teach our Annie to do anything at all
different. Do see, Beth."

They twittered and chirped and danced around her
till Hester felt quite dizzy. She looked around for help
and met the twinkling eyes of a gentleman who had not
yet been introduced. He was standing with Julie and
Geoffrey and now leaned over to Julie and said something. Julie turned around, caught Hester's desperate
look, and came to her rescue, bringing with her the
merry-eyed gentleman.

"Hester, you must let me present Mr. Boscroft to
you. He was kind enough to remind me of my duties.
Dear girls, you are neglecting those young men I
invited especially for you. See . . . they're all looking
this way so wistfully. You must come and entertain

them at once." She whisked them across the room with all the expertise of a matron in her forties. Hester watched her in amazement. "Well done, little sister," she silently applauded. She turned to Mr. Boscroft. "How do you do, sir. You will forgive me for standing here gape-mouthed. I cannot help it. You see, I am used to taking charge, and to see my sister doing it so masterfully leaves me breathless with admiration."

"Ah, you have not been so much in your sister's company recently. We here at Littlecomb are quite used to it. I collect this is your first visit?"

"You are right, Mr. Boscroft. It is my first visit here. I used to spend some time with Julie in her London home. I cannot but think that being mistress of a manor in the country has been beneficial. Not that there was ever a want of conduct in Julie, she had always pretty manners. But she was very young, and so shy. But now she has address *and* beauty!"

"Certainly not the only beauty in her family, Miss Wyckham."

Hester looked at him sharply. She was not much given to mild flirtations, considering them missish and a waste of time. But he was smiling at her so pleasantly that she felt it would be rag-mannered to give him a setdown within five minutes of meeting him. She changed the subject.

"Do you live here also, Mr. Boscroft?"

"Yes, not twenty minutes away, so we shall be seeing a great deal of each other, I promise you. Do you ride, Miss Wyckham?"

"Yes, I love it. Are there good rides in the neighborhood?"

"Very pleasant ones, I do assure you. You will
allow me to ride with you, I hope?"

"With pleasure, Mr. Boscroft."

"Shall we say at ten in the morning?"

She laughed, realizing she had been led very cleverly
into this. "I thank you, sir, but I think not on my first
morning. I haven't seen Julie in an age, and you know
how sisters are. They must have a good long talk
together."

"I'm afraid I don't know, Miss Wyckham. My own
sisters were ever at odds over everything imaginable.
You are fortunate in your relative, and so is she."

"Yes, I am well aware of it," said Hester, looking
across at Julie, radiant in primrose silk, more daringly
low-cut now that she was a matron, with tiny puffed
sleeves, and tied under the bosom with deep gold
ribbons whose streamers fell to the floor. Delicate
diamond drop earrings threw sparkles of light over
her face, and she smiled bewitchingly up at a tall,
rather hawk-faced man who loomed over her . . .
possessively?

Hester caught herself up immediately. What on
earth was she doing, starting a hare like that? She
wondered who the man could be. She was quite sure
she had not met him, it was not a face one could forget so easily. Could it be one of the young men
invited for the Lithey girls? She turned to find Mr.
Boscroft watching her quizzically and flushed.

"Oh, forgive me, Mr. Boscroft, I find looking at
Julie often sends me into a daze. Even after all these
years I find her amazing to behold."

"Ah, just so, Miss Wyckham," he answered solemnly.

"No, really, I . . ." she spluttered to a halt and glanced up at him. His eyes were twinkling at her.

"Are you sending me up, Mr. Boscroft?"

"Oh, never, madam. But just for a moment there, it seemed to me more curiosity than amazement showing in your eyes."

She laughed. "Well, then, you are right. I was wondering who that man could be, for I'm sure we were not introduced."

"That, Miss Wyckham, is our local 'catch.' Rich as Croesus, unmarried, and wined and dined by every matron in the vicinity with an unmarried daughter. And the daughters swoon when he deigns to turn that brooding glance on any of them. If he stands up to dance with a girl more than once, the gossips have them engaged before midday."

"Yes, but who is he?"

"Why, Lord Markham, to be sure."

"Well, other than his money, of course, I can't think why he should be so doted upon by all the mamas. He certainly cannot claim to be out of the ordinary as far as looks are concerned. In fact, he is quite forbidding looking."

"Ah, but that is what ladies most admire. It puts them in mind of the heroes of their romances, don't you see?"

"Romances? Pooh, I care nothing for that sort of reading, any more than I enjoy fairy tales, now that I'm grown up."

"And speaking with the weight of your many years, what would you advise as suitable reading for young ladies?"

"I always recommend a course of sermons first to

elevate the minds of the young, then a careful selection of volumes of an historical nature for self-improvement and reflection," she said gravely.

"No doubt you speak from personal experience, Miss Wyckham?"

"No doubt."

They looked each other in the eye, daring the other to laugh. He gave in first and she joined in, enjoying laughing with him and liking him better than she had at first when it seemed he would turn out to be one of those smarmy complimenters, forever flirting.

"We insist on knowing the joke, sister," Julie put her arm through Hester's. Behind her was Lord Markham.

"The merest trifle, Lady Hallam," said Mr. Boscroft, "and now, sadly, I must go make my bow to Lady Breckinridge who is giving me reproachful looks. She is an incurable flirt, you know," and with this outrageous assertion he moved away.

"Hester, you must let me present to you Lord Markham, our neighbor."

Hester gave him her hand, and after looking intently into her eyes for a moment, he bent to kiss it lightly. His hand felt warm and his lips on her hand were almost burning. Hester, strangely flustered, withdrew her hand perhaps too hastily, causing him to bend upon her again that intent look, this time questioningly.

Hester took herself firmly in hand, wondering at her reaction. This kind of missish behavior was foreign to her nature. Though she was but nineteen, she had been out for two years, and behind this was what seemed a lifetime of being in charge. She had had many beaux, being blessed with a handsome dowry and what she characterized as "healthy" good looks, and had learned to deal with suitors with good common sense. She now refused to allow herself to blush and behave like a ninnyhammer.

"How do you do, Lord Markham. Julie is lucky, indeed, to have so many good neighbors," she said as coolly as possible.

"Also lucky in her choice of sisters," returned Lord Markham.

"Oh, no, Lord Markham, I cannot allow that. It was not luck, but good sense on my part. I chose Hester especially, and I congratulate myself on my own taste every day."

Hester, watching Julie's face during this speech, felt her heart turn over with love for the goodness shining there.

"Don't refine too much upon Julie's testimony, Lord Markham. I do not. She is as prejudiced as she is beautiful."

Lord Markham, whose eyes had fastened upon Julie's face while she spoke, answered this sally almost absently with "Yes."

Hester had to remind herself that she had often seen this bemused expression on men's faces when they looked at Julie. But for some reason she could not fathom she resented the look from Lord Markham. It could not be envy, for she had never been envious of Julie; as well be envious of the beauty of moonlight. Nor could it be jealousy. Lord Markham was an acquaintance of a few moments, and in spite of the magnetism that had given her a flustered instant, his hard, unhandsome face did not appeal to her at all. But was it possible that Julie's eyes sparkled up at him a little too much? Surely Julie would never lead such a man on to dangle after her. She had not been given to casual flirtations before marriage and would certainly never be guilty of such a lapse in taste now. But was there something a trifle too hectic in her gaiety? Hester determined to keep a discreet watch over this situation till she knew what to make of it.

Now Geoffrey joined them and took possession of his wife's arm.

"Come alone, my love, we must go in to dinner. You'll take Hester, won't you, Markham?"

When all the ladies had been provided with escorts, they proceeded to the dining room, resplendent in dazzling white linen, silver, and crystal. During the first course Hester dutifully chatted with Lord Markham. She found him well read and well traveled and a pleasant conversationalist. But she noticed his eyes ever straying to the end of the table to watch Julie. And Julie was aware of his looks, becoming more animated as the dinner progressed. With the first remove, Hester turned to her other side with relief. Here was Lord Breckinridge, puffing out his mustaches and preening under her gentle raillery. He had obviously always had an eye for women and was a vain little peacock, but was certainly harmless.

The ladies retired when the port came; and when the gentlemen joined them later, a whist table was set up for some of the guests, and the young ladies entertained at the pianoforte. Each of the Misses Lithey complied willingly with requests for songs, but Hester smilingly declined, claiming she had no talent for music. The evening was pleasant, but for Hester, it was happily over at a comparatively early hour. She had enjoyed herself, but was tired from her journey that day and had many impressions she wanted to mull over. She therefore asked Julie to forgive her for not staying to talk after the guests were gone, for she must take herself to bed. They would have the whole day tomorrow for a long coze.

III

HESTER woke slowly and deliciously to the scent of roses being wafted in on the sheer, billowing curtains. Though the sun had not yet touched the windows, the world outside her window was filled with sunlight and birdsong, and the sky assured her of a clear, cloudless day. She became aware that her door was opening slowly; then a mass of silvery curls poked slowly around the edge, followed by a pair of blue eyes. "Julie, dear one, come in, do. What hour is it? I feel that I must have overslept disgracefully."

"Oh, no, Hester. It is but ten. I would not let anyone wake you, though Moreton insisted on coming in to open the drapes about half an hour ago."

"And a good thing she did, or I might have slept here all the day. Now, hand me my robe, dearest, and I will come down to breakfast directly."

"Stay where you are. I have the maid just outside the door with your breakfast tray."

"Oh, please, Julie, you must not spoil me this way. Besides, you know I never take breakfast in bed."

"Please, this once, let *me* spoil *you*. I have so looked forward to taking care of you, after all the years you took care of me," Julie said wistfully.

"But, my love, of course you shall. Bring on the tray, and you must sit here on the bed with me, and we'll talk about dinner last night, and you shall tell me all about everyone."

Soon they were chattering away, and while Hester drank her tea, Julie absentmindedly ate her sister's toast. As she reached for the last triangle, Hester put out her own hand and snatched it away, laughing, "Well, pet, you seem to have a hearty appetite. Did you not have breakfast?"

"Oh, hours ago. Well, at least an hour ago. But I do seem famished this morning. Now tell me, Hester, which gentleman caught your eye last night? Have you developed a *tendre* for any of them yet? I vow it will be Lord Markham. All the girls swoon over him."

"Not even a tiny twinge yet. I found him pleasant enough, if rather forbidding."

"Oh, do not say so, Hester. I have kept him titillated for weeks with bits of news of you. I do believe the only reason he has stayed in the country so long is on the chance of seeing you."

"Well, if there was any interest there, I'm sure it was well hidden. He was courteous, but cool—and it seemed to me, abstracted. I had always the feeling that he was thinking of something else the whole while."

"Nonsense, that is just his way. Believe me, he has been most eager to meet you."

"Why, you minx, is it possible that you are trying your hand at matchmaking?"

Julie had the grace to blush, for she well knew in what scorn Hester held this kind of meddling.

"Oh, Hester, just the least little bit. He is really such a catch for a husband, and all the silly girls here are dangling after him. I could not help thinking how you would put all their noses out of joint if he could but meet you. And he's so romantic looking—and *so* much money!"

"Pooh, I make nothing of that. I have quite enough money to be going on with and have no need to be hanging out for a wealthy husband. And I'm sure I don't know what you mean by 'romantic' looking. To my mind he has a very hard, cold look that I cannot like."

Julie thought this over for a moment, then her face brightened, "Well, then, what of Mr. Boscroft? He is ever so popular here in Littlecomb. I cannot imagine why he has never married, he is the most pleasant person, always ready to be part of any plans one may make. And he did seem much taken with you."

Hester, watching her earnest face, first smiled, then began to laugh, and finally collapsed into fits of giggles, so infectious that Julie had to laugh with her.

"Oh, why do you laugh—you do not take me seriously!" Julie sat up and wiped her eyes.

"If you could see your face, poppet. So serious and . . . and . . . calculating. I never thought to see the day that you would try to be marrying me off,

Julie. I vow, you think me on the shelf already and I but nineteen."

"But you should be married, my love. You are perfect at managing a household and wonderful with children and everything, and you've been out quite two years already."

"Well, I'm not exactly so long in the tooth that I am in despair, so let us have done with all this on your part and just enjoy being together. Now, what are the plans for today?"

"When you're dressed you must see *all* over the house. There is so much there wasn't time to show you yesterday. Then I want you to see my lovely gardens, and Geoffrey wants to show you the stables, and Lady Breckinridge has asked us to tea, and the Litheys sent around a note to ask us to come riding this morning, but I sent back our regrets—I didn't want you to wake up till you'd had your sleep out—then they sent again to ask us to tea, but I'd already accepted Lady Breck . . ."

Hester held up her hands protestingly, "Oh, wait, please, no more I beg you. My head is spinning. Ring for Moreton, darling, do—and let me get up and dressed, and I will take your hand and be led wherever you wish."

In spite of Hester's protestations that she couldn't possibly touch a morsel of food after such a late breakfast, Julie prevailed upon her to sit down to a light nuncheon of baked eggs. And after all, Hester found it possible to eat, having worked up quite an appetite touring every inch of the house and grounds

and stables, exclaiming and praising Julie for her taste
in furnishings and Geoffrey for his taste in horseflesh.
She had picked out a very beautiful mare for her own
use, which Geoffrey said was a regular high-stepper
who would give her a good ride.

Julie's excited chatter throughout the morning continued unabated with one small exception: while showing Hester Geoffrey's old nursery, she had faltered for
a moment, but then rushed her hurriedly away to see
the master bedroom and the sewing room, where Miss
Ninby was making ". . . oh, the most exquisite evening gown ever!"

Her conversation throughout this tour was larded
with references to Lord Markham, who seemed to be
the arbiter of taste in Littlecomb. Hester tucked away
the incident in the nursery and her thoughts about
Lord Markham for speculation later when she could
be alone.

Now, after a leisurely nuncheon, they both hurried
upstairs to change their gowns. Geoffrey was to take
them for a short drive around the countryside and
then to Lady Breckinridge's for tea.

That formidable lady was ensconced on a sofa that
seemed frail indeed, her stout body bursting the seams
of a purple bombazine, unsuitably decorated with rows
and rows of ruffles. In attendance was her daughter,
Susan, sitting mouselike, to one side of and slightly
behind her mother.

Hester saw immediately that Mr. Boscroft was smiling at her from his place before the fireplace, but
before he could come forward she was introduced to
two young sprigs of the local gentry, Mr. Hallison and
Mr. Dalton, both dressed in the latest fashions featur-

ing collars so high that they could hardly turn their heads. Though they seemed near strangling they were cheerful, well-mannered young gentlemen who quizzed Julie amiably and professed themselves delighted to make the acquaintance of Miss Wyckham.

"I see you are well on your way to capturing the heart of every gentleman in the neighborhood," said an amused voice at her elbow. She turned to find Mr. Boscroft.

"Oh dear, have I met *every* gentleman in the neighborhood?" she asked in disappointed tones.

For one second he stared at her, then threw back his head to laugh delightedly.

"I now consider myself as having been properly set down, Miss Wyckham. However, to answer your question, I believe you have met all the eligible ones. Since I'm sure it's much too early for you to have bestowed your heart, I will set about trying to fix your interest with me before any of the other gentlemen have a chance."

"Really, Mr. Boscroft, I'm quite persuaded that a gentleman of your qualities has been bespoken already," she rallied him.

"Alas, dear lady, gratifying as your opinion is to me, I must report that I have been ever unfortunate in my dealings with the ladies. They seem blind to my 'qualities,' I fear."

"I am convinced that quite the reverse is true, Mr. Boscroft. I'm sure you are much sought after by mamas with eligible daughters but have so far succeeded in eluding capture. I fear you may be too nice in your taste, sir."

"I am indeed particular, Miss Wyckham, but when

my standards are met I am instantly aware of it," he said, giving her a most meaningful look.

Before this interesting discussion could be pursued, they were summoned by Lady Breckinridge to attend her. Hester was directed to a seat beside that lady, who instantly investigated her background, present acquaintances, and future aspirations with great expertise. Hester emerged from this interrogation shaken and pink in the face from restraining her inclination to giggle. Declaring that she felt quite warm, she requested Geoffrey to give her his arm for a stroll on the terrace. Geoffrey, eagerly accepting a chance to escape, led her outside with alacrity.

Hester made a great play with her fan, in what she hoped was a convincing show of one suffering from the heat and, as soon as they were out of earshot, she began to giggle helplessly. Geoffrey looked quite alarmed and glanced fearfully over his shoulder.

"I say, Hester, this is not good form. What on earth has come over you, going on like that?"

"Oh, Geoffrey, that *outrageous* woman! I declare I feel that I have been taken apart and put back together again—and that perhaps all the parts are not exactly where they were before. Oh, dear . . . dear . . . I think I will go into whoops again," and proceeded to do so.

"Nonsense, my girl, Lady Breckinridge may be a bit on the inquisitive side, but she means well, poor woman."

"Geoffrey, you are a complete hand. How you can call her a poor woman is quite beyond me. Whatever do you mean by it?"

"Well, she's . . . she's . . . ambitious, don't you know?"

"*Ambitious*? Now, what can she be ambitious about?"

"Oh, Hester, it should be plain as a pikestaff. There's that antidote of a daughter, nearly on the shelf by now she's been out so long, and not a single offer. Except the curate, of course. He's forever dangling after her. And I must say she seems to go along quite famously with him, always on about Roman history and Greek plays and such like. But Lady Breckinridge has greater plans for her daughter than a mere curate, and gives him a very definite setdown every time he comes around, and the poor fellow can't get up the nerve to declare himself. Course, the chap ain't a complete cabbage head. He sees well enough which way the wind is blowing."

"But surely the girl is old enough not to need her mother's consent, if she really wants the curate?"

"Can you see that mouse going against her mother? Oh no, Hester, that won't wash for a moment."

"But what can her ambitions for her daughter have to do with me?"

"Now *you're* being a cabbage head. Surely you can see that the addition of an attractive girl to our small circle would put her guard up a bit?"

"But, Geoffrey, I'll be gone in a few weeks."

"It doesn't take a few weeks to attach a man."

"Well, but tell me which men I am to beware of, and I will make it clear to her that I have no interests there."

"Who else but Markham? And I think she wouldn't

object to Boscroft. He's very warm in the pocket, you know. Very large fortune there, must be almost as big as Markham's."

"Yes, I see. But they must have been neighbors these ages, Geoffrey. Why hasn't one of them come up to scratch by now? If they aren't interested in the Honorable Susan, there must be many other attractive girls around. I admit I've wondered why they are neither one married. Lord Markham must be five-and-thirty if he's a day, and Mr. Boscroft—well, perhaps five-and-twenty. Surely both of an age to have been snapped up by now by some enterprising miss?"

"Oh, well, they do say Boscroft is a bit too nice in his tastes for any of our local damsels, and Markham —well—I've heard quite a bit about him in London from time to time. Not much of it fit for your ears, I'm afraid. Must say he behaves himself down here, though I don't quite like the way he hangs around Julie. Never stepped out of line, but his reputation . . ."

Hester laughed at him, "Really, Geoffrey . . . *Julie!* As if Julie would ever . . ." and with that she collapsed again into giggles.

"Hester, for goodness' sake, you will oblige me by stopping that this instant. You'll have them all out here in a moment. Come now, I never thought for a moment that Julie would ever look at him—it's just his way of looking at her that I object to."

"You are a goose, Geoffrey, and no mistake. Now, let us beard the lioness in her den again. She'll think me quite rude as it is, I fear."

Upon re-entering the drawing room they found a distinct change had taken place. For one thing, Lord Breckinridge had joined the party and was standing in the middle of the room looking about with such an air of accomplishment and excitement that Hester was immediately intrigued. This was aside from the fact that Lady Breckinridge was looking triumphant and almost dangerously red in the face.

Clearly something momentous had occurred. Seeking enlightenment, Hester applied to Julie.

"My dear," whispered Julie, obviously herself in a high gig, "it is really the outside of anything. I declare I was never so surprised in all my life. It seems Lord Markham has asked Lord Breckinridge's permission to pay his addresses to Susan, and, quite naturally Lord Breckinridge has agreed. Well, I mean to say, it is what Lady Breckinridge has been angling for this age."

Hester slid a very discreet look at Susan, and found that young lady still sitting primly and quietly beside her mother, but, if such a thing were possible, she looked more crushed than ever. Her eyes were downcast so that it was impossible to see their expression, but it was obvious that she was agitated. The color came and went furiously in her cheeks, and her hands, which before had been quietly and serenely clasped in her lap, were now clenched together till the knuckles were white.

Meantime, Lord Breckinridge was expounding excitedly to Geoffrey, and Lady Breckinridge, retaining a firm grip on Mr. Boscroft's arm, was beckoning imperiously to Hester.

"Miss Wyckham, oh, Miss Wyckham, I think we shall all shortly be demanding your felicitations. You have heard our good news?"

"Miss Susan, I most certainly and sincerely do wish you happy," instantly responded Hester.

"*No!* Please . . . I . . . I . . . you must excuse me," said that damsel in a smothered voice and flew across the room and out the door.

Lady Breckinridge, looking distinctly put out at this display, said, "You must excuse Susan, Miss Wyckham. Poor girl is quite overcome with happiness at her good fortune. Not usually so rag-mannered."

"Of course, my dear Lady Breckinridge, I quite understand. Absolutely no need for apologies," replied Hester. But she couldn't help thinking that she'd be willing to lay a wager that it wasn't "happiness" Susan was overcome by. She had the feeling there would be trouble in that quarter, in spite of Geoffrey's opinion that "that mouse would never go against her mother."

IV

HESTER placed her foot in Mr. Boscroft's hands and was expertly thrown up into her saddle. The mare danced about excitedly, but Hester had no difficulty calming her. She was delighted to see the mare so fresh.

In fact, she was thoroughly delighted with everything. The chill of early morning, the knowledge that her claret-colored riding dress was extremely becoming to her, and the courtesy of Mr. Boscroft, who had arrived quite a half hour early and busied himself checking her saddle girth and adjusting the stirrup perfectly. Julie, who had cantered impatiently a short way down the drive, now came prancing back to urge them on. They all rode down the drive and across the fields to a gentle rise and stopped to admire the view of the countryside, sloping gently down and away from them. In the early morning hush it was like a beautiful painting. On the lower ground the morning mist had not yet lifted and this added a softness to the scene. The checkered fields, broken here and there by a row of poplars or a seemingly artfully arranged grove of trees, had an ethereal delicacy that made Hester catch her breath in wonder.

"What do you say, Miss Wyckham, shall we let them out for a run? I vow that mare of yours is eager."

"Oh yes, do let's. I've so longed for a good gallop. Are you with us, Julie?"

But Julie, without answering, put her heel to her horse and took off, laughing back at them. They set off after her gleefully. She led all the way and finally pulled up laughing and breathless in the shade of a huge spreading oak beside the road.

"Oh, you are regular slowtops this morning!" she chided them.

"I give you best this time, my lady. But I must protest you caught us out. Another time we'll be more prepared for your tricks," rejoined Mr. Boscroft.

"Come, sir, face your losses like a sport. Well, Hester, did you like your gallop?"

"Famously! Now which way do we go?"

Mr. Boscroft pointed toward the hillside ahead of them. "I like very much to go up there and through the woods at the top of the rise and so back the way we came. It looks a short ride, but will take quite three quarters of an hour—unless you mean to race us back, Lady Hallam?"

"Oh no, I'm quite content now. We'll have a gentle ride back. You young folks are obviously not up to us old troopers, eh, my beauty?" she inquired of her horse, patting her gently. "Now, come along, children,

I shall lead the way till we get to the woods. Then we may ride three abreast and have a good chat."

By the time they reached the trees, the sun had burned away the mists and was shining warmly on their backs, warning them that the day would be hot, and making them grateful for the sun-dappled shade. Hester and Mr. Boscroft came up with Julie, and the three rode along together.

"Now, Mr. Boscroft, you must tell us your impressions of the startling news at the Breckinridges' yesterday. What do you think?"

"Why, as to that, I'm sure I wish them happy, Lady Hallam."

"Oh, that is not what I mean at all, and well you know it. What I mean is . . . well . . . it was such a surprise, do you see? I'm sure I have been as much in their company as anyone, and I never suspected Lord Markham's intentions for a moment. I don't believe I've ever seen him even talking to her above what was necessary for courtesy's sake. Of course, I am not in Susan's confidence, I doubt anyone is except the curate, but I'm sure if anything had been afoot in that direction I would have noticed at once."

"Now, Julie, surely he could have been courting her this age with morning visits or with love letters that you would know nothing of?" said Hester.

"Well, of course, but he could hardly have been doing so without some reaction from her. I mean, surely she would have blushed when he spoke to her or . . . or . . . something!"

"Perhaps she is not a blushing person," said Mr. Boscroft.

"Oh, I can answer for it that she is," said Hester.

"Did you not see her yesterday when I offered my congratulations?"

"Well, there you are then," said Julie, "and I protest I never saw her do that when he spoke to her before. Cool as could be always, as though she could hardly be troubled to answer. Do tell us, Mr. Boscroft, had you any knowledge of what was going forward?"

"Not the least in the world, but then I'm not a very noticing sort of fellow, I'm afraid."

"Now that is a Banbury tale if ever I've heard one, Mr. Boscroft. Not much goes on that misses your eye, I'll be bound," retorted Julie.

Mr. Boscroft protested laughingly and tried to change the subject. "Are you ladies all prepared for the Litheys' party next week? I hear they have hired musicians and mean to have at least twelve couples to stand up."

"Of course, the very thing. We shall really see them together then and will be able to see how they go on," said Julie craftily.

Hester and Mr. Boscroft both laughed at this. "Julie, my dear love, you are becoming like a gossiping old dowager. What will Mr. Boscroft think of you?"

"Oh, pooh, Hester, Mr. Boscroft knows me quite well. Besides, it is my belief that Mr. Boscroft is holding out. I'm sure he could tell us a bit more about this affair than he has."

"Please allow me to assure you, Lady Hallam, that I am not in Markham's pocket. I would be the last to know anything of his affairs."

Hester turned to look at him thoughtfully. "I read just the least bit of . . . dislike? . . . in your voice."

"No, no, Miss Wyckham, not at all. I'm not well

enough acquainted with Lord Markham to claim like or dislike. One meets him wherever one goes, of course. Only natural in a small place like this. But our interests are quite different. In fact, our conversations rarely rise above the commonplace. Certainly never an exchange of confidences."

"Did you know him in London at all?" inquired Hester.

That she had scored in some manner Hester was sure, but exactly how she could not fathom. His eyes had turned cold and his lips set in a grim line for just a moment, then he brushed her question aside with a brief "hardly at all."

Naturally, Hester was much intrigued and caught Julie's eye to see if she had noticed this exchange. Julie raised her eyebrow significantly at Hester.

Mr. Boscroft suggested they make plans for a picnic party to take advantage of the good weather, and they began to discuss whether they would all ride, or take carriages, and who would be included. They set it for the day after tomorrow, provided the weather held.

They arrived back to find Geoffrey waiting to show off his new mare, and he carried Mr. Boscroft off to the stables to discuss her many fine points, while the ladies went to change out of their habits. When they came down, they found Mr. Boscroft again astride his horse and waiting for them. He declined the invitation to luncheon, claiming business to take care of, but assured them they would undoubtedly meet later in the day at the Litheys', where they had all been asked to take tea.

The ladies retired to Julie's morning room to gossip. Hester picked up her embroidery frame and began to sort out some silks for the border while Julie wandered about.

"What is it, little one? You seem uncommonly restless."

"Well, I guess I am a bit. Oh, make no mistake, I adore the country, but I do wish sometimes I had more to do. Now that I have the house and gardens in order, I miss having some work to occupy me."

"My dear, take advantage of your leisure. In no time at all you will have the house filled with young ones who will give you no peace from morning till night."

Julie gave her one stricken look and collapsed on the sofa beside Hester and caught her hands. "Oh, Hester," she cried and buried her head in Hester's lap and sobbed.

"Why, Julie, whatever is it, my little love? Please, my darling, tell me. What have I said to hurt you so?"

"Not you, oh no, Hester . . . it's just . . . just . . . oh, Hester, I do so much want to give Geoffrey an heir. That was the main reason I wanted to come here. It has been five years, and I thought perhaps racketing about in town was preventing . . . well, so then we came here, and it has been so many months now, and not a sign yet. I know Geoffrey is most disappointed, though of course he would never, never say a word for fear of hurting me."

"My dear, I'm sure you are imagining the whole thing. Geoffrey is far from being disappointed about anything. He seems to me to be merry as a grig down here, and I've never seen him look so well content."

"Yes, but you know he has never had his own family, his parents died when he was still so young. He's always been alone. He told me once that he wanted to have a fine big family of children tumbling about the house to make up for his lonely childhood. I know he feels it terribly that we've had no children yet."

"I'm sure he will be happy when the time comes, but I'm equally sure he does not brood on it. And I know he would be most distressed if he thought you were doing so. Why have you not discussed this with him?"

"Oh, I cannot. I feel that it must be my fault. Perhaps because I am so small . . . or . . . or . . ."

She faltered to a stop as Hester threw back her head in a great peal of laughter.

"Julie . . . oh, Julie . . . forgive me, dear heart, but I cannot help myself. Wherever do you come by such ideas? Too small?"

Julie raised her face, shining with tears, to stare at Hester intently.

"You mean . . . you do not think. . .?"

"Most definitely not! You are worrying for nothing on that score, I do assure you. Size has nothing whatever to do with it. Probably you are worrying too much. Put the whole matter out of your mind as much as possible, and I have no doubt that nature will take its course in due time."

"Truly, Hester?"

"I'm sure of it. Now stop being such a wet goose and mop up your face like a good girl before Geoffrey comes in to find you like this."

Julie sat up obediently and dried her tears. She declared that she felt ever so much better, as she had been sure she would as soon as Hester knew all and had taken charge. Hester quailed but accepted the

responsibility. It had always been thus with Julie. Her
open heart could brook no "secrets." It was no wonder
Geoffrey had thought Julie "mopish" if she had been
carrying around this worry for all these years, never
confiding it to anyone. Her complete confidence in
Hester's assurances that all would be well might have
been frightening to a less sturdy spirit than Hester's.
But she shouldered it without a qualm, as she had
always done for Julie.

The afternoon tea party at the Litheys' proved to be
an exciting affair—with the news of Susan's offer, the
plans for the evening party, and an animated discussion
of gowns. The Lithey girls were in great form, pelting
Julie and Hester with rapid-fire questions whose answers
they never had time to wait for.

The eldest, Miss Letitia, was all but promised to
the rather stout, but pleasant, older son of a prominent
local resident. However, this did not seem to deter her
in the least from flirting with any other gentleman
present and joining her sisters in their dizzying conversation. Since the girls were sixteen, seventeen, and
eighteen, they were as close as triplets and very much
alike in looks and disposition.

Mr. Boscroft had not yet appeared, and evidently
Mr. Lithey was awaiting this reinforcement before
joining them. The young gentleman seated beside Mrs.
Lithey and watching Letitia with an adoring if bemused expression was evidently her suitor.

The girls swirled around their guests, laughing and
talking all at once, asking and answering their own
questions.

"Julie, do tell, had you the least idea that Lord

Markham was trying to fix his interest with Susan? Of course, you could not, none of us did, but how . . ."

"Miss Wyckham, we are so happy that you arrived in time for our party, it will be a famous rout indeed. Do you dance the waltz? But, of course, you must, you are used to London and Bath."

"Caro, darling, please stop bouncing around and let me but make my curtsy to your mother. I vow, you girls are like a flock of birds. There always seem to be more than three of you. Come along, Hester, take my arm for protection, and I will see you safe," laughed Julie, leading Hester towards their hostess.

"Miss Wyckham, you will excuse my girls, they do get overexcited now and again, but there is little I can do, they are so high-spirited," said Mrs. Lithey indulgently.

"Oh, I like their manners fine, madam. I have never had a liking for those shy, wishy-washy creatures who blush if you speak to them and can never raise their eyes and have no conversation. However, I admit that three at one time . . . but never mind, I'm sure I shall get used to it very soon," said Hester, twinkling with suppressed laughter at Mrs. Lithey.

"You are too good, Miss Wyckham," said that lady with a twinkle of her own. "Won't you sit here with me? Perhaps we can get in a moment of quiet conversation. I have been longing to ask you about your gowns. You must have such a clever seamstress." They settled down to talk of patterns and fabrics, while Julie and the three girls discussed Susan's good fortune and the mystery of Lord Markham yet again.

Shortly they were joined by Mr. Lithey with Mr.

Boscroft in tow. Hester was happy to see him again.
She wondered if Lord Markham would also drop in.
But Mrs. Lithey told her that Lord Markham had
sent his regrets. No doubt he would be with the
Breckinridges, she thought. Julie came and urged Hester to take her place with the girls and let her rest
quietly with Mrs. Lithey for a moment. Hester rose and
was immediately swept up by the chattering girls for a
walk in the shrubbery with Letitia's swain and Mr.
Boscroft. Since the day had turned very warm indeed,
Hester was happy to escape to the cool of the garden.
She found herself walking a little apart with Mr. Boscroft after a few moments.

"I do believe Julie is right, there must be more than
three of them," she said laughingly.

"They are a bit lively, are they not? But they make
every gathering a jolly time around here."

"I can see that one is never allowed to be dull with
them. I admire them exceedingly, I must say. For all
their high spirits, they are very kindhearted. They
don't seem to envy Miss Susan her good luck at all in
capturing Lord Markham. One would think that at
least one of them would have had a *tendre* for him
and be cast into the glooms by the announcement."

"Oh, it is my belief that they all have had a *tendre*
for him, one after the other, taking turns, you know,
along with every other unmarried girl hereabouts. But,
I have never seen him talk above a quarter of an hour
with anyone except your sister. Perhaps he feels safe
with her."

"Well, if that were a requirement, there are any
number of safely married ladies in the neighborhood
—Mrs. Lithey, Lady Breckinridge . . ."

"Ah, yes, indeed there are, but none of them are pretty, and Markham has a decided taste for pretty faces."

'Good God, no wonder Geoffrey said . . ." she stopped abruptly, almost biting her tongue in vexation with herself. What was there about this man to make her confide in him so freely?

"Yes, I'm quite sure Geoffrey did," said Mr. Boscroft, smiling at her discomfiture. "But I'm sure Geoffrey is quite used to men flirting with Julie by now. And I'm equally sure he has no reason to fear that Julie could not deal with any such danglers with dispatch."

"Oh, decidedly. She is really quite besotted with Geoffrey. She never had time for any young man after she met him. She used to try to pass them along to me to deal with. Poor things, they were not happy to take second best."

"Now, surely you are angling for a compliment, Miss Wyckham, for never under any circumstances could you be considered second best."

"I'm afraid I did rather force your hand there, didn't I? But it was unintentional, I assure you. I feel that I might have known you for many years and therefore am easy with you and tell you many more things than I would ordinarily. I hope you will not mind?"

"You do me great honor, Miss Wyckham. And now, I will ask you to do me another. May I have the pleasure of standing up with you for the first dance at the Litheys' rout?"

"With pleasure, Mr. Boscroft. You are very kind."

"I assure you kindness has nothing whatever to do with it."

"Do you tell me that you are not kind? But I have heard everywhere what a very pleasant person you are. Surely a man who is everywhere judged to be pleasant must be kind?"

"Madam, I am kind to those who stand in need of kindness—lonely old ladies, shy young girls, animals— all objects worthy of one's kindness."

"And I do not qualify?"

"I must admit, my dear, that kindness is hardly the emotion you have aroused in me." With this he raised her hand, kissed it, and wheeled to walk quickly away.

V

THE DAY of the Litheys' evening party arrived after an interval filled with delightful entertainments for Hester. Mr. Boscroft's picnic had been a huge success; the whole party on horseback had made their way to the picturesque ruins of an abbey, followed by servants with a most sumptuous repast. The next evening there was a formal dinner party at the Breckinridges'. Miss Susan was present, calm and inscrutable as ever, her plain but pleasant face revealing nothing. Lord Markham had, most unfortunately according to Lady Breckinridge, been called to London on business and would not be able to join them.

There had also been many rides and visits in the neighborhood and many people called to meet Lady Hallam's sister. Hester declared that she was so exhausted from changing her gown for the many occasions that she would have to go away for a rest cure.

But in spite of everything, she had never looked better; her cheeks were like roses and her dark blue eyes sparkled.

Julie was telling her this in the sewing room, as Hester sat watching the seamstress pin up the hem of Julie's new ball gown. Miss Ninby, her mouth filled with pins, crept around Julie on her knees, waiting dumbly and patiently whenever Julie twirled around in rapture.

"Pooh, nonsense, Hester, you know perfectly well that you love to be forever jaunting from one party to the other—your health always improves and you begin to glow. Is she not a rare beauty, Miss Ninby?"

"M–m–m, m–m–m–m," said that lady through the pins.

"Julie, you will completely turn my head. You know well that I never refine too much upon what you say about me. You are much too prejudiced to be objective on this subject."

Julie continued unheeding, "And your gown, Hester—truly magnificent. Nothing like it has ever been seen in Littlecomb. Such style—and that color! Oh, you will break hearts in that color! You look like an angel."

Hester laughed at this extravagance and thought to herself that no one could possibly look more angelic than Julie in her white gauze trimmed with silver ribbands. However, she could not help regarding with satisfaction her own rose pink silk gown on its hanger awaiting Miss Ninby's attentions. She had to admit that the color was wonderful and exactly matched the color in her cheeks. Also, nothing could improve the cut. It hung straight from the dark garnet bow beneath the bosom and Hester knew she looked taller and wonderfully slim in it. It had tiny puffed sleeves of lace and her satin slippers matched perfectly. Julie had insisted that she wear their mother's pearl necklace, given to Julie as the eldest at the time of her marriage. Hester's own beautiful diamond drop earrings completed the picture. She was very close to feeling smug about this costume.

When Julie and Hester entered the drawing room at the Litheys' on the evening of the party the reaction was certainly more than gratifying. Of course, Hester discounted the raptures of the Lithey girls, who she felt would react the same if they had appeared in gray bombazine. But she did not discount the many other admiring glances, including the stunned look on Mr. Boscroft's face. She hoped fervently that for once she was the object of that look rather than Julie, and was surprised at the thought. Never having been vain of her looks or envious of Julie's, it was certainly a startling reaction on her part. Certainly she had never been conscious of desiring the admiration of any young man, as she definitely did in this instance.

As Julie was claimed and moved away, Mr. Boscroft's expression did not change; Hester blushed and lowered her eyes. She knew he was coming toward her and waited for him breathlessly.

"Hest . . . I beg your pardon . . . Miss Wyckham, but your beauty has so dumbfounded me I forgot myself. I call you Hester in my thoughts, you know. Do you mind?"

"Of course not, Mr. Boscroft. And I thank you for

your compliment. You are most ki . . ." she stopped
in confusion.

"Ah, you remember my strictures on the word
'kind,' I see?"

"Yes . . . ah . . ." she hesitated for a moment
and then, calling herself a goose, she faced him
squarely and resolutely changed the subject. "This is
quite a formidable crush, is it not, Mr. Boscroft? I
think there will be many more than twelve couples
standing up tonight."

"Many more. The Lithey girls have a host of friends,
and I imagine once started they are hard to stop."

"They are lucky in that. In our part of the country
we are much too quiet. There are too few young
people to make an informal rout such as this possible.
We do have balls and assemblies, of course, but they
must be planned well in advance to insure a crowd."

"How very interesting, Miss Wyckham," he said
with awful gravity.

"I thought you would find it so, Mr. Boscroft," she
returned, matching his tone. "Would you care to hear
a description of some of our local families and their
lineage?"

"Not in the least, Miss Wyckham. I would much
rather discuss you."

"Oh, my lineage is quite unexceptional, I do
assure you, if rather dull as a topic of conversation."

They eyed each other solemnly for an instance, and
he began to smile. "I give you best, Miss Wyckham,
but another time . . ."

"Oh, I believe we are evenly matched when it
comes to sending someone up, Mr. Boscroft."

They were interrupted at this point by the arrival

of the Breckinridge party, including Miss Susan, but without Lord Markham. There was an interested buzz of speculation around the room as to what his conspicuous absence could mean. Though there had been no formal announcement, Lady Breckinridge had made one very close to formal that day at the tea party, and word had not been slow to spread. Everyone had been looking forward to seeing the happy couple together for the first time at this party.

However, the guests had not much time to speculate over this tidbit, as the Breckinridges were now joined by a most dashing gentleman in the uniform of a well-known Hussar regiment. The buzz became an excited hum.

Mrs. Lithey hurried forward to greet these important guests, and Lady Breckinridge proudly introduced her nephew, Captain James Frampton, in a voice loud enough to be heard over the entire room. And indeed, she had reason to feel proud. Captain Frampton was at least six feet tall, with dark hair and eyes, and teeth exceedingly white in his tanned face. He was dazzlingly handsome in his uniform.

As Captain Frampton bowed gracefully over Mrs. Lithey's hand, the three Lithey daughters appeared like magic and he was duly introduced. He greeted each in turn and so expertly fenced with their barrage of questions as to be able to answer them before they could do so themselves.

Hester strolled away into the next room with Mr. Boscroft to escape the crush and was shortly followed by Julie and Geoffrey. Julie was all agog to impart various *on dits* garnered from the assembly as to the whereabouts of Lord Markham, some opinions being that he had cried off. Julie was sure that this could not be so, but she was puzzled to explain his absence.

And so the Litheys' party was assured of being a rousing success almost before it had begun. Everyone exclaimed over the decorations and the gowns and the pleasantness of the company. When the music started the first dance was formed enthusiastically, and Hester was claimed immediately by Mr. Boscroft. After honoring several importunate young men with her hand in the dances that followed, she declared herself in desperate need of a chair and rest. Her partner obligingly took her to the sidelines where she sat gratefully and gently waved her fan while exchanging pleasantries with her escort. Her idle gaze fell upon Captain Frampton, just entering the ballroom. He was alone and stopped inside the door to stare deliberately about him. His eyes moved slowly around the room, and Hester clearly saw him stop and his jaw go slack when he espied Julie dancing with Geoffrey and dimpling up at him enchantingly. Captain Frampton visibly pulled himself together and continued his leisurely study of the guests. He was joined by Mr. Lithey at that moment and immediately leaned over from his great height to ask a question. That he was desiring some information about Julie was perfectly obvious to Hester. She could see the small moue of disappointment as Mr. Lithey informed him of Julie's status. But Captain Frampton bore up bravely, shrugged his shoulders, and continued his survey. Hester was much amused at this byplay and looked forward to telling Julie about it when they were home. She was smiling absentmindedly in his direction when she became aware that his glance had finally reached her and that he was staring at her fixedly. With great aplomb she fastened her gaze on Miss Susan standing with her mother just a few feet to one side of the Captain and broadened her smile in greeting.

Hester could see from the corner of her eye that Captain Frampton was again bending questioningly over Mr. Lithey. She felt quite sure that they would shortly be coming in her direction, and she could hardly blame the Captain for believing that she had been smiling at him in a most forthright way. To avoid the encounter she knew was coming, she requested her partner's arm and went off with him in the other direction. But the captain had not reached his status in the military for being behindhand in the matter of maneuvers. He sauntered slowly but purposefully around the other side of the room and presently came face to face with Hester, taking her completely by surprise. Mr. Lithey, who had obviously been dragged along to accomplish an introduction, did so and the captain clasped her hand firmly and bent over it lingeringly.

"A very great pleasure, Miss Wyckham. May I beg the pleasure of standing up with you in the next dance?"

"Why, I thank you, Captain Frampton, but I am already engaged for the next dance."

"Then the one after that," he persisted.

"Well—but of course, captain." She turned gratefully to her next partner who had approached and took his arm. "If you will excuse us, sir." He bowed and they moved away. She could feel her heart thumping in a most uncomfortable way, yet in spite of this, she was not looking forward to their future encounter.

And this she could not explain to herself. It was most unlike her to act like a girl just out of school. She had never behaved that way, even when she had been that age. But there was no denying she was unusually flustered by Captain Frampton and, not being accustomed to such feelings, didn't know quite how to behave with him. Consequently, she suddenly felt quite embarrassed.

However, by the time the set was finished, and she had been led to a sofa by her partner, she had gained some measure of control of herself and was able to smile up at Captain Frampton calmly when he came to claim his dance. They moved onto the floor.

"Have you lived long in Littlecomb, Miss Wyckham?"

"I have not lived here at all, Captain Frampton. I am only here on a short visit to my sister, Lady Hallam."

"Lady Hal . . ." he hesitated for only an instant, "Hallam is your sister?"

"Yes, have you met her?"

"Why no, I have not had that pleasure."

"Oh, I made sure you had met her on some previous visit."

"I have never visited Littlecomb before."

"I see. Then I must be mistaken."

"Mistaken about what, Miss Wyckham?"

"Why, I thought I noticed you trying to catch her eye when you first entered the ballroom and supposed you knew her."

He eyed her for a moment. "Yes, you are mistaken, but it is gratifying to know that you noticed me when I first entered the ballroom."

Touché. The figure of the dance forced them to part after this sally, and Hester had to admit that he had bested her expertly. She would have to watch her step in future when she took it upon herself to tease him.

He took her by surprise when they came together again by asking if he could take her down to supper. She had not yet promised herself to anyone for this, since she had secretly hoped that Mr. Boscroft would ask her. As he had not, she could hardly refuse Captain Frampton. When the dance ended he led her back to a chair, talked pleasantly about the quality of the music until her next partner came up to them, and then departed with the promise that he would come back to claim her when the supper hour approached. With a dark look at the gentleman waiting expectantly before her, he walked away.

Now Hester was not sure that she was altogether pleased with the way her evening was turning out. She had caught sight of Mr. Boscroft several times during the evening, dutifully dancing with some of the older ladies, and some of the younger ones not so dutifully. He seemed to be enjoying himself enormously and smiled at her warmly each time she saw him. But he had not come back to request another dance, and he had not requested her to have supper with him, and she had to admit to a feeling of disappointment. But then she shrugged it away. She was *not* going to develop a *tendre* for Mr. Boscroft. No doubt he had been merely amusing himself with a mild flirtation to pass the time and had his affections firmly attached elsewhere. As for herself, she was not interested in any serious feelings yet. But he was a very nice person and she had felt comfortable and relaxed in his presence.

That was it, she thought—comfortable. There was much to be said for a friendship like that, but it could sometimes fool a person into thinking affection was developing where there was nothing more than ease and pleasantness. And after all, she had always hoped that when the right gentleman came along she would know it at once. Excitement would be engendered, she had always supposed, that would make it instantly clear to her that the moment had arrived. She remembered the feelings she had experienced in her encounter with Captain Frampton. Oh no, she thought, in dismay, not an accomplished womanizer like that.

Why she should feel that he was a womanizer she found it hard to say. Something in his eyes as he had gazed around the room, as though judging this one too plain, that one too silly, and so on. Perhaps he was just an accomplished flirt, well up on all the games to be played without getting hurt. Well, she had now warned herself. And she was very well able to play those games also if it amused her to do so. And why shouldn't she, after all? Feeling comfortable with someone wasn't always the way to go on either.

By the time Captain Frampton appeared she had talked herself into a more forthcoming frame of mind and felt quite equal to the cut and thrust of his conversational style. And he was quick, she had to admit that. She ended by enjoying the experience, and the rest of the evening was somehow heightened by knowing that he was watching her when they were not dancing together. She could feel his eyes following her around the room. She could also feel Mr. Boscroft's eyes, and they were watching her at first with some surprise and later with a decided frown.

When he came to ask her for a dance during the second half of the evening, she acquiesced courteously, and he led her onto the floor.

"You are enjoying the evening, Miss Wyckham?"

"Oh, very much, Mr. Boscroft, it is a lovely party, is it not?"

"Indeed it is, and part of its success must be laid at your door. You have many devoted admirers to-night."

"Everyone here has been most courteous and pleasant. I don't know when I've seen so many gracious people assembled in one room. I'm sure the Litheys are to be congratulated on their friends. They all seem intent that I shall have an enjoyable time."

"Yes, I have noticed. Is Captain Frampton a previous acquaintance of yours, Miss Wyckham?"

"No, indeed. Why should you think so?"

"You seemed to be old friends. I believe you stood up with him for several dances and took supper with him."

"He did but ask me, Mr. Boscroft, as anyone might."

"To be sure."

After that he seemed to have no more to say. At the end of the dance he escorted her back to a chair, waited for her next partner to come forward, bowed coolly, and walked away. She saw him no more that evening.

But she did see Captain Frampton, who promptly asked if he could take her riding the next morning which she as promptly accepted. She knew she was accepting in what could only be called defiance if she examined it carefully. But this she took care not to do. She didn't want to admit even to herself whom she was defying.

VI

THE NEXT MORNING found her seated at the breakfast table well before any other members of the household found their way to it. When Julie came in, Hester had finished what looked to have been a substantial breakfast and was drinking her tea.

"Why, Hester, up so early? I made sure you would have a long lie-in this morning."

"But I never have done so, my love. An evening party never tires me. And I promised Captain Frampton I would ride with him this morning. I was just now thinking I must go up and put on my riding dress, or I will have to make him wait. And you know how gentlemen hate to be kept waiting."

"Hester, how intriguing! Have you made another conquest?"

Geoffrey entered at her question and immediately

demanded to know about conquests. On being told, he declared that he and Julie would ride with them.

"Oh, Geoffrey, I don't believe I want to ride this morning. I am feeling a trifle fagged after last night."

"Nonsense, never looked in better health. Besides, you will never tell me that you would let Hester go off *alone* with a perfect stranger?"

"But he's Lady Breckinridge's nephew. I'm sure there can be nothing wrong with it. He seemed quite unexceptionable to me."

"Not quite the thing, just the same. I would not feel right. Responsible and all that, you know. Promised her father I would take good care of her."

"I do assure you, Geoffrey, I am well able to take care of myself, and I found Captain Frampton everything that was gentlemanly and courteous."

"We'll go with you," said Geoffrey firmly and turned to his mail. "Why, here's a note for you, Hester."

Hester took the note curiously and opened it. As she read she was aware of Julie, waiting expectantly to be told its contents.

"Well, here's a strange thing. Miss Susan Breckinridge presents her compliments and requests me to go for a ride with her in her carriage this afternoon. Reply requested."

"Susan? Now that *is* strange," cried Julie. "She has never asked *me* to go with her, nor anyone else that I've ever heard of. Whatever can she want?"

"I am sure she is just complimenting *you*, Julie, by doing her bit to entertain your guest."

"Most unusual, just the same. Will you go?"

"Of course. I'll just go into the library, if you'll

excuse me, and write an answer. I don't want to keep her servant waiting."

The note sent off, Hester went to her room to put on her riding dress. She came down to find Julie waiting for her, already similarly attired.

"How quick you are, my dear!"

"Well, when my lord speaks, I obey instantly. He's gone around to the stables to bring up the horses. And if I mistake not, here comes your beau," she said, peering down the drive.

Captain Frampton cantered up, greeted the ladies, and raised his eyebrows at the sight of Julie in riding dress and Geoffrey approaching from the stables with the horses. If he was displeased at this addition to the party, he made no comment. He dismounted, tossed Hester up into her saddle with ease, and remounted. They all trotted slowly down the drive, chatting about the beauty of the morning and the pleasures of the party the evening before.

Captain Frampton dropped back deliberately, allowing Geoffrey with Julie beside him to take the lead, and turned to Hester.

"Well, Miss Wyckham, did you not trust yourself to be alone with me?"

"Oh, I felt perfectly safe on that score."

"But evidently your brother-in-law was not quite so secure in his feelings."

"Well, Geoffrey is rather old-fashioned in his ideas. He is also very protective of the women in his family."

"With two such women I can't say that I blame him. Must keep him busy though."

She laughed. "Now that is rather a backhanded compliment, sir, but I will accept it nevertheless."

"I never make compliments, Miss Wyckham. I leave that to those languishing fellows with nothing better to do. I've no time for it. I simply say what I think straight out."

"And are you just as apt to be uncomplimentary when the occasion demands it?"

"*If* the occasion demands it. I am not so ill-mannered that I express myself to hurt unnecessarily."

"Well, that is reassuring. I can relax my guard a bit."

"Oh, I wouldn't advise that, Miss Wyckham, even if I thought you could."

"Why, Captain Frampton, do I give the impression of being ever *en garde*?"

"Oh, you're needle-witted and no mistake. But that suits me. Never cared for stupidity in a woman, no matter how beautiful she might be. Are you bespoken, Miss Wyckham?"

Startled, she turned to stare at him. "I beg your pardon, sir?"

"Now don't go all missish on me, madam, it doesn't become you at all."

"I am never 'missish,' and I believe it must be *my* decision about what becomes me so far as my behavior is concerned. Now, I think we must catch up the others," and so saying she urged her horse forward.

He reached over to lay his hand over her reins. "Now *don't* go flying up into the boughs. I will beg your pardon," he said in a humoring voice.

Though still feeling indignant at his abrupt and rude question, she realized that it would appear childish in her to make too big a fuss over it. After all, he had explained that he was an outspoken man. Perhaps the best way to deal with him would be to give as good as she got.

"Not exactly a heartfelt apology. However, I suppose I must be grateful for getting any at all."

"There now, that's more like you."

"I protest, sir, you cannot know what is *like* me. We cannot have spent more than two hours at the most in one another's company."

"Oh, never fear. I am used to judging immediately what will be worth bothering with and what will not."

"I think you may be the rudest man I have ever met, although I must admit that I am already familiar with your habit of making judgments. I saw you at it last night when you entered the ballroom. I was happy to notice that there was one who gave you more than a moment's pause."

"I beg to differ with you. You gave me not a moment's pause."

"I was not speaking of myself, sir, but of my sister. I noticed you standing gape-jawed for at least one full minute."

"Yes, I admit she stopped me cold. Most amazing woman to look at I ever saw. But wouldn't suit for me, even if she were free. Wouldn't stand up to my kind of life, you know."

"I'm afraid you've left me behind, sir."

"Well, it's a rigorous life, don't you know, being a soldier's wife."

"Ah, I believe I begin to see daylight. I take it that you are in the market for a wife?"

"Exactly. Why I asked if you were bespoken."

"You didn't want to waste your time?" she asked with gentle understanding, trying to keep her mouth straight.

"Got it exactly! Knew you were needle-witted the moment I saw you. I'm never mistaken."

"Well, I'm afraid you have made one mistake, Captain Frampton."

"Yes?"

"I am not looking for a marriage into the army, nor indeed, any marriage at all at this time."

" 'Spected you would say that. Natural enough in a well-brought-up girl," he said complacently.

"I *assure* you . . ." she began, but realizing the hopelessness of arguing with him, determinedly changed the subject. "I am going for a drive with your cousin this afternoon, Captain Frampton. I must say I am looking forward to becoming better acquainted with her. I understand she is quite a scholar."

"Oh, she ain't a bad girl at all—quiet, you know, but at least not silly like most her age. When they get left on the shelf too long like Susan, females tend to go a little silly, I've found."

"Have you, Captain Frampton? How very interesting. Oh, dear, I'm afraid I forgot my manners completely. I did not congratulate you upon the good fortune that has befallen your family."

"What good fortune is that?"

"Why, Miss Susan's betrothal, to be sure. A most happy occasion for you all, I'm sure."

"Oh, well, as to that . . ." his voice trailed off and, not wishing to appear inquisitive, she did not pursue it, but she had to admit that she was most intrigued by what could only be called concern in his voice.

"Will you be making a long stay in Littlecomb, Captain Frampton?"

"That depends upon my reception."

"But I'm sure no one could be more delighted than Lady Breckinridge to have you for as long as you will stay."

"Oh, not her. You," he answered with great simplicity.

"Me!" She felt her voice rising to almost a squeak with the surprise.

"Of course, you. I liked you the moment I laid eyes on you, Miss Wyckham. To give you the word with no bark on it, I hope to attach your affections as speedily as may be. I'm not a man to waste time."

"No more you are," she replied faintly. But her sense of humor betrayed her, and she began to laugh. She laughed so heartily that Julie and Geoffrey pulled up to wait for them to come up in order to share the joke. But by the time they had caught up, Hester was laughing so much she could hardly control her horse, let alone speak.

"Hester, I wish you will stop this unseemly laughter," said Geoffrey, sounding much abused. "You were never used to laugh so immoderately, surely. I don't remember it at any rate. But since you've been here you seem to be continuously overcome with hilarity."

This only set Hester to laughing more. Geoffrey said he washed his hands of her and would no longer answer for her good manners. Julie said that she would get hiccups and Captain Frampton, usually imperturbable, begin to look worried. When finally Hester could speak she begged pardon of all.

"I blame Captain Frampton's humor, at least this time, Geoffrey. I'm afraid I cannot take responsibility for my conduct when he is around."

The rest of the ride continued sedately and most

pleasantly, though Hester could see that Julie was twitching with curiosity.

After reaching the house again, Captain Frampton declined any refreshment and bade them all farewell. Not, however, before begging permission to accompany Hester and Susan on their drive in the afternoon. Hester firmly declined.

Julie tore up the front steps, calling that she would join Hester in her room immediately, and did so much sooner that it seemed possible. True, her gown was not completely fastened in the back, and her hair was all tumbled, but she said she couldn't wait for it to be done by her own maid, and that Moreton could take care of it while they talked.

"Tell me immediately, Hester. You were going along so famously with Captain Frampton! I could see that he was completely captivated."

"Oh, as to that, I do believe it is true," laughed Hester.

"*Really,* Hester? And you? Never tell me you have fallen in love so soon?"

"Why, Julie, why not? Only a few days ago you seemed eager to marry me off."

"Now, don't tease, Hester. You know perfectly well what I mean."

"Yes, pet, I know what you mean—and the answer is no. Very decidedly no!"

"Why not? He is a most attractive man, and I know his family is frightfully good—been here since the Conquest or something."

"Oh, just that we do not suit. Or at least he does not suit me. I admit that last night I found him most attractive and that he made me flutter a bit. But closer acquaintance has shown me that it will never do."

"Don't tell me that he insulted you by offering you a . . . a . . . oh, what is that expression?"

"If you mean did he want me for his light o' love, he did not. Far from it, indeed. He made me a most honorable proposal. Told me 'the truth with no bark on it' that he intended to attach my affections."

"No! Just like that? Why, he hardly knows you."

"And so I told him. But Captain Frampton is a man used to making instant judgments, and he evidently took one look at me and decided that I was in good enough health to take on the job of a soldier's wife."

"Oh, Hester, you cannot be serious. What else did he say?"

"Not much more of consequence. He's a man of few words," Hester said, laughing at the memory. Julie began to laugh with her and soon they were quite helpless, begging each other to stop.

"Oh, Julie, you cannot imagine a more droll proposal. I had the distinct feeling that at any moment he would inspect my teeth and question me about childhood diseases. He is the *most* arrogant man. I thought last night that he was very sharp-witted, but I think it's just outspokenness."

"But, Hester, you are outspoken yourself. I should think you would go along quite well together."

"I hope, however, that I am not arrogant, dear one?"

"No, never, sister. You are the best person in the world, and well you know it."

"Ah, now we are getting down to the truth. Julie, you goose, I love you. Now, what gown shall I wear for my outing with Susan? Do you think the craped muslin with the twill jacket will be too warm?"

They decided it would be fine, and when Hester was arrayed in this costume of pomona green with a tiny jacket and a chip straw bonnet with wide green ribbands, they went downstairs.

VII

AS THE CARRIAGE bowled smoothly along beneath the trees on the road to the village of Littlecomb, Hester covertly examined what little was visible of Miss Susan Breckinridge's face. Susan was wearing a poke bonnet tied with lilac ribbands, so that there was very little to see.

When Susan arrived, she had greeted Hester and Julie calmly and, after an exchange of courtesies with Julie, she invited Hester to step up into the carriage with her. It was a very smart, open barouche and Hester was delighted to oblige her. So far Susan had conversed in generalities, her gaze straight ahead, her beige silk-gloved hands loosely clasped in her lilac muslin lap. Hester had to admire her taste. She had a plump little body and was undoubtedly doomed to become stout with age, but she knew better than to emphasize her size by loud colors or unsuitable decorations.

As the carriage approached a lovely grove of trees, Susan leaned forward and asked the coachman to pull up. He did so and the footman jumped down and ran around to let down the step and hand the ladies out. He solemnly handed Susan a light carriage robe.

"I hope you will not mind, Miss Wyckham. I thought it would be pleasant to sit under the trees. It is quite dry, I do assure you."

"I should like it very much, Miss Breckinridge."

Susan led the way into the trees, found a grassy mound, and spread the robe. They arranged themselves comfortably, and Hester looked about approvingly. It was indeed beautiful; the deep shade was pleasantly cool on such a warm day, wild flowers abounded, and the sound of a running stream came to them faintly.

"This is delightful, Miss Breckinridge. However did you find it?"

Susan blushed and looked down at her hands for a moment without speaking.

"I come here frequently, Miss Wyckham. I find . . . well . . . often I'm . . ." her voice trailed away.

"I have such a place at my own home, Miss Breckinridge, that I often slip away to. There are times, I find, when one needs absolute solitude."

"Oh, yes, exactly so. I was confident you would understand. When you smiled at me so warmly the night of the Litheys' party, I quite felt that I had found a friend."

Hester's conscience gave her a sharp tweak, to remind her that she had not been smiling warmly at this girl so much as trying to avoid the eye of Captain Frampton.

"My dear Miss Breckinridge," she replied with great warmth to assuage her conscience, "I am honored indeed. I hope you will continue to think of me as your friend."

"Will you not call me Susan then? It would make it more comfortable. You see I have never had a friend . . . of my own sex," she added.

"Gladly, Susan. But it seems to me you have many lovely young people in the neighborhood who would happily have been your friend all these years. You grew up with the Lithey girls, did you not?"

"Oh, yes, and they are ever so nice . . . but I'm afraid they found me poor company. I could never take an interest in the things that interested them, you see."

"Yes, I can see that that might be so. They're charming girls, but, well, perhaps frivolous. You are a scholar, I understand?"

"I take great pleasure in the study of history and the classics. I had a very good governess who inspired me to learn. Too much, I fear, for my dear mama's happiness. One of the Litheys would have made a much more satisfactory daughter for her, I think."

"Oh, no, Susan, you must not say so. Your mama loves you very much, I can see it."

"Yes, certainly she loves me, but she would be better pleased if I were pretty and made a great thing of gowns and balls and beaux. I know that I am a disappointment to her, Miss Wyckham," said Susan simply.

Hester laughed. "I protest, I can hardly call you Susan if you continue to call me Miss Wyckham. My name is Hester."

"Yes, I know. Th . . . thank you, Hester. Now that we are truly friends, I wonder if you will mind if I confide in you? I would like to ask your advice about something."

"I would be only to happy to help, though I don't know that I am qualified to offer advice."

"The problem is, you see, that I have always been used to obeying my parents in everything. I think you can see that my mother is a very . . . strong-minded woman. Oh, very good and kind to me always," she hastened to add. "But she has always entertained . . . hopes for me that I'm afraid I am not able to satisfy."

"Yes, mothers quite often do feel that way about their daughters. Only natural that they should want the best for them."

"Oh, I understand that perfectly. But I do feel they do not always *know* what is best for them."

Now Hester knew perfectly well that Susan was preparing to confide in her about Lord Markham's proposal. And she felt sure she knew what the problem was. After all, she had seen Susan's reaction at tea the day Lady Breckinridge had made her announcement, and she had heard Susan's protest. That protest might have been taken for maidenly shyness by others who had witnessed it, but Hester had never taken it so. She quailed before the confidence about to be entrusted to her, for how could she advise Susan? Was it even proper in her to presume to advise her? But Susan, having once begun, was rushing on.

"You were present, Hester, when . . . when my mother . . . when Lord Markham . . ." She paused for a moment, as though to gather her forces. "No, I am going about it the wrong way. I must simply speak straight out. The thing is, you see, Lord Markham asked papa's permission to pay his addresses to me, and papa gave him that permission. Naturally, mama was delighted. It was what she had wanted above anything. But I . . . I . . . oh, Hester, I cannot obey them in this. I do not *like* Lord Markham, and I know that I have not the least attraction for him. I cannot think why he should have made me an offer at all. He has always shown such a great preference for pretty girls, and I am not in the least pretty."

She raised her hand to stop the protest she saw forming on Hester's lips.

"No, Hester, do not say it. We are friends, and we must be straight with one another. I am plain and over-plump, and that's all there is about it. Anyway, as I was saying, Lord Markham has never made any bones about his indifference to me, and it cannot be my dowry, for he is known to be rich as can be himself. He surely has no need for my money, so what can he want from me?"

"Well, perhaps he has come to see your true worth as a suitable wife for a man in his position."

"Even you cannot believe that truly, Hester. He is much in London and is very popular there, I understand. If he found none of the local girls suitable, I am sure there are hundreds of pretty, suitable girls in London who would be happy to become his wife."

Hester could not in honesty deny this and could

think of nothing to say. She therefore could do no more than murmur a rather inadequate "Yes, I suppose that is true."

"Yes. Well, so, feeling as I do about him I could not accept him, and naturally, my mother is quite put out with me. And Lord Markham is furious and stormed off to London to give me time to think it over, he said. But there is nothing to think over. I will not have him."

With this last statement she raised her eyes and gazed directly into Hester's own, and Hester was astonished to see the steel in them. Certainly here was a will as strong as Lady Breckinridge's. Hester was also not a little astonished to discover that those eyes were quite beautiful—Susan's best, if rarely revealed, feature. They were a cool, clear gray with darker rims around the irises, and fringed with short, but luxuriant, black lashes. She stared into them for a few moments, and then realized that some comment was being awaited.

"You are quite right, dear Susan. If you do not like him, then of course you will not have him. No one could blame you. And I feel sure your parents will not insist when they know your true feelings."

"Oh, but they do know my true feelings, and they still insist. They say I must believe that they are doing what is best for me, even though they well know that I have already . . . " She stopped abruptly.

"You have already what, Susan?"

"Hester, have you met our curate?"

"Why, no, I haven't yet."

"Will you come with me now to meet him?"

"Happily."

They gathered up the carriage robe and shook out their skirts and straightened their bonnets.

Once back in the carriage, Susan turned to Hester and took her hands. "Crispin . . . Mr. Ebershaw . . . is my only other friend in Littlecomb. I . . . we . . . he declared himself to me over a year ago, and I accepted. But my parents will not allow it, and Crispin will not marry me without their consent. I have told my mother that we love each other very much and intend to marry, but she pretends it never happened. And now she acts as though I were just a twittery girl reacting to her first proposal and that it was perfectly natural that I should behave that way. She makes sure I will come around and only laughs indulgently when I try to tell her differently. I believe she is living in some fantasy of her own making, since I have *never* in my life behaved like a twittery girl."

With this vehement statement Susan came as close to losing her composure as Hester had seen her, but for one other time. Oh dear, she thought, what shall I do? Surely I have no right to urge her to go against her parents' wishes, but as her friend I would be sadly wanting if I advised her to do what I would not do myself. I suppose the best way is to wait until I can take the measure of the curate. So thinking, she patted Susan's hands reassuringly, made some understanding but noncommittal noises, and sat back to await events.

The carriage soon pulled up again in front of the church, and a young gentleman came hurrying out. As he approached the carriage Hester felt her jaw dropping. In her imagination she had pictured a middle-aged, colorless, perhaps old-maidish, curate as Susan's would-be fiancé. She could not have been more wrong.

Crispin Ebershaw looked like a Botticelli angel. A crown of waving golden curls surrounded a face of unbelievable beauty and sweetness. His blue eyes were as innocent as a baby's and, as he hurried up to Susan, as filled with adoration as it was possible to see anywhere.

"My love," he said to Susan fervently, looking deep into her eyes as though he were a thirsty man drinking from a cool stream. "I thought that perhaps you could not make it after all."

"Crispin, here is Miss Wyckham, come to meet you. Miss Wyckham, allow me to introduce Mr. Crispin Ebershaw to you."

"Oh, yes, Miss . . . ah . .."

"Wyckham," prompted Susan gently, as one long accustomed to the task.

"I beg your pardon, Miss Wyckham, I am very happy to make your acquaintance. Susan has told me about you and said that she would ask you to accompany her today. Won't you step down? We can walk in the gardens. Or perhaps you would like to see the church? It is very beautiful, is it not? Norman architecture, you know, and quite the oldest church in the county."

"Yes, Mr. Ebershaw, very beautiful, but perhaps I could see it another time. Shall we not walk in the lovely gardens I see over there and become acquainted?"

Mr. Ebershaw had placed Susan's hand through his arm, and she walked along looking at him with such open love on her face that Hester did not know whether to laugh or cry to behold it.

As the conversation consisted of mere common-places, it was possible for her to study them both without losing her part in it. It did not take her more than a few moments to realize that here were two people as ideally suited as it would be possible to find. He was a gentle, rather vague, person, who would naturally turn to someone as soft-spoken and protective as Susan. Her own attitude was one of adulation and almost maternal care. She guided him carefully over the stones of the walk, furnished him with information when he seemed to lose his way in the middle of a sentence, and nodded in agreement with his every utterance.

That he was completely unaware of his own beauty and the effect it had on the onlooker was very evident. He was as unself-conscious as a child and obviously had more important things to do with his time than fuss about his appearance. Not that he was sloppy in his dress, but it was evident that he had not given much thought to prevailing modes. She could see how such a man would appear to Lady Breckinridge as completely beyond consideration as a suitor for her daughter.

Presently, Susan turned him gently back in the direction of the carriage, while he continued his enthusiastic discourse on a bit of Homer he was in the process of translating from the Greek. When they arrived in front of the church, Susan waited patiently for him to finish his thoughts before interrupting him.

"Crispin, I am afraid we must be going now. I will contrive to send you a message tomorrow."

"Oh, my love, I have neglected you shamefully. Is all well? Are they making you very miserable? If *only* I could make it easier for you in some way."

"I am not miserable in the least, Crispin. You are not to be worrying yourself about that."

"Exactly, my dear. We will neither one of us worry. All will come right for us, you will see."

He took her hands and bent over to kiss her plump fingers with great tenderness, then raised his head to look into her eyes. For a moment she returned his look with equal love, then gently turned him towards Hester.

"Of course, Miss . . . ah . . . Wyckham. So kind of you to come. I am so happy to know that Susan now has you for a friend. I'm sure it will help her enormously. You will come again?"

"Be assured that I will, Mr. Ebershaw."

The ladies climbed into the carriage and were driven away. After turning to wave one more farewell, Susan turned to Hester and said simply, "You see?"

"Yes, indeed, I do see, dear Susan. I see more love than is usually given to us poor mortals to experience. I wish you joy with all my heart."

"And you do see that it is impossible for me to go along with my mother's wishes and marry Lord Markham?"

Hester pondered the wisdom of becoming embroiled in what was surely a family matter and not her business. But then she thought she was being chicken-hearted. She had offered Susan her friendship, and Susan had entrusted her with her dearest secret and was confidently awaiting her reply. She could not back out now.

"Yes, I understand. I think you are absolutely right, Susan. You must just stand firm. Tell me, has Mr. Ebershaw any . . . er . . . prospects?"

"He has a small competence from his family—only about five hundred pounds a year—but he is sure to get his own church soon, and then we will do very well, especially if my parents will but consent and give me my dowry. It is quite an enormous one, you know, Hester. Much more, really, than we would need. If only I could make my mother see. I'm sure if he were vicar of his own church she would feel differently about it."

"Would she so?" asked Hester, musingly. In her mind she was moving amongst her friends and acquaintances to see if she had heard from any of them where there might possibly be a vacancy.

"Well," she continued, "we must set about it and see what can be done. Do not despair, my love, we will come about. I have no fears about your being able to hold out against your mother, especially now that I have seen the reason for it. He is well worth holding out for."

"You cannot think how happy you have made me, dear Hester. I knew I could not be mistaken in you. I will stop worrying immediately and together we shall contrive something that will answer, I'm sure."

These were brave words, but wonders can be done when two strong-minded young women take on a problem.

VIII

HESTER did not feel that she would be betraying
a confidence in revealing to Julie the conversation she
had had with Susan regarding the latter's feelings about
Lord Markham. She felt sure Susan would have expected Julie to ask and, since she had laid no strictures
about speaking of it, felt no compunction in telling.
She well knew that Julie would never reveal it.

Julie was greatly intrigued and claimed she too had
wondered why Lord Markham should have proposed
so abruptly.

"He could have done it any time these past ten years,
had he so minded. And I agree, it hardly seems
possible he could be in need of her dowry. She is right,
she should not have him!"

Naturally, Hester had not spoken of Susan's hopes
with regard to the curate, for she felt that that *would*

be betraying a confidence. But she was curious about one thing.

"We drove through Littlecomb and saw the church. We also met the curate, though the vicar was not around. Have you met Mr. Ebershaw, Julie?"

"Well, of course, I have met him."

"Well, I must say, I think it rather unusual that you have never mentioned him."

"Mentioned him? But . . . but . . . why should I have?"

"Why, Julie, he must be the most startlingly beautiful young man I've ever laid eyes on. You must have noticed him."

"Oh, yes, he is uncommonly good-looking," replied Julie indifferently.

Hester knew Julie well enough to understand her attitude. She knew the her indifference stemmed from Julie's feelings about personal beauty in general. She had never *seen* her own, having always felt deprived in the matter of inches and embarrassed about her 'woolheadedness' which made it impossible for her to deal with problems immediately as Hester always had. Her pale blond curls had been a source of much pain for her, and Hester had many memories of Julie's tear-streaked face as Nanny relentlessly pulled the brush through her tangles. Julie admired dark, romantic looks and tall, willowy figures. Knowing all this made it perfectly possible for Hester to believe that Julie could look upon Mr. Ebershaw's beauty with indifference.

Since at that moment Mr. Boscroft was announced,

Hester did not pursue the subject. Mr. Boscroft said that he had come to ask Miss Wyckham to accompany him on a drive in his curricle.

Hester protested, laughing. "Why, I thank you, Mr. Boscroft, for your kind thought, but I have just returned from a drive with Miss Breckinridge. Won't you join us instead? Julie has ordered tea, and Geoffrey will be coming in soon."

"With pleasure, if you are sure it will be no intrusion."

They settled down to await their tea and chatted quite amicably. Hester was happy to note that there seemed to be no sign that he was still displeased with her as she was certain he had been after their last exchange at the Lithey party.

However, when the footman appeared to beg Lady Hallam to speak for a moment with her housekeeper about some domestic problem and Hester was left alone with him, Mr. Boscroft became more constrained. After making a rather limp comment upon the weather he fell silent, and Hester resolutely took up the direction of the conversation.

"I was taken by Miss Breckinridge to see the church in Littlecomb, Mr. Boscroft. Lovely building, is it not?"

"Yes, it is a great attraction in this part of the country—twelfth century, you know."

"So Mr. Ebershaw informed me. You have met Mr. Ebershaw?"

"Oh, certainly. Quite an unusual young man to look upon."

"He is beyond anything beautiful! I don't know that I've ever seen a more beautiful face on anyone—with the exception of Julie."

"I understand the vicar is well pleased with the way he handles his duties. So we in Littlecomb can rest assured that we have not simply acquired a beautiful face."

"I am so happy to hear you say that. I have it in mind to see if I cannot help him to find a living of his own, if I can but think of someone of my acquaintance with a vacancy. Would you know of anything, Mr. Boscroft?"

"I will put my mind to the problem. But why are you so eager to divest Littlecomb of his good services?"

"Oh . . . well, I . . . I thought perhaps it would be a good thing for him and I would like to help him if I could."

He looked at her so particularly for a few moments that she felt quite embarrassed. Surely he could not think that she . . . She rushed into speech.

"He is surely of an age where he should have a living of his own; he has been curate here quite five years, I understand, from . . . well, never mind . . . I should think it must be certain that he will like to marry soon, and, of course, that would be almost impossible until he has secured a position for himself . . . and . . . and . . ." she floundered to a halt before his laughing regard.

"I think I understand, Miss Wyckham. All the ladies of Littlecomb are concerned for Mr. Ebershaw's good. I don't think he is aware of it, or at least, perhaps in one case he may be, though even there, one cannot be sure with him. He is rather vague at times. No doubt his mind is too much occupied with more scholarly thoughts."

"He is somewhat 'not of this world,' I must admit,"

Hester laughed. "But no doubt the worldly side of things could be attended to by the proper wife."

"And had you someone in mind for that position, Miss Wyckham?"

"Yes, I do," she said, with a secret smile.

"Not yourself," he asked quickly, a note of alarm in his voice.

"Goodness, *no*! How can you think so? No one I have ever met could be farther from my picture of an ideal husband. I would be driven into the boughs after the first hour and would probably never come down."

"No, no, I did not think he would do," he soothed her. "I feel quite sure I *know* what would be more suitable for you."

Her startled look met his own bland gaze, and she dropped her eyes in confusion.

"No challenge, Miss Wyckham? Not at all like you. However, I feel sure you will recover momentarily. But to return to the matter of the curate's wife, had you anyone in particular in mind for the post?"

"Oh, no," she said as airily as possible.

"I see. And how *is* your friend, Miss Breckinridge? All overcome with prenuptial blushes?"

Hester was saved from having to respond to this quizzing by the entrance of Julie and the footman with the tea tray. But she felt quite certain that Mr. Boscroft had learned all he needed to know regarding the state of affairs between the curate and Miss Breckinridge, and surely he could not be unaware of Susan's feelings regarding Lord Markham.

Since Geoffrey soon arrived, the conversation became

general, and shortly thereafter Mr. Boscroft took his leave. Not, however, before reiterating his invitation to be allowed to take Miss Wyckham up in his curricle for a drive the following afternoon.

Hester was delighted to agree and smiled so warmly at him that he impulsively carried her hand to his lips and kissed it. Hester felt suddenly almost giddy with pleasure. She tried to scold herself for behaving like a silly girl, but the pleased smile continued to creep back to her mouth when she thought of him. Even Geoffrey, usually so unaware, began to twit her gently about her beau.

After spending the next morning in the garden, following Julie about as she directed the several gardeners on various improvements, Hester was happy to retire to her room after lunch for a short rest and to change her gown. She spent an anxious half hour upon its selection, finally settling on a white dimity sprigged with tiny blue flowers and flounced at the hem. With it she would wear a wide-brimmed Italian straw tied down with a blue gauze scarf, and carry her white ruffled parasol.

That she presented a most fetching picture was made perfectly apparent by Mr. Boscroft, as he handed her into the carriage. He followed her, and ordered the footman to let go the horses' heads. As they rolled smoothly down the drive, Hester, aware that the boy had not swung on behind as was usual, wondered if it was quite the thing to go driving, quite unattended, about the countryside with a gentleman. But then she chided herself for being lily-hearted. After all, she decided, Mr. Boscroft was held in such high esteem by his neighbors that his reputation must be quite unassailable.

With this consoling thought, she dropped the whole problem and looked about her delightedly. The day was not too warm to enjoy the bright sunshine, and the countryside seemed bursting with a sort of ripening activity, every tree and flower busily growing and expanding. The hedges were green and burgeoning, and the wildflowers in the ditches seemed almost to be jostling each other for room.

Mr. Boscroft, accustomed to his horses and the road, spent most of his time watching her face, glowing under the white sunshade, her eyes sparkling and made an even deeper blue by the color of her scarf. She looked altogether adorable, and he ached to stop the carriage and gather her into his arms and kiss her. He wondered what her reaction would be to that, but an instant's thought gave him his rueful answer. He had no reason to suppose that her feelings for him were deeper than for any other gentleman of her acquaintance. He could only hope they were not already seriously engaged by some man she might be acquainted with at her own home or in London. Oh Lord, he thought, how many men must already have tried their luck with her. But if her affections were engaged she would surely have contrived to let him know. She was not the kind of girl to try to set all the men dangling after her whether she wanted them or not. Having come to this conclusion, he relaxed and breathed easier.

"I can see that you enjoy the country, Miss Wyckham."

"Very much. And this part of the country is, I

believe, more beautiful than our own. Everywhere one looks is some more enchanting vista. The eye can hardly grasp it all."

"But Littlecomb must surely seem dull to you after all the delights of town. We are very quiet here."

"Oh, not as quiet as we are at home. However, I assure you that I am much more a country mouse than you seem to suppose."

"I find that hard to believe. You seem to enjoy all entertainments heartily."

"Oh, certainly I do, most decidedly. I do not like to be dull at all. But I find the country entertainments more to my liking than the social whirl in London. There one may be required to attend as many as three or four parties in one evening, besides the endless activities of the day. One becomes too exhausted to truly enjoy any of it finally. I know that I am always glad to escape after a very short stay."

"I am truly happy to hear you say that."

"Why is that, Mr. Boscroft?" she asked, trying desperately not to sound coy.

"Because that is precisely the way I feel, and I am glad to know that we agree on it. I would not call myself a 'country mouse' exactly, but I cannot pretend that I don't prefer it to the city. It is becoming very important to me that we agree as much as possible," he said.

"I also find that . . . agreeable," she responded with a smile.

"Then we are . . . agreed," he smiled back, and they looked each other in the eye. This time they both burst into laughter at the same time.

"We seem always to have these words that stick and will not be dismissed, have we not?" she said.

"Yes, and it will be a *kindness* if you will always *agree* to be so agreeable and kind to me."

"I don't believe kindness is the correct description of my feelings," she answered.

"I would be most happy to have a more precise definition, Miss Wyckham."

"I don't think I can be more precise at this point," she said, suddenly serious.

"Perhaps if I defined my own first?"

"No, please do not . . . I am not . . . it would not . . ."

"No, of course," he reassured her gently. "I will wait, my dear, for as long as may be necessary."

Hester was in great agitation, for though she felt greatly attracted to Mr. Boscroft, and had already had several hints from him that his feelings for her were growing, she was not yet sure enough of her own to commit herself in any way. She felt that for the moment the attraction was enough. It should be allowed to grow and strengthen before it could be spoken of. Although she had never felt quite this way about anyone before, still they had known each other but a short time. Much too short for events to have reached this point. Thank heaven, he was sensitive enough to perceive this too.

She sat staring off over the fields they were passing until she had brought her feelings under control, and then turned to him to question him about a building she could see in the distance. He answered her calmly, without the least sign that anything out of the way had happened, for which she was most grateful. They managed to carry on quite a tolerable conversation that grew into an animated discussion of preferred architectural styles. Finally they reached home again, much pleased with each other and the way the day had turned out.

Although Mr. Boscroft had hoped for more, he was content that the door had not been closed, that he had only to go on as before, and that there was good reason to hope that one day she would accept him.

IX

THE BOUQUET of flowers that arrived the next morning sent Julie flying up the stairs to Hester's room.

"Just see what came for you, Hester. Have you ever seen more beautiful roses? Quickly, read the card, who sent them?"

Her heart beating wildly, Hester opened the note with as much equanimity as she could muster. But her face showed her disappointment before she could stop herself.

"Oh," she said disinterestedly, "from Captain Frampton."

"Well, but what does he say?"

"Oh, here, you may read it. Nothing interesting, I'm afraid."

Julie read Captain Frampton's greeting which simply presented his compliments and the message that he would look forward to seeing her at dinner that evening. Julie looked at Hester with interest. She had not missed that look of disappointment and couldn't help hoping that it was because the flowers were not from Mr. Boscroft. She had also been sharp enough to read more than the usual happiness in Hester's face when she had returned from her drive the previous afternoon.

She knew better than to question Hester at this point, however. Hester would always tell her first, Julie was sure, when she was ready to talk about her feelings.

Now she merely asked Hester's opinion on the menu for dinner. Julie had asked the Breckinridges and their nephew for a very small gathering. She had sent round a note to Lord Markham also but had been informed that he was still away from home, though expected back tomorrow. Julie was just as glad. From what Hester had told her she knew that, had he accepted, the party might have been most uncomfortable for all concerned. In all honesty, though she owed the Breckinridges a dinner, she had to admit that the main purpose of asking them for tonight was so that she could see whether anything further had happened so far as Lord Markham's suit was concerned. She deplored this light-minded curiosity in herself, but managed to calm her conscience with the knowledge that she must entertain Hester after all.

She now went to find Geoffrey and tell him about the flowers and consult him about what Hester's disappointment could mean. Geoffrey was always so wise.

But that gentleman disclaimed any knowledge of how women reacted to such things.

"You need not concern yourself with it, my love. Sensible girl, Hester, no fear that she will lose her head and shame her family."

"Of course not, Geoffrey. But think if it should be Mr. Boscroft! Why, we should be neighbors! Oh, the heaven of having her next door practically. It would make me happy above all things."

"Now don't start that matchmaking nonsense, Julie. Besides, doesn't do to get your hopes all set in one direction. Women are such fickle creatures, I vow I don't believe they ever make up their minds except on the spur of the moment."

"Oh, how can you say so, you wicked creature? Did I not make up my mind when first I set eyes on you?"

"Spur of the moment, just as I said."

"Why, Geoffrey, not true at all. It must have taken me the better part of . . . a week!" she said, dimpling up at him so entrancingly that he pulled her to him suddenly and held her so tightly that she gasped.

When the Breckinridges were shown in, Lady Breckinridge, bedecked with enough glitter for several dowagers, steamed across the floor and grasped Julie's hands with a sad but speaking glance. Julie knew immediately that something untoward had happened and looked to see if Hester was aware. Hester nodded imperceptibly and came forward to greet the guests.

When she came to Susan, she knew instantly that the battle had been joined, and obviously Susan had won. She had her chin well up and her shoulders back and looked at Hester with such triumph in her eyes that no one could doubt her victory.

Lord Breckinridge looked troubled and unhappy but did his best to hide it. And Captain Frampton had the hunted look of a man whose good nature has been tested to its limits. He had obviously become embroiled in a family situation that was more than he had bargained for when he had contemplated repairing to the country in search of a healthy country girl who would make a proper soldier's wife.

Julie, all charm and graciousness, did her best to soothe all sensibilities and, with Hester's assistance, finally succeeded in making the evening, if not a resounding success, at least not a crashing failure.

When the ladies left the table, Julie managed to maneuver Lady Breckinridge into her morning room to look at the new carpet, giving Hester a chance for a few words alone with Susan, thus ensuring that she would find out what had happened when they had all gone home.

"Hester! I have prevailed. And I owe it all to you. I could never have been so strong if you had not given me the courage."

Hester tried to discourage the idea that she had had anything to do with it, but Susan would not allow her to.

"Oh, yes, indeed, you gave me strength. I told Mama that nothing—nothing—would ever make me change my mind. That I would not have Lord Markham and that, if she persisted, I would *elope* with Mr. Ebershaw. That brought her up short, I can tell you. She pretended to swoon, but I just ignored it. She

never swoons. Then she called in papa, and he began
to look as though he were having apoplexy, and she
began to berate me for an unfeeling daughter. My
cousin came in, and she appealed to him to talk to me
to try to make me see reason, and he kept saying it
had nothing to do with him and trying to get out of
the room. Oh, it was a grand set-to, believe me. But I
never raised my voice, except to make myself heard,
of course. I just kept repeating that I would elope with
Mr. Ebershaw if they persisted, and finally my papa
said they must give in then, he supposed. So I made
him sit down and write Lord Markham immediately
and tell him that it would not work . . . and he did!"

Hester had listened to this long outpouring with
astonishment and some amusement. So the mouse had
spirit. Bravo, she thought. Really, Lady Breckinridge
was a very foolish woman to persist in her pretensions. She had the means at hand to make a most suitable marriage for her daughter, certainly a most
happy one, and if she cared for Susan more than herself she should have seen it and been grateful for it
long ago.

She heard Julie approaching with Lady Breckinridge and immediately picked up her embroidery frame
and began showing her stitches to Susan. The gentlemen soon followed, and there was no further chance
for discussion between Susan and Hester.

Captain Frampton advanced upon Hester purposefully and requested that she walk with him upon the
terrace. Actually, Hester could not help thinking it
was more a command than a request, but she gave in.
She knew he would not listen to her anyway, and at

least there could be some amusing story to tell Julie later.

Pulling her arm through his, he strode off down the terrace so fast that she had to run to keep up with him. Finally, gasping breathlessly, she pulled him to a stop.

"Captain Frampton, had you a goal in mind for our walk?"

"Goal? No, no, just a walk, you know, to take the air."

"Ah, good, then you won't mind if we set a more leisurely pace, will you. I like a nice walk myself after a large meal, but I must confess I don't care for a run."

He laughed. "Right you are. A walk it shall be. I had something else on my mind and quite forgot our purpose."

"And what had you on your mind, sir?"

"Oh, to escape the sight of my aunt's sad look fastening upon me. Perhaps I should not be speaking of it, but it really is beyond anything, Miss Wyckham. There's my aunt spending the whole afternoon enacting Cheltenham tragedies, and the whole house in an awful uproar. I vow, it's not right to make such a thing out of a simple engagement. Either they suit or they don't. No use to make such a fuss about it."

"I agree, Captain Frampton. And did you think they suited?"

"Why, I had no opinion one way or the other. Don't know the fellow. But I could have told 'em they were wasting their breath when they tried to force Susan to do something she didn't like. She was always like that, even as a little girl, I remember. She could be pushed only so far."

"Well, I admire her for that spirit, Captain Frampton. And so should Lady Breckinridge. After all, I'm sure a great deal of it was inherited from her."

"And so I told her. But she wouldn't have it. Said Susan was always such a biddable good girl, had never crossed her, and on and on. Ha! I set her straight on that score. Oh, let us talk of something else. My aunt puts me out of all patience."

"Certainly. What would you prefer to talk of?"

"You," he answered promptly. "I've hardly thought of anything else since I met you, and that's a fact, Miss Wyckham."

"I would prefer that you did not, Captain Frampton."

"Well, we cannot always have things just as we want them, can we, Miss Wyckham? But I am sure that in time you will come to see my point of view with better favor."

"I assure you that I will not, sir. Can we not now move on to some other topic of conversation?"

"No, dammit . . . beg your pardon, I'm sure . . . but I've been thinking of this meeting all afternoon. And there's my aunt giving me no peace. I've forgotten most of the things I had planned to say to you."

"Put your mind at rest, Captain Frampton. It is much better so."

"Now look here . . . I mean to have you for my wife, Miss Wyckham. Had my mind set on it the moment I saw you and have learned of nothing since to change my mind."

"You've been making inquiries then, have you?"

"Well, of course. You're a dammed . . . pardon . . . fine-looking girl and all that, but can't go buying a pig in a poke, you know."

"Oh, indeed I do know. And, to continue with your metaphor, what did you find? Do you think it is possible to make this pig's ear into a silk purse?"

"Oh, have no fear, nothing at all against you that I can learn. Good family, respectable dowry, well behaved."

"How very gratifying, to be sure," she gurgled, hoping that she would be able to remember every word of this remarkable dialogue for Julie.

"Well, there you are then. I'm sure your brother-in-law will be able to tell you anything you may wish to know about me. Won't find anything to my discredit, let me assure you. I've never had the time to fribble-frabble my time away on loose women or gambling or anything of that kind. And I'm well fixed, you know. You would always have the necessary."

"Oh, I'm sure that must be true, Captain Frampton. But I'm afraid I must again refuse your kind offer."

"Expected you would. But I'm a patient man. You may have all the time you like to consider it."

"But I'm compelled to tell you that I would not suit your requirements at all. I suffer somewhat from nosebleeds and am prone to complain a great deal of the cold. Most unsuitable for a soldier's wife, I fear."

He studied her deliberately for a moment, then said, "Oh, I expect I could keep you warm, Miss Wyckham."

At this she blushed and turned quickly to the door. But before she could move away his hand shot out

and caught her around the waist and pulled her to
him.

"Now, if I were not a gentleman, Miss Wyckham,
and very serious about marrying you, I should kiss
you. I know you would not like it, but I think you
must own that you deserve it."

Hester did not struggle, but stood perfectly still
and looked him in the eye. She had to acknowledge
that he was right, that she had been teasing him, and
that in spite of his single-mindedness to get what he
wanted, he had meant only to honor her.

"I'm sure I beg your pardon, Captain Frampton.
You are right, I was behaving inexcusably, but you
did not seem to hear me when I refused you."

He let her go and stepped back. "That was well
done of you, Miss Wyckham. I accept your apology
and offer mine. Now that we understand one another,
I think we shall go on famously together. Now, I wonder if you have a sable cloak, Miss Wyckham?"

"A . . . a . . . sable cloak," she stuttered, bewildered at this abrupt change of subject.

"Yes, you said you suffered from the cold. I
thought if you did not possess a good warm cloak,
that I might make you a present of one. Damme, if
that won't keep you warm when you follow the
drum."

Hester looked at him in perplexity for a moment,
then as his meaning burst upon her, she began to
laugh helplessly.

In the drawing room Lady Breckinridge heard
these peals of laughter and looked much put upon.
She turned to Geoffrey and asked in her most for-

bearing voice who could find so much to be merry about.

Geoffrey said, "Oh, that must be Hester. Must be the air in this part of the country. She's been carrying on like that since she arrived."

After the company had all departed, Hester told Geoffrey and Julie about her encounter with Captain Frampton. At least, she told them most of it, leaving out only the last part of which she was ashamed and had yet to settle with her conscience. Even Geoffrey laughed and enjoyed the story and told her she might do worse.

Julie was indignant at this and declared she would never forgive Hester if she married some soldier and went traipsing off around the world where they could never see each other. Hester assured her there was no danger of this. While they were still talking, the butler entered with a note that had come, he said, earlier in the evening for Miss Wyckham.

Hester scanned it quickly and then read it to Julie and Geoffrey. It was from Mr. Boscroft to announce that he would be away for a few days on urgent business and to please forgive him for not being able to call upon her tomorrow.

Hester took the note to her room and once in bed read it again. She felt all at once quite deflated. Several days, he said. What could have called him away so suddenly, she wondered. Just when they . . . She hurriedly put that thought aside. But all the same, she said to herself defiantly, I *am* disappointed.

X

HESTER'S VISIT had been, so far, most satisfactory.
Set in such idyllic surroundings, with the slow-paced
social life of Littlecomb fitting her mood exactly, she
was most content. The tiny ripples in the pond created
by Susan's rejection of Lord Markham's proposal,
Julie's small cloud that she was sure would soon be
cleared away, the entrance of Captain Frampton into
her life, and the first stirrings of her own feelings, all
acted to keep the waters from stagnating. Just enough
to make each day interesting, she thought smugly, but
not enough to agitate the spirits.

Reclining on the golden chaise in her bedroom, with
a book from Geoffrey's library and the whole afternoon
her own, she reveled in the peaceful scene spread for
her view from the windows. Beyond the rose gardens the
fields began, and lovely groves of trees beckoned with
their shade in the haze of sunlight, the stillness so com-

plete that the only sound was the hum of insects or an intermittent birdcall.

She heard the sound of hoof beats, but slow-paced, not signalling urgency. She supposed it was one of the stablemen or someone else about the business of the estate. She very much hoped so, because this was her first afternoon entirely to herself since she had arrived. Julie had gone calling on one of their tenants, and Hester had begged to be excused from accompanying her this once. She was feeling languid and peaceful and completely enjoying her solitude.

She turned her eyes back to the poems of Lord Byron and read:

> Man's love is of man's life a thing apart;
> 'Tis woman's whole existence.

Oh how exactly right, she thought. At that moment there was a tap on the door.

"Yes, come in," she called.

"Begging your pardon, miss, but Baynes sent me to tell you there's a gentleman," said the little maid.

"A gentleman? Well, I'm sure he wants Lord Hallam."

"Please, miss, master's from home."

"Well, did he tell the gentleman that?"

"To be sure, miss. And he told how mistress was away, and the gentleman said as how he would see you."

"Me? Who is the gentleman?"

"'Tis Lord Markham, miss."

"Good God! Now what to do? Oh, very well, tell Baynes to show him into the drawing room, and I'll be down directly."

The maid withdrew and Hester sat for a moment, not only reluctant to spoil her lovely rest, but even more reluctant to meet Lord Markham. She had not liked him, and added to that was her uncomfortable knowledge about Susan's rejection of him, which he must have had already. However, she did not like to appear rude to a guest of Julie's and Geoffrey's, so she knew she must go down to greet him.

She went to the mirror and cursorily tidied her hair, decided the rather plain, even if somewhat rumpled, gown she was wearing would do for Lord Markham, and slowly proceeded down to the drawing room.

He turned from the window and crossed to meet her, taking her hand and kissing it warmly. She retrieved it as quickly as possible and asked him to be seated.

"Thank you, Miss Wyckham. I hope you will not mind my calling. I only returned last night and came as soon as I could attend to my household problems."

"Why, I'm sure that is very kind of you, Lord Markham. But I am puzzled as to the reason for your haste. If it is something to do with Geoffrey, I'm sure he'll be back presently, and you are most welcome to wait."

"No, no, not at all. My business is entirely with you."

"With me?"

"Of course. You must know, Miss Wyckham, since the night we met I've thought of little else. I hope you will not think me too forward and precipitate, but I can remain silent no longer. I must declare what is in my heart."

Throughout this speech Hester stared at Lord Markham, first in puzzlement, then in amazement, finally with real distaste.

"Sir, you will oblige me by ceasing instantly. I do not

believe that I have ever said or done anything to indicate that I would welcome such a declaration from you, but you may take my word for it that any such idea could only have been a misunderstanding on your part."

"I protest, Miss Wyckham, I made sure I had revealed myself only too plainly."

"Lord Markham, we exchanged a few words at dinner on various books and places of interest. Beyond that there was no conversation of any personal nature whatsoever."

"I am devastated . . . that I could have been showing my heart to you, and you so completely unaware. Never have I spoken of those things to anyone."

"Then your conversations must be very thin on content," she replied drily.

"Mere flirtations, to pass the time, I assure you. You are the only woman I've ever met with whom one could have a 'conversation.' It was a revelation to me, believe me. You will allow me to hope? I know you cannot be so heartless as to say no."

"I'm sure you mean to do me honor, Lord Markham, but I must decline. Now I must ask you to excuse me. I have a headache and must retire to my room. Goodday."

So saying, she held out her hand. For a moment he held it tightly clasped in both of his, gave her one of his dark, brooding looks, and bowed.

"I warn you, I will not take no for an answer," he said abruptly and turned and stalked out of the room.

She tottered over to the sofa and collapsed upon it and sat stunned for a few moments staring vacantly into space. She was still there when Geoffrey walked in. He spoke to her, but at first she was not even aware of it. Then it seemed his voice finally broke through her thoughts and she turned to him, startled.

"Oh, Geoffrey, I beg your pardon, I didn't hear you come in."

"Must say you look strange, Hester. Something happen? Please—whatever it was—don't start giggling again."

"No, Geoffrey, laughing is the farthest thing from my mind at the moment. I've just had the most unusual experience, and I simply cannot account for it."

"Well, it couldn't be ghosts, if that's what you think— house was never haunted to my knowledge, and my family have lived here forever."

"Geoffrey, sit down and let me ask you something. You know Lady Breckinridge told us that Lord Markham had asked for Susan? Then you remember I told you of Susan's refusal. Well, at least, I told Julie, and I'm sure she told you."

"Yes, yes, get on with it, Hester."

"And he has been away from home since that day?"

"Yes, and he got back last night, I know. Billson my stableman told me, had it from Markham's coachman this morning."

"Yes, so he said to me."

"Who said to you?"

"Lord Markham, haven't I been telling you?"

"Hester," began Geoffrey, with great patience, as though he were speaking to a child, "start again and take it very slowly. We'll come about, you'll see."

"Geoffrey, please don't speak to me in that tone of voice. You can see that I am trying to tell it all from the beginning. Now just listen without interrupting—please."

Feeling unjustly censured, Lord Hallam sat back, folded his arms, and looked put upon.

Hester began again. "Lord Markham left here not two minutes before you walked in. He was told you and Julie were out and asked for me. I felt that I must do the honors for the house, so I came down. He began instantly, with no preamble whatsoever, to tell me that . . . that . . . well, actually, he made a declaration. He told me he came as soon as possible, had been thinking of me since we met, and would I allow him to hope."

"Well, you must be used to these things by now, Hester. Been out two years, dammed pretty girl—must have had more than your share of proposals."

"Geoffrey, are your wits wandering? Please pay attention. Did I not ask you, to begin with, about Lord Markham's proposal to Susan?"

"Yes, by God, you did. Now what's this? What sort of blackguard game's he playing?"

"Exactly. I knew you would come to it eventually," she replied sweetly.

"Never liked that fellow above half. Oh, I could tell you things, if I'd a mind. Not fit for your ears. Fellow's got a bad reputation in London, from all I've heard. Must say he's always behaved himself down here though."

"Well, I'm afraid he's up to something very strange. If he came back last night, and by the way, I could stand to know why he went tearing off to London in such a hurry after Susan's first refusal, he must have had

Lord Breckinridge's note with Susan's definite refusal as soon as he returned. And then this afternoon he comes strolling in here as cool as you please and proposes to me. Not a sign that he was in any way distressed by Susan's turndown. Come to think of it, not a sign that there had ever been such a thing in his mind as a proposal to her. What can he mean by it?"

"Devilish deep, that's what he is, and I for one won't put up with any of his tricks. I'll call on him immediately and ask him what he thinks he's up to."

"No, no, Geoffrey, please don't do anything. I've told him no, and I mean to have no more to do with it. If you go rampaging over there, you'll blow it all up to more importance than it deserves. Let's just forget it and hope he is sensible enough to say no more about it."

She could not bring herself to tell Geoffrey of Lord Markham's parting words. She was sure that he had only to hear them and he *would* call on Lord Markham. She could only hope that she would hear no more of the matter. At least from Lord Markham. Naturally, she would tell Julie.

Julie didn't hesitate to give her opinion the moment she heard the story. "He doesn't believe we know. He must believe the Breckinridges would not speak of it until things were settled. Oh, what a cabbagehead he must be! To have known Lady Breckinridge all this time and not understand her well enough to think that she would keep silent about such a thing."

"Yes, but why rush around to propose to me?"

"Well, perhaps it was love at first sight, and he only realized the depth of his feelings after he had spoken to

Lord Breckinridge, and then he rushed off to London
in despair and . . ."

"Julie, Julie, what a lot of romantic faradiddle,"
laughed Hester. "What novel are you reading now?"

"Well, just the same. . ." Then she broke off and
started again. "Oh, dear heaven, I completely forgot.
We are to dine with the Halseys tonight. You know, the
parents of that beau of Letitia's, who sits and stares
at her all the time. They are very nice, and I'm sure you
will like them excessively. They have just come down
from a stay in Scotland or someplace and sent round
to ask us. I wonder who will be there? What shall you
wear? Oh dear, I wonder if my lilac will do. I must go
check on it."

She rushed from the room, and Hester followed her
up and rang for Moreton. She tried to decide on a
gown and how she would have her hair arranged. It
didn't seem so important as it had on other occasions,
and she was not long in discovering the reason. Mr.
Boscroft would not be there. A few days, he had said.
Perhaps he would be back tomorrow. At least she
could begin to look for him then.

She wished for him more than ever when she entered
the Halseys' drawing room and caught sight immediately of Lord Markham, leaning languidly against
the mantel and listening to a very fetching Letitia.
Young Halsey was struggling valiantly to make conversation with Mrs. Lithey.

Lord Markham detached himself instantly and came
to Hester's side, taking her hand and kissing it with
great, and most embarrassing, fervor. Hester felt sure

it must be remarked upon by the whole company and didn't know where to look. Julie shepherded her away most expertly towards their hostess, and Geoffrey, at her urgent signal, came up on Hester's other side. For the moment she felt safe. But she could not spend the evening between them. She smiled at them both, patted their arms reassuringly, and turned back to the company, resolved to defend herself.

And she did need that resolve. Lord Markham made a determined set at her, leaving no one present in any doubt of his intentions. She fended him off as best she could. Fortunately, she was not required to be his partner at dinner. But she was aware of his eyes upon her throughout the agonizingly slow meal, and she became so discomfited that she could hardly carry on a coherent conversation with her kindly host on one side and Mr. Lithey on the other. Finally, after the gentlemen had rejoined the ladies in the drawing room, Markham succeeded in getting her into a corner and, standing with his back to the room, began to plead his case again. Hester was ready to sink through the floor with embarrassment.

"Please desist, Lord Markham, you are making me the object of attention of the whole room, and I do not like it."

"My beautiful love, Hester . . . you do not mind that I call you Hester . . . I feel that I have known you always. You look, if such a thing were possible, even more bewitching than the last time we met. My heart is quite overcome."

"Well, mine is not. Now please stand aside, sir, and let me pass."

"Please hear my case, Hester. I love you. I will go tomorrow to speak to your father."

"You will do no such thing, Lord Markham! I really do not wish to discuss this further. If you persist I'm afraid I may forget myself and say what might be better left unsaid."

"Say, my dear love, say what you like. I will answer."

"Very well, Lord Markham. If you insist. To begin with, may I ask why, if you were so overcome with love for me the moment you met me, you proposed to Susan Breckinridge the very next day?"

The dark face went instantly still, and Hester noted with interest that he seemed to be white around the lips. She watched him and waited without speaking for a moment. When he did not answer, she continued.

"No answer, my lord? Then I will try you with another. Why, if your heart was so stirred by passion, did you go haring off to London the very next day?"

He stared at her so bleakly for a moment that she felt positively chilled. But she refused to acknowledge any feelings, continuing to stare back at him as dispassionately as possible.

"Hester," he finally said, through clenched lips, "there are many things you cannot know about and that I cannot tell you now. They do not matter in the least. When we are married . . ."

She stamped her foot in anger and amazement that he could continue spoiling her pose of calm disinterest.

"We are not to be married. What must I say to make you believe that you are the last person in the world I would even consider. I do not like you, Lord Markham. There, I can't say plainer than that."

He simply smiled tolerantly, as one watching a favored child being mischievous.

"You will see, I will make you love me, my dear love."

"I am not . . ." she began indignantly, ". . . your dear love," she trailed off more quietly, as he turned away and she became aware of a number of interested eyes.

When she could be alone with Julie she berated her. "Why did you not come to my aid? Could you not see how much I needed you?" she said, nearly in tears.

"Oh, Hester, my darling, I am so sorry. But when I tried to rescue you earlier, you seemed to want to handle it yourself. I didn't like to interfere."

And with that, Hester, though feeling very sorry for herself, had to be satisfied. She *had* wanted to defend herself. She *had* felt completely competent to dampen the pretensions of such a man as Lord Markham. She wondered what there was in her to have attracted two such seemingly insensitive, arrogant men as Lord Markham and Captain Frampton. She even wondered wildly for a moment if there were any other kind of man. But then she remembered Mr. Boscroft and was comforted. He was sensitive . . . and kind (she apologized silently to him, but he *was*) . . . and would never make her an insane proposal and not hear her refusal. Of course, she had to admit, he might not make her any proposal at all. But she remembered his eyes that day in the curricle. She could not be mistaken about his feelings for her. Could she? And did she really *want* his proposal? Ah, she thought, there is the crux of the problem. While she liked him better than any man she had ever met, she had no mind to marry so soon. She felt that there were many things in life to be done, many places to go, that, once saddled with home and family—and she did want a family—she would no longer have the heart for. She was in great hopes of persuading her father to take her to Italy next winter. He was not averse, having a great longing himself to see the classical ruins *in situ,* after having viewed Lord Elgin's loot. He called Lord Elgin a pirate and was indignant that those beautiful marbles were no longer adorning the Acropolis to be seen in their true glory. He was most anxious to get there before "those damned bandits" completely denuded the country.

So, Italy and Greece loomed large in her immediate plans. She was not averse to a gentle summer dalliance, but she must guard herself against any more serious assaults on her heart. Feeling that she had thought things through, calmly and reasonably, she resolved to keep her wits about her in the future and not allow anything to assume more importance than it deserved.

XI

HESTER accompanied Julie the next morning into the nearby town of Barnes in quest of long white kid gloves to wear to the Barnes Assembly the next evening. They had settled upon their costumes for this ball earlier that morning. Julie, torn between a pale green gauze over white satin and cream lace over blue, had finally settled on the green, while Hester had little choice but to wear her spangled white spider gauze over white satin. She had brought only two ball gowns with her, feeling that surely this would be sufficient for such a short stay in a country town, and she had already worn the pink to Mrs. Lithey's rout. Julie had nearly swooned at the smartness of the white gauze, declaring that nothing like it had ever been seen, and that she would make all the other ladies quite green with envy.

They were now seated in Mr. Shrubsole's emporium, while that bustling gentleman flung bolts of fabric about for their inspection. The store was like an enchanted fairyland, with shimmering satins, frail silks and gauzes, demure muslins and dimities, and French cambrics in every color. Hester felt she must simply have a length of silver gauze to drape across her elbows in the newest style. She selected her white kid gloves and could not resist another dainty pair of palest lilac, and an irresistible pair of claret kid half-boots to go with her riding dress.

Julie chose several lengths of fabric that she felt life would be insupportable without, and altogether they had a fine time.

Into this very feminine atmosphere strolled Mr. Boscroft. Hester felt her heart perform a very complicated movement, creating a shortness of breath. However, having resolved to be sensible in the matter of these susceptibilities, she bravely took a deep breath and greeted him with what she felt to be an admirable coolness. Could she have seen the welcoming warmth that glowed in her face, she would not have been so complacent in her feelings.

"Mr. Boscroft!" she said, holding out her hand, "you are back!"

"I am back, my d . . . er . . . Miss Wyckham," he corrected himself with a hasty glance at Julie. He held Hester's hand for only a fraction longer than was necessary and then turned to greet Julie.

"Oh, Mr. Boscroft, this is wonderful. You are back in time for the Assembly tomorrow evening. You will be there?"

"I wouldn't miss it, Lady Hallam. I hope I am not too late to claim the first dance, Miss Wyckham?"

"No, Mr. Boscroft, you are not," she said demurely.

"And since I am so happily circumstanced as to advance myself before you are quite beseiged, I will make so bold as to claim at least three more and the supper hour. Will I seem a very greedy fellow in your eyes? Or do you perhaps fear that we will create a scandal?"

"Oh, I believe my reputation can withstand any such assaults upon my character. At any rate, I will chance it."

Julie took this opportunity to tease them both. "You will have your work cut out for you, Mr. Boscroft, to have so many dances with Hester. She has captured several hearts in your absence."

"And may I inquire the names of my competition? Forewarned, you know."

"Well, let me see now. There's Captain Frampton and Lord Markham amongst the crowd who seem to besiege her when she but appears."

Mr. Boscroft's face darkened. "Lord Markham?" he inquired in an icy voice.

"Why, yes, I forgot that you could not know of it. This has all come about while you were from home."

"I do not understand you, Lady Hallam. *What* has all 'come about'? If I mistake not, Lord Markham was well on the way to a firm offer to Miss Breckinridge. Has he cried off?"

"Oh, no, Mr. Boscroft, that is not the way of it at all. It was she who cried off. She would not have him, and managed finally to convince her parents that nothing could prevail upon her to accept him. Is that not famous? I declare, nothing could have so shocked us all as that. I'm afraid we had not taken the true measure of Miss Breckinridge," said Julie.

Hester put her hand on Julie's arm in gentle warning. She did not like this gossiping in a shop about the affairs of a neighbor. Julie had the grace to blush and lowered her eyes in confusion. She was ashamed to think that she could so have forgotten her manners and her sense of what was right.

"I beg your pardon," she said faintly, "I'm afraid I sometimes forget my surroundings."

"No real harm done, Julie. Now let us forget it," said Hester and turned to the counter to pick up the length of silver gauze. "Is this not delicious, Mr. Boscroft? I declare it will go perfectly with my white ball gown. I am so delighted to have found it."

But Mr. Boscroft, though acknowledging it to be beautiful, could not seem to give it his entire attention. His eyes strayed off into the middle distance and stayed there, while his lips seemed to tighten, and the muscles in his cheeks were quite visibly twitching.

"Is anything wrong, Mr. Boscroft?" inquired Hester, who had not missed this display.

"What . . . oh, I beg your pardon, Hes . . . Miss Wyckham . . . you were saying?"

She laughed at him, "Oh nothing of any importance at all, Mr. Boscroft. Mere women's twitterings, I'm afraid."

"I have never heard you 'twitter,' Miss Wyckham," he replied firmly, "and I'm quite sure you would be incapable of it."

This response was enormously gratifying to Hester. She felt that nothing nicer had ever been said to her. She smiled at him so wholeheartedly that he looked completely bemused for a moment. Then pulling himself together, he asked them to excuse him, that he

had several things to attend to, much as he detested
the idea of leaving their company.

When he had bowed himself out, Julie stood staring
after him with a most speculative look in her eye and
turned to inspect Hester's face, in search of information. Evidently she found it, for she nodded to herself
in a congratulatory way, and looked extremely pleased.

Having exhausted the possibilities of Mr. Shrubsole's stock, they took themselves home, well satisfied
with their morning's foray. The afternoon found them
entertaining several callers, including the Litheys and
the doctor's wife. It turned into a cozy, women's tea,
with much talk of dressmakers and the latest French
fashions, and genteel gossip of the neighborhood. All
the ladies being well-bred and kind-hearted, it never
became malicious, to Hester's great relief.

The evening—happily, they felt—held no engage-
ments, so they spent a very quiet dinner with Geoffrey
and were grateful to retire quite early to their beds.

The morning of the ball in Barnes dawned bright
and warm and found Julie and Hester enjoying an
early ride. They took the now familiar way, and Hester could not help hoping that Mr. Boscroft might join
them. He did not appear, but when they arrived home
she found that he had not forgotten her altogether.

Nor, evidently, had he been so inattentive as she
had supposed when she was gushing about the gown
she would be wearing. For there on the hall table was
the most enchanting bouquet for her to carry, a tight
little circle of palest pink and white rosebuds nestling
in a collar of silver lace paper and trailing silver ribband streamers. Hester felt her heart quite melting with

the sweetness of it. The card said simply, "Not with kindness. Philip Boscroft."

Philip, she thought. Will I ever be able to call him that, having thought of him all this time as Mr. Boscroft?

Julie did not ask to see the card, but contented herself with exclaiming that nothing could be more perfect to match her costume, and hurried off to find Geoffrey and relate this latest news. She knew he would only warn her not to set her mind on such an uncertain event, since he could not bear to see her disappointed in any way. She knew full well that he was right, but just the same she was unable to keep from almost dancing down the hall.

The day brought two more posies for Hester—both perfectly unexceptionable as to taste and beauty, and both equally suitable to carry with her that evening. But she only glanced at the cards disinterestedly and asked the butler to carry them away. Julie watched all of this with great interest and inquired casually who were her admirers.

"Oh, Captain Frampton and Lord Markham. How they have the nerve after the setdowns I have given them both, I cannot think. I believe they must be completely caper-witted to carry on this farce," she replied in great annoyance.

But this irritation had entirely disappeared by the time she entered the Assembly rooms in Barnes with Geoffrey and Julie. Mr. Boscroft, who seemed to have been waiting just inside the door, immediately presented himself and eyed his floral offering with enormous gratification. She thanked him prettily for it, saying he must know more of women's fashions than he allowed, to have chosen the bouquet with such perfect taste.

They made their bows to all the dowagers arrayed along the wall and, duty done, turned to each other and to a general inspection of the room. It had been decorated for the occasion with great swags of blue and white bunting and an enormous profusion of flowers. The ballroom was quite crowded, and the orchestra was already tuning up for the dancing. Julie and Geoffrey led the way, and they strolled about the room to greet their many acquaintances. They were besieged by a diaphanous cloud of pink, blue, and primrose, which resolved itself into the Lithey girls, breathless with excitement as usual, all talking at once and surrounded by a hedge of attendant swains. When the master of ceremonies announced the first dance, they were swept away as precipitously as they had appeared.

Mr. Boscroft made Hester a formal bow and extended his arm. She took it happily, and he led her out onto the floor. Over his shoulder as they waited for the music to begin, she saw Lord Markham enter the room. His eyes found her instantly, and he scowled as he noticed the bouquet she was carrying. She looked away as though she had not noticed him. She knew she would have to contend with him during the evening, as well as with Captain Frampton, but she felt quite equal to these encounters. Nothing seemed able to depress her spirits tonight.

That she had need of a light-hearted attitude was made abundantly apparent when she was led to the side of the room by Mr. Boscroft after the first set. Lord Markham appeared instantly and asked for the next dance. Since she knew better than to appear for two consecutive dances with one gentleman in such a small place as Barnes, she felt it was better to accept and get it over with. She threw Mr. Boscroft a speaking glance and took Lord Markham's arm, and allowed herself to be led away.

Lord Markham remained coldly silent for a few moments to signify his displeasure.

"You are very quiet, Lord Markham," said Hester. "How can you be out of sorts with so much gaiety about you?"

"You received my flowers, Miss Wyckham?" he asked heavily.

"Why, yes, how forgetful of me. Thank you very much for such thoughtfulness, Lord Markham."

"You did not find them suitable to carry tonight?"

"They were lovely indeed, sir," she replied, "but these arrived first, you see," she said blandly.

He merely raised his eyebrows at this, knowing full well that ladies would contrive any excuse to carry the bouquet of the man they most wished to honor.

"I do not like to see you carrying another man's gift. People will not know who sent it to you, of course. But I do not think it is fitting."

She gave him a look of great astonishment. "I must tell you, Lord Markham, that I do not feel that I require your approval for anything I choose to do."

He seemed not hear this protest, pursuing the subject as though unaware of her anger. "In these small towns any such mark of favor is pounced on immediately and fanned about within hours. Some of these women will have no compunction about inquiring of the florist as to who ordered the bouquet carried by

Miss So-and-So at last night's ball. They are uncon-
scionable," he said with indignation.

"They may inquire to their hearts' content, for all
of me. In fact, I will most happily give them the information myself, if applied to," she declared.

"Yes, you are much too open to be able to dissimu-
late, Miss Wyckham. That is why I felt I should warn
you. It will not do to set the whole neighborhood gossiping," and on this pronouncement was carried away
by the figure of the dance so that she was unable to
squelch him with a reply. But she felt a smoldering
anger beginning to build at his presumption. She realized, however, that if she gave way to it, she would
spoil the wonderful mood of the evening. She was determined to enjoy herself, and so by the time they were
carried face to face again, she had swallowed her rage
and was able to meet him with a cool smile. She replied noncomittally to his further remarks, and the
dance finally ended. She allowed him to lead her to
Julie, talking with several gentlemen at one end of the
room, and deliberately turned her back on him. Mr.
Dalton, one of the Lithey beaux, immediately claimed
her hand for the next dance, and she accepted gladly.

She was now dismayed to note that the Breckinridges
had arrived, accompanied inevitably by Captain
Frampton. She cast about rather wildly for Mr. Boscroft and saw him in a group quite nearby. As though
sensing her glance, he turned and smiled at her warmly.
He came to her briefly to remind her that the next
dance was his and then returned to his conversation.
But she felt reassured immediately.

After the next set she knew she could delay no
longer greeting the Breckinridges. Susan was looking at

her so expectantly that Hester had not the heart to keep her waiting. Mr. Dalton obligingly led her to them, and she made her curtsy to Lord and Lady Breckinridge and turned bravely to hold out her hand to Captain Frampton. He bent to kiss it heartily and claimed there was not a woman in the room could hold a candle to her, that she would break hearts at his officers' balls.

Her heart sank at this possessiveness, but she knew she must simply depress his expectations as much as possible and hope for the best.

She turned to Susan, noting that she was looking, not beautiful, of course, but very different from her usual self. For one thing she held her head up and looked about her with great interest. No more the retiring mouse, she had an eager, glowing look that quite became her. She was dressed most tastefully in the palest blue, with a breathtaking necklace of sapphires and diamonds set as tiny flowers.

Lady Breckinridge seemed to be wearing the entire contents of her jewel box, all draped or pinned randomly about her person. She appeared very depressed, and Hester wondered uneasily how she would react when she became aware of Lord Markham's very obvious behavior.

There was some bewilderment on the part of the other guests, who were, of course, unaware of Lord Breckinridge's note of refusal to Lord Markham and were therefore unable to understand the greetings exchanged between them. Lord and Lady Breckinridge, coming face to face with Lord Markham, bowed gravely. Susan, though she flushed painfully, stared him straight in the eye defiantly and did not move or blink in acknowledgment. Lord Markham stared coldly back, then with a nod barely within the bounds of civility, passed on. Lady Breckinridge looked completely crushed by this snub, but Susan's mouth seemed to have all it could do to keep from breaking into a smile.

There was an excited hum over the ballroom as conjecture abounded. Caroline Lithey, talking to Hester at that moment, allowed her mouth to fall open as she quite frankly stared.

"Miss Wyckham, did you see! Whatever could it mean?" gasped Caroline, a remarkably terse statement from that usually verbose young lady.

"It would seem to me that Lord Markham's suit has not prospered," was all Hester would say. She excused herself immediately and went to find Julie. She was determined not to be teased for information about Susan's affairs. Also, she hoped to be able to avoid Lord Markham as much as possible, now that the Breckinridges had arrived.

XII

IN ONE CONTEXT, the Barnes Assembly always afterward separated itself into two distinct parts. The first half of the evening, before the supper hour, was the Lord Markham half. She had not only to contend with his hovering, sometimes disapproving presence and his ability to appear as by magic at any moment when she was not provided with a partner, but she was also aware of the unwavering icy stare of Lady Breckinridge. She was only too sure that that formidable lady was laboring under the misapprehension that, but for Hester, things might have prospered in Lord Markham's suit for her daughter.

Hester could think of no tactful way to inform her that not only had she not encouraged his attentions, but that she absolutely abhorred them. Certainly the old lady could never accuse Hester of flirting with him or encouraging him in any way.

The second part of the evening was the Captain Frampton half and presented just as many frustrations as the first. Lord Markham, after claiming two dances and being turned down for supper, retired from the ball and was seen no more that evening. Captain Frampton seemed to feel that he must do his duty dances first and resolutely pushed Lady Breckinridge around the room before turning to Susan. These obligations finished, he was able to step in just where Lord Markham left off.

After a strenuous country dance with him, she asked him to take her to one of the French windows for air. They pushed through the heavy draperies and found a tiny balcony. She fastened the drapes back on their holders, for the last thing she wanted was to be shut off from the rest of the room in the company of Captain Frampton. Not that she thought for one moment that he would behave in any way badly, but she knew tongues would wag nevertheless.

He took her fan from her to wave it gently across her face and she was grateful for the lovely June night and the breeze he created on her flushed face. She thanked him kindly.

"No great thing, my dear. I would do a great deal more than this for you, you know well."

"Most kind—however, the fanning will be enough."

"Do not say so. I have great plans for all the things I want to do for you. When I get back to London, I will look into the matter of the sable cape immediately."

"Pray do not go on with this foolishness, Captain Frampton. You know my feelings full well." She was exasperated, but at the moment too hot and tired to say anything more.

"I am convinced those feelings are just the whim of the moment, dear Hester. I am sure that with time your heart will change."

"And I am more than sure that it will not. I beg you will not go on with this. It is useless, I assure you," she said with as much sincerity as she could muster.

"I have never been one to be overset by obstacles. I believe that one must always forge ahead, convinced of victory, to win wars. Small battles lost are of no importance in the overall," he replied blithely.

"Captain Frampton, this is not a battlefield you are on, and I am not an opposing army. I do not need to be out-maneuvered to be won. You made me an offer, I declined that offer, and I wish no more to be said about it. Can we not be friends from now on and be easy with one another?"

"I am always easy with you. I feel that I have known you always. Oh, Hester, my dear love, please allow me to hope," and so saying, he grabbed her hands, turned them over and began kissing her palms. She tried to pull them away, but he was determined.

"Captain Frampton, you are creating a scene. People are beginning to stare. Please . . . Captain Frampton!"

Hester wanted to sink through the floor. They must look to anyone who cared to watch, like two people engaged in a tug-of-war.

"Ah, Miss Wyckham, our dance I believe," said a calm, somewhat amused voice.

Captain Frampton straightened up abruptly, Hester

snatched her hands away from his loosened hold, and turned gratefully to her savior.

"Why, I believe you are right, Mr. Boscroft," she said with as much dignity as she could muster. "If you will excuse us, Captain Frampton," and with that she took Mr. Boscroft's arm and walked away.

Literally, they waltzed away, for he took her onto the floor and danced with her the daring new waltz. She was delighted to find him so knowledgeable in the intricacies of the steps. She herself had danced it often in London and the Bath Assemblies, but had not expected to find a partner in the waltz in so small a place as Littlecomb. She must revise her ideas about Mr. Boscroft.

Very few couples were on the floor for the waltz, so she knew they were the cynosure of all eyes and undoubtedly speculation was stirring, since she had already danced with him twice during the first half of the evening and taken supper with him. But somehow, it did not matter in the dipping, whirling exhilaration of the dance and the warmth of his hand upon her waist. She laughed up into his face from sheer happiness.

When the music ended they strolled into the next room for a glass of punch. They spoke together of the things that mattered to them, they exchanged previous histories and experiences, as lovers are wont to do when in search of the essence of the beloved, when the need is strong to know all in order to know more completely.

Though they felt at ease with each other, they explored tentatively, Philip from the desire not to frighten her away by too determined an assault, realizing full well her independent spirit that would not be pushed.

Hester's reasons were simply to allow time to show her whether this friendship could ripen into a love that would demand and should be given expression. Her very practical nature rebelled against the swooning romanticism of most of the young ladies of her acquaintance. She had read and rejected the novels of the day, filled with dark, brooding heroes and dark, brooding love affairs. She felt instinctively that for her love must be a thing of light and singing joyousness and must include shared ideas and interests. The idea of a marriage built on the basis of a few moments of physical attraction was repugnant to her. She had had her share of infatuations as a schoolgirl, of course, but her own level-headed inner voice had quickly discovered that the handsome face often concealed a vacuous mind, or that the dashing character revealed more sensitivity to his horse than to any human being of his acquaintance.

So the Barnes ball was a thing of shining happiness for her, in spite of being divided in her mind into the Markham half and the Frampton half.

When she awoke the next morning, she lay lazily in her bed, calling first one moment to mind and then another. Remembering now, with amusement, Captain Frampton's discomfiture on being discovered bending passionately over her hands. She could smile indulgently to remember Lady Breckinridge's cold eye. These things could not touch or change her feelings of gladness.

Moreton came in with her morning tea and a large, informal sheath of garden flowers with the dew still on them. She buried her face in their freshness and laughed with joy.

Moreton watched this display for a moment and then said drily, "Don't you want to see the note that came with them? For heaven's sake, you don't even know who sent them yet."

"Of course, I know who sent them. And, of course, I want the note," she said, snatching it from Moreton's hand and reading it avidly.

These are not a proper tribute, but I will continue the search. Philip.

She lay back on her pillows with a secret smile. Moreton sniffed and said, "I suppose you know you have a very silly look on your face."

"Oh, Moreton, don't be such a sourpuss. Be happy with me this morning. Such a beautiful day!"

"Yes, well, I'm sure you know there's none would begrudge you happiness less than me, my lady."

To her amazement her mistress leaped from the bed and hugged her warmly, then said, "Hand me my wrapper. I want to take these down and find a suitable vase and arrange them."

"You'll do no such thing. I'll go down and find something proper and bring it up to you." She stumped out of the room, muttering to herself about them as didn't know any better than to go flittering about the house in a wrapper in front of all the servants.

Lady Breckinridge descended upon the household before the afternoon was out and, when the butler came to announce her presence in the drawing room, Julie and Hester looked at each other with dismay. They had been pottering about in the garden since lunch time, and they knew their dresses were no longer presentable.

"Oh, bother!" said Julie. "I had planned to go up for a long lazy bath and a nice little nap before dinner. Now she will stay for hours, and we must give her tea and from the look of her face last night, I know she has come for no good reason."

They reluctantly went upstairs to change and presented themselves in the drawing room as speedily as possible. It never did to keep Lady Breckinridge waiting about.

That lady wasted very little time on the amenities. Staring at Hester, she inquired acidly if the neighborhood could look forward to offering her their felicitations in the very near future.

"Well," said Hester, trying to put off the inevitable, "it would be a great pleasure to receive them, but I cannot think why they should do so."

"I'm sure that most of us present last night felt that some announcement was imminent."

"Announcement?" said Julie, all innocence.

"Yes, madam, an announcement. Miss Wyckham seemed to all of us to have *three* gentlemen making such a dead set at her, that one could only hope their intentions were honorable and that she would accept *one* of their offers."

"I am sorry to disappoint the neighborhood, of course, Lady Breckinridge, but I'm afraid I have no news of import for them. I have accepted no offers."

Lady Breckinridge eyed her blankly for a moment, her mind obviously working on the best way to extract the information she wanted.

"I believe you are aware, Miss Wyckham, that Lord

Markham had asked Lord Breckinridge's permission to
address our daughter?"

"Yes, I am aware of that. She refused him, I
believe?"

"Pooh, I make nothing of that. Any young girl is
expected to refuse the first time. A gentleman of
honor expects it and makes his offer several times."

"Then, no doubt, Lord Markham will do all that is
required of him as a gentleman," answered Hester
quietly. But inside the thoughts were rushing wildly.
She cannot know of his proposal to me, Hester thought,
no, no one knows but Julie and Geoffrey and myself.
Surely Lord Markham cannot have told anyone. She
wondered why Lady Breckinridge was pursuing this,
since it was by now a dead issue, Lord Breckinridge's
letter with Susan's unequivocal refusal having been sent
and received.

"It seemed to me," continued Lady Breckinridge
ponderously, "that you were unwise to encourage Lord
Markham's advances in quite so forthcoming a way
last night. You will not mind my saying this?"

Hester felt her entire body flush with anger, and
before she could prevent herself replied, "But I do
mind, *very* much! I have never behaved in a deliberately forthcoming way in my life, and certainly feel
that you can have no occasion to censure me!"

"Hester, my dear . . . " warned Julie faintly.

"Really, Miss Wyckham, there is no reason for you
to take that pert tone with me. I am but speaking as a
mother to a daughter," replied the old lady, and to
Hester's surprise her eyes seemed to glisten with tears
and her mouth to quiver.

Hester was instantly repentant. She was only a poor

soul with a dream for her daughter, still trying to foster that dream with the idea that all was not lost, and if she could but persuade the young, attractive newcomer to step aside, her hoped-for son-in-law would reappear.

"Please, please accept my apologies, Lady Breckinridge. My sharp tongue will be my downfall one day. I had no right to speak so to you. But please do believe me when I tell you that far from encouraging Lord Markham, I have done everything in my power to *discourage* him."

"Dear child, that was prettily said. Of course, we will forget all about it. I was only . . . I have wished so much . . ." She seemed unable to continue that thought, perhaps because the realization that the dream was finally over was beginning to take hold of her mind.

Hester felt very sad for her, in spite of her silliness and snobbery and blindness about her daughter. She realized that, as a mother, Lady Breckinridge left much to be wished for, but still she knew that she loved Susan. Perhaps, now, she would not stand in the way of her daughter's happiness any more.

When she finally took her leave, with many protestations of friendship and affection, Julie and Hester collapsed on the twin sofas in front of the fire and looked at each other. Suddenly they both began to laugh, and naturally Geoffrey walked in upon this scene of hilarity. He looked at them in a pained sort of way that only made them laugh the more.

" 'Pon my soul, I wonder how your parents dealt with this continuous giggling. Must have driven them nearly mad."

XIII

THE NEXT MORNING, very early in order to escape the censure of Geoffrey, Hester was cantering off down the drive. She had wakened before the sun was full up and had sat in her window for a short while, musing over the events of yesterday, dreaming of the possible events of today . . . Mr. Boscroft . . . Philip . . . and suddenly decided to go for a ride before breakfast. She had hurried into her habit and slipped quietly out and round to the stables. The sleepy stable boy obligingly saddled her mare and offered to accompany her, but she said blithely that she would not need anyone with her today. She hoped the boy would not get into trouble with Geoffrey for it, but she would make everything right for him.

She rode along happily, glad that she was out in the lovely morning and that she was completely alone to enjoy it. She rode to the top of the rise, studied the view for a while, and then continued down and across to the woods on the opposite rise, the path she had taken with Julie and Mr. Boscroft that first time.

When she reached the trees she stopped again to look around her. The woods were alive with the sounds of animals going about their morning business. She heard hooves behind her and turned. Oh, dear Lord, she thought with dismay. For there was Lord Markham, looking very pleased with himself.

"This is wonderful, Hester. I had hoped I might see you riding this morning, but of course, never expected to see you so early."

"Were you waiting for me, Lord Markham?"

"I must confess I was. I could not sleep and rose very early and came here, hoping that you would come."

"But how could you know I would ride in this direction?"

"Oh, this is a favorite ride in the neighborhood. I made sure that if you came out at all it would be this way. And such good fortune to have you alone. Where is Geoffrey this morning—and the beautiful Julie? Still in bed, I'm sure."

"Yes. Well, it has been a pleasure. I must get back now, or they'll begin to wonder where I can be."

"Oh, surely not for hours yet. It is very early, not gone seven I'm sure. I'll just ride along with you."

Realizing she could not stop him and must just make the best of it, Hester toed her horse and started along the path, Lord Markham beside her.

He studied her cold face covertly for a moment and then said, "I know you must think me an impetuous fellow, Hester, but I assure you nothing could be farther from the truth. I have thought this out most carefully and believe it is the right thing. If you will but relent . . . open your heart but an instant . . . I am sure you will have no trouble changing your mind. I am not considered such a bad catch, you know."

"I am sure there are any number of lovely girls who would faint with pleasure to have your attentions, Lord Markham. Unfortunately, I am not one of them. I do not mean to be unkind, indeed I am sure I am doing you a great kindness by telling you this. For surely you cannot want someone who does not love you. That would be a most unhappy marriage for you." Hester hoped that all of this sweet reasonableness would accomplish what she had so signally failed to accomplish before.

"I believe," said Lord Markham, "that you will come to love me *after* we are married if it does not happen *before*. If I had had more time . . ." he broke off abruptly.

"But you had all the time in the world, Lord Markham. There was no need for you to propose to one girl and then immediately propose to another. Perhaps, given time and some indication of sensitivity and patience, Susan might have accepted you. I must own that I would not, even then, but . . ."

At that word Hester felt some heavy object strike her on the head. She felt herself sway, felt his arms catch her, and then . . . blackness.

It seemed many hours later when she began to rise slowly to the surface of a black bog. She opened her eyes but immediately closed them again, as the light striking them sent needles of pain into her head. She moaned, and felt something cold on her forehead. She sent a signal down to her hand that it must come up and protect her eyes. All happened in very slow motion, but finally she felt her own hand against her face and dared to open her eyes again behind this shield.

"There now, you're coming around. I knew that cold water would do the trick. Do you feel better?" It took her another moment to realize that the voice belonged to Lord Markham. Where on earth was she, what . . . ?

She looked around and recognized nothing but the face of Lord Markham hovering over her.

"Where are we? What happened?"

"Why, you did not look where you went and walked your horse directly into a low bough. It knocked you out completely. I brought you here to a tenant's farm on my property. The building is empty now, unfortunately, so there is no woman here to attend you, but I think I have done very well. You'll be all right in a moment."

"But . . . but . . . why didn't you take me to Julie? It must have been closer?"

"Oh, no. This was the nearest place. I wanted to get you comfortable as soon as possible."

Somehow, this did not seem quite right, but her head ached so badly that she could not make her mind grapple with the problem at the moment. She closed her eyes again and the mists came swirling around. She felt extremely nauseous and knew that she must lie quite quietly for a little longer or she would disgrace herself.

When she could open her eyes safely again, she asked him for her horse. He assured her the horse had come to no harm at all and was safely tied up outside.

She tried to raise herself, but the pain in the back of her head at the movement caused her to cry out and fall back.

"Please, Miss Wyckham, rest easily. You must not try to get up yet."

"But I must get back. Julie will begin to worry."

"Yes, yes," he said soothingly, "in a little while, when you are feeling better, we will think about what is best to do."

She had to agree that it was almost impossible to force her mind to work at this moment with such a headache. She closed her eyes, thinking, "I will just rest for a moment and then I will sit up and go away from here."

When she next opened her eyes she had no idea where she was. She was aware that she had been deeply asleep, and from the looks of the light seeping in through the one, terribly dusty small window, it was late afternoon.

Late afternoon! She sat up suddenly and a slight dizziness assailed her. She steadied herself and waited and then looked about. Where . . . what . . . and then slowly it began to come back to her. She had been riding and Lord Markham had been with her and she had walked her horse into a bough, he said, and he had brought her . . . here. She looked at "here." A nearly empty, very dusty, and shabby room. The few bits of furniture left in it were so worn that the previous tenants had obviously not considered them worth taking. She was lying on a horsehair sofa of undoubted antiquity, whose stuffing was erupting in various places, and which smelt mouldy. This was the vacant house of a former tenant farmer of Lord Marham's.

Lord Markham! Where on earth was *he*? She remembered everything now, and he had been here when she had dropped off to sleep. He would never have deserted her in this dreadful place. No, she reassured herself, he had in all probability gone for a carriage to fetch her home.

She lowered her feet to the floor carefully and sat for a moment before attempting to rise. When she did she felt momentarily dizzy again, but the room quickly steadied and she walked slowly across to the window. But it was so small and dirty and so obscured by vines and weeds that she could see nothing. She made her way to the door and tugged. It was stuck, drat the thing, so she pulled and struggled with it but it would not budge. Well, she was in the main room of the tiny hovel, and perhaps this door was never used. She turned and made her way to the kitchen to try the back door. It seemed loose, and the doorknob was not dusty, but try as she would, she could not move it. She bent down, and yes, there was a keyhole. Could it be locked? But surely Lord Markham would not go out and lock the door after himself. For what reason would he do such a thing? To protect her? But protect her from what? She stood quite still for a long while to try to puzzle this out.

She could think of no logical reason for him to lock her in. She went back to inspect the front door. It too had a keyhole, but she could see nothing through it. It was either locked also, or stuck completely through years of disuse. Now what should she do? She went back to the sofa and sat down. She would wait. If Lord Markham had gone for a carriage, he surely must be back very soon.

She certainly hoped it would not be long. She was becoming aware now that she had left the house very early and without breakfast. If the light was anything to go by, it must be the middle of the afternoon. Hunger pangs were beginning to make her feel even more nauseous.

She was unable to be sure how long she waited, it seemed interminably, but she knew it must have been quite late when she first heard the sound of a horse approaching, for the sun was well down in the sky.

She rushed to the window, but again could see nothing. She begin shouting as loudly as possible. What if it were only someone passing! Good God, they might not hear her, and she renewed her shouting and pounding on the door.

"I don't believe anyone will hear you, you know," said a voice behind her. She whirled around to see Lord Markham standing in the kitchen doorway, arms filled with various bundles, watching her with a smile.

"Oh, thank God, you are here. What took so long? Did you bring a carriage? It doesn't matter really. I feel so much recovered that I am sure I can ride back."

"I am happy that you feel better. Perhaps you would care for a bit of refreshment. I'm afraid I can't build a fire, but I have brought cold milk and bread and cheese, and let me see . . . what else have we here . . . a bit of ham and . . ."

"What are you talking about?" she demanded. "Surely you do not think I will stay to eat? I must leave instantly. Poor Julie will be frantic by this time."

"I think it will be best to have something first, Miss Wyckham. Now you sit here on this bench, and I will pour you some milk."

"I think you have gone mad. Milk! I am leaving." With that she strode across to the door and gave it a sharp tug. But it did not yield. She whirled to him again.

"Why is this door locked? I demand that you unlock it immediately!"

"I'm afraid I can't do that, Miss Wyckham. Won't you please come sit down and have some of the milk? I'm sure you must be famished."

"I wish you will not speak of that milk again. I want to leave this house, sir, and I require that the door be unlocked. After that I will trouble you no longer. I am perfectly able to ride back. I am fully recovered."

"Now look here, Hester . . ."

"Please don't call me Hester. I have never given you permission to do so."

"All right, Miss Wyckham, if you will have it that way. But I assure you, it won't make the least difference by morning which name I call you."

"What do you mean, 'by morning?' By morning, sir, my brother-in-law will no doubt call upon you to find out what you mean by detaining me here."

"By morning your precious brother-in-law will know perfectly well what I mean," he declared cryptically.

"I could do with an explanation now, if you will be so kind."

"Happy to oblige. I mean to keep you here for the night . . ." he held up his hand at her gasp of outrage, ". . . oh, have no fear. I will not harm you or press my attentions upon you. But by morning it won't matter one way or the other, for by that time you will have to marry me."

"*Never!* Geoffrey will . . ."

"Lord Hallam will be only too happy to have me for

a brother-in-law by morning, I do assure you. Not even *your* reputation can withstand spending the night alone with me, and your precious Geoffrey will beg me to marry you to save your honor."

As coldly as possible, she turned her back on him and walked into the front room and sat down upon the shabby sofa. She folded her hands in her lap and stared stonily ahead.

He followed her and stood watching her for a moment. Then he threw back his head and laughed, "Oh, well played, my lady. Well played, indeed."

She ignored him, not even deigning to look in his direction.

"I knew you were a game one, and see how right I was. What can't be cured, must be endured, eh, Hester? That's the sort of spirit I like. I think I can begin to like you very much."

She would not answer him nor look at him. She had decided the only thing she *could* do was to wait out her imprisonment with dignity. The night would pass eventually, though there would certainly be unpleasant repercussions when news of this leaked out, and she had no doubt he would make sure it did leak out. But surely she had enough credit to override it. If it happened that she had not, she still would never give in and marry this monster.

Oh, Lord, I am so hungry, and my hair is a mess, she thought, and wondered briefly about her saucy, plumed riding hat that matched her costume so perfectly. Probably fell off when he carried me here, and he didn't bother to retrieve it.

And her head was so sore . . . I probably have an enormous lump back there, she thought, as her fingers went to the spot to explore tenderly . . . wait a moment! Why would I have a lump on the *back* of my head if I walked into a bough?

Her eyes flew instinctively to Lord Markham, and she saw the smile on his face.

"I wondered how long it would take you to figure that one out, my lady," he smirked.

"You hit me!" she exclaimed in disbelief.

"Nothing to speak of, just enough to stun you, so that I could bring you here."

"That's why you were waiting in the woods! But what if I had not come riding this morning?"

"It was a chance. I decided that I would just be available for whatever opportunity presented itself."

"You mean you would have been lurking about all day to get me alone someplace?"

"Oh, for several days, if need be."

"You are mad," she said simply. But she felt cold inside with a rage such as she had never experienced before. That he would *hit* her was beyond anything. Very well, she thought, it is full-scale war, and anything goes. I must see what I can contrive.

But first, she thought, I must *eat*. Without looking at him, she rose and walked into the kitchen, picked up the flask of milk and poured a drink into the cup he had thoughtfully brought along. She cut some bread and cheese and took a slice of ham in her fingers and begin to eat as slowly as she could. It was difficult to do as by now her hunger was so great she wanted to wolf the food down, but she refused to give him the satisfaction of seeing it. She felt she was fortifying herself for a battle, and while she did so she looked about to see what weapon she could discover.

There was nothing obvious to be seen, the room containing only a rickety-looking table and a bench. The fireplace was a yawning, black hole with not even a piece of half-burned wood in it. Her mind's eye roved over the other room. Had she seen anything there that would be useful? The sofa, a small stool by the fireplace, some empty shelves. Nothing.

She sat down on the bench, eating slowly, her mind working at the problem. Surely she could think of something. As she stared fixedly at the table and munched, she slowly became aware that one of the table legs did not match the others and splayed out slightly. Perhaps it was only propping up the table there . . . *not attached.*

Hester darted a look into the other room. Lord Markham still sat on the stool by the fireplace, leaning completely at his ease, watching her. She put down the cup of milk and rose, brushing the crumbs from the skirt of her riding dress. She paced slowly into the other room, and lay down on the sofa, moaning softly as though her head still hurt, and closed her eyes.

XIV

WHEN JULIE had finished her breakfast and Hester had still not appeared, she sent the maid to inquire of Moreton if Hester was still sleeping.

"If you please, my lady, Moreton says Miss was up very early and evidently went riding," said the little maid when she returned.

Julie was not feeling at her best this morning, so she decided to spend the time in her morning room catching up on her letters. She detested writing letters, but it was too hot for the garden, and she didn't feel up to riding. Besides, by the time she could change Hester would be coming back.

She settled down resolutely, and soon became immersed in describing the events of the past week in a letter to her papa. By the time she had finished, three quarters of an hour had passed, and Hester had still not returned. But Julie, feeling her duty done, put down her pen and went to find Geoffrey. He was just coming in from the stables.

"Well, kitten, you look unusually beautiful this morning," he said, tilting up her chin to plant a hearty kiss on her rosy lips.

"Oh, Geoffrey, do I? I feel so dragged out today."

She followed him into his library and while he busied himself with some papers she wandered about restlessly, pulling books off the shelves and putting them back after a brief glance.

"You're acting very mopish, I must say. What's the matter? Are you becoming bored with the country already? Where is Hester?"

"She went riding early and has not returned. And of course I am not bored with the country. I love it here, and the past weeks with Hester have been wonderful. Also, I am *not* mopish. I was not feeling quite the thing this morning, but I feel wonderful now. I just don't want to start anything till Hester comes back. Then we shall plan what to do with our day."

She came around the desk to smooth his hair, bent to kiss his cheek, and informed him she would find something to keep her busy and went off.

She found the housekeeper, and they went together to check through the linen cupboards and before she was aware of it the morning had passed and it was time for lunch. She went to Hester's room, to find Moreton sitting there mending a torn ruffle on one of Hester's gowns.

"Did my sister go down to lunch, Moreton?"

"Why, my lady, I have not seen her. I made sure she was with you."

"I have not seen her all morning. Where could she be? She surely cannot be riding so long."

They stared at each other for a moment, and Julie could see the alarm growing in Moreton's eyes.

"I'll just go speak to Geoffrey," she said hastily. "No doubt Hester met someone on her ride and went to have lunch with them—the Litheys perhaps."

She hurried down to the library, but it was empty. Without ringing for a servant to ask his whereabouts, Julie hurried through the rooms in search of her husband. Not finding him, she decided he must be in the stables and went rushing out the door and round the drive. And there he was, talking in the stableyard to one of the boys.

"Geoffrey, I cannot find Hester, and she has not returned, and I think we must send to the Litheys to see if she is with them. . . ."

"Whoa . . . pray slow down, Julie, and tell me what is wrong."

"I *am* telling you, Hester went out riding early . . ."

"Did she go alone?"

"I don't *know!*"

Geoffrey turned to the boy. "Were you here when Miss Wyckham took out the mare?"

"Yes, m'lord. I saddled it for her and offered to go with her, but she would not have it. Rode off alone, she did."

"You should have insisted; you know I do not like the ladies to ride unaccompanied."

"Sorry, master, but she'd not have it. Rode off before I could saddle a horse for me own self."

"Oh, Geoffrey, please don't waste time scolding. It

was not his fault. Just go and inquire at the Litheys'
if she is with them. Quickly, please!"

"Yes, yes, my love, immediately, don't fret yourself.
You know well how capable Hester is of taking care of
herself."

He had his mare saddled and, kissing Julie, he
mounted and cantered off down the drive. When he
returned an hour later, it was to find Julie waiting at
the top of the steps and an anguished Moreton hovering in the background, wringing her hands. Geoffrey
wished he could think of some way to avert the tears
he felt sure were coming when he divulged his news.

"Now, Julie, you must not fly up into the boughs.
She was not at the Litheys'. I did not tell them I was
looking for Hester, no need to get the whole neighborhood in an uproar. Same with the Breckinridges.
Ran into Boscroft in Littlecomb, so knew she couldn't
be there. I am now going to follow the ride up to the
woods and back here, just to take a look around."

"Oh, my God, Geoffrey, do you suppose she was
thrown and . . . and . . . she may be lying someplace with a broken leg or something . . . oh Geoffrey! Wait, I'll change and come with you."

"You'll do no such thing. I'll go much faster alone."

"Please do not say no, Geoffrey. Two pairs of eyes
will do better than one. Besides, I will go mad doing
nothing . . . I cannot bear just to be waiting."

He looked at her for a moment and then decided it
would be best for her to come along. He nodded his
assent and told her not to fuss but change as quickly
as possible. She gave him a look of love and gratitude,
turned and ran into the house, calling for her maid as
she flew up the stairs.

In ten minutes she was galloping beside him down the drive. When they reached the first rise they paused to look about and then continued over the familiar ground more slowly. Among the trees at the next rise they coursed in and out through the trees, calling, but saw nothing. They rode back through the trees to search the ground farther from the path on each side, and by accident Julie spied a speck of deep red color under a bush. She dismounted to push aside the foliage and then called to Geoffrey excitedly. He came hurrying up and dismounted and together they stood staring down. There on the ground was a claret-colored hat, the brim pinned up on one side and a black plume trailing down the other. Geoffrey picked it up, and Julie took it from him.

"It's Hester's . . . part of her riding dress. Oh, Geoffrey, I am so frightened. What can have happened? What shall we do?"

"Now, now, kitten, you must be calm. I will find her, have no fear. Let's turn back now. We'll search the trees again on the way out and then follow the path back to the house. If we don't turn her up by then, we will think what will be best to do."

They remounted and walked their horses back slowly. But there was no sign of Hester all the way back to their home. They could see Moreton at the top of the steps waiting for them, and a by now thoroughly frightened stableboy standing in the drive. Several maids huddled in the front hallway, agog with excitement.

Geoffrey dismounted and came around to hold his arms up for Julie. She slid down into his embrace and putting her head against his chest began to cry. He patted her ineffectually and held her, but he couldn't think of any way to give her comfort.

"Julie, you will oblige me by not crying and being as brave as you can. You know perfectly well that nothing terrible can have happened. She has just taken it into her head to go off somewhere without bothering to send word. We'll give her a scold when she comes home, believe me."

"B–b–but, her h–h–hat, she w–w–ouldn't go riding ab–b–bout hatless," sobbed Julie.

"Now you will go in the house and wash your face, and lie down," he said firmly, motioning to Moreton to come take Julie, "and I will ride in the other direction, towards Markham's."

Moreton hastily dried her own tears on her apron and hurried down to take Julie in her arms.

"But she never goes that way, Geoffrey," said Julie, a small gleam of hopefulness in her eyes.

"Well, perhaps she met up with someone and they took her off to show her a new ride and . . . and . . . well, we cannot know standing about here, so I'll be off. Now no more tears, Julie."

"No, my love, I'll be brave, I promise you. Only do not be too long."

"Back in a trice and probably will have her with me. Now do you go change out of your habit and lie down for a bit." And with that he mounted and rode off quickly down the drive.

But the sun was well down in the west before he returned, and he was not accompanied by Hester. Julie had spied him as he turned in the drive and flew down the stairs and out to meet him.

Geoffrey dismounted wearily, and the stableboy

came running to take his horse. Julie simply looked at her husband, her eyes huge and terrified.

"No, my dear, I did not find her. I rode all the way to Markham's. Ran into him just leaving his place with a number of parcels. Said he was going to see one of his tenants with some supplies they had requested. Rather odd thing for him to put himself out for one of his tenants. However, I didn't mention Hester. Knew if he had seen her thereabouts he would have mentioned it and I didn't want to start any hares."

Geoffrey fully expected Julie to go into hysterics, but she surprised him. She held herself a bit stiffly, to be sure, and she bit her lower lip when her eyes seemed ready to fill with tears, but somehow she held herself together. She was determined to show Geoffrey that she could cope and be useful.

"You must come in now, my darling Geoffrey. You are exhausted and must be famished. I have some supper waiting for you, and there is hot water in your room to wash away some of that dust. Robert has laid out a change of clothes and is waiting to help you. Do you go straight up, and then you will eat, and *then* we will talk."

Geoffrey had never been so proud of his wife as he was at that moment. Grit to the backbone, he thought. Looks as though a breeze could waft her away, but when trouble comes she's like a rock. He felt tears begin to form in his own eyes, and without saying anything for fear of disgracing himself he stumped off up the stairs.

When he had washed and changed, he came down to find Julie waiting for him in the dining room, determined to wait on him herself, in spite of the hovering footmen and the slightly disgruntled butler. She waved them all away, refused to sit down, saying she could eat nothing, and served Geoffrey his supper. When he had finished, he sat toying with his glass of port trying to think of what to say to her. He reached for another glass and poured port for her.

"Here, drink this. Do you good," he said gruffly, pushing the glass to her.

She obediently picked it up, took a sip, and set it back down carefully. She would not speak of what was in both their minds. She knew she would not help by nagging him about what he was going to do next.

Finally, reluctantly, he spoke. "I'm afraid, my dear, that we can no longer keep silent about this. We must ask our neighbors for some help."

"Whatever you think best, Geoffrey."

"I will ride round and ask Lithey and Breckinridge. I'll take all the stablehands with me, and they can ride into Littlecomb and ask the Daltons and the doctor."

"Geoffrey, you must do as you think best, of course, but I would go first to Mr. Boscroft."

"Boscroft . . . yes, of course. I suppose I didn't mention him because I hoped to avoid giving him this news. His attentions have become so marked that we can no longer be in doubt of his love for Hester . . . damned hard to tell him . . ."

"'I know, my love. But I think you must. He would want to help."

"I'm sure everyone will be only too glad to help. There will be quite a large number of us, and we can divide up and search more thoroughly."

"It is very nearly dark, Geoffrey. Do you think it will be any good searching at night?"

"We will do what is possible. Fortunately, the light lasts a long while in the summer."

"May I come with you?"

"I think it would be better not to, my darling. I know how you feel. You have the most difficult job of all—to wait. But I think you should be here. If she should somehow make her way back alone and find us both gone . . ."

"You are right, I wasn't thinking clearly. I must wait here. You go along now, Geoffrey, and don't worry. I will get everything ready in case she has been injured and . . . and . . . I will be fine," she declared stoutly.

Geoffrey rose and, coming round to her, lifted her from the chair, embraced her heartily, and hurried from the room.

XV

HESTER carefully opened one eye the merest slit and looked across the room. It was completely dark now, and she had been lying there for what seemed years. She had forced herself to breathe quietly and evenly so that he would think she had fallen asleep. Evidently the ruse had worked.

He was still leaning against the wall by the fireplace, but his arms were folded, his legs extended and his chin was on his chest. He was asleep, she thought triumphantly, and was even snoring slightly.

Moving only inches at a time, she carefully eased herself upright and waited. When he did not move, she removed her boots and rose barefooted. She then began, one slow step at a time, to cross the floor to the kitchen.

Her heart stopped completely as she stepped on a loose board and it creaked. She froze, midstride, and waited, watching him. But his breathing continued evenly. She pulled her foot back, moved it onto the board beside it and tested gingerly. It seemed solid enough, and she started out again.

She reached the kitchen table and sat down, suddenly weak from nerves and excitement. Then she reached out to the corner that had the unmatched leg and with one hand on the leg, she gently tried to raise that corner of the table. But she did not have enough leverage sitting down. She stood up and tried again, still holding the leg. She did not dare let go for fear that if it was not attached it would fall. She slowly raised the table a few inches. Thank God, the leg came away in her hand.

Now, sir, she thought triumphantly, we shall see something. She turned to begin the slow, heart-stopping trip back across the room, expecting each moment to cause a creaking floorboard to protest loudly enough to waken him. But he didn't move, and the snoring continued. Poor fellow, she thought, with a grin, he is exhausted from his labors.

She reached his side without wakening him and, with no compunction at all, raised the table leg and brought it down with all her strength on his head.

He fell sideways off the stool without a sound except a slight thud as his head hit the floor. She knelt beside him and searched his pocket for the key and found it with no trouble. She rose and rushed to the kitchen door, unlocked it, and going out, locked it behind her. She threw the key as far from her as she could and looked about to see what way seemed best to go. She had no idea where she was and could see nothing in the least familiar. It was dark, but the moon might be coming up. Well, she thought, I shall just follow the cart path and that must bring me to a road and from there I will see where I must go next.

She started off across the yard, and almost immediately stepped on a stone and cried out in pain. Good God! My boots, she thought, and turned back—but then thought of the key sailing through the air and the direction it went. Which way was I facing? I'll never find the key in the dark. I must just go barefoot and make the best of it and stop wasting time. She turned and started off, her tender feet smarting from sharp stones in the path.

The path eventually came to a cross path, not the road. Now which way to go? She stood looking in first one direction, then the other, and saw little to choose between them. She shrugged and turned right.

She walked down the center where there seemed to be a bit of grass left to cushion her feet as much as possible, and the path seemed to curve back and forth aimlessly. There were dense growths on either side, and the trees seemed to loom larger and larger. Finally she seemed to be walking on leaves and looking down, realized that there was no path left. It had petered out completely in the trees. She could make out what seemed to be tree stumps, so evidently this was the path a farmer used to collect fire wood. Now what to do? Should she waste time and go back, or follow the footpath winding off through the trees? If she knew anything of farmers, this was probably a shortcut to the next farm, and there perhaps she would find people and a horse or a farmer's cart to take her home. She set off down the footpath, going cautiously but as quickly as possible.

The path seemed to go on forever, and was sometimes so overgrown with brambles she had to force her way through. She distinctly heard her skirt rip, but went on just the same. Then, without any preparation she walked right into a pool of water, tripped and landed on her hands and knees in the mud. She waded out and sat for a moment on a fallen tree to get her breath back. She raised first one foot and then the other to inspect them carefully but blindly with her fingers. She could see nothing, the blackness was so dense beneath the trees, but she was aware of cuts and felt sure they were bleeding. Her hair had come loose and had tumbled down around her shoulders. She pulled it back and wished she had something to tie it with. She finally reached down and tore a strip from her petticoat and tied her hair back. When Moreton saw that petticoat! But the thought of Moreton brought one of Julie, and she firmly pushed both thoughts away. She must keep moving, try to find the correct direction to go, and not give in to self-pity.

If only she could get out of these trees and find a rise somewhere to see about her. She rose and doggedly set off down what she hoped was the path. After, surely, miles, the trees thinned out and she could see empty sky ahead. Hurrying forward she stumbled over a large stone, her ankle twisted beneath her and she sat down abruptly. Biting her lips, she held the ankle tightly for a few moments, refusing to cry out. She struggled to her feet again and tried her weight on it and knew immediately that she had sprained it, and the going promised to be even more difficult. No matter, she set her mouth in a hard line, *I am free and that* is all that matters. I am out of the woods and there is surely a field ahead and that is where I will go.

Sure enough, there was a field ahead, and quite a distance beyond them, she could see the land begin to rise gently. I will go there, it doesn't look to be too far. But the fields were plowed slantwise to the direction she was heading, so that she was continually stepping over the rows, and it took much longer than she had thought it could take.

She stumped along grimly, ignoring the quite painful ankle, the cut feet, the bruised toes, holding her heavy riding skirt up and over her arm to make the walking easier. She fell a number of times, but each time picked herself up and plowed determinedly ahead, her eyes reaching for that hill.

Geoffrey, meanwhile, had ridden straight to Mr. Boscroft's and interrupted that gentleman at his supper.

"Sorry to burst in on you like this, Boscroft. Felt you'd want to know. Hester's gone missing," he blurted out, knowing of no way to put the matter delicately.

"Gone . . . ?"

"Missing. Went off this morning for a ride before any of us were about, never came home. Been everywhere I can think of looking for her with no luck. Felt the best thing was to ask everyone to help look."

During this blunt speech, Philip Boscroft had stood absolutely frozen, his face slowly draining of color. Without moving he continued to stare at Geoffrey, then threw down his napkin and moved to the door of the dining room.

"Billings," he shouted, "send round to have my horse brought up immediately."

Billings, his round face eloquent of disapproval of this interruption of his master's meal, appeared in the doorway.

"Your *horse,* sir!"

"Immediately," replied Philip in a voice that brooked no questions or delay.

Billings, recognizing defeat, turned and snapped his fingers at the hovering footman, who hurried off to the stables.

Within a very few minutes, the two men were riding down the drive at a breakneck pace. They separated to rouse various neighbors, agreeing to meet in front of the church in Littlecomb as soon as possible.

Everyone applied to stayed only to call for a horse and give orders for their people to saddle up and follow them. Soon a large group had assembled at the church.

Captain Frampton very naturally began to organize the men into smaller parties and give each of them a certain territory to cover. No one, least of all Philip or Geoffrey, resented his taking command. He assumed control so naturally that they were happy to comply and grateful that he was there to do it. The parties soon set off in all directions, armed with torches and lanterns.

No one had thought to send for Lord Markham, for his manor lay quite a distance beyond Littlecomb in the other direction. The party assigned to that direction were instructed to stop there and see if he would join them.

They were all instructed to search only the roads in and around Littlecomb. They could not profitably search the fields and woods in the dark, but if they had

no success tonight, that would be their objective tomorrow.

Julie, left alone, had first to deal with a by now
hysterical Moreton. She tried to administer a few drops
of laudanum to quiet her. This Moreton refused, saying it might put her to sleep and she must wait up for
her dear Miss.

"Then you will oblige me by behaving sensibly. You
are no help to me at all this way," said Julie firmly.

"Yes, my lady, to be sure I will. What will you have
me do?"

"Go up and wash your face. Then when you are
calm, we will think what best to prepare."

Julie called for the housekeeper and ordered water
to be heated. She was not quite sure what the hot water
would be needed for, but resolutely set her mind against
thinking of anything too dreadful. She simply told the
housekeeper that Miss Hester would surely want a hot
bath above all else.

When Moreton came down, red-eyed but calmer,
they decided that the men might come back and be
hungry, and Moreton was sent off to the kitchen to order whatever refreshments were available.

These preparations in hand, there seemed little
else that could be done. Too restless to settle down,
Julie called her dogs and set off for a tour around the
house, checking, though she knew it to be irrational,
behind bushes and hedges. Hearing a carriage coming
up the drive, her heart nearly stopped. She ran around
to the front in time to see Susan stepping out of her
barouche with the assistance of Mr. Ebershaw.

Susan rushed to Julie to put her arms about her. Julie pushed her gently but firmly away.

"Please, do not . . . I can't . . . I must not break . . ."

Susan was instantly contrite. "Of course, how thoughtless of me. You certainly don't need anyone to depress your spirits at a time like this. I promise we will not commiserate and pull sad faces. But I thought it might help just to have someone with you. Lord Hallam said that you were alone."

"You are very kind. Won't you come in, and we'll order some tea and be comfortable," said Julie. She realized that only kindness was meant, and now that she thought about it, it might be a good thing to have company for a while. She greeted Mr. Ebershaw belatedly and led them up the steps and into the drawing room.

When they were settled and each holding a cup of hot tea, Julie inquired, "How is Lady Breckinridge? I hope she will not feel left alone, with your papa so kindly helping Geoffrey and you with me?"

"Oh no, Lady Hallam, mama does not mind. She wanted to come with me, but I felt sure you would not want . . . that is, I thought . . ." she floundered to a halt.

"I'm sure your mama would prefer to wait for her husband to come in. It may be quite late, and she would want to be there to greet him," said Julie smoothly.

"Yes, yes, of course, that was the very thing. So I came alone, that is, I persuaded Mr. Ebershaw to accompany me. I thought it would be better to have a man to lean on at such a time," said Susan, perfectly seriously, looking at Mr. Ebershaw with such pride and love in her face that Julie felt compelled to nod a solemn agreement. Well, well, she thought, so that is the way of it. She wondered if Hester had found out the day she met Mr. Ebershaw, and if so why she hadn't mentioned it. What a sly boots was Hester, and so I'll tell her when . . . oh Hester, she cried in her mind, where are you?

However, she contrived to hold herself steady and converse with Susan with some composure. Mr. Ebershaw contributed very little to the conversation, occasionally murmuring an agreement or patting Susan's hand in a consoling way. Finally, Julie could contain herself no longer, and jumping up, she inquired if they would care to stroll down the drive with her for some air. They both agreed heartily that that was what they would most enjoy, and the three set off down the gravel. Though they walked slowly, it seemed but a moment later they were again at the steps.

Much as Julie appreciated the kind thought behind this visit, she felt that if she had to sit and make polite conversation with them for another moment she would scream. Thankfully, Susan must have sensed something of this, for she suggested that perhaps Julie would like to lie down for a while since it was now quite late. Julie agreed that this might be best, and with many reassuring words they climbed back into the carriage and took their leave.

Julie went back into the drawing room and took up her embroidery frame. This managed to keep her attention for two minutes. She tossed it impatiently aside and paced to the front door to stare down the drive and then into the breakfast room to the French windows. She went out onto the terrace and stood there for a few minutes. Then she went back into the house and ordered candles to be lit in every room. Perhaps Hester was out there, somewhere in the dark, trying to find the house.

And so she was, and it was *very* dark. She had reached the rise at last, and was forced to sit there for a few moments' rest. The dew was so heavy now that the grass was soaked, but she was beyond caring for that. In fact, she was grateful for the feel of it on her feet, which she knew were cut and bleeding, and for her ankle, which was puffed and throbbing with every step. She tried to gather some of the dew in her hands and laid the coldness against her ankle as she attempted to pierce the darkness about her for a recognizable signpost. Dear God, she thought, how can I have walked so long and not come across a single house or even signs of one? These fields cannot be unattached to some farm, they are all planted and plowed. The very real fear that she was walking away from Little-comb rather than toward it was waiting just beyond consciousness to leap up and send her into a panic.

Lord Markham had said that they were in a tenant's farm on his estate, but he might well have been lying. He could have taken her anywhere, and since she had no idea how long she had been unconscious, she had no way of knowing how far they had gone from the place where he had struck her.

That . . . that . . . monster! she thought, with such a rush of fury that had he been present she would have cheerfully hit him over the head again. To have put us through all of this anguish—poor Julie, she must be quite ill with worry by now. Oh dear heaven, where can I be? I must decide which way to move.

She tried to think logically of directions. The ride
she had taken had been to the east of the house; she
had therefore been heading back west when she encountered Lord Markham. That meant that Littlecomb was further to the west beyond the house, and
she had heard that Lord Markham's estate was beyond
Littlecomb in the same direction. *If* she had been on
his estate, she would therefore have to walk east to
get back to Julie's. Now if I only knew where east
could be found! Her hope for moonlight had long ago
disappeared. The sky was dark and ungiving, not even
a star showed through. She could only be grateful that
it wasn't raining.

Well, she thought, I will never get anywhere by sitting here. She stood up, but not daring to turn for fear
of losing her sense of direction, she only turned her
head as far to her right as it would go, looking for any
sign of a light. Surely to goodness, everyone in the
world can't have gone to bed. Nothing on the right.
Very, very slowly she scanned it again and then
turned to her left. Slowly now, she thought, her eager
eyes trying to probe the thick darkness as far as possible. Her eyes jerked back a fraction. Was that . . .
there . . . a tiny flicker. She stared fixedly but could
not be sure. She closed her eyes for a second, then
snapped them open . . . and there . . it *was* . . .
a minute, wavering spot of light. And now, dear God in
heaven, was it possible? There seemed to be more than
one tiny flicker. It was very far away, seemingly miles,
but never mind, it was something, some living someone
somewhere. Feeling vastly comforted and somehow
light-hearted in spite of her painful ankle and sore and
burning feet, she set off toward the lights.

XVI

THE CHIMES finally finished tolling their dreadful message, and there was no way for Julie to deny any longer that it was eleven at night and not only had Hester not returned, her husband was still out, and she was slowly beginning to give in to an unreasoning terror. Something dreadful had happened, she felt sure, and Geoffrey was forced to stay away to attend to . . . Gruesome pictures presented themselves to her mind . . . Hester's broken body being carried into the doctor's office . . . a blood-stained body in a ditch, recognizable only by the claret riding dress as . . . NO! She caught her breath on a sob and pushed the picture frantically out of her mind.

She turned and almost ran to the open front door and out to the top of the steps, to stare fruitlessly down the drive, her head cocked for any smallest sound. Still nothing. Perhaps she should have asked

Susan and Mr. Ebershaw to stay. These hours alone
had nearly undone her. She could not let go for she
had promised Geoffrey that she could cope alone.
Added to this was the pitiful figure of Moreton, huddled on a bench in the hall, never moving, never taking her eyes off Julie as she passed. And Julie knew
full well the housekeeper had her hands full keeping
the maids, always prone to hysteria, under control.

She passed as calmly as possible toward the breakfast room at the back of the house, her little spaniels
padding along behind her. Even they seemed to sense
trouble. They had not left her side all evening, had
never barked or whined or begged her to play.

They all went out on the terrace, out to the very
edge beyond the glimmer of candlelight. Julie sat
down on the top step, the dogs around her. The night
was so dark, so heavy, but at least there was no rain
. . . the picture presented itself of Hester lying unconscious, the rain beating down into her face . . .
she fought the image down and dashed her hands angrily across her eyes. I will *not* cry, she vowed silently.

She stared off down through the rose garden so intently that it seemed the very bushes moved. Only
imagination, of course. But *was* it? Some denser darkness seemed to detach itself from its surroundings and
move. Julie shot to her feet, her eyes straining, tearing at the darkness . . . a flicker of white . . . Julie
knew beyond any shadow of doubt that here was her
sister. All the blood that had momentarily turned to
ice and frozen in her veins, melted with a great rush.
She shrieked, *"Hester!"* and began to run, the dogs
barking wildly and chasing after her.

"Hester . . . wait, my darling . . . I'm coming . . .

Julie's coming . . . everything will be all right . . . wait . . . wait." She ran as though her very feet had eyes, for she dodged in and out of the bushes, never once so much as brushing against them. Then she was there, she was touching her, holding her, and yes, it really was Hester, who sighed, "Julie," as Julie's arms went around her.

Julie was sobbing and laughing and patting Hester's head and shoulders, as though still not convinced that she held her. The dogs were jumping and barking joyfully, and Hester, with the tiniest laugh, said, "Well, poppet, all to pieces as always . . ." and fainted dead away.

Julie, still holding her, sat down quite suddenly when the full weight sagged into her arms, and that was where they still were as Moreton came chugging down through the rose bushes. She fell to her knees beside them and tried to take Hester, but Julie could not let her go. She was not even aware of Moreton, but still bent over Hester, crying and crooning to her that all would be well now that she was home.

Moreton blew her nose vigorously and mopped her face. Then she touched Julie on the shoulder and said very gently, "My lady, let us take her up to the house. She'll need attention. My lady . . . my lady . . . please, my lady . . . let her go now. You must help me get her up to the house."

Julie sat up slowly and turned her huge drenched eyes to Moreton. "What . . . ? What did you say?"

"You can't give in now, my lady. You must be brave yet a bit longer, and help me get Miss up to the house."

"Of course. Yes, you are right. Do you have a

handkerchief for me, Moreton? Oh, never mind, what am I saying? Yes, yes . . . help me get her up, Moreton."

Moreton simply picked up Hester in her arms, stood and strode off up through the rose garden, as though Hester weighed no more than a feather. She went so fast that Julie was almost running to keep up with her. As they reached the terrace, it was obvious that that blood-chilling shriek of Julie's had reached more ears than Moreton's. The entire staff was on the terrace, the maids crying in each other's arms, the housekeeper shushing them quietly, and even the stately butler was seen to wipe the corner of his eye surreptitiously.

"Hot water, buckets of it, immediately in Miss's room," barked Moreton, as they opened a path before her. She never stopped once until she had reached Hester's room and laid her gently upon her bed. Then she stood with Julie and they both stared in horror.

Hester's face was scratched and smudged, her hair falling out of what appeared to be a ribband made of rag, her beautiful riding dress torn and stained, and soaking almost to the knee. But worst of everything were her feet. They were already bleeding onto the coverlet, and it was clear that something was dreadfully wrong with her ankle—it was swollen and had a puffy blue look that was most unpleasant. Moreton began to moan softly, reaching out hesitant hands to pat Hester's body here and there. But then the footsteps of the servants could be heard, bringing water, and she straightened up, ready to be sensible and take charge.

Julie, still in a state of shock, stood helplessly for a

few moments and watched Moreton struggling to raise Hester in order to remove her jacket, and then leaped forward to assist her. Together they undressed Hester and began to wash her. When they began on her feet, Hester moaned, and then slowly regained consciousness. Then she started up, staring wildly about her, and Julie was there, pushing her back on the pillow, murmuring to her reassuringly.

"There, there, my darling, you are safe. You are home, and Julie will take care of you. See, here's Moreton, and you're in your own bed. Just lie still, my love."

Hester reached out and touched Julie's face wonderingly, then sighing, closed her eyes, and fainted again. Julie turned to the maid, hovering in the doorway.

"Fetch my hartshorn . . . quickly!" The maid scurried away.

"Excuse me, my lady. 'Twould be best, perhaps, to let her be till we finish binding up her feet. They are in such a terrible condition. I'm afraid I must hurt her cleaning out those cuts properly. Not to speak of that ankle. I'll be quick as I can. You," she snapped, turning to the doorway and the cluster of servants, "go down and fetch up a basin of hot water!"

Moreton finished washing the torn and bleeding feet, applied some salve and bound them up expertly, clucking and muttering to herself all the while. Julie fetched Hester's brush and began trying to untangle the snarls in Hester's hair. She held up the piece of white rag that had tied it back and looked at it wonderingly.

"I wonder where she came by this?"

"Oh, I can tell you that. It's the hem of her petti-coat. I noticed it when we were undressing her."

"Dear heaven, Moreton, what can have happened to her? Where can she have been all this time?"

"Well, I don't know, I'm sure. She looks as if she'd been dragged backwards through a thornbush."

Julie, delicately trying to separate a strand of hair, pushed Hester's head to the side on the pillow, and then gasped.

"Good God! Look at this. Why, she's got a lump the size of a goose egg on the back of her head. She must have knocked herself unconscious somehow. No wonder she looks this way. Why, she might have been lying somewhere for hours, and then . . . her horse must have bolted, that must be the way of it. She was thrown and landed somehow on the back of her head. Oh, the poor darling! What she must have been through this day!"

"Must have run a far piece, that horse, for it to take her till near midnight to make her way home."

They continued their work in silence, awed by the pictures of poor Hester's trials. Julie became aware of voices below in the front drive and moved to the window. There was Geoffrey, thank God. Telling Moreton that she would be back immediately, she sped downstairs just as Geoffrey entered the front door.

"Geoffrey . . . my love . . . she is here . . . she is back!"

She threw herself into her husband's arms and hugged him fiercely.

"Oh, Geoffrey . . . if you could but see her . . . she looks dreadful . . . her feet all bleeding. I'm sorry to cry, but it is so sad, and the strain has been so dreadful. You won't believe what I've been imagining."

"Yes, my little one, I *can* believe it . . . I'm afraid I've been imagining far worse. Where is she?"

"We have her in bed. I wish you could have seen Moreton . . . she carried her all the way from the bottom of the rose garden!"

"The rose garden? She came that way? Good God, where can she have been?"

"We weren't able to ask her anything, Geoffrey. She fainted, and then we carried her in, and she only regained consciousness for a moment and then fainted again. Moreton wouldn't let me revive her. Said it was better so till she had finished doctoring her poor feet. And her ankle, Geoffrey! We must get Dr. Noble at once. Can we send one of the stableboys to ride into Littlecomb and fetch him?"

Geoffrey turned to give the order to the goggling stableboy, still standing in the drive.

"But take that poor brute off to the stables at once and have him taken care of. You take a fresh horse and fetch Dr. Noble, quickly now."

By the time the doctor arrived, the household had settled down somewhat. Geoffrey had been fed, telling Julie the story of the hopeless search, and how good everyone had been, and how reluctant to give up even in the darkness.

"Oh, good Lord, should have sent word to Boscroft. Looked like death when I left him down the road. I'm not even sure he went home. Looked as if he was prepared to keep going all night."

"Oh, we must send to tell him, poor man." She

rang for the butler and gave him instructions to send
yet another boy over to Mr. Boscroft's with the message that Miss Hester was home safe, and that she
was sleeping, and would he please wait till morning
to call.

The doctor arrived and bustled off up the stairs
with Julie. He saw a pale but calm Hester, propped
up against her pillows, allowing herself to be fed gruel
by Moreton.

"Well, Miss Wyckham, you look better than I expected, I must say. You've given us all a fright this
evening."

"Good evening, doctor. Very good of you to come
around so late, there was no need, truly."

"No bother at all. Just let me have a look at that
ankle for a moment. I won't bother those bandages on
your feet. I'm sure we can trust your maid to have
cleaned them well, eh, my girl?"

"I should think so, doctor. Nothing serious there,
all cleaned and put some of my own special salve on
them and bandaged them up good and proper. They'll
be well in no time. That ankle, though, I'm sure I
don't know . . . "

"Yes . . . yes . . . I see." His fingers probed the
puffing gently, and then he nodded. "Only a sprain,
but you've given it quite a workout tonight. Must have
walked miles on that foot to get it into such a condition.
Painful, I'll swear."

"Very," said Hester, simply.

"Well, we'll have some wet compresses on it, to
take the swelling down. Then you must stay off it for
a few days, you know."

"Oh, never fear, doctor, I will . . . happily," she said with a slight smile.

He stood staring down at her for a moment, his eyes full of questions, but he only said, "Hmmm," and then packed up his case and took his leave, giving Moreton instructions to give her a few drops of laudanum if she had trouble sleeping.

Downstairs, he reported to the waiting Hallams that there seemed to be nothing serious, and that he was confident Hester would be up and about in a few days. He cautioned them to keep her off that ankle, shook hands with Geoffrey, and bade them good-night.

Geoffrey asked the butler to see that all the candles were out, and arms about each other, he and Julie went slowly up the stairs to Hester's room.

Hester smiled up at them wearily and held out her hands. Geoffrey took them in his own and kissed them, then leaned over to kiss her cheek.

"Well, old girl, you've led us all a merry chase today. What do you mean by it, eh?"

"Oh, Geoffrey, you look so tired. I am so sorry," she said, the tears glistening in her eyes.

"Now, now . . . none of that, if you please. You'll have us all sniffling and carrying on disgracefully. Glad you're back, and that's all about it. Now . . . can you tell us what happened?"

"Not tonight, Geoffrey," interrupted Julie firmly. "She is almost too tired to hold up her eyelids as it is. Tomorrow will do just as well. Isn't that right, my dear one?"

"Yes, if you won't mind. I don't believe I could be coherent tonight. I think I will sleep for a week."

"Don't think you'll get a chance to do that," said Geoffrey gruffly, "not if I know anything. We'll have a certain gentleman here at sunup, sure as we stand here."

"A certain gentleman. . . ." said Hester faintly, a look of fear in her eyes.

"Boscroft," said Geoffrey succinctly.

"Ah," sighed Hester, relaxing back into her pillows, her mouth curving up in a sweet smile, her eyes closing.

"Well . . . if you don't look like the cat that just swallowed the canary. Will you look at that, Julie?"

"Yes, my love, I see. Now come along. Time you were in bed, too. You must be nearly dropping. Good-night, Hester, my dear love, sleep well."

XVII

AND HESTER did sleep well. Moreton crept in twice to check her breathing and crept out again. Julie came in to stand looking down at her and tiptoed away and the clock hands reached twelve before Hester even stirred. She woke slowly, deliciously, to the sweet smell of the garden wafting in the open window and the sunlight dancing on the carpet. And just as slowly memory returned—of the previous day and night and all its terrors. But so completely had her deep sleep healed her that she could review the whole episode calmly.

She gave a brief thought to Lord Markham, wondering if he were still locked in that house. If he had managed to break out he would be home by now . . . if his horse had not wandered . . . she sat up straight in bed . . her mare! Where could it be? She remembered now that when she had left the house she had not seen the horses. Granted she had been in something of a hurry, but *he* had come in the back way, so the horses, one would think, should have been standing there. She *had* heard him ride up. He must have tied them some place out of sight in the trees so that no one passing would see them, she supposed. She must tell Geoffrey about the mare, and they must do what they could to recover her.

The door opened slowly, and as on Hester's first morning here, a mop of silvery curls and two large blue eyes peered around.

Seeing Hester sitting up, smiling at her, Julie laughed, turned to call down for Hester's breakfast to be sent up immediately, and came rushing to the bed to crush Hester in a bear hug.

"You slugabed! I thought you would sleep forever. We've all been on tiptoe for hours, the cook has re-heated your breakfast several times, and oh, Hester . . . if I don't hear what happened soon, I think I shall burst."

Hester laughed at her and straightened her hair and patted the side of the bed.

"Sit down, love, and you shall help me eat my toast, but I shan't talk about it yet. I must *eat* . . . I don't know when I've ever had such an appetite. Then I'll dress and come down and tell you both together, for I'm sure Geoffrey will want to hear the story, and I can't tell it twice."

"Oh, indeed he does want to hear it. He and Mr. . . . oh, my goodness, I completely forgot . . . Mr. Boscroft has been here all morning. He came almost before we were up, and hasn't stirred from the house. He just sits there so . . . so . . . implacably, Hester."

"Well, then, you shall all hear the story at once and save me telling."

"But you can't get up, Hester. The doctor insists that you not stand on that ankle. Have you forgotten?"

"Now that you mention it, I have had a twinge or two. I remember I sprained it, but surely not so badly that I must stay in bed?"

"Dr. Noble said . . ." began Julie firmly.

"Oh, stuff! I hope I'm not such a namby-pamby I must stay coddled in bed for a sprained ankle."

"Well . . . I know, we will compromise. You will put on your prettiest robe, and Moreton will carry you over to the chaise and you can receive the gentlemen here."

Moreton entered then with the breakfast tray which Hester attacked voraciously. Julie had only one tiny piece of toast, and then forbore to deprive her of any more. When she had finished a porridge, three eggs soft-boiled just the way she liked them, four pieces of toast, and two cups of tea, she lay back with a contented sigh. Julie took herself downstairs to inform the gentlemen that Miss Wyckham would receive them in her room presently.

Moreton brushed Hester's hair till it shone, then helped her into a dark blue velvet robe, and carried her to the chaise. She arranged the folds of the skirt becomingly and then went away to fetch the guests.

When Geoffrey had kissed her good-morning, Hester turned to Mr. Boscroft and held out her hand with a glad smile. He took it in both of his and gripped it tightly, then bent to kiss it, first on the fingers and then on the palm. Hester felt her heart leap in that same strange way she had experienced with him before, and hoped he could not feel how her pulse was racing.

She asked them all to sit down and, when they were settled and looking to her expectantly, she began. She started at the very beginning, with her need to have a solitary ride in the early morning, and went steadily ahead, never with the slightest tone of self-pity, making it all as unmelodramatic as possible. Julie's eyes became larger and larger and, when Hester told of Lord Markham's plans for her, Julie gasped indignantly.

"But this is beyond anything! The man is insane without doubt. Geoffrey . . ."

"Hush, let me finish it all now, little one. Then we will talk of what is best to do."

She went on to the end, then sat there looking at them. Mr. Boscroft cleared his throat.

"Let me understand this very clearly. You hit him with the table leg and left, locking the door after you?"

"Yes, and then I threw the key as far away as I could. Stupid, I know, to do that and then remember I had left my boots. I blame only myself for the condition my feet are in."

"Blame *yourself*," began Julie indignantly, "and whom, I would like to know, do you hold responsible for your being there in the first place?"

Mr. Boscroft, his face set and a very peculiar light in his eyes, stood up and came to Hester. He again lifted her hand to his lips.

"My love, you will forgive me. I must attend to something immediately. I will return as soon as may be," and with that he turned and strode from the room purposefully.

Geoffrey sat staring after him for a startled moment, then hurried out of the room.

"Here, Boscroft, wait up. I think I had better come with you."

"They're off to Lord Markham's, you may be sure," said Julie solemnly. "I would very much like to be there with them. I have a few choice words for that gentleman."

Several hours later, both ladies looked up resignedly as the sound of hoofbeats came to them from the gravel drive. Julie put aside her paper and went to the window.

"Now who can it be? I declare I don't believe we know anyone else."

For they had not been left to while away the time alone. There had been a steady stream of callers, and Julie had been up and down the stairs more times than she could count. Some only stayed for a moment to inquire, but others, Lady Breckinridge and Susan in particular, declared that they could only be satisfied that the dear soul was safe if they could see her. Julie showed them up, and they settled down to hear what had happened.

Hester and Julie had decided, however, that until Geoffrey and Mr. Boscroft returned, the best story to give out was that her horse had bolted and taken her in a direction that she was unfamiliar with; she had been thrown and was unconscious for some time, and that when she regained her senses, it was to find that her horse was gone. She had made her way on foot back

to the house. Lady Breckinridge and Susan found this
a satisfyingly horrible tale and went away, with many
kisses and expressions of sympathy.

Hester had entertained the Litheys with her lunch,
and the Daltons and the doctor's wife later. But she
did it all gladly, happy for the chance to express her
gratitude to all of them for their concern and help the
night before.

It had seemed finally that they had seen everyone.
Julie went to the window and leaning out saw that it
was not more visitors, but the men come back.

"They are here, Hester. And what do you think?
They have your mare with them. I wonder where they
found her?"

On the ride to Lord Markham's, the two men had
spoken very little, but Philip did say that he had a
notion of where the untenanted farm lay, to which
Markham had taken Hester, and if Geoffrey didn't
mind they would go there first. They made their way
off the main road by a cart track to a run-down,
deserted-looking cottage, almost overgrown with weeds
and bushes. Without stopping to try the front door,
they made their way around to the back and found that
door hanging half off its hinges. The cottage was empty,
but the table still held the remains of food on its precariously tilted top, and in the other room, by the sofa,
a pair of dark red kid half-boots stood forlornly.
Philip stood staring at them for a moment, then went to
pick them up.

He turned to Geoffrey and lifted his eyebrow.
Geoffrey nodded, and still not speaking, they went
back out into the yard. It took very little searching to

discover Hester's mare, tied to a tree only a little way into a small copse. They drew up some water from the well for the horse, and then remounted and set off grimly, leading her.

When they reached the Markham manor, they were told by the butler that Lord Markham was still asleep and could not be disturbed.

"You will tell him we are here, and be quick about it, or I will go up and wake him myself," said Philip tightly.

"That will not be possible, sir, but if you come back . . ."

"At *once*!" repeated Philip quietly, but with a look in his eye that convinced the butler that waking his master was the lesser of two evils. He scurried off up the stairs. In a very few minutes a very disheveled Lord Markham came storming down the stairs, demanding to know what they meant by coming round here and forcing their way into his house.

"I would have thought both of you gentlemen would have more address than to behave so rudely. What can you mean by it?'" he demanded.

Philip held out the red boots. Markham started visibly, but blustered, "Well, well . . . I am waiting. What is it you want?"

"We have heard a very nasty story this morning, Markham, from a lady who has suffered much pain and distress at your hands. It is we who are waiting for an explanation."

"I'm sure I don't know what you're on about. What *lady*?"

Philip handed the boots to Geoffrey and with his

riding crop slashed Lord Markham so hard across the face that he staggered back and fell to the floor.

"Why, how dare you? How *dare* you? I'll see you dead for this, Boscroft. I am the one insulted, and my seconds will call on you tomorrow. I'm a prime shot, you know, and I'll chose pistols. You'll be dead by sunup."

"You cannot think that I would duel with *you*. I would not so lower myself. What I mean to do is thrash you within an inch of your life, as one would any villain."

Geoffrey here interposed. "One moment, Boscroft, if you please. I would like to ask this . . . this . . . scum if he could seriously believe that I would ever allow my sister to marry him."

"Oh, I think you won't be so toplofty, when this story gets around, Hallam. She may say differently, but she can't prove she didn't spend the night with me."

Geoffrey stepped back, bowed politely to Philip, and said, "You may proceed, Boscroft."

And Philip did, coldly, but with such fury that Markham was powerless to defend himself against the onslaught. He finally lay curled on the floor, protecting his head with his arms as best he could, and Geoffrey touched Philip quietly on the shoulder.

"That should do it, eh, Boscroft?"

Philip stopped and looked around, then he handed the riding crop to Geoffrey and took back the boots. He looked down at the wretch at his feet disdainfully.

"If it ever comes to my ears that you have so much as spoken Miss Wyckham's *name* to *anyone*, I will make it my business to come and administer another dose of the same. But first, I will make sure that everyone knows the real reason you were so desperate to make her your wife."

With that he turned on his heel, and he and Geoffrey marched out of the house, mounted their horses, and rode away.

When they came back into Hester's room, Philip crossed over and held out the boots to her. She looked up at him wonderingly.

"But how did you know where they were? And how could you have gone and come back so quickly? It must have been far away—I walked for hours last night."

"Well, you more or less took the long way around, as it were. We went by horse and rode straight there by the road. They were just where you had left them."

It was Geoffrey who told them what happened. How they had found the cottage and her mare and then had gone to Lord Markham's.

"He tried to bluster it out, but when he saw the boots, he knew that we knew everything. Philip gave him a thrashing, and we came away."

"Oh, Geoffrey, you're leaving out everything, I'm sure," Julie complained.

"No, told you the whole thing just as it happened, I promise you."

"But, Geoffrey," interposed Hester, "this won't be the end of it. He can still spread unpleasant gossip and set the whole town talking—and I'm sure he won't hesitate to ruin me if he can."

"I don't think so," said Philip.

"But why would he hesitate? Such an unscrupled man would take great pleasure in spreading stories," said Hester.

"He will not. Believe me, my dear, he will not," said Philip firmly. "Now, let us speak of more pleasant things. The whole nightmarish business is over, and we have come through it with flying colors. Or rather, I should say, you have, Hester. There cannot be many women so brave as you. And such slyness—such cunning! I think we must all be very careful what we are about in the future."

Hester laughed, "I was clever, was I not? To have spotted that table leg and put it to such good use?"

Philip was prevailed upon to stay for dinner, and carried Hester down to the table. She refused to go back to bed, declaring she had never felt better, and could not bear another meal in bed. They made a merry time of it, and Hester forgot her scruples against flirting, and engaged in that very delicious activity with Philip with the best will in the world.

When it was time to say good-night, Julie tactfully pulled Geoffrey to his feet and walked with him to the door, turning his back deliberately on the couple.

Philip bent over Hester's hand, kissed it warmly, and then held it close for a moment.

"Good-night my dear, my very dear Hester. Thank you for letting me stay. I don't know that I could have gone away, even if you had not wanted me to be here."

"How could I not want you to be here? . . . after all you've done for me?"

He bowed and with a gleam of mischief in his eyes, said, "Too kind."

"Not nearly . . . kind . . . enough, sir," she returned, with an answering gleam.

XVIII

IT BECAME EVIDENT in the days following Hester's ordeal that Philip Boscroft's prediction that Lord Markham would not speak was a true one. How he could be so positive they did not know, nor did he vouchsafe any information.

However, it was apparent that the neighborhood had fully accepted Hester's story of the bolting horse, since the flow of visitors never ceased, and there was never a suggestive pause nor a lifted eyebrow to express a doubt.

Hester, though unable to walk about, insisted on getting up and dressing every day. Geoffrey made it his business to spend most of his time in the house and be available to carry her whenever it was needful: from bed to breakfast room, and from there to Julie's morning room or to the drawing room, and so on throughout the day.

"I feel it must chaff you dreadfully, dear Geoffrey, to be forever kicking your heels about the house. I cannot tell you how it distresses me to be the cause of it," apologized Hester one day.

"Pooh, nonsense. I suppose I am not so ill-natured a fellow as to complain of such a small thing, Hester."

"You are the best-natured brother one could hope for. I'm sure my sister never did anything half so fine for her family as when she married you. Bless you, Geoffrey."

Geoffrey chuffed and puffed, but looked very pleased, nonetheless. He had just settled her in the morning room, for the doctor's expected visit. That doughty gentleman came every day, though he declared there was little enough for him to attend to, since, besides her ankle, Hester had taken no real harm from her adventure.

"I could wish any number of my patients had such constitutions as yours, Miss Wyckham," he declared, as he gently unwound the bandage from her ankle. He examined it briefly, then put the bandage back into place. "Course, some of 'em do, confound 'em, but refuse to admit it. All the style nowadays to pretend one's sensibilities are so delicate that the sight of a pricked finger causes one to reach for the hartshorn. Lot of damned nonsense, begging your pardon. All the stare to swoon away at the blink of an eyelid. Most of 'em never honestly fainted in their lives!"

Hester had to laugh and admit he was right. She liked this crotchety doctor enormously and had begged him not to bother himself by coming every day, but he ignored her and came anyway.

Hester, indeed, felt somewhat guilty that perhaps she had disrupted everyone's summer. There were daily calls from all of their close neighbors: the Breckinridges, the Litheys, the doctor's wife, the vicar, the Daltons. And of course, Mr. Boscroft.

He, however, came at different times each day, and never stayed more than an hour, and had not stayed for dinner again this past week, though he was urged to do so by all of them. Hester could not help wondering what could be the reason. He was as warm to her as ever, flirted gently, teased, and laughed with her, but nevertheless she was aware of some subtle . . . withdrawal? She hesitated over the word in her mind, but could think of no other that exactly expressed what she felt. She had speculated briefly over the possibility that on further thought he may have suspected that she had encouraged Lord Markham in some way to cause him to behave the way he had. But she could not harbor such a thought for more than a moment. She *knew* he could not think so of her. But there was *something*. Oh well, she thought, it will work itself out if it is meant to.

Considering the busy social life she had experienced on first coming to Littlecomb, there seemed to be a decided lull at the moment. She did not know whether this was a usual lull of midsummer, or whether her mishap was in some way responsible for it. She certainly hoped not the latter reason. There was no denying, however, that she was the object of what little social life was still going on.

Julie and Geoffrey refused to leave the house for any reason whatsoever, though Hester urged them to take a morning ride at least or accept a dinner invitation. They simply laughed at the idea that they would want to go without her.

"Too dull," declared Julie, "besides, I couldn't enjoy myself. I would keep wishing I had stayed home with you. You're much better company, you know."

The week had therefore gone by very pleasantly for Hester. She felt in tearing good spirits, even though hobbled to a chair, and her wit and gaiety lit up all the visits and impromptu supper parties that resulted from them.

Friday brought the first sobering event, in the form of a note from Mr. Boscroft excusing himself for not being able to attend her the next few days. He had, he wrote, a number of matters of business taking him away, but hoped to be with her again early in the next week. Dampening—but she refused to allow her spirits to sink. After all, though she liked Philip better than any man she had ever met, she was not so far committed that she could not bear to be without his company for a few days. She told herself this very firmly, in her best no-nonsense voice, and added that she was not altogether sure, in any case, that she was ready to give her heart to anyone. There was her trip to Europe with papa, there was next season's London visit, and all her plans to remain independent for several more years. She showed the note to Julie who demonstrated her willingness to commiserate.

"Oh, just as well, I think, don't you really," said Hester airily, "must be a dead bore for him to hover around an invalid day after day."

Julie did not look entirely convinced by this pronouncement. However, she said nothing. She went away to bring in the visitors, whose carriage they had heard approaching down the drive.

It turned out to be Miss Susan Breckinridge, unaccompanied by the redoubtable Lady Breckinridge as she usually was.

She flew across the room with a face so full of radiance and excitement that Hester's heart lifted in spite of herself.

"Hester! Oh, my dear, you will never guess! The most wonderful thing has happened."

"Your mama has given her consent to your marriage to Mr. Ebershaw," replied Hester promptly.

"Well, no, not yet. But I think we can be confident that she may very soon. You see, Mr. Ebershaw has been given his own church!"

"Oh, my dear! That is above everything most wonderful. I am *so* happy for him. But how did this come about so unexpectedly?"

"Well, yesterday, Mr. Ebershaw had a letter from a Lord Berkwell, who introduced himself as a cousin of Mr. Boscroft's. He wrote that he had applied to Mr. Boscroft to inform him if he knew of any suitable candidates, since he had several livings within his gift, and would be needing someone directly, and that Mr. Boscroft had given him Mr. Ebershaw's direction. Is that not amazing? Just when we were so desperate!"

"Most amazing and wonderful, indeed! Mr. Boscroft! Well, I'm sure he is a most kind and thoughtful man," responded Hester, while inside her a voice was singing "Philip, oh, dear Philip."

"Yes," continued a glowing Susan, "and Mr. Ebershaw is to go as soon as everything can be arranged.

Lord Berkwell was most insistent that everything be done as expeditiously as possible."

"And have you told your parents about all this?"

"Indeed I did! You can imagine how proud I was to make such an announcement. Mama has always been so positive that Mr. Ebershaw would never amount to a row of beans, said he was only a dreamer with a pretty face, who'd never be entrusted with a parish. But Lord Berkwell assured Mr. Ebershaw that it was a very large and important parish and that he had come most highly recommended by our vicar. Mama was speechless for quite five minutes, I do assure you!"

"I can believe it. So you think it is possible that she may be brought into the way of thinking more seriously of Mr. Ebershaw as your husband?"

Susan blushed and said demurely, "Oh, I think that will be the way of it, if we proceed carefully. She has invited him to *dinner!*"

"Oh, *Susan!*"

"Yes, and it's the very first time. And not just a family dinner. He is to be guest of honor, to celebrate his appointment, and the Litheys and the Daltons are to be there. Oh, Hester, I do wish you could come . . . and Mr. Boscroft. But he had to decline, he said, since he was called away for a few days. Had you heard?"

"Yes, I heard. The dinner, I take it, is to be soon?"

"Monday night. We had wanted it for Saturday, but so many people were already engaged that mama couldn't make up her table at such short notice. Perhaps the doctor will let you be up by then."

"Perhaps," smiled Hester, absently, while her mind dealt with the fact that Mr. Boscroft did not expect to be back by Monday, since he had declined. She brushed the thought aside impatiently, and gave her attention to Susan, who prattled on with such a lack of her usual reserve, that she seemed a new person.

". . . and so we have decided that if the evening goes well, and mama seems pleased with Mr. Ebershaw and encouraging, he will speak to papa that very night. We cannot be too long about things."

"Well, in that case, I will come however much the doctor may forbid it. But, I'm sure he won't. He cannot pretend that there could be any possible reason to keep me sitting about here any longer. I'm sure I express Julie's and Geoffrey's happy acceptance for the evening also. You'll tell your mama?"

"As soon as I reach home. Now—*now*—I am perfectly happy. To have you there will make the evening better than ever. I'm sure you shall bring me good luck . . . since I have known you, my whole life has changed so much that I can only hold you responsible."

She refused to listen to any of Hester's protestations of innocence and very soon took her leave. She wanted, she confessed, blushing scarlet, to pick up Mr. Ebershaw for a short drive. He had so little chance to rest and breathe fresh air.

Hester agreed gravely that this would be most effacacious for Mr. Ebershaw and that Susan was to be congratulated for her thoughtfulness. Susan laughed and hurried away.

At dinner that evening she told the whole story to Julie and Geoffrey, who were as delighted as she at this happy turn of events.

"And you say Boscroft had a hand in the whole thing? I wonder what made him think of it? Wouldn't have thought he would have even been aware of the situation."

Julie looked at Hester archly and said, "Oh, I think we could perhaps work out the way of it if we put our minds to it, my lord."

Geoffrey looked at her and then at Hester, and grunted, "Ah, just so. Should have known a woman had a hand in it. Forever matchmaking, you women. Not the sort of thing a man would meddle in unless pushed to it by some woman."

"I protest, Geoffrey," said Hester, "I certainly *never* dreamed of pushing Mr. Boscroft in this. In fact, it never occurred to me that he had arranged it until Susan told me so. I *did* ask him if he would let me know if he heard of any vacancies, but I assure you, I had meant to make a push to find something for Mr. Ebershaw myself. It seems I was a bit slow off the mark. However, Mr. Boscroft certainly let no such grass grow under his feet. Was it not thoughtful of him?"

"Very good sort of man," declared Geoffrey. "I can tell you I like him more than a little. I never was more impressed in my life than I was with his handling of Markham. Hardly spoke, you know. Didn't need to. Course, I wanted to do the same thing—thrash the bounder—but somehow felt he had more right."

He said this with a sly look at Hester, which she grandly ignored.

"Yes, Geoffrey, I'm sure we are all most thankful to have such a friend as Mr. Boscroft. Now, shall we leave you alone with your port, or will you allow us to remain?"

However blithely she may have spoken, Hester could not help being gratified that Mr. Boscroft had made it

his business to take on the handling of Lord Markham.
Nothing had been seen of that gentleman since their
morning call on him, and though there was much speculation in the neighborhood as to his whereabouts, most
people assumed that he had gone off on one of his trips
to London. There was even more speculation about
the engagement of Lord Markham and Susan Breckinridge. Since no formal announcement had ever been
made, and no formal disclaimer of the hints made by
Lady Breckinridge, hints strong enough to be considered
an informal announcement, everyone was too discreet
to approach her on the subject. She never referred to it
in any way, nor indeed, did she ever mention Lord
Markham's name after that awful visit to Hester after
the night of the Barnes Assembly.

For Hester many questions remained to be answered.
Why had Lord Markham proposed to Susan, why he
had left for London so precipitously the next morning,
why had he come back and pursued *her,* and above
everything else, why he had been so relentless in his
pursuit that he felt it necessary to abduct her? She felt
quite sure, in spite of all his easy lovemaking, that he
did not love her, or indeed, even like her above half.

It seemed quite possible, however, that they would
never learn the answers to these interesting questions.
Such a strange and unpredictable man might do anything and never provide answers. She had to content
herself with the knowledge that he had "answered" for
one of his misdeeds.

XIX

THOUGH SATURDAY was cloudless and beautiful and sure to bring its share of visits, Hester found it almost impossible to keep her spirits from sagging. The days had moved by at a very stately pace, in spite of all she could do to entertain herself.

It was this unaccustomed inactivity, she thought to herself irritably. She was in the ordinary way a very healthy girl and used to a great deal of exercise. She had nearly all her life ridden every morning, and was used to going for long walks almost daily. These activities, together with a varied social life and the management of her father's household, had given her little time for introspection or quiet pursuits. She was a good needlewoman, but only for short periods of time. And although she was very well read for a girl of her time, she was no bluestocking. An hour with a book at one time was all she had ever been used to.

It was so galling to be confined. She could now only think that this was the worst part of the whole experience. She raised herself gingerly, supporting herself on the arms of the chair, and tested her weight on the ankle. It was not pleasant, but not unbearably painful, either. Just a trifle delicate. Probably would be fine with a bit of exercise. She limped slowly across to the window and turned to come back. She realized somewhat ruefully that she should have made her first trip a shorter one. Half way back to her chair she was biting her lips to keep from moaning, and onto this scene walked Julie.

"Hester! Are you mad? I distinctly heard the doctor tell you this morning not to put your weight on it yet." Scolding all the way, she led Hester back to the chair, insisting on taking as much of her weight as possible. Hester laughed at her big-sisterly manner but was most grateful for her support. She sank back into the chair.

"That was stupid, I suppose, but I am in such fidgets from sitting here. Really, Julie, I'm afraid I shall go mad if I can't move about soon!"

"I know, my sweet, but if you cannot you cannot, and that's all about it. Someone will no doubt be coming along presently to keep you company."

"Please forgive me, Julie. I'm so sorry to add ill temper to your other burdens. You have had so much to bear this past week, and you've been so good to me. I'm afraid you're fagged to death. As a matter of fact, you're looking a bit pale this morning. Are you sure you're quite the thing?"

"Now that is all in your head, you silly goose, you are just trying to find something to feel guilty about.

I hardly have a thing to do anyway, and only a short time ago I was complaining to Geoffrey that I wished there were more for me to be responsible for. For heaven's sake, let us say no more on the subject. I'm sure I should be bored to tears if you had not been so thoughtful as to sprain your ankle and so give me a reason to feel useful."

Hester had to laugh at this and determined to complain no more, no matter how dragged she felt.

Julie said suddenly, "I have a capital idea! Let us have the servants carry out some things and we'll set you up in the garden under the elm. It's lovely and shady there, and it will be a change for you. Would you like that?"

"Oh, above all things, darling Julie. What a wonderful idea. It will be so delicious to be out in the air again."

Julie rang for the butler and, after some consultation, they decided that a rug should be taken out first and then the large wing chair with a stool for Hester's feet. Then they would require a table for her book and embroidery frame. Everyone began bustling about, and presently Geoffrey came to carry her outside.

He set her down carefully in the chair, lifted her feet onto the stool, and stood back. Julie had also had cushions carried out and strewn about the rug, so that the whole thing looked comfortable and quite inviting. Hester let her head go back against the chair and looked straight up into the leaves over her head. She couldn't help the tears that flooded into her eyes. It was so lovely to feel the soft June breeze on her face and to see the sky all around her.

Julie threw herself down on one cushion and Geoffrey on another, and they both seem quite delighted to be there and extremely pleased with themselves. Hester laughed in spite of her tear-filled eyes at their expressions.

"You look like two children escaped from the schoolroom," she exclaimed.

"Tell you what, Julie," said Geoffrey, "should take our luncheon out here."

"What a wonderful idea, my love. Better yet, let's send word around and have people come a bit later in the afternoon and have a picnic. What do you think, Hester, will that not be delightful?"

"Famous. Just the thing. Do you think it possible we'll be able to get anyone at such short notice?"

"Oh, have no fear, we'll just ask everyone and let who comes come. I must go in and speak to the housekeeper and the cook. Geoffrey, do you think you would like to take a ride into Littlecomb and pass out the invitations?"

"No problem. But why don't you just let me ask them as I meet them. No need to bother writing invitations. Let us make it all impromptu and simple. What time do you think I should ask them to come?"

"Well—it's just ten o'clock. What do you think, Hester. Would two be a good time?"

"Very good. But won't all this make too much work for you? Oh, I wish I could do something to help."

"Oh, presently there will be plenty for you to do. I'll attend to things from the house, and you'll direct the servants at this end. Come, Geoffrey, let's begin at once. Oh, what a lark! I'm so glad I had such a good idea," and she hauled Geoffrey up from the pillows, and they went running off hand in hand across the lawn like two children.

In a very short while she waved to Geoffrey as he cantered down the drive, and not long after that came a steady stream of footmen and maids from the house, carrying more chairs for any older guests who might not feel equal to sprawling on the pillows, and various loads of napkins and cutlery. Hester directed the placement of everything and spent quite a long space of time without giving a thought to her restlessness or *anyone's* absence.

Geoffrey presently cantered back up the drive and crossed the lawn to tell her that he felt quite sanguine about the appearance of a good crowd. Julie flitted back and forth, happily reporting various appetizing dishes being prepared by the cook, who had quite entered into the spirit of the thing.

In no time at all she spied several carriages coming up the drive, frothing with pale-colored muslins and lawns. It was the Lithey girls and their friends, accompanied by several young blades of the neighborhood. They all called and waved their parasols at Hester, erupting out of the carriages almost before they were halted. They came dancing and tripping and laughing across the lawn like a flock of butterflies. They were in exceedingly high spirits, as though this sudden invitation had released them all from some drudgery.

She welcomed them happily as they descended upon her in their usual dizzy spin, kissing and petting her, and asking and answering their own questions in their best form. They finally settled down on the carpet and

the cushions, all disdaining anything so rubbishy as
sitting on a chair at a picnic, and the conversation
bubbled.

They were followed shortly by Lady Breckinridge
and Susan, who were greeted gaily by the company
under the trees, and all the young men jumped to their
feet to bow to Lady Breckinridge and assist her in
settling into a chair. She was rather perspiring and red-
faced from the warmth of the afternoon, but seemed
in very good spirits, Hester was glad to note.

Captain Frampton cantered up the drive on his
horse, and Hester could not help a slight sinking feeling, but after all, he could be amusing also when he
was not harping on the subject of marriage, and she
welcomed him warmly. He at first displayed a tendency to want to stand in attendance beside her chair,
but as she had little time to talk to him, he presently
gave in to the request of Caro Lithey to come and tell
her all about his experiences on the Peninsula.

Mrs. Lithey and Mrs. Dalton made a very sedate
entrance onto this jolly scene, and not too much after
this came the doctor's wife with Mr. Ebershaw.

Hester watched in astonishment as he crossed the
lawn, solicitously holding the lady's elbow. The party
was in full swing by this time, so that his arrival went
almost unnoticed by most. Susan, of course, had been
very much aware almost from the moment the carriage
had turned into the drive. She had looked a little
surprised at first, then exceedingly pleased. She blushed
and lowered her eyes for a moment, then when she had
herself under control she looked up to smile quite
openly and warmly upon him. He went straight up to

Lady Breckinridge in her chair and bowed. She looked startled but nodded quite amiably and asked him how he did.

Hester silently blessed Geoffrey for making sure the curate had been included in the party. Now, if only Philip . . . but no, she was not going to spoil her party by regretting anything. She was determined to enjoy every moment.

The servants began making their way across the lawn laden down with plates and trays and baskets and were welcomed with a cheer by all the young people. They fell hungrily on the refreshments, the gentlemen making a great thing of serving all the ladies instantly.

"You will allow me to bring you some more of that chicken, dear lady?" said Captain Frampton at her elbow.

"No, indeed, I think I might burst if I try to force another morsel of anything into my mouth."

"Must keep up your strength, you know," he replied.

"Oh, well, I'm bursting with that also, after all these days of lying about. Believe me, it is a matter of regret for me—everything tastes so wonderfully out in the air, does it not?"

"I have not noticed it in particular. But then, you see, I am quite used to eating out of doors. Part of soldiering, don't you know?"

"Yes, of course, how forgetful of me."

"However, we don't often do so in such charming company as this. I have really enjoyed my stay here."

"I'm sure we are all gratified to hear you say so. Have you been having some good rides this week?"

"Oh, certainly, but I have missed having you to ride with me."

"Not as much as I have missed my rides, I do assure you. Oh, there is nothing so hard to bear as confinement!"

"Yes, so I imagine. Had you a tendency to weakness in the ankles?" he asked, a slight frown appearing on his brow.

Hester didn't miss this frown, and the uneasy look that appeared in his eyes. The very thing, she thought, gleefully. She cast down her eyes and tried to appear overcome with guilt. Then looking up she allowed him to watch her make up her mind to confess.

"Yes," she said faintly, "I have suffered all my life from this sort of thing. And always in the same ankle. The doctors have always said I must be particularly careful of it. Oh, the hours of agony I have spent on my bed, waiting for the sprains to mend."

" 'Pon my soul," he exclaimed in dismay, "how very unfortunate. Won't do, won't do at all, you know."

"What won't do, Captain Frampton?" she asked innocently.

"Well, a wife who follows the drum must have the constitution of a horse, don't you know. No time for lying about. Perhaps you should consult your doctor about some exercises to strengthen those muscles."

"Alas, that has been our object since I was a child, Captain Frampton. But to no avail. *Nothing* seems to help it at all."

There was a long, thoughtful pause, while Captain Frampton stared off into the distance. Hester gave him plenty of time to picture in his mind a wife, forever being laid up with a sprained ankle, and the unsuitability of such a partner for a soldier. She could see these images flitting through his mind, as he frowned and chewed on his lip and shook his head slightly. Finally she saw him come to a decision, brace his shoulders, and turn gravely towards her.

"Miss Wyckham . . . ahem . . ." he began.

"No, Captain Frampton, say nothing. I am afraid I am the guilty party here and must make my confession at once. It was wrong of me not to tell you of this fatal flaw in my health long ago. I can only ask you to forgive me and release me from any understanding we may have entered into." Hester presented this speech with the sad, but resolute, tones of one willing to make her sacrifice for the greater good.

He cleared his throat solemnly, "Bravely done, dear lady. I cannot tell you how I appreciate . . . er . . . admire your courage. I accept in the same spirit." He bowed profoundly, did a very military about-face, and marched off the the other side of the carpet, and seated himself beside Caro Lithey. Hester turned her head away to hide her smile. He was a ridiculous man, but somehow it was impossible to dislike him.

She looked about the party and thought what a nice group of neighbors they all were. This would be a pleasant place to spend one's life . . . for Julie, she amended quickly. And, of course, I shall enjoy it also since I will visit quite often.

The party was still filled with animation, and now, the food finished, the servants began moving among them to remove all traces of the repast. Everyone seemed happy and relaxed, and one of the young ladies began to sing a popular ballad and was soon joined by most of the company.

The shadows of late afternoon were slanting across the lawns, but everyone seemed content to linger. Even Lady Breckinridge had relaxed back into her chair, and her fingers gently beat time to the song.

Julie came up to drop down on a cushion beside Hester with a happy sigh.

"Well, sister, was this the best picnic ever? I declare I've never seen a hungrier crew . . . there is not a crumb left of anything. Isn't that grand?"

"Except that I ate most of it and shall probably have to see my dressmaker about letting out all my dresses."

"Pooh, you hardly ate anything that I could see. I notice that Captain Frampton is still being most attentive."

"Oh, Julie, the most famous roast, I can hardly wait to tell you it."

"What happened?"

"Not now, I wouldn't have anyone know for the world. I'll tell you when we are alone."

Hester happened, at that moment, to catch the eye of Captain Frampton and gave him her best sad, regretful smile.

XX

GEOFFREY strolled into the breakfast room and casually asked the ladies if they would like to go for a Sunday drive.

Hester and Julie stared at him speechlessly for a moment.

"But . . . but . . . Dr. Noble said . . ." began Julie.

"Said nothing about going for a drive that I heard. Course, wouldn't have done at first, but I can see no harm in it now. And nor does he, for I just rode over and asked him!"

"Oh, Geoffrey, you are wonderful!" squealed Julie and ran off to fetch bonnets and shawls. When all was in order, Geoffrey carried Hester out to the waiting carriage. A cushion had been thoughtfully placed to protect her ankle from a chance bump or jolt, and they set off. Hester felt as though she were literally flying as Geoffrey let the horses out for a good run.

They stopped frequently, first to chat at the vicarage gate, then at the doctor's. Later they met Lady Breckinridge and Susan, out for an airing in their own carriage. In Littlecomb they pulled up at the Litheys' gate, and the whole family swarmed down the path to greet them and exclaim over their happiness at seeing Hester out and about again.

After much persuasion, the Hallam party agreed to stop for luncheon. Hester was carried into the Lithey drawing room. There she found, already seated and waiting patiently for the return of his hosts, Captain Frampton. They greeted each other gravely, both exhibiting a solicitous kindness for the other.

During luncheon she and Julie carefully avoided each other's eyes as Captain Frampton monopolized Miss Caro Lithey. From time to time the delicious trills of Caro's laughter could be heard rippling out in answer to the very serious pronouncements being poured into her ear. Hester wondered if he were making careful inquiries as to the state of Caro's health.

Altogether it was a most happy day, and since tomorrow would bring the diversion of Lady Breckinridge's dinner party for Crispin Ebershaw, it too could be looked forward to with, if not eagerness, at least without dread.

Since Dr. Noble had heard of her exploit of trying to walk before he gave permission, he had absolutely forbidden any more attempts until he expressly told her she might, and that it could only be in his presence.

This required that she make her entrance at the Breckinridges' in Geoffrey's arms, not the best way to display one's gown.

"However, you may imagine what a great saving in slippers," quipped Hester gaily.

Mr. Dalton, a wicked gleam in his eye, advanced on his wife purposefully. She shrieked and dodged away from him.

"I declare, Mr. Dalton, what will everyone think of you, behaving so in public," scolded Mrs. Dalton with pretended outrage.

"Well, Emmie, there's no denying that point about slippers. At the rate you seem to require new ones, you'll soon have my pockets to let. I thought I might save us from the poorhouse by using a little muscle."

Lady Breckinridge turned to her husband, "Well, Breckinridge, I will be willing to make a contribution to the saving of shoe leather. I've always despised walking anyway, as you well know."

Lord Breckinridge looked at her with his eyes goggling, then began to splutter with laughter. One by one the whole company succumbed to merriment as the picture presented itself of the diminutive husband hoisting in his arms the very stout body of his wife. Lady Breckinridge joined in with a high-pitched whickering giggle, proving that she could enjoy a joke on herself as well as the next one.

The tone of the evening was set well in advance of the entry of Crispin Ebershaw, his golden curls brushed to a glow, his angelic face wreathed in a shy smile.

He bowed gallantly over his hostess's hand. She greeted him with, for her, great joviality. When they shortly all went in to dinner, she took his arm possessively and could be heard twitting him, with a ponderous flirtatiousness, about all the hearts he would be sure to break in his new parish, and the dangers of being an unmarried vicar.

Hester could not but feel that things boded very well for Susan and Crispin, and that without a doubt felicitations would be in order before many days were over.

They were a large party to sit down to dinner, for besides the Breckinridges and Mr. Ebershaw, there were the entire Lithey family, the Daltons and their son, Captain Frampton, and the eldest Miss Lithey's young man. There seemed to Hester to be a very obvious lack of a dinner partner for herself, but she refused to give in to self-pity and senseless pining. Tomorrow would surely bring *him* back, and then they should see . . . well . . . whatever. There was no denying that she missed him sharply and most surprisingly to herself. Some time in the last few days, in spite of all her good resolutions, it had quite simply happened . . . she acknowledged that she loved him very much. It was apparent that though she had pressed down the growing feeling as determinedly as possible, all the while it had been quietly building and now, without a fanfare or a drum roll, it was just there, firmly rooted and flourishing.

She became aware that Mr. Ebershaw on her left was speaking.

"Please forgive me, Mr. Ebershaw, I was contemplating this happy group of people and thinking how fortunate we all were to be so well met. I'm afraid you shall miss all of us very much when you go away," she teased.

"Well, not all of you," he said, daringly, darting a small mischievous smile at her.

She stared at him for a moment, then caught his meaning and gurgled with laughter, "One to you, Mr. Ebershaw . . . and I cede the point most cheerfully."

He blushed with pleasure and said shyly, "I hope that *she* will not be homesick . . . but, a vicar's wife has much to do, you know. I doubt she'll have much time to grieve."

"Nor will she anyway, you may be sure, Mr. Ebershaw. And after all, it is not so far away that you cannot visit back and forth often."

"I am very much aware of how much we owe to you, Miss Wyckham. I hope I may find a way of repaying you some day."

Hester pooh-poohed such an idea, declaring that she had done nothing. As he well knew, it was Mr. Boscroft who . . .

"I hope you are speaking well of me, Miss Wyckham," said a cool voice and in strolled Mr. Boscroft. "I realize I am dreadfully late for dinner, Lady Breckinridge, and unexpected, but will you allow me to beg my dinner from you just the same. I have only just returned and dare not ask my own cook to turn out at this hour."

Lady Breckinridge rose impetuously and swam around the table to him.

"My *dear* Mr. Boscroft. This is famous, indeed. You have honored us by treating us like family, which I'm sure we all feel you to be. Please, please . . . come along and sit down here."

She bustled about, ordering a chair to be placed beside Hester, requesting Mr. Dalton to oblige her by moving over just the least trifle. When a place had been made for him and he had gone around the table to greet everyone, Boscroft slid in beside Hester.

"Well, Miss Wyckham, what responsibility were you laying at my door in my absence?" he inquired, appropriating her hand, kissing it, and retaining it in his own.

She was sure everyone was watching and in great confusion dropped her eyes and felt a blush flooding her face. She tried gently to disengage her hand, but his grip was firm. Finally she forced herself to look up at him, and reply with all the composure she was capable of at the moment.

"Only one that is rightfully yours, Mr. Boscroft, and to your great credit. Your help in procuring a vacancy for Mr. Ebershaw."

"Ah," was his sole comment on this. He obviously had more important things on his mind. She tugged against his clasp on her hand and looked at him so imploringly that he relented and released it.

"And how do you go on, my dear? Are you up and about yet?"

"Not exactly skipping around," she laughed, "but at least able to get out of the house, as you can see. Geoffrey carries me about. Not a very dignified method of traveling, I fear, but better than moping at home. I'm coming quite to like it."

"Well," he replied, in a considering tone of voice, "I shan't object to that, if it gives you pleasure, as long as I do the carrying in the future."

At this she was so overcome that she could think of no reply and addressed herself to her dinner with great concentration. She was afraid to look at him too closely, at any rate, for fear that he would see that she had fallen in love with him. She felt it must show quite clearly in her eyes. And though she felt very nearly sure he returned her feelings, he had not made a definite declaration of them yet. He had come very close on the day he had taken her for a drive in his carriage, but he might very well have changed his mind since that day.

"I am happy to see that your appetite has not been impaired by your misadventure," he said politely.

"What? . . . my appe . . . oh, yes, I am quite famished tonight, and Lady Breckinridge always sets so many delicious things before one."

"She does indeed. She seems in very high alt tonight."

"Oh, she *is*. I feel quite sure you are responsible for that too."

"Well, that is certainly gratifying to hear. She has always flirted with me terrifically, you know, but I never dreamed her feelings were so deeply engaged."

Hester laughed delightedly. "Oh, charming, but please, no confessions of your romantic dallyings, it is most unfair to dear Lady Breckinridge."

"You are right, most ungentlemanly of me. I must apologize for my behavior. Now, what *am* I responsible for?"

"I feel sure that Lady Breckinridge is feeling so gay tonight, because she has reconciled her ambitions for Susan with reality, and it has not turned out to be so very terrible after all. Her future son-in-law is to be a vicar—not a titled gentleman, of course—but she is able to accept a vicar. Indeed, seeing Susan's happiness she must be happy herself."

"Do you mean that he has asked for her already and been approved?"

"Oh, not yet, but Susan has every reason to be sure that he will ask tonight . . . and be accepted. And that is your doing, for you found him a place."

"I? I do assure you, my dear, it was my cousin . . ."

She interrupted him rudely, "Please do not try that story on me, Mr. Boscroft. Do you take me for a complete ninnyhammer?"

He laughed. "Very well. So, they are to be married and will shortly be leaving us. What else has happened since I went away?"

"Well, it is far too early to be positive, but I would say that Captain Frampton may be trying to fix his attentions with Caro Lithey."

"What? Why, I made sure he would have no other than yourself. What a fickle fellow he is, to be sure!"

"Yes, but I am bearing up under the blow wonderfully well."

"You are the picture of courage, I do assure you. What, if you don't mind my asking, caused him to change his mind in this very irresponsible way?"

"I was forced to confess that my constitution was not all that could be wished for in a soldier's wife."

He positively whooped with laughter at this, and she could not help joining in so that several people demanded to be let in on the joke. They protested it was but a small thing and directed the conversation into other channels by each turning to speak to their other dinner partners.

When Lady Breckinridge rose to lead the ladies to the drawing room, Geoffrey automatically got up and came around the table to carry Hester. But before he could attempt it, Philip laid his hand on Geoffrey's arm.

"Sorry, dear fellow, but I claim this privilege," he said very positively, and without waiting for an answer, swept Hester up in his arms and strode out of the room with her. When they reached the drawing room he stopped to inquire solicitously, "Would you care for a stroll on the terrace, my dear?"

She gurgled with laughter at this, but demanded that he put her down immediately.

"But I am convinced a quiet stroll and a breath of air will do you good."

"Idiot," she dimpled up at him, "please put me down. Everyone is staring."

Still holding her, he turned to survey the ladies who, having followed them into the room, now stood drawn up in a row, very interested spectators to the little drama before them.

"Dear ladies, I was just inquiring of Miss Wyckham if she was desirous of a stroll on the terrace. What is your opinion?"

They stared at him silently for a moment contemplating the mental picture of him pacing up and down the terrace, Miss Wyckham in his arms being taken for a "stroll," then Lady Breckinridge began to giggle, and one by one they all began to laugh.

"Mr. Boscroft, you are too ridiculous," said Lady Breckinridge. "Please put Miss Wyckham down here in this lovely chair. You are embarrassing her."

"Oh dear me, of course, I would not want to embarrass her for anything in the world," and he placed Hester in the chair prepared for her.

"Now I'm sure you'll be wanting your port, Mr. Boscroft. Rest assured, we will guard Miss Wyckham carefully while you are gone."

He bowed and withdrew. Wherever Hester looked a pair of eyes, filled with speculation, slid tactfully away from hers. All except Julie's. That lady was postively beaming. Now that he was out of the room it was all Hester could do to keep from bursting into fits of giggles.

Julie came up and sat beside her and said, "Well, I believe that you must very soon be making a decision."

"Oh, as to that . . . I have made it already."

Julie looked into her eyes very intently for a moment, then laughed happily.

"And it is the right one, I feel very sure. I will be so happy, dear Hester, so *very* happy."

XXI

JULIE was directing the footman and Moreton on the placement of cushions in the carriage, while Philip waited contentedly in the drive, Hester in his arms. The morning was still cool, so Moreton was holding shawls and a light carriage rug.

Philip had insisted the night before that a drive in the morning freshness would be beneficial for Hester and that he would arrive for her at ten sharp. No one felt inclined to deny him, least of all Hester, who now showed not the smallest sign of embarrassment at being held in his arms.

She felt particularly attractive this morning in a new pale green cambric round gown sprigged with tiny white flowers and a parasol to match. She hoped Julie would take her time and see that the cushions were arranged *very* carefully.

Finally all was done, and she was placed in the seat

and Moreton moved forward with much clucking to bundle her up against any possible morning chill. Hester waved her parasol gaily to them, and they set off down the drive.

They didn't speak for a while, content to be together. From time to time he smiled around at her and she smiled in return. As they approached a familiar copse of trees, Hester pointed it out to Philip as the meeting place of Susan and Crispin Ebershaw.

"Although she did not say so in so many words, I felt sure of it. Her coachman seemed very familiar with the place, and she blushed when she told me that she came here frequently."

"Well, if it was good enough for Mr. Ebershaw, it will do quite well for me," said Philip. He drew up the horses, leapt down and, pulling the carriage robe from her lap, walked off to the clearing to spread it on the grass, then came back for Hester.

As he seated her carefully, he inquired, "Are you warm enough, my dear?"

"Oh, yes, of course. I am not at all invalidish, you know, just a sprained ankle. In fact my health is generally so robust as to be embarrassing. I've never been able to swoon properly as nearly all truly genteel ladies do."

"Are you reassuring me as to the state of your health, as you had need to do for Captain Frampton?"

Hester giggled. "Oh, that was wicked of me, I acknowledge. But he *is* so ridiculously pompous, one can't help trying to set him down. The unbelievable part is that he is rarely aware of being set down, so there is little satisfaction in it."

He seated himself beside her and took possession of her hands.

"Enough of Captain Frampton. I want to speak of you—and me. Your father, by the way, sends you his love."

"My fath . . . ! You have seen my father? When?"

"While I was away. In fact, I went away especially to visit him. Did you miss me?"

"Yes . . . I mean . . . but why did you visit my father?"

"You cannot guess?" he said, teasingly.

"Oh, please, Mr. Boscroft . . ."

"*Mr.* Boscroft? Surely you do not mean to go on being so formal with me, my love?"

"Oh . . . well . . . Philip," she said faintly, looking down at her hands with great concentration.

"There, that was not so difficult, was it?"

"Won't you please tell me about seeing my father?"

"With the greatest pleasure in the world. We got along famously and had several most interesting discussions about history, and he told me of your proposed trip to Italy together. I took dinner with him twice and found that he has a most excellent cook."

"You know very well that is not what I mean. *Why* did you . . . I mean, how came you to . . ."

"I went to see him, as you must know, to ask his permission to pay my addresses to you."

"You . . . he . . . I didn't . . . what did he say?" she asked, finally, only a bit breathless.

"He gave me his blessing."

"Oh!"

"Hester?"

"Yes, Mr. Bos . . . Philip?"

"*Now* may I speak to you of my feelings?"

"Oh, yes . . . please!" she said softly, her eyes finally seeming to weary of looking at her hands, raised slowly to his.

He groaned and snatched her up into his arms and kissed her firmly, as though his feelings, too long held in check, had broken through like a dam bursting. He then kissed her entire face, murmuring, "Oh, adorable creature, how much I love you," and other exciting things as her arms went about his neck.

Hester felt as though her bones were melting in a most delicious way and hoped that she would not *now* swoon. She could not bear to miss any of this wonderful moment.

"Hester, my darling, please say that you love me, I have waited so long to hear it."

"Oh, I *do* love you, I do. But I must protest you have not waited so long. We met barely two weeks ago."

"It has seemed years to me."

"I was afraid you must have tired of me after the accident."

Philip looked at her incredulously. "Tired of you? How *could* you think that?"

"Well, it did seem that you came less frequently . . . or at least that you stayed for a very short time. I made sure something was wrong. I even imagined for a few moments that you might have believed I had led Lord Markham on to behave the way he did."

"What a little goose you are. I did stay for shorter times, but I did it for a purpose. I did not want your feelings to be affected in any way by my dealings with Markham."

"Your dealings with Lord Markham? I don't understand."

"I didn't want you to let gratitude affect your feelings."

"Now *you* are a goose. My feelings were already irrevocably set, I fear, by that time."

The conversation continued along these lines for over an hour, with long, deliciously detailed remembering of first meetings, first feelings, and first misunderstandings, so interesting to lovers.

When they became aware of their surroundings again, the sun stood straight over the tops of the trees. Philip suggested they drive back immediately and share their good news with Julie and Geoffrey.

Philip gathered all the belongings and soon they were driving back down the road.

"That turned out to be a very short thing as drives go, but I'm sure it was everything that is . . . pleasant," teased Hester.

"Pleasant is one of those words that belong in the same category as 'kind' as far as I am concerned. I like words more positive than that," he replied.

"Then I will substitute . . . wonderful."

"That is coming nearer the mark," he encouraged her. "I will expect much better words in the future. I wonder what you will say to a honeymoon in Italy?"

"Oh, Philip . . . Philip . . . truly? I will say . . . heavenly! . . . divine! . . . rapturous! . . . whatever pleases you."

"There then, I am glad your father gave me such a happy thought. I hope you will not mind, but when he told me of your proposed trip with him, I suggested he might like to join us there after, say, a month."

"You are indeed wonderful. I do love you so much, Philip. Was he agreeable . . . pleased?"

"Both. Said if you accepted me, therefore making a honeymoon necessary, he would join us later with great happiness, if you liked the plan."

"I will love it—after a month."

"Do you suppose you will be so bored with my company by that time even your father will be a welcome change?" he asked seriously.

"Idiot!" she said laughing delightedly at such a ridiculous thought. "I have every intention of never being bored by you. But I am so happy that I want to share it with everyone. I wonder if Julie and Geoffrey . . ."

"Hold up there, if you please. You may be putting too great a strain on my amiability."

"Oh, my goodness, they must be wondering what can have happened to me all this while."

"I have a fairly good idea that they know exactly what has happened to you."

As they drove up to the front steps, Julie came running out of the house, her face wreathed in smiles, to stand looking up at them expectantly. They both had to laugh at her.

"Shall we pretend nothing has changed, and so keep her in suspense for a while longer?" whispered Hester in a pretended aside.

"Oh, Hester, please do not tease. I must know instantly any news," exclaimed Julie.

"Then I will tell you instantly. Mr. Boscroft has asked me to be his wife . . . and I have accepted," said Hester softly.

"And I wish you both . . . oh . . . so very much

happiness . . and with all my heart." She whirled around and ran back into the house, calling excitedly for Geoffrey. Philip lifted Hester down and carried her into the house, pausing for only an instant to steal one more kiss while Julie's back was still turned.

Geoffrey came hurrying down the hall to greet them, arms out as though to embrace them both.

"Well, well, I wish you happy, my dear people, I wish you very happy indeed. This is the most welcome news. Come into the drawing room, and we will all have a glass of wine to wish you well."

As soon as healths were drunk, and the excited chatter had died down, the questions began. When, where . . .

"Well, as to when," laughed Hester, "it will be one month from today, and where will be at our own church at home."

"A month," exclaimed Julie, "my dear, will we ever be able to get you ready in so short a time? . . . your clothes . . ."

"Oh pooh, I don't care for all that. I'm sure Miss Bumbry can fix me up in an instant," sniffed Hester, with a most unusual disdain for such a trifle, which used to be of such intense interest for her.

"Then we are off to Italy," Philip said, happy to be able to contribute something to the conversation, so far exclusive to the two ladies.

"Italy, oh, I say, that *is* something like," said Geoffrey, "we have always wanted . . ."

"Next year," interrupted Philip hastily, "we shall all go together. This year we shall stay one month alone, and then Hester's father will join us for the second."

"Of course, dear chap, of course. Then we shall see you back here, I hope?"

"Indeed you shall. We shall all be neighbors and go along famously together."

Julie was looking off into the distance, trying to figure out something in her mind.

"Julie, my love, what are you thinking about so intently?" asked Hester.

Julie blushed deeply, and then said, "To see if you would be back before . . . in time . . ." she floundered to a stop.

Hester stared at her, and then looked to Geoffrey and had her suspicions confirmed. He had turned quite red himself, and his chest seemed to have swelled out quite five inches. He was grinning from ear to ear.

"Good God!" exclaimed Hester, "it has happened, you are to have a child!"

"Yes, yes, darling Hester, just as you predicted. Has there ever been such a happy day in all the world like today?" Julie exclaimed exultantly.

Philip went for the wine decanter and poured everyone another glass, saying, "This calls for another toast. 'To all of us, and our happiness. May it go on forever.'"

They all went into luncheon in a very happy frame of mind, Hester declaring her head to be swimming from the wine, but Julie said it was only happiness.

Once finished with a very hearty meal, they all sat back contentedly, no one making a move to desert the table.

"Well, dear ones, I don't know about the rest of you, but I can find it in my heart to forgive even Lord Markham today," declared Julie.

"It is hard, you know, even to remember that unpleasantness now," said Hester, "though I could bear to have my curiosity appeased over several questions."

"I know exactly what you mean," said Julie. "I've wondered myself about one or two things. Why he proposed to Susan Breckinridge is the first one."

"Oh, I think I can answer that for you," said Philip, lazily, "he was very badly dipped, and his creditors were snapping at his heels."

"Why, you don't tell me," said Geoffrey in astonishment, "I had always thought him to be extremely comfortable. Don't say it was all a hoax?"

"Oh, I know he *had* plenty from his father, but he has been gambling heavily—very heavily—and was in quite desperate straits. I heard this last time I was in the city."

"Well, why didn't he have a try for one of the heiresses there? I'm sure there were enough lures set for him," asked Julie.

"In that you are wrong. No respectable young female was allowed near him these past several years—his reputation has become so bad. He is a rake and a libertine and has created a scandal by flaunting his lights o' love in the faces of all the matrons. He was barred from Almack's, that I do know, and no mother with an eligible daughter would invite him to anything."

"So he was forced to come down here and try for our local heiress?" guessed Julie.

"Well, I can understand that, but then why did he go haring back to London the very day after he had proposed—and received a 'no'?"

"I imagine he paid no attention to that refusal,

thinking it but maidenly shyness. In fact, he probably expected it. I'm sure he went tearing back to London to reassure his creditors that his expectations were very great and that he would soon be able to make them all happy."

"Well, of all the infamous things to do," said Julie, her eyes flashing.

Hester laughed at her outrage. "Yes, but he is a most outrageous man, so you must have pity on him now. Besides, that was not the most outrageous thing he did."

"Oh, never think I am forgetting his treatment of you, nor ever shall. I suppose I will forgive him, in honor of this day, but I won't forget," declared Julie stoutly.

"I think I now begin to understand his making a dead set for me," said Hester thoughtfully.

"Yes, not so hard when you know the basic fact of his great need for money," responded Philip.

"Well, I guess I can understand that too," said Julie, "when he couldn't get Susan, he went for Hester."

"Got it in one, Julie," applauded Philip. "And when she wouldn't have him, he became so desperate that he felt the only way for a quick marriage was to *force* her to agree, by disgracing her name. Oh, he is as smart as he can stare—but, fortunately, he met his match." He turned and toasted Hester with his glass of wine.

Julie avowed that the servants must be waiting this age to clear the table, and they all rose. Philip hurried around the table to claim his prize.

"I have to admit, I thought you would never all want to leave the table. I have been itching to do this for at least an hour," he said, lifting Hester and holding her close for a moment.

Laughing, they all trooped out of the dining room, but instead of turning into the drawing room, Philip kept going towards the front door.

"Philip, where are you going?" asked Julie.

"Why, to take Hester for a stroll in the shrubberies, dear Julie. Poor Hester is full as a tick from her hearty luncheon, and I feel she is in need of exercise," and with that he swept out the door.

MERRIE

a novel by

Grace South

FAWCETT COVENTRY • NEW YORK

MERRIE

This book contains the complete text of the original hardcover edition.

Published by Fawcett Coventry Books, a unit of CBS Publications, the Consumer Publishing Division of CBS Inc., by arrangement with Doubleday & Company, Inc.

ISBN: 0-449-50196-5

Printed in the United States of America

First Fawcett Coventry printing: July 1981

10   9   8   7   6   5   4   3   2   1

*For my mother, Betty Watson Burton,
with love and gratitude.*

Prologue

Candlelight flickered over a gaunt and shabby woman, far from fashionable, no longer young. The servant led her down a dark hallway. "My lord, the lady has arrived."

The chamber was populated with ghostly shapes swathed in Holland covers, cobwebs and dust. In the marble fireplace were neither embers nor ashes, and the silence was that of the tomb. He sat in a satin-backed chair, a decanter on a table at his elbow.

It was the dead of night, March 10. A fitting time to return to England, she thought, this dark midnight of the day that had witnessed the birth of the Emperor Napoleon's long-awaited heir. One hundred cannon shots had reverberated throughout Paris; all the rulers of Continental Europe had rendered homage to the infant King of Rome. Here in London no celebrations were held, nor in Portugal where Wellington battled the encroaching French. "You sent for me. How did you learn my whereabouts?"

The glimmering half-light cast his aquiline features into harsh relief; great pools of dark shadow drowned his pale eyes. "You should not be surprised to discover that I possess considerable tenacity."

"And temerity." Her voice was cold. "I've come, as you wished—though I cannot imagine why you should request such a journey of me, and after so many years." Exhaustion was obvious in every line of her slender, almost emaciated figure. Abruptly he gestured her to a chair.

"It was necessary to speak with you," he said as she pulled off her black bonnet, revealing white-streaked hair. "You've lost your looks. I did not expect that." His words were brutal, shaped by thin and humorless lips.

7

"How fortunate," the woman retorted with her first trace of feeling, "that I no longer seek to please you." Thin hands, neatly encased in mended gloves, twitched in her lap. "Have done with this! What do you want of me?"

"To ask a favor." She gazed at him in startled wonder. "One for which you will be well paid."

With faint laughter for his proposed benevolence, she leaned back in her chair. "I wonder what possible thing *I* might do for *you*."

"It will be necessary to improve your appearance." On the hand he stretched out for the decanter gleamed a magnificent black opal ring. "It does not suit my purpose to have you an antidote."

An antidote, was she? "Of course your purpose must be mine."

He blew dust from an empty glass. "There is an advantage to it," he continued, as if she had not spoken. "You have so greatly changed that your own brother would not know you now."

She took the brandy snifter from him, cupped it in her palms. "It grows increasingly obvious that *you* have not changed at all."

Only a slight quiver of his nostrils betrayed that she had pierced his armor. "I want you to return to London. I have need of a female relative who knows how to go on in Society, one whose presence in my home won't cause raised eyebrows, and whose cooperation won't mean favors I have to repay."

So astonished was she by this suggestion that she nearly dropped her glass. "I require no further proof: You are gone quite mad!"

"Consider the advantage to yourself." He gestured impatiently. "It is quite obvious that you are in need of financial assistance—assistance that I can provide. What is required of you is simple enough, and you need not fear you'll be recognized."

"No one would dare recognize me, or recall my history, while I am under your patronage." There was a faint mockery in her tone. "Still king of the castle, I see. What is it you require of this female relative?"

Brusquely, bluntly, he explained. "I hold to my earlier conclusion," she remarked, when he had done. "You are mad

8

as Bedlam! I am the *last* person of whom you should ask this thing."

"On the contrary." So brilliant was his pale gaze that it might have blinded her. "You are an excellent choice. Your particular talents will suit me admirably."

"Fiend!" A strange expression fled across her face. "Surely you must realize this could be a dangerous game."

"You were not so timid, once." His voice was cruel. "This bickering is pointless. You have very little choice. Am I not correct?" She regarded him steadily, but spoke not a word. "Shall we consider the bargain struck?"

"And the consequences?"

"Any consequences will be on my head." The black opal flashed fire as his long fingers tapped the chair arm. "An interesting tale you must have to tell, if only you could be induced to confide in me."

She raised her glass as if it were a shield. "To pour my secrets into the devil's ear? I think not! You have secured my compliance in this scheme, though I doubt your motives and suspect that what you have told me is not the entire truth. You can ask no more."

"Can I not?" He glanced up sharply, but saw only the candle's dim image in her tarnished eyes. "You have forgotten a great deal if you think that of me."

Chapter 1

I do not know why everyone over a certain age assumes that those less ripe in years are automatically deficient in both wit and hearing, but I found it often so, particularly in the case of one's relatives. It signified not that I was twenty years old, almost of sufficient age to be considered on the shelf, although I must add that my unwed state was due to my father's long illness and subsequent demise and not to any particular deformity of person, for my appearance was generally held to be pleasing enough. With an incongruity that I had learned to expect from them, my worthy elders remarked in one breath that I held various opinions which were most unsuitably strong-minded for a lady of my gentle upbringing and tender years, and in the next murmured vaguely that a particular topic of conversation was unfit for my unsullied ears. I wonder that they did not, at those most interesting moments, send me outside to play!

So it was on that particular morning, when I first heard the name of Lady Sara Cainneach. I can claim no especial foresight, no unaccountable frisson or sensation that someone trod on my grave; though, in view of what later came about, I consider it most disappointing that I did not. If ever a moment called forth premonition, that one must have done! But it seems I am sadly lacking in sensibility. The only reaction roused in me by mention of the lady's name was curiosity, for Mephisto uttered it in a tone that suggested depths of meaning which I could not fathom. Any sort of mystery is anathema to me, much as a red flag to a bull, and I immediately assumed my most innocent expression and listened intently for what might come next.

Our hostess, Lady Penelope, known to the world as Pen,

11

seemed as bewildered as I. This was not an unusual state for her. Pen possessed a heart of gold and a mind filled, to put it kindly, with feathers. She could speak quite knowledgeably of pleasure and amusement, the next rout and her newest gown, but divergence from these subjects left her gasping, like a fish on dry land. This detracted not a whit from her charm, which, coupled with bronze curls, baby-blue eyes, a rosebud mouth and a peaches-and-cream complexion, was considerable enough to prompt London's most notorious rake to offer her his hand and name, allegedly the only honorable act in a long and infamous career. Nor did the marriage founder on matrimony's rocky shoals, despite the dire predictions of cynical friends who expected Sir Jason to cast his frivolous wife overboard within a year. I admit a certain curiosity concerning Jason, curiosity little connected with his profligate past: I failed to see how so notoriously discerning a gentleman could nourish such extreme devotion to a pretty widgeon like Pen. That he was devoted could not be questioned, as evidenced by eight years of wedded bliss with nary an indiscretion remarked by the world, and five extremely lively offspring.

But to continue: Pen evinced blank confusion at her half-brother's remark. (Mephisto was the sole product of the old Duke's first marriage; Pen, and her twin brother, the offspring of a later Duchess, the sixth, I believe.) "Lady Sara Cainneach?" she repeated vaguely, and set down her teacup. "Forgive me, Christian, but should I know the name?"

I'll credit Mephisto with this much: I never heard him make a scathing remark to Pen, or berate her lack of intelligence, despite his legendary intolerance for the rest of the world. Perhaps this is a timely moment to explain that Mephisto had been named not only one of the executors of my father's estate, but also my guardian. It was not a situation that suited either of us overly well. Mephisto was the last person in the world to relish the responsibility of a dependant female of impressionable years, and I was far too independent—*not*, as he claimed, headstrong—to enjoy being under the thumb, so to speak, of so autocratic a gentleman.

To gaze upon my guardian's cold, harsh features was to understand how he had come by his nickname. His remote and chilling eyes moved to rest on me, and I wondered if any enterprising lady had ever succeeded in rousing a spark of

12

passion in their unfathomable depths. That many had tried I instinctively knew. No man of Mephisto's wealth and position could avoid the ploys and strategems of the more rapacious type of female.

Mephisto's dark brows twisted into a frown. "The name should not be unfamiliar," he advised Pen, in a voice that warned against further protest. "May I recall the Irish branch of our family to your mind? Lady Sara has kindly agreed to oversee Merrie's debut."

"Oh." Pen retrieved her tea-cup from a carved gilt side-table, replete with carved strings of bellflower and honeysuckle fluting, and blinked at her half-brother over its rim. "I do not believe I've made Lady Sara's acquaintance, but it is very kind of her all the same." I received a gentle smile. "Merrie must be vastly excited about her come-out."

"Truly, Lady Penelope, you have no idea." I cast Pen a demure look, nicely tinged with shyness, that caused her to regard me most approvingly. Mephisto snorted, and moved to a window-seat with scrolled ends and straight legs. My guardian and I had taken each other's measure upon our first meeting, and neither of us had yet been inspired to alter that initial, unfavorable, impression.

Pen's children invaded the drawing-room at that moment, followed by their harried governess, and I was spared further tedious assurances that I would do quite well in Society and might even take the *ton* by storm. Mephisto rather spoiled this last prediction by adding the provision that I keep my mouth closed and my face blank. Not that his disapproval worried me. I was well enough acquainted with the world to know that great heiresses are invariably met with superlative kindness, even the plainest of them, which I was not. Nor was I particularly interested in amassing eligible suitors, for I had already met Ninian—but more of him later; it is not yet time for Ninian to enter this tale.

"Tedious brats," remarked Mephisto, observing with distaste the particular specimen that perched upon his knee. "Do send them away, Pen. I wish to speak to you seriously." There was some merit in his request, since the whole troop of young Palmerstons clamored for their mother's attention at the top of their undeniably healthy lungs, while the governess hovered and wrung her hands ineffectually. Pen disengaged herself from various grubby little paws, patted the

13

youngest's head as one might a favorite puppy, and shooed the lot of them away.

"You want a favor," she remarked, apparently oblivious to the slamming door. "What is it you wish me to do?"

"Plan one of your incomparable *soirées*." Mephisto's voice dripped boredom; for once, we were in accord. "Meredith will be guest of honor, and thus we will launch her into the world." I shot him a look of extreme dislike, not caring to hear myself spoken of in terms more aptly applied to a great strapping battleship, before donning the requisite air of excitement. This whole matter of my come-out was distasteful to me, and I would have dispensed with it altogether, if only I could. But, since Mephisto would only gain pleasure from an overt battle of wills with me—a battle which, due to my damnable situation, I would likely lose—I acquiesced as best I could and bided my time. As if he could read my thoughts, Mephisto smiled, with singularly blood-curdling effect. "I will of course stand the expense."

Pen's contorted features indicated that plans already tumbled willy-nilly through her mind. "Poor child!" she murmured. "To have your debut delayed so long." I did not care to reflect that I would be sharing the Season with insipid, giggling schoolgirls who were bound to consider me an aged spinster and act accordingly. What pleasure it would be to put their collective noses out of joint! "Your father could not have picked a more unfortunate time to fall ill."

"I doubt that he chose it, Pen." Mephisto was wry. "Nor is it a subject that Meredith will care to dwell upon." I was grateful for Mephisto's interference—my acerbic father had been dear to me and his long illness a grave ordeal—but one glance at my guardian's pitiless face assured me my gratitude was misplaced. Mephisto had no more feeling for me than for the chair in which I sat. I wondered if Fate might be induced to give him the set-down he so richly deserved, and immediately determined to offer Dame Fortune a helping hand.

"Oh!" wailed Pen. "I did not mean that your papa *wished* to—my wretched tongue! Jason swears I chatter like a magpie. Don't dare say I make as little sense, Christian, or I shall never speak to you again!"

"I should never," retorted Mephisto, "invite such a horrid fate." He had the knack of easy banter, when he chose to employ it, which was seldom. I was intrigued anew by his gentle treatment of his half-sister, who could easily have driven the most sanguine of men to temper, and sanguine Mephisto most definitely was not.

Lady Penelope laughed, an enchanting trilling sound. "You wish me to the devil, and well I know it! But I shall be good and get on with the matter at hand." Immediately she set out upon ambitious and grandiose plans for my entrance into the *haut ton*, eliciting indifferent agreement and occasional protest from Mephisto, while I sat back, apparently listening with an appropriate humility, and reviewed my frustrating circumstances.

The reader may have observed that I am not short in wit. I knew full well that Mephisto so little relished his guardianship that he meant to get me married and off his hands with all possible speed—an impossible task during my time of mourning since I could not then be jettisoned into Society. How he must have regretted my great wealth, for without it he could have disposed of me quite easily, without exciting undue comment. Heiresses are a far more noteworthy commodity than impoverished females of gentle birth.

Not that I have ever regretted my fortune! Without it I should probably have been forced to hire myself out as a governess, an occupation that would doubtless have ended in my hurling my charges out an upper-story window or applying my hairbrush to that portion of a recalcitrant child's anatomy which a lady is supposed never to name. *Derrière*, to be precise. I am not long on patience, nor prone to prudery. No female who grows up in a rural setting can long remain in ignorance of the bizarre rituals indulged in, most indelicately, by farmyard animals. Although I have no great faith that mankind in general is superior to the beasts of the field, I have the utmost confidence in Ninian, who has repeatedly assured me that he intends to employ a great deal more finesse.

My guardian, therefore, wished me alternately married off or impoverished, so that he might be rid of an unwanted responsibility. I did not particularly concern myself with Mephisto's little whims; his wishes were of no consequence to me, except that they were invariably in exact opposition to my own. Perhaps I should pause to explain Mephisto, as best I can. He plays an important part in this tale—far too

15

important, to my mind! For without his infernal interference, we might all have gone on much more prosperously.

The Most Noble Christian Mortimer Carlyle Vansittart, Duke of Denham and Marquis of Rye, Earl of Charnwood, Baron Vansittart of Heywood, Baron Vansittart of Needham, and Baron Vansittart of Arles, is a ruthless, autocratic and cynical man of ancient and honored lineage. I hardly need add that Mephisto is almost universally feared. Of course, *I* never harbored that particular emotion towards him. Rage, resentment, an unladylike loathing, yes; but it took a far more dastardly man than the dangerous Lord Denham to make *my* knees knock together with fear, an affliction that my maidservant suffered each time she heard the Duke's gruff voice. But Mephisto *will* persist in his unpleasant habit of killing his opponents in duels—not that many remain who are sufficiently mutton-headed to challenge him—and ruining others at play, so it is his fault alone that the majority of his acquaintance consider him a demon straight from hell.

My thoughts were interrupted when Jason—Sir Jason Palmerston, to give him all due honor—entered the room. He had just come from riding, and wore the blue coat with brass buttons, leather breeches, top-boots and pristine cravat that were *de rigeur* for that pursuit. Mephisto and I both watched—I with interest, he sardonically—while the reformed rakeshame of London dropped a kiss upon his wife's blushing brow. Said Jason, in a bored tone belied by the doting expression in his brown eyes, which were fixed on Pen's dirt-smudged gown, "The children have been here, I see."

Pen giggled and touched his hand. Their devotion to each other caused me a pang of envy; but Mephisto, a stranger to the gentler emotions, looked even more saturnine. "In full force," Pen agreed, "with Marie traipsing after them and clucking like a broody hen." A small frown appeared. "Do you know, Jason, I fear she doesn't exercise *quite* the control over them that one might wish."

"Pen," remarked Mephisto, addressing himself to me, "excels at understatement."

Jason regarded his brother-in-law without enthusiasm, appearing to debate whether to take exception to this remark. The men had once been intimates, one reason, no doubt, why Mephisto had so violently opposed Jason's marriage to Lady Penelope. Pen had, however, neatly spiked his guns

16

by steadfastly refusing to wed anyone else, and finally Mephisto yielded, allowing Jason to triumphantly bear his bride to this fine stuccoed house, with its round bow windows and low-pitched roof, in Queen Anne Street.

Jason ungently grasped my chin and forced my face up so that my eyes met his. "Sir!" I gasped, disliking such rough treatment. Jason smiled, and I immediately perceived the reason for his legendary success with the fair sex. He was at the time forty-two, two years older than Mephisto and twelve years older than his wife, but neither advancing age nor abstinence from his libertine ways had dulled his charm. It seemed that Pen was a fortunate lady indeed, and her bemused expression, as she surveyed her husband's muscular back, indicated a full awareness of this fact.

"Not precisely a beauty," Jason announced, and I glared at him. He released me, thoughtfully. "But perhaps something more." Mephisto looked to be on the verge of speech, but heroically refrained.

"Jason, a little less frankness, if you please!" Pen feared my feelings had been wounded and was quick to make amends. "Meredith is an extremely attractive young lady!"

She need not have worried: I have spent sufficient time before the looking-glass to be aware of both my assets and my deficits, and was consequently unchagrined. At that moment—in my simply cut gown of white muslin trimmed round hem and sleeves with a floral design worked in white embroidery floss, my pelisse of beige Merino cloth, buff-colored gloves and chip straw hat—I was a masterpiece of understatement. Even Mephisto had remarked, in relieved tones, that I looked just like a young girl should.

Jason moved to a serpentine-fronted cabinet of fine elevation and poured himself a brimming glassful of some lethal-looking brew, no doubt the better to tolerate Mephisto's presence in his drawing-room. "The chit will do well enough. You'll have no trouble establishing her, if that's your aim."

"Then our endeavor has your blessing?" murmured Mephisto, as I demurely contemplated the Aubusson carpet. So that the reader may better follow this conversation, I here offer a brief catalogue of my virtues, to wit: curly black hair; deep green eyes, rather large and surrounded by sooty lashes; a heart-shaped face; a delicately formed little nose of which I am rather proud; a mouth that though wide is nonetheless well-

17

formed; and an equally well-shaped chin which only my detractors claim is stubborn. Although it is my great misfortune to stand only five feet tall—I console myself that this is a perfect height for listening at keyholes—Ninian assures me that my figure leaves nothing to be desired, and it is true that my endowments, though not over-ample for one of my small stature, are just where they should be. Add to this a portion of some hundred thousand pounds and it becomes apparent why Jason's lukewarm praise did not cast me into despair. All the same, I contemplated making him eat his words.

"My blessing?" repeated Jason, as if Mephisto's query had been devoid of sarcasm. "Certainly, if that is what you wish." The men gazed at each other with the utmost dislike and Pen quickly drew their attention to herself, leaving me to reflect upon my guardian's unadmirable character.

In appearance, Mephisto was well enough, with that imperious world-weary air that inspires the less clever sort of female to make an absolute gudgeon of herself. (I shall never understand such creatures, for it was obvious from Mephisto's dissipated countenance that he had already done all in that nature that he cared to do!) His face was intriguing, despite its debauched traceries; his features were stern and almost savage; grey was sprinkled liberally through his black hair. The effect was diabolical, and an excellent portrayal of the soul within. Lest the reader think I draw too severe a picture of my guardian, I must protest that I have tried to the best of my ability to be fair, which, considering Mephisto's abominable treatment of me, is more than he deserves. Every unflattering adjective in existence must have at some time been richly merited by that callous gentleman, and I have magnanimously limited myself to only a few.

Suddenly I became aware of Pen's blue eyes, fixed anxiously on me. "I beg your pardon?" I inquired hesitantly. "I was wool-gathering, I fear."

"Meredith," remarked Mephisto, "has not yet recovered from the rigors of her journey here." His icy eyes inspected me as if I were a not-particularly-appealing piece of horse-flesh. "You must bear in mind, Pen, when you make your plans, that she is not robust."

"Nonsense!" I retorted sharply, then recalled myself. The wry twist of my guardian's lips did not deceive me: Mephisto

18

seldom smiled, and was even less often amused. "It is simply the excitement—I am used to a quiet country life."

Jason, glass in hand, had moved to stand beside a dainty composite article, a fire-screen with fall-down front which when open formed a writing-table with an array of pigeon-holes, drawers, and stationery cases tucked away in its depth. He observed me with more interest than he had hitherto shown, an interest that I did not find unflattering. "Soon," I added, "I will be myself again."

"An unthrilling prospect," murmured Mephisto, perhaps remembering the occasion when I had kicked him smartly in the shin. "Is there no way in which this dire event can be postponed?"

"Christian!" Lady Penelope was too kind, or too muddle-headed, to comprehend our enmity. "What will Meredith think of you if you persist in such odd remarks?"

"Nothing at all," I replied immediately, then smiled. It would not do for Mephisto to realize that I was an opponent worthy of his mettle. This was not cowardice on my part, but caution: Mephisto's reputation may have been exaggerated, which I've since taken leave to doubt, but no man was so dreaded without *some* reason. I preferred to lull him, to deceive him into thinking me a demure nonentity. I would boldly secure my own happiness and my guardian's ignomini-ous defeat, once I caught him off-guard. That I had thus far failed to convince Mephisto of either my innocence or malle-ability discouraged me not one whit.

I leaned forward, the better to radiate sincerity. "I am fast becoming familiar with Lord Denham's inclination toward levity, Lady Penelope. His little witticisms cause me no offense. But what did you wish to say to me? I cannot apologize enough for failing to attend."

"Piffle!" Pen waved an airy hand and was off again, this time in plans for refurbishing my neglected wardrobe, with the unstated objective of bringing all London's eligible bache-lors to languish at my feet. Since this was a matter that little interested me, although I had no doubt it would come about, with or without dashing new attire, I left her to it and returned to my reflections.

I daresay I might have liked Mephisto well enough, for his wits were as keen as his tongue, had it not been for the legal control he exercised over both my fortune and me. Though

19

Mephisto was an intimate of my father's, an association founded solely on their mutual interest in government—Papa had been a high-ranking official in the Admiralty, and Mephisto wielded more influence than even the Prime Minister—we had scarce set eyes on each other before the sad events that left me to his reluctant care. That Mephisto meant to sternly and rigorously fulfill the obligations that my deluded father had laid upon him was speedily and painfully made clear. As a result of that previously mentioned interview, I dined for a week upon bread and water in the solitary splendor of my room, and Mephisto spent a fortnight with a richly merited limp. But it is not my wont to brood over the inequities of fate. Since open defiance would not serve, I immediately set about hatching schemes to more subtly achieve my ends.

I beg I will receive no pity for my orphaned state. It is true that Mephisto, Lady Penelope and Sir Jason were virtual strangers to me; I had been among them a scant ten days. However, being plunged abruptly amid strangers is no harrowing experience for a young woman with my particular interests and abilities. To begin with, I am not missish, nor do I possess the slightest sensibility. To continue, I have an incurable curiosity—what my dear Papa called, in a rare moment of jest, a nose for mischief—and a most scientific way of solving the puzzles that people pose to me. Can there be greater satisfaction than unlocking family closets and seeing mouldering skeletons tumble out? I think not.

And I must take this moment to violently refute the unkind allegation that I snoop. I do not. I *investigate*, which is quite another thing. Nor is it true, as others have claimed, that I reap intrigue from hitherto-barren soil. Did I not discover the liaison between our housekeeper and a groom? And solve the mystery of Mrs. Brown's unaccommodating cow? The unfortunate matter of the parlor-maid has no bearing here, and I adamantly deny that she deliberately drowned herself in the village well. It was sheer accident. Girls in that interesting condition are prone to spells of dizziness, and she had the additional matter of her mistress's missing diamond brooch preying on her mind, as well as fastened to her petticoat.

I hoped that Mephisto knew nothing of my proclivities—it was not a matter which my father bragged upon, castigating my inquiries as "meddling," and my behavior as unfitting for a young lady of gentle birth—for I fully intended to exercise my abilities in regard to my guardian as they had never been exercised before. I had simply, in the past, found it advantageous to learn all I could of the people around me. Now it was of paramount importance that I do so. Mephisto stood planted most firmly between myself and what I wanted most in the world. Unless I was, for the first time in my life, to admit defeat, he had to be removed. In short, I meant to blackmail him.

Chapter 2

A Spin of Fortune's Wheel

Lady Penelope sat in her tranquil drawing-room, quietly stitching a miniscule costume to be used in the private puppet theatre that had been erected as a last-ditch attempt to distract the younger generation of Palmerstons from such hair-raising pursuits as enacting the various battles of the Napoleonic Wars under the priceless dining-room set, while Sir Jason recounted to her a rather shocking *on-dit* concerning Sophia, youngest of the Princesses.

"Ireland!" said Pen, interrupting her devoted spouse in mid-sentence. "Search my memory as I will, I can recall no branch of the family residing there."

The drawing-room had delicate damasked walls and an ornate marble fireplace, and was furnished with a gilt suite that included small and large sofas, a confidante and armchairs, all with very light frames on straight turned legs. An elegant commode of similar design replaced the usual sideboard, and an exquisite harpsichord sat in one corner.

Seated at this instrument, and admirably manipulating its ivory keys, was Lady Penelope's twin brother, Luke Vansittart, the Marquis of Camden. The resemblance between them was

21

startling, and superficial. One disgruntled dowager, after failing to snare the elusive Marquis for her daughter, a plump damsel with an unfortunate fondness for garlic, had commented acidly that the Almighty's attention had wandered during the creation of the Vansittart twins, and He had thus given Pen all the countenance and Luke all the brains. Whereas this may have been a slight exaggeration, it was generally agreed that Lady Penelope was indeed inclined to be feather-headed, and Lord Camden a trifle too serious.

"Why this interest in Ireland?" Lord Camden abandoned the harpsichord and moved to a gilt arm-chair.

"Christian," said Pen, surveying her twin thoughtfully, "brought his ward here to meet us. I am to help with the girl's come-out, but her titular chaperone will be a female relation imported from Ireland, one Lady Sara Cainneach."

"I should think that would please you." Luke made a fine appearance in a bottle-green coat, fawn pantaloons and Hessian boots. "Giving you as it does the perfect opportunity to racket about London, indulge in all sorts of dissipations, and spend so much money that poor Jason must pawn the family plate." Sir Jason, known to be one of the warmest men in London, smiled.

"That is not the point." Severity sat so strangely on Pen's enchanting features that both gentlemen laughed. "Wretches, both of you! Pray stop quizzing me, Luke. I wish you had been present to observe the extraordinary attentions paid the girl by Christian. Jason will tell you it was very odd."

"I will?" inquired Jason. "To say the truth, I'd as lief not speak of Mephisto at all. The mere mention of that name inspires me with an overwhelming desire to lay violent hands on the man."

Lady Penelope made no reply. Although she would cut out her tongue before saying so to her husband, she could well comprehend Christian's opposition to their marriage, and had long ago forgiven him. It was one of her dearest wishes that Jason might one day do the same, for she greatly regretted that she had been the catalyst that changed friendship to frigid enmity, but it seemed that nothing short of an outright miracle was likely to bring this about.

"What does the girl look like?" asked Lord Camden in his tactful way.

"*I* found her quite pleasing." Pen stressed the words, as if

22

trying to convince herself. "A slight little slip of a girl with huge emerald eyes. She'll go off, no doubt of it, for she is a considerable heiress beside. Her only rival will be Fanny Allingham, and Fanny's lineage is far inferior."

"Fanny is the most obnoxious young lady I have yet to meet." Jason planted a kiss on the nape of his wife's slender neck. Pen blushed. "But the Allingham fortune more than atones for her lack of breeding. She'll doubtless be one of the most sought-after misses of the Season."

"Meredith's fortune is almost as large," Pen protested stubbornly, "and she is a great deal handsomer. I predict that she will be a great success." As if he found it of more interest than the conversation, Luke contemplated a gleaming boot.

"Meredith," said Jason, in the tones of one who knows from vast experience that whereof he speaks, "is an incorrigible minx. If you don't keep a sharp eye on her, my love, you will find yourself embroiled up to your pretty ears in hen-witted escapades."

Pen abandoned her needlework to gaze upon her husband with dismay. "Of all the absurd things to say! I am quite out of charity with you. As if Christian would bring into society a girl who he suspected might conduct herself in an improper way—and Christian, I might remind you, should certainly know! He is a devilish high stickler."

"In matters regarding his family," amended Jason wryly. "Thank you, but of *that* I am aware."

"Darling!" Aghast at her unthinking words, Pen stretched out an apologetic hand. "I did not mean—"

"Of course you didn't." Sir Jason pressed a fervent kiss upon her palm. "Nor have you wounded me, my love."

Luke, witness to this moving scene, thought it incumbent upon him to intervene before these peace-making activities became positively embarrassing. "All the same, it is deuced odd, you know." Two pairs of bemused eyes turned towards him. "Why should Mephisto concern himself with a school-room chit? He could have easily left her to you and this unknown chaperone."

"There," replied Jason with approval, "you've hit the nail upon the head—though I might point out that the girl is hardly a schoolroom chit, being, I believe, twenty years of age." He stretched a muscular arm along the back of the sofa and absently toyed with his wife's bronze curls. "Yet Mephisto has concerned himself to a remarkable extent in the girl's affairs. I no sooner set eyes on her—as Pen says, she is a taking little thing—than I asked myself why."

"Meredith is a great heiress." In the tradition of her sex, Pen chose to be perverse. "And no matter what you say, Christian has a strong sense of propriety. Since he has been saddled with the responsibility, surely it isn't wonderful that he means to see the thing done properly? After all, if she should come to grief, the blame would rebound on him."

Jason gave a great shout of laughter at this notion of Lord Denham conducting himself as befit a proper gentleman, and even Luke looked stunned. "Darling Pen," said the lady's doting spouse, "you are a great deal too credulous! It is mere child's play for Mephisto to hoodwink you." His amusement faded. "I fear, my love, that your half-brother is very devious. What queer start he's off on now I cannot anticipate, but if he involves *you* in any of this deviltry, I mean to remonstrate with him *most* sternly." Sir Jason's eyes gleamed as if the prospect was not altogether a displeasing one.

"You are talking fustian," Pen said crossly. "What ulterior motives could Christian nourish, pray?" This question, though reasonable, was perhaps ill-advised, for it promptly reminded her of Lord Denham's mistress, Delilah, discovered by him in a Temple of Health conducted by a shrewd and unethical medical practitioner who promised the gullible rejuvenation through use of milk baths, balsamic tonics, a magnetic throne and a celestial Bed. Delilah's *rôle* in this arrant quackery had been that of Goddess of Health, and her *forte* nude erotic dances around the aforementioned bed, which was canopied, supported by twenty-eight glass pillars, and rented out for £100 a night to those who sought cures for impotence and sterility. Mephisto had removed Delilah from this setting and established her as the most dashing of the *demi-monde*.

But rumor claimed that Denham's interest was on the wane; and that the Duke had finally awakened to his responsibilities and meant to set up his nursery. "Good God!" Pen gasped. "Surely Christian doesn't mean to *marry* Meredith!"

Luke was taken with a choking fit and Jason observed the twins with a tolerant eye. "I think," he drawled, "*that* fear may be laid to rest. Mephisto didn't seem to be particularly smitten by Miss Meredith's charms."

"But he wouldn't!" In real distress, Pen plucked at the

flowers on her gown. "It would be the most improper thing—of course he would wish no one to know!"

"Why so overwrought?" Jason captured her hands before the silk was reduced to shreds. "You have often said you dearly wish to see *both* your brothers wed." This shot did not miss its mark; Luke flushed to the roots of his golden hair.

"But not to a girl so much younger than he!" Pen protested, apparently forgetting that her own husband was older than herself by a good number of years. Jason grinned. "I cannot say why, but I feel it would be a most grievous mistake." Luke cleared his throat and received a pointed look. "Though it is true I would like to see my brothers as happily established as myself."

So relieved was Lord Camden to be spared further discomfort that he bore with equanimity the advent of the junior Palmerstons *en masse*, despite the determined efforts of the youngest to exercise his gums on the brim of his uncle's elegant hat.

"I am not happy about you, Luke." Pen coped admirably with the three children who vied for possession of her lap. "You seem so blue-devilled of late! Will you tell us what is bothering you?" Lord Camden was saved a reply by Miss Samantha Palmerston, who applied herself with unharmonious gusto to the harpsichord's keyboard. Lady Penelope dropped a kiss upon the brow of the toddler who had successfully claimed the seat of honor; ruffled the curls of the losers, who sought to bear defeat manfully; then sat abruptly upright. The winner wailed. "Jason! 'Twould be the perfect thing!"

"Pernicious brats," remarked their father, observing the young lady clambering astraddle his knee, hopeful of what was known in the family as "playing horsey." "What would be the perfect thing?"

Pen clapped her hands and fair jiggled with glee. "Luke! Luke shall marry Meredith!"

Jason surveyed his brother-in-law, who looked every bit as vexed as a cat whose fur has been rubbed the wrong way. A very tolerant husband, Jason did not disabuse his wife of the extremely addle-pated notion that her sober twin and the volatile Meredith might suit. "Perhaps we should leave that matter to Luke, my love. Personally, I am a great deal more interested in Mephisto's mysterious Lady Sara than in your Miss Meredith Sherrington."

25

"As am I," said Luke wryly. "Mephisto is riding after prime quarry, or I don't know my foxes and hounds." His sister's puzzled brow indicated that she had, happily, been thrown off the scent. "And I do *not* think we claim among our family any Irish Cainneachs."

Chapter 3

It was a grand time to be in London, those first glittering months of the Regency. In January, Parliament had conceded that George III was irrevocably mad (conversing as he did with angels, Cardinal Wolsey, and his two dead sons, a condition which the royal physicians explained as gout that had flown to his head) and passed the Regency Bill, formally appointing as Regent our extravagant Prinny, whose debts amounted to £160,000 by the time he was twenty-three. Mephisto was among the advisers to the throne, who unanimously mistrusted their new sovereign—but then, Mephisto trusted no one, including my Aunt Tayce and myself. How I should have loved to see my guardian's face when, at the swearing-in ceremonies, Prinny confronted his Tory Ministers with a bust of that great Whig, Charles James Fox, displayed most prominently! Tayce believed that Prinny retained his father's Tory advisers, Mephisto among them, thus alienating his Whig friends, because a change of government would have further retarded the King's recovery. Whatever the reasons—and my aunt was always remarkably well-versed in such matters—the act did not bring Prinny any great popularity.

I found her in the library. Tayce had not been in Denham House for more than a day before she appropriated this chamber for her own use, and only I was permitted to interrupt her scholarly pursuits. Mephisto's housekeeper was

26

grievously offended that Tayce would not even allow the parlor-maid to polish the grate, though judging by the condition of the rest of Denham House, this pique was inspired not by thwarted cleanliness but by frustrated curiosity. Tentatively, I cleared my throat, and was ignored. My aunt was aggravating enough to make a parson curse!

She was seated at a knee-hole library table, inlaid with ivory and ebony. Papers were scattered in wild disarray across its broad surface. My aunt's pen skipped in leaps and bounds across a sheet of foolscap, and she frowned ferociously through the ill-fitting spectacles perched on the very tip of her nose. Knowing better than to further interrupt Tayce's communications with her Muse, I seated myself on a simple backless sofa with scrolled end-pieces and straight legs and waited impatiently to be granted an audience.

Tayce, Mme. Dore, was my mother's sister, a French aristocrat of the *Ancien Régime*. My mother, Lucile, fled France when the Terror began, but Tayce remained an additional four years, and barely departed her homeland with her head intact. Escape in those evil times had not been easily accomplished, but Mme. Dore at length reached Brighton in paradoxical company with one of the Revolution's most mysterious leaders, Jean Larousse, who then promptly—as was his habit—disappeared. I once asked Tayce about her relationship with this man—for danger stimulates passion and my aunt had an eternal eye turned toward expediency—but received only a curt request to tend to my own business in reply. *"Oh, la vache!"* she muttered, and I prudently ceased to tap my foot against the hardwood floor.

Tayce's first action, after parting with Jean, was to seek out her sister. Her second, when she learned that Lucile had both married and died in the interim, was to descend upon my father and take over my upbringing. This arrangement hardly suited Papa, but Tayce soon had him so firmly wrapped around her finger that he cherished a life-long feud with those who questioned her loyalty. The English and their mania for spies! Tayce was not the only *émigrée* to be accused of espionage.

"Well, *petite?*" One would never suspect from my aunt's appearance—she was then fifty years of age, angular and unlovely, with grey hair that came forever unpinned in her struggles with Clio and Calliope and Melpomene—that she

27

had once been a favorite of that gentle giant Louis XVI, and every bit as gay and extravagant as the beautiful Marie Antoinette. But Tayce had left all foolishness behind her in blood-hungry France, and now she embraced female emancipation as ardently as ever she embraced those well-bred *beaux* who left her arms for those of Madame Guillotine.

I shrugged. "It is as we expected. Lady Penelope is a charming nitwit, and is already contemplating eligible *partis.*" Tayce squinted at me rather like a cannibal thirsting for blood. Mme. Dore was opposed to marriage as a matter of principle, and had once shocked poor Papa greatly by inquiring why I should consider it a privilege to give over my fortune into some gentleman's spendthrift hands. "You can imagine my great relief to learn they think I'll take." I grinned. "Just think, dear Aunt, I may even become the rage!"

"Imbeciles." Already Tayce wore that look of glazed and slightly cross-eyed concentration that betokened a return to her literary endeavors.

"Lady Penelope is to give a party for me. Will you attend?"

I might as well have offered to break her on the wheel! It is incongruous in one who had been a leading figure in the old French court, but Tayce had an often-expressed disgust of English society and kept herself as sequestered as if she had taken up the cloister and the veil. Her revulsion quickly changed to shrewd appraisal. "Why should I, pray?"

I rose and restlessly paced the floor, once more pondering the infamous will that made Mephisto my guardian. "Something," I announced, "is afoot. Have you ever heard mention of Lady Sara Cainneach?"

Tayce's lips pursed, but she refrained from reiterating past occasions when I had, she claimed, allowed imagination to run riot. "No. Who is she?"

"That," I retorted, "is precisely what I wish to know. Mephisto positively shrouds her in mystery and informs me she is to join us as my chaperone."

My aunt's interest abruptly evaporated. Some years past she had announced that I had attained the theoretical age of reason and that she henceforth absolved herself of any part in my various follies. I took no offense. Beneath her gruff exterior Tayce nourished no soft heart, but I believed she was sincerely fond of me.

"Curtail your impatience, *ma petite!*" said she. "If the

Cainneach female is to reside beneath this roof, you will have ample opportunity to unearth whatever wretched secrets lie hidden in her past." My aunt, as grows apparent, did not share my avid curiosity, preferring instead to direct her not-inconsiderable intellect toward unravelling the tangled threads of the Revolution. She had been engaged for several years in the preparation of a *magnum opus* on the subject, a learned exposition from the novel point of view that the Terror would never have come to pass had women been allowed a more active role in government.

"Perhaps," I said pettishly, dropping again onto the couch and defiantly tucking my ankles beneath me, "you will regret your disinterest when I am found murdered in my bed!"

"*Mon dieu!*" Tayce observed me over the top of her spectacles. "Who do you anticipate will be driven to such lengths? The only candidates I can envision are Mephisto and myself, and I doubt that either of us would go about the matter so crudely."

I nibbled at my thumb and reflected that one who had survived the late occurrences in France could not be expected to nourish a properly horrified view of sudden death. "You mock me!" I snapped, first removing the thumb. "It is even more likely that I shall be married out-of-hand to some brainless dolt."

"In that case,' said Tayce, without enthusiasm, "I should feel obliged to interfere." She sighed so soulfully that, had I not known perfectly well that my aunt was in excellent physical condition for her age, I would have imagined her teetering on the brink of the grave. "Do take steps, *petite*, to see the contingency does not arise."

I ruminated gloomily upon the selfishness of my nearest and dearest kin. "I tell you, something very odd is going on."

"What?" My aunt set aside her pen and briskly pushed her wire-rimmed spectacles up to the bridge of her nose, where they stayed perhaps ten seconds before again beginning their inevitable descent. I did not voice my reservations concerning Mephisto. Tayce had already stated her intention to reserve judgement of my diabolical guardian, an act prompted not by a love of fairness but by supreme indifference.

"I wish I knew," I sighed. Could I but persuade Tayce that my future was as meritous of her vituperative attention as

29

was France's past, I would gain an invaluable ally. Not one to waste precious time in verbal play, my singularly unethical aunt awarded me a severe look before settling her spectacles once again on the bridge of her nose and returning to her manuscript.

In truth, it was little wonder that Mme. Dore had been transformed into this gaunt and black-clad figure who was so determined to keep herself aloof from the world. Tayce was willing enough to supply macabre details of the blood-bath in France—such as a hair-raising description of that black day when the executioner, Henri Sanson, held up the Queen's severed head for an admiring populace to view—but for all she said of her life before the Revolution, she might have sprung full-grown into life on that fateful day in 1789 when the *sans-culottes* took the Bastille. Nor did she explain how she so long survived her debonair husband, one of the first aristocrats to dangle by the neck from a lamp-post.

As sharp as ever the guillotine was, her eyes rested on me. "I mislike that look, *petite*, and furthermore you are a devil-ish distraction!" snapped my doting aunt. "Concoct your schemes elsewhere, if you please."

"I have been quiet as a mouse!" I was all wounded innocence. "Very well, I will go, since I can see you do not wish my company." Suiting action to words, I rose. "You will be sorry, I daresay, when asked to identify my corpse."

A sense of humor is among the artifacts Tayce left behind her in France. So exasperated as to have liberally splattered herself with ink, my aunt reached for her silver-topped cane, and I took a prudent step toward the door. "Never mind! Not for anything would I have you bestir yourself on *my* account."

"Stay where you are!" I stood stoically while Tayce limped across the room, wondering whether the dratted cane would connect this time with my shins or my *derrière*. Lest the reader think me victim of brutality, I will add that Tayce's cane was never wielded with sufficient force to cause injury—except when, upon first meeting Mephisto, she cracked him sharply on the knuckles, causing him to curse her *most* fulsomely. Today I received a hearty nudge in the ribs with the silver knob, a rare sign of affection. Then she placed one surprisingly strong hand beneath my chin and turned up my face to hers. (The reader will note that, due to my lack of height, people have a most annoying tendency to thus manhandle me.)

Tayce's glasses had again slipped down to the end of her nose; her eyes, faded and surrounded by countless tiny lines, were unnervingly acute. "Humph!" said she, and released me. I glared at her, and she pinched my cheek. "You're looking much too glum. I suggest a spot of dalliance with your rascally young man as an antidote for dreaming up mysteries."

I stared speechless as she returned to her work-table, too shocked to experience the pity that customarily assailed me when Tayce so slowly and painfully manipulated her cane, dragging the crippled leg that was her only visible souvenir of her homeland. "How long," I asked weakly, "have you known?"

"Forever." Tayce dismissed Ninian with the nonchalance that characterized her dealings with the opposite sex and solved the problem of her spectacles by shoving them to the top of her head. "Do you know, *petite*, that if anyone ever offers you bodily harm, it will be because you have poked your nose into what you should not?" Neither of us could have known that she uttered a harrowing prophecy.

"Twaddle!" I retorted. "I trust you will conduct yourself properly at my funeral. You recall, of course, that in the event of my maidenly demise, my fortune reverts to the American branch of the family?" On this infinitely cunning thrust—the disposal of my fortune was another of Papa's posthumous crimes against Tayce, who was penniless—I whisked myself out of the room.

"*Allez vous coucher, ma cocotte!*" Tayce's irate voice was muffled by the heavy door. Having taken the first steps in insuring that my aunt would concern herself with my welfare, I went, not as requested to blazes, but to plan an assignation with Ninian.

31

Chapter 4

Between Scylla and Charybdis

An elegant closed *coureuse*, from the famed French carriage builder R. M. Duchesne, rattled over the cobbled London streets, and stopped before one of the great houses that stood between Sackville Street and Hyde Park Corner. Set one hundred feet back from the street, the mansion was protected by a high wall surmounted by ornamental lamps. Two gates, with a tall classical pedimented arch between them, led into the oval courtyard.

Gabrielle St. Erth, the new Lady Randolph, exhibited little pleasure at this charming view of what was to be her home. London, to Gabrielle, meant noise and confusion, boisterous and rowdy people, the smells of horse manure and sweat and smoke that lingered even in this exclusive thoroughfare.

A lovely creature, with that shade of red-gold hair immortalized by artists, the newly-created Countess had soft brown eyes and translucent skin that, just then, was alarmingly pale. With great solicitude, her husband of only a few days assisted her to mount the steps to the massive front door. Though Adam St. Erth was a very handsome man, his wife shivered at his touch.

The footman who opened the door gaped speechlessly at his master. "Stand aside, idiot," advised Lord Randolph, and propelled his lady inward.

Gabrielle gazed through the three arches stretching ahead to the Great Stair, adorned by classical statues standing in recesses, that filled the whole central space of the house to the roof. The uppermost step, she thought, was an excellent spot from which to put a period to her life.

Lord Randolph dealt, rather impatiently, with his distressed servants and led his bride into the sitting-room. She moved toward the hastily-laid fire. "So cold," she murmured, unthinkingly.

"My dear, what can you expect?" The Earl removed his hat and gloves. He wore a long-tailed coat of fashionable blue, breeches of an equally fashionable yellow, and polished top boots. "May I remind you that we were not expected for another sennight?"

Lady Randolph surveyed her hands, icy even in their little lilac gloves. Her head ached, and she felt faint. "I'm sorry," she whispered. Perhaps quick repentance might appease this uncertain-tempered man.

The superior butler entered the room, bearing a silver tray, on it a single goblet. Gabrielle, too, would have enjoyed some refreshment, but was too timid to ask. "My dear," said Adam wearily, "do you think you might give Pomeroy your cloak and bonnet? Or, having been so eager to arrive here, have you now decided that you do not wish to stay?"

Gabrielle flushed and bit her lip, but removed her lavender velvet pelisse with its broad turned-down collar, and the charming velvet bonnet with lilac ribbons that tied beneath her chin. These, with the gloves, the butler bore away. Lady Randolph turned once more to the fire. She was sure the servants despised her, most of all the very proper lady's maid that her husband had provided, and all waited maliciously for her to put her foot wrong. It would not be long; Gabrielle's background had not prepared her to be mistress of so grand an establishment. Again she wondered why Adam had chosen her.

He had come to stand behind her, so close that his breath ruffled her short curls. "Well, Lady Randolph?" The title was mockery. "Are you pleased with your new home?"

"It is lovely, my lord." And it was, though the heavily-fringed dark curtains resembled funeral palls.

"My name is Adam." His hand on her arm was ungentle, and forced her to face him. "Must I insist that you call me by it, Gabrielle?"

"No"—she trembled lest his unpredictable anger be roused— "Adam."

Lord Randolph stepped back and surveyed, with disapprobation, his wife's simple muslin dress. "What of the gowns I provided? Why have you chosen to attire yourself in that ridiculous rag?"

Gabrielle clenched her hands nervously. Adam could hardly be expected to understand that she felt as uncomfortable with those new gowns as with this fashionable hairstyle that he had ordered. An obedient girl, Gabrielle had suffered silently as her long ringlets had fallen prey to the hairdresser's skilled hands, and as a result the face that confronted her each time she passed a mirror, with those short curls clustering from a center parting, was that of a stranger. Even the *modistes* had been quick to assess the new Lady Randolph's ignorance, and bullied her into purchasing all manner of things that she didn't want or even like. It was useless to mention such things to Adam, who would only say, among less kind remarks, that she must be firm. "I thought this would be more comfortable to travel in, and no one would see."

"You were wrong, weren't you?" He watched her as if she were a rodent and he one of the fighting terriers that he had in great and gory detail told her about. "It is I whom you must please now. You are Lady Randolph and shall appear as such, not as a schoolroom miss. Do you understand?"

Gabrielle thought resentfully that it would take more than a brilliant marriage to transform a young lady barely seventeen years of age into a sophisticated Countess, but was too wise, or timid, to give voice to that opinion. "Yes, Adam." As Lady Randolph, she would see that her younger sisters, when the time came, married well—not for convenience, as she had done, or for money, but for love.

" 'Yes, Adam,' " sneered the Earl. " 'No, Adam.' 'I fear I am going to be ill, Adam.' By God, I believe I've married a mocking-bird!" Roughly, he grasped her shoulders. Gabrielle gasped. "Haven't you sufficient spirit to voice an opinion of your own?"

"I don't think," Gabrielle flashed, "you would care for those opinions, my lord!" She knew as soon as she spoke that she had done exactly as he wished, a grave mistake. The familiar, dreaded warmth leapt into her husband's eyes. "Not now, I beg you! I still feel unwell."

"Tell me, do you mean to pass the years of our marriage being continually ill? It will avail you little." The Earl did not release her and his grip was cruel. "You are a fool, madam, if you think I am to be put off by excuses, or even tears."

34

"I told you I am prone to carriage-sickness." With great effort, Gabrielle kept her voice even. "It has been always so with me."

"And damned unpleasant for your fellow-travellers, as I have good reason to know!" He released her so abruptly that she almost fell. "You'll make me the laughingstock of my entire acquaintance with this short-lived bridal trip."

Gabrielle recalled, in mortification, that ill-fated journey with unplanned stops at coaching-inns where everyone from the ostlers and boots to the interested stagecoach passengers knew of her indisposition. "Perhaps you might say that it was a matter of government that called you home."

Adam laughed unpleasantly. "I may, I suppose, claim such great dismay that Grenville and Grey have called for peace at any price that I wrenched myself away from my wife's loving arms? Or shall I lay blame on the Continental Blockade which has so injured British trade?" Knowing nothing of such things, she remained silent. He sneered. "Never fear! I shall hardly say that I was driven back to London by a disgust of my wife's inadequacies in the marriage bed. It is a matter that I speedily mean to rectify, after all." Gabrielle turned pale. "My dear, you cannot forever shake like a *blancmange* each time I come near you!"

"It is the chill of the house," Gabrielle lied, not wishing to inspire Adam to once more demonstrate his mastery. "I fear I have been a sad disappointment to you, my lord—Adam—and I apologize." But the disappointment was not all on his side! The handsome man who had courted her in so charming, if casual, a manner did not make an equally amiable bride-groom. Gabrielle recalled her mother's gentle soliloquy on the more distasteful aspects of conjugal bliss and concluded that her mother, despite the production of seven children, was a veritable innocent.

The family had been so pleased at Gabrielle's brilliant marriage, dowerless as she was. As Adam's wife she would brush shoulders with the *beau monde*, whereas before she had not been considered elevated enough in rank to be admitted into such high company. It had been folly of the highest order, but Gabrielle's delighted family did not understand that she was terrified of these aloof aristocrats, so intolerant of those unfamiliar with their ways; or that, of all

35

the alien things that surrounded her, Adam bewildered her the most.

He was watching her. "My dear, you have no need to apologize." So kind was his tone that she wondered if she had misjudged him, if these past days had been a simple nightmare. Disillusionment was prompt. "You have sufficient sense to know why I married you. I mean to get an heir, and you are of good breeding stock. You are also young enough to be molded to my particular tastes."

Gabrielle swallowed hard, but didn't trust herself to speak. She was shocked by his frankness, as Adam very well knew. Having discovered in his wife a modest prudishness that he castigated as fit only for commoners, he had proceeded to enlighten her in the ways of the *haut ton*. Consequently, Gabrielle learned with dismay of the Annual Cyprians' Ball at the Argyle Rooms, where well-bred gentlemen who had been seen at Almack's the night before abandoned themselves to a wild orgy of delight; of Mother Windsor, the notable procuress in King's Place; of the innumerable lovers of both the fat, well-corseted Regent and the Princess of Wales.

"You are looking positively haggard," said Lord Randolph with mock solicitude. "Your rooms should be ready now. I suggest you rest awhile."

Gabrielle would have liked nothing better, but had already learned caution. "And you?"

He smiled. "Such concern for my welfare! But set your mind at ease, I do not mean to join you." He moved toward her and she forced herself not to flinch. "Not just now. I shall set about some likely tale explaining our return."

"What will you say?"

"Can it be you do not wish me to leave you?" With one finger, he traced the perfect structure of her face. "I shall attribute it to the complexities of the Sherrington estate. There is a very large fortune involved, and Denham is no fit custodian for a green girl. I wonder—" He grew thoughtful. "There is a possibility that you may help me there."

Gabrielle suspected her husband's interest in the Sherrington estate derived from his long and virulent animosity for his co-executor, but it was little of her concern. "Certainly," she murmured, "if you wish it. And now, if you will excuse me, I *am* weary, and believe I will retire."

It was, of course, not to be that easy. She cried out as Adam's fingers twisted in her hair. "My dear!" mocked Lord Randolph. "Is it the anticipated anguish of separation that fills you with such pain? But I vow I shall seek succor in no other arms but yours!" With strength inspired by fear, Gabrielle broke away from him and ran towards the door. The Earl laughed. "These nervous agitations," he chided, "will grow to a very serious height if they are not checked. Surely you do not mean to run away from me?"

Gabrielle could easily imagine the consequences attendant upon that particular thing. "No, Adam," she said, and paused by the door. "It is only that I am so very tired."

"Very well." He had lost interest. "I believe you *may* be of some assistance regarding Miss Sherrington, but perhaps you would wish to be more composed before we go into further detail."

"Yes, Adam." While Lord Randolph gazed contemplatively into the marble fireplace, seeing unknown visions in the crackling flames, his young Countess lifted her skirts, sped up the mahogany staircase, and with shaking hands uncapped the forbidden bottle of laudanum hidden away in her portmanteau.

Chapter 5

Monday 8 April 1811

"Lady Sara Cainneach?" Ninian's noble brow wrinkled as he searched his erratic memory. "Loath as I am to disappoint you, I don't recall the name."

"Ninian," I replied, with perfect sincerity, "I doubt that you'll ever disappoint me." He possessed the ability to distract me from more mundane trains of thought, being the finest specimen of the male animal that I had ever been privileged to set eyes upon.

37

"Do you know," he inquired, with a bewitching smile, "I rather hope I don't? Tell me more about this female dragon that your guardian's set to watch over you."

"I can't, or very little." It was my turn to frown, though I quickly erased it lest I invite premature lines. One grows careful of one's appearance when enamored of a handsome rascal like Ninian Northcliffe. I was not sufficiently small-minded to resent the drooling admiration that half the ladies of London lavished on him, although it was a matter of some perplexity that the married women among them devoted less time to their husbands and families than to pursuit of an arrant fortune-hunter, albeit one who had the *entrée* everywhere. "I know only that she is a widow whose home is Ireland, and that she has agreed to oversee my come-out. Beyond that, no one seems to know anything about her, except Mephisto, and he won't tell. Even Pen, who is addle-pated but knows everyone, drew a blank at Lady Sara's name. It is decidedly queer."

"You surprise me." Tenderly, Ninian took my arm. "I thought by now you would have ferreted out all sorts of information, and would have brought Denham firmly to heel."

"Would that it were so easily done! Mephisto is a secretive devil, but I haven't yet despaired of him."

"I rather wish you would." Ninian was unusually serious. "Denham doesn't make an amiable enemy."

"Pooh!" I adjusted my scarf. "Surely you aren't suggesting that I should be afraid of him?"

"Not man nor beast nor, probably, the Deity." Ninian's eyes twinkled. "Your fearlessness is part of your charm."

"The other part," I retorted complacently, "being my great fortune." Ninian laughed, a most delightful sound.

Since this seems an admirable opportunity, I shall indulge myself with a brief description of my comely companion. He was then four-and-twenty years of age, a veritable Adonis, as I have said previously and will doubtless say again, with blond hair so pale as to seem spun flax and roguish, dancing eyes. He was cheerful, charming, and happy-go-lucky, without either conscience or scruple to disturb the easy-going tenor of his mind, and his delightful manners and easy address made him a hostess's dream. Of his lithe and muscular physique, so admirably suited to a notable sportsman, I shall say little, lest I wax more eloquent than is suitable for a young girl of gentle upbringing and supposed inexperience.

"A penny for your thoughts," Ninian offered, the twinkle more pronounced. "Whist, my darling, shall we be off to Gretna Green?"

I turned my head to better observe him, a pastime that rates high among my favorites. His taste in matters of dress—in all matters, in fact—was impeccable. That day he wore an admirably-fitting coat of green cloth, kerseymore breeches of a buff color, highly-polished boots, hat and gloves. His cravat was arranged with stunning intricacy, and again I marvelled at his expertise in the process known as "creasing down." Ninian explained it, at my request: the man of fashion lays back in his chair, and the stock—twelve inches broad—is wrapped around his throat. He then lowers his chin slowly and, if heaven smiles, pleats the twelve inches of material into five inches' worth of regular tiers. I understand that this is no small accomplishment. "We shall do so," I replied, "the moment I come of age. At this particular time, it would be a trifle ill-judged, since an elopement would leave Mephisto in charge of my fortune."

"Well thought out," observed Ninian, and gallantly kissed my hand. "Though I am, of course, dismayed that I must wait so long to introduce you to the joys of wedded life."

"Fudge!" said I, poking him with my parasol. "You are dismayed that you must wait so long to introduce yourself to my fortune. There are other heiresses, you know. Would you prefer that I release you from any obligations to me so that you may wed one of them instead?" It was a magnanimous offer, and I didn't mean a word of it.

The reader may note a hint of uncertainty in the preceding passage, and I hasten to explain that this emotion assailed me only in regard to Ninian. He may have been a gazetted fortune-hunter, but he was mine, and I was occasionally beset by fear that, due to my accursed situation, I should be forced to watch him flit away, like a carefree butterfly, to a more accessible bloom.

"That," replied Ninian, incensed, "is a damned silly question! The only other heiresses *I* know are either fubsy-faced old maids or have gorgons of mamas who won't let a penniless wastrel like me get within a mile of them." He grinned. "No, my poppet, it will have to be you, and wait I shall, even if it be an entire year. In return for my patience, I shall receive a wife who is not only rich as Croesus, but who also possesses the face of an angel and the body of a Salome. The trifling discomfort of existing awhile longer in my usual penurious state is a trifling price to pay for such largesse."

I blushed. Such praise from Ninian was rare, and I vowed to renew the application of my favorite recipe for preservation of the complexion, a mixture of a good many white flowers, cucumber water and lemon juice, combined with seven or eight pigeons beheaded and minced fine, the whole then digesting in an alembic for eighteen days before use.

"Surely," Ninian added, in impassioned tones, "you cannot doubt my devotion, Merrie?"

I could, and did, but saw no more reason to confess this than to reveal my nightly entreaties to the Almighty that a more bedazzling, and even wealthier, heiress might not burst upon the *ton*. "It may not be a year," I added, with determination, for I had no intention of tempting Fate by allowing Master Northcliffe to kick his heels so long. "Not if I can oblige Mephisto to knuckle down!"

Ninian looked thoughtful, but remained silent. He was not precisely poverty-stricken, and would come into his father's money when he turned twenty-five; but until then, Ninian was forced to exist on an allowance that was scarcely adequate to support the appearance of a leisured gentleman. Even with his inheritance, Ninian would be barely comfortable—hence his need to marry advantageously. He candidly admitted as much on our first meeting, when I taxed him with seeking out my acquaintance from ulterior motives, and I returned his frankness by voicing *my* immediate determination to marry *him*. Unfortunately, over the intervening years, matters had not noticeably progressed.

"Denham," he mused, "is a damned high stickler. They say he seldom loses his temper—he has little need to, having other and more effective ways to deal with those who offend him—but they don't reckon with you." His gaze was appraising. "*You* may find yourself obliged to knuckle down."

"Never!" I said grimly. "Confound the man!"

Ninian laughed and abandoned his grave manner. "You are looking more than usually fine today. May I hope it is for my benefit?"

"This is hardly the time for flattery," I retorted, not ill-pleased. It was true that I'd taken extraordinary pains with my appearance, and had carefully selected a dress of pink Trafalgar net with a satin Hungarian vest ornamented with silver frogs, cords and tassels. With it I wore a velvet Roxborough jacket, the color of a pigeon's breast; a jonquil-shaded poke bonnet in imperial chip; a scarf of deep salmon with an Indian border; and a large parasol of hinged pink silk with a folding wooden handle and a whalebone frame. I would not own that Ninian had inspired my efforts, though excessive female admiration had thus far not given him a swelled head. He was perfectly aware that I intended to marry him for unspecified reasons of my own. There was no need to further inform him that he had taken my fancy to an alarming degree. "We must forthwith plan Mephisto's downfall."

Ninian pulled one of the dark curls that I had allowed to peek daringly from beneath my bonnet's rim. He was in an unaccountably merry mood. "Very well, my highly capricious darling! I will refrain from telling you that you are the most adorable creature in existence, and that I have missed you abominably! Nor will I express my relief at finding you as impractical and impetuous as ever, so far from being deflated by your siege of mourning that you now unconscionably plan your guardian's ruin." He drew me into a deserted corridor— we were exploring Bullock's Liverpool Museum while my romantically-minded and somewhat imbecilic maid kept a sharp lookout lest Mephisto, for some incredible reason, also decided to venture within—and embraced me thoroughly. "At last! I have been wanting to do that for the past hour."

With hands that were not quite steady, I straightened my abused bonnet. "Heavens!" I said weakly. "One would think you have been denied my company for at least a year." My feeling for Ninian was not precisely comfortable, nor did I trust it totally. He aroused in me exactly the sort of weakness that I detested in other women and which led them to grave folly. This did not in the least affect my determination to marry him.

"It seemed like a year!" Ninian grasped my hands. "Are you sure you don't wish to throw caution to the winds and summarily elope?"

"I take it," I said crossly, disengaging myself, "that your

41

pockets are again to let. You have no more sense of economy than a newborn babe!"

"I haven't a feather to fly with," Ninian admitted cheerfully, and tweaked my nose. "You haven't answered my question."

"What I wish has nothing to do with it." Pleasant as this interlude was, it brought us no closer to a solution of our difficulties. I had no intention of being disinherited for marrying a penniless adventurer, and even Tayce didn't doubt that Mephisto, in his current loathesome position, would do that very thing. "Were it not for my wretched fortune, I would straightaway fly to the Border with you; but, contrariwise, if not for my fortune, *you* would not wish to run off with *me!*"

This piece of admirable logic affected Ninian in a strange way: He immediately enclosed me in another ardent embrace. "There!" said he, with obvious satisfaction, as I emerged both breathless and dishevelled from his arms. "We will speak more of *that* matter at some other time, when you are more willing to devote your entire attention to what I say." He restored my parasol to me—it had, during our antics, fallen to the floor—and conducted me sedately to an exhibit of curiosities from Africa, North and South America. Fishes, insects, shells, zoophytes, minerals and the like were displayed, in an area called the Pantherion, in a state of preservation hitherto unattempted.

Despite my knowledgeability on the subject—a necessary precaution when dealing with so shrewd a man as Mephisto—I am afraid I did not award Bullock's marvels the study that they merited. "What a strange mood you are in today," I remarked, with a sideways glance at my escort. His unexpected ardor had left me feeling unaccountably shy.

Ninian's excellent teeth flashed in a smile. "I am anticipating your entrance into Society, and the resultant contretemps." He assumed a visionary air. "You will act as a perpetual-motion machine, stirring up the salons, defending female foibles and advocating social and political emancipation for the weaker sex."

"And you?" I inquired. Ninian might not be in wholehearted agreement, but he did not argue with my views. "What pursuits will *you* engage in while I am creating such a stir?" This must not be construed as jealousy, that most demeaning of emotions, but a natural interest in the prospective activities of my unofficially-betrothed.

"I?" Practical as may have been Ninian's emotions toward myself, there was a definite gleam in his grey eyes. "I shall be among your throng of gay and profligate admirers, exclaiming that it is quite charmingly original for you to run counter to conventional behavior, and proclaiming my heart completely enslaved." He took my arm. "It is, you know."

"Palaverer." I pinched him smartly. Whatever the reason for Ninian's avowals of devotion, which I swallowed with a liberal seasoning of salt, they were undeniably welcome. I, of course, did not advertise that fact.

He hugged me impudently, but his cheerful face grew serious. "All the same, I mean to stick as close as a courtplaster to you, poppet. You are to be shortly thrown alone into the midst of the most dangerous class of society in London."

I turned and stared at him with the utmost astonishment. "Ninian! Is this wise? If Mephisto realizes I favor you, he may take grave steps."

Ninian's pleasant face was shuttered, a curious fact that roused in me a lively apprehension. "Ah, yes," he said, with curling lip. "One with my relatively impoverished background is hardly eligible to woo a great heiress. I suppose I shouldn't be surprised that you think I would have greater concern for my own skin than for your safety."

I fear my mouth fell open in most unbecoming surprise. "My safety?" I repeated, with a disgusting lack of originality. "Whatever are you talking about, Ninian?"

"There are," he retorted, "countless pitfalls for the unwary in this town, and I mean to see that you tumble head-first into none of them." He eyed me with no small severity. "With or without your cooperation, my girl."

"Yes, Ninian," I replied meekly. It was one of my inconsistencies that I adored my suitor in this masterful mood.

"You need not fear Denham will, er, interfere with me," Ninian continued, with what I considered commendable, if foolhardy, bravery. "I will be merely one of the admirers that flock around you. You will bestow no particular recognition upon me, but flirt indiscriminately with us all, as is your habit."

"Yes, Ninian." *He* was most deflatingly free of jealousy.

43

"And then, we shall see what we shall see."

"It will be as you say, Ninian." His frowning countenance prompted me to an admission that I would not otherwise have made. "And it is extremely unjust of you to accuse me of thinking you place your welfare above my own! I have *never* considered you selfish, only practical." An odd tickling sensation assaulted my nostrils. There was no help for it; I sniffled belligerently. "Mephisto is a dangerous man, and I should not be at all happy if you were made uncomfortable on my account."

"Curse Mephisto!" retorted Ninian, his good humor restored. Heaven only knows what shocked horror was suffered by Bullock's other visitors that day, for my disgraceful descent into sensibility was awarded by yet another kiss, this one delivered not only with overwhelming enthusiasm, but publicly.

Chapter 6

Irons in the Fire

Lord Denham had already that day visited the fencing rooms in St. James's Street, examined the latest acquisitions at Tattersalls, and exhibited himself briefly in White's bow window. He had also been privy to the complaints of his Regent regarding the arch-conservative Duke of Cumberland, an individual of menacing aspect and worse reputation who had been convalescing at Carlton House ever since his valet tried to murder him the year before. Cumberland occupied himself by following the Regent wherever he went, warning him against Whigs, reform and Catholic emancipation. Prinny, as a last resort, had moved to the Stable Yard to avoid his brother's company.

Mephisto, however, exhibited greater interest in a certain house on the New Road in Marylebone. This was an enchanting and imposing Gothic *cottage orné* with a thatched roof and mullioned windows and brick walls rendered in colored plaster. Larch trees and pines encircled the lawn; tall elegantly-shaped chimneys rose above the reeds of the roof. Lord Denham's expression, as he gazed upon this masterfully-executed flight of fancy, was more than usually sardonic. He moved along the thatched verandah, supported by rustic columns entwined with ivy and honeysuckle, that extended along the cottage's south front. He gazed with even deeper irony upon the large glass conservatory at its eastern end. But Lord Denham had not come to savor the more frivolous details of this whimsical masterpiece. He inserted a key into an ornate scrolled lock and stepped quietly within.

The bedchamber was done up in the Chinese style, the walls papered with figures which resembled nothing of God's creation, fanciful scenes that continued round the whole room. Clad in a dressing-gown that was reminiscent of a frothy white beribboned cloud, Delilah lounged artistically in a pagoda-like alcove of carved wooden couches and sipped her morning coffee. She was an extraordinary combination of perfect physical beauty and total amorality, and she had been Lord Denham's mistress for the past three years. "Mephisto! To what happy accident do we owe so unexpected a visit?"

Mephisto returned her sleepy, slanted-eyed regard with an expression of what might have been vague amusement on his harsh features. Delilah fit in well with the strange motifs—waterfalls and dragons, strange elongated birds and lattice work—for she was even more exotic than her surroundings, an indolent golden-skinned creature with unbound jet-black hair. Aware of the pale gaze fixed on her, Delilah stretched luxuriously, revealing a voluptuous body, and glanced pointedly at the oversized bed.

Lord Denham ignored this invitation and walked to the fireplace, where Chinese heads leered from the chimney-piece. Delilah sighed. She owed much to this man, who had with his patronage enabled her to give her unusual talents full play, with the result that she was now as notorious as any fallen woman who ever lived. When Delilah drove in Hyde Park, a crowd of horsemen trotted beside her, begging for a smile of recognition or a nod. Her evening parties were attended by dandies and foreign gentlemen of the *corps*

45

diplomatique, peers of the realm, foolish young bucks down from Oxford and Cambridge, all of whom agreed their hostess knew exactly how to titillate the most jaded appetite.

Delilah cast Lord Denham a smouldering glance, to no avail. Here, it seemed, was an appetite that she could no longer whet. "You mean to be as disagreeable as usual, I see." She settled more comfortably among her myriad pillows. "I vow, you are the greatest rascal unhung! I suppose you have come to relieve me of my companion?"

Lounging against the chimney-piece, Mephisto was as enigmatic as any of the carved heads. "As you say." A faint smile touched his lips. "I doubt you will be lonely long."

Thus ended their relationship. Although it rankled that he should think to dismiss her so casually, no hint of dismay showed on Delilah's golden features. "No," she agreed, thinking of the dolorous fop of a lawyer who so persistently courted her, a vain silly fellow who was allegedly as rich as he was vulgar. An ugly little quiz to be sure, but he could be counted on to deal with the pile of *post-obit* bills stuffed away in her dresser drawers. She glanced up to find Lord Denham regarding her quizzically.

"I am practical," said Delilah, with a shrug. "We know one another too well, I think, for it to avail me to dissolve in tears. But tell me one thing, if you will: What do you mean for this so-sorry little Sparrow as you call her that you brought to me?"

"I trust you will not take it amiss," Lord Denham replied, abandoning the fireplace to sit beside her, "when I tell you I would rather not say." His unamiable tone discouraged further questioning. "You have done as I asked?"

Delilah admitted to herself that there would be certain advantages attached to her new unfettered state. Mephisto was known as a most dangerous man, and one uninclined to share his belongings. "Exactly," she replied, setting the coffee aside. "You are the most reckless devil that ever existed! Your Sparrow has undergone a transformation and will be received everywhere with enthusiasm, if that is what you wish."

Lord Denham was not disposed to either affirm or negate this subtle query. "How did you and she get along?"

"We rubbed on very well together"—beneath Delilah's languorous exterior dwelt a keen sense of both intrigue and

46

revenge—"for all her initial state of alarm and fainting-fits. One would think her a delicately nurtured lady whom you have kidnapped and starved into submission!"

"You may think what you like," replied Mephisto, taking her wrist in his strong fingers. The lover-like gesture, and the chill in his voice, caused Delilah to wince. "As long as you do not attempt to throw a rub in my way."

"Stuff!" said Delilah, with more bravado than she felt. "I have other fish to fry. Since you have given me my *congé*, I no longer need concern myself with your eccentricities."

"Well said." Lord Denham's hand moved to her lovely throat. "All the same, I think I must ask for your word that you will refrain from noising this matter abroad." Delilah stared at him, fury in her slanted eyes, and his grasp tightened. "It would displease me greatly were you to attempt to feather your nest at my expense—particularly when I recall that I built that nest myself and at considerable cost." Delilah grimaced, finding it difficult to breathe. "Well, madam? Have I your word?"

Mephisto might have done well to remember that Delilah was a creature of strong passions, which she indulged with great latitude. But she only nodded, though she wished nothing more than to claw out his mocking eyes. "I'll be silent as the grave," she gasped, rubbing her sore throat. "Good God, what's it to me if you foist a straw damsel on the *ton!*"

Lord Denham smiled unpleasantly. "Nothing at all, as I'm glad you realize. Now, where is she?" Sulkily, Delilah rang for her maid. She had no idea of this Sparrow's true identity, but assumed she was to be Mephisto's newest *chère amie*. Well, Sparrow was welcome to the brute! He was as mean as Satan, with the most vicious and untrusting nature ever possessed by man.

The Duke reached into his pocket and produced a jeweller's case, thus affecting Delilah with a rapid change of sentiment. Avarice shone from her dark eyes. With a saturnine expression, Mephisto fastened the gems around her neck, the diamonds cold against her bruised skin. "For, shall we say, services rendered?" he murmured. "Though I know your mind is of too fine a tone to care for such things. And in return for the silence you have promised me."

Passion, inspired by such generosity, briefly got the better of reason, and Delilah pulled his brooding face down to her own. "Will you not reconsider?" she whispered huskily. "You know I please you very well—far better than will that frail scarecrow."

"You are flogging a dead horse, my sweet." Lord Denham disentangled himself. "I have discovered belatedly that I have an uncontrollable penchant for clever women, among whom Sparrow definitely numbers."

"I thank you." Sparrow stood in the doorway, an extremely slender woman of medium height with a very pale complexion and hair that was an odd combination of brown and gold, as if streaked by the sun. "High praise, I vow." She wielded mockery like a sword.

Delilah drew her wrapper closer about her, but Lord Denham rose, so in control of the situation that he might never have been caught in a compromising position. He examined Sparrow as critically as if she were a mare he wished to buy. "I applaud your handiwork, Delilah," he remarked at length. "You've wrought a near-miracle."

"It was nothing." Delilah shrugged again. "After all, I was well paid." They made a good pair, Mephisto with his dispassionate nature and this woman who hid so well behind her ironic mask. Despite their weeks of enforced intimacy, Delilah had learned nothing more of Sparrow than that she was twenty-nine years of age.

"Well, Sparrow?" Lord Denham's sarcasm was even more pronounced, as if he meant by brute force to shatter that facade. He would not succeed, thought Delilah. This one would die before she let herself be cowed. "Are you prepared to play your role?"

Sparrow moved gracefully into the room, elegant in the grey silk gown that perfectly matched her eyes. "As ever I will be." Her lack of warmth matched his own.

Lord Denham reached for the pelisse that was offered by Delilah's discrete maid. "You once possessed a fair ability in that respect, as I recall."

There was little humor in Sparrow's laughter. "I did. More than you know."

"Why are you doing this?" Delilah asked, inspired not wholly by sympathy. Not lovers then, perhaps never to be. But they spoke with the familiarity of long acquaintance, and Mephisto's hands lingered briefly at Sparrow's shoulders as he helped her don the pelisse.

Even had Sparrow wished to answer, she was given no opportunity. "Your association with Delilah is at an end," Lord Denham said crisply. "You need not concern yourself with her questions."

"Ah, yes." Delilah stretched lazily. "I am to avoid you altogether from this moment on, never to mention you, or inquire about you, and if possible never to think of you again." Her white teeth flashed in a dazzling smile. "Good luck to you, little Sparrow! And be assured that if the occasion should arise, I will stand your friend."

"I am more grateful than I can express." Briefly, some emotion struggled to free itself from behind those opaque eyes.

An infuriated muscle twitched in Lord Denham's cheek. "I assure you," he said icily, "the occasion will *not* arise."

No longer did Delilah need to tread carefully, lest she arouse Mephisto's displeasure. "Do not let me delay you," she begged sweetly. "I assure you I shall endeavor to bear with resignation the sad loss of your company." With a pungent oath, Lord Denham practically shoved Sparrow from the room.

Delilah reached again for her cup and sipped her coffee, never even noticing it was cold. Her fingers moved to the diamond necklace. So Mephisto meant this to be his last present, the means by which he bought her silence and his freedom? Perhaps it would serve as such, and perhaps not. Delilah meant soon to learn the motive behind all this mummery.

Chapter 7

Tuesday 9 April 1811

Never shall I forget that large and gloomy mansion in Cavendish Square, the sprawling house with its pillared portico that resembled the front of a Roman temple, the brooding windows with their heavy pediments and glazing bars. Tree-branches scrabbled futilely at the mellow brick, ivy climbed the rustic columns of the great front gate. Tall chimneys and blind garrets peered over the high wall that barricaded Denham House from the rest of the world. It could easily have been a prison, or an institution for the insane.

Wiggins met me at the front door. He was an individual of singularly macabre aspect, although this evil air might be partially attributed to the nasty squint in his left eye. Wiggins was Mephisto's superior valet, responsible for such sartorial miracles as boots polished to mirror-like perfection, flawlessly ironed clothes, hats brushed to a fine gloss. In short, Wiggins spent his days performing trivialities and contriving to make them seem essential to his master's peace of mind.

I knew myself to be the subject of much speculation in the servants' hall. Though I could hardly make friendly overtures to my guardian's staff, most of whom would have been appalled by such familiarity, my maidservant was not similarly restricted. Being of a confiding nature, she had quickly settled in belowstairs, where she lauded me to the skies, puffed up my consequence without heed of either my blushes or the truth, to such good effect that I received the nod of approval from the starchiest members of the domestic hierarchy.

But my guardian's valet had no soft spot for diminutive ladies with little heart-shaped faces and saucy manners!

Doubtless Wiggins considered dimples, of which I possess two, infallible signs of frivolity. He regarded my black curls, the modish bonnet which was somewhat askew, and my flushed cheeks; and his sinister features grew censurious.

"Lady Cainneach," said Wiggins sourly, "has arrived. I thought you should be informed, Miss, since his lordship is not on the premises." Tayce would have been a more proper recipient for this news, but my aunt had inspired the household with such awed terror that they would have dared disturb her for no occasion less monumental than a Heavenly Visitation.

"Marvelous!" I stepped blithely into the hallway and Wiggins looked even more severe. I suppose he thought it ill-bred to flaunt such enthusiasm. "Where is she? I will go to her at once!" I pulled off my bonnet and dangled it by its strings.

"Her ladyship is in her chamber, resting after her journey." Wiggins did an excellent impersonation of an icicle. "She will not wish to be disturbed."

Of course I could not overlook this impertinence. I drew myself up to my full stature and stared haughtily at him down the length of my nose, a feat more difficult than it may sound since Wiggins, though slight in stature, was at least six inches taller than I. "Your conclusions do not interest me, Wiggins," I announced. "You may go." He glowered, but dared not offer further insolence. I gaily mounted the stair, little knowing this was a victory for which I would dearly pay.

I had made it my business to learn which rooms were to be assigned Lady Sara and paused only briefly in my own chamber to dispose of my bonnet and parasol before proceeding there. Not being of retiring disposition, I had no qualms about invading Lady Sara's solitude. Indeed, it seemed positively providential that our first meeting should take place in this manner rather than under Mephisto's sharp eye. With my plan of attack fixed firmly in mind, I raised my hand and knocked energetically on the door. I found myself confronted suspiciously by Lady Sara's maid.

Bridey—this was the creature's name—was Irish from the top of her carroty head to her stubby toes. Her freckles were so numerous that she looked to have tumbled headfirst into a vat of brown ink; and across her snub nose was a faint scar, a souvenir of a flying pepper pot I later learned. Her cap and black stuff gown gave her an entirely spurious air of docility.

"Good day!" I exuded conviviality. "I have come to welcome you and your mistress to Denham House." Bridey muttered—blasphemies, I have no doubt—as I firmly pushed her to one side and stepped into the room, there to blink in amazement. Mephisto had done Lady Sara fine, assigning her a lavish suite exotically and romantically furnished in the style of Louis XV. The walls were decorated in heavy silk, and rare plants grew out of lacquered rosewood boxes. I hope I do not sound small-minded, but it did not escape my notice that my chaperone was housed far more grandly than I.

"Arragh!" said Bridey, claiming my startled attention. She did not appear to appreciate my proffered hospitality. "If it's my lady ye'll be wantin' to see, she's in her boudoir. Asleep."

I considered her. It might behoove me to secure this creature's gratitude, for no one is more privy to a lady's secrets than the lady's maid. "I have," I offered, "an excellent recipe for freckle removal, comprised of crushed strawberries, green grape juice, and asses' milk. If you like, I will make it up for you."

"By the Holy!" muttered Bridey, her plain features screwed into a ferocious scowl. "It's a sad cross to bear, stab me if it's not."

Further conversation in this fascinating, if incomprehensible, manner, was forestalled by Lady Sara herself. "Bridey!" she called, "to whom are you speaking?"

"Sure and it's not meself!" Bridey retorted, with a shocking lack of subservience. She jerked her head toward the boudoir door. "Be off with ye then. Herself will be wishin' a word with ye." I moved towards the inner room, passing by rosewood furniture, a sofa covered in Beauvais tapestry, and a handsome Venetian mirror, not at all certain whether I was meant to go or stay. "Chancy as the Irish weather," observed Bridey enigmatically. "May the devil trip the man!"

Lady Sara's dressing-room contained velvet and satin draperies, a floral patterned carpet and a great wardrobe from which spilled forth a startling array of gowns. Judging by their dashing style, these had been created not by any provincial Irish seamstress but by London's most fashionable modiste, and quite recently. Leather-bound volumes sat awkwardly among crystal cosmetic jars on a dressing table, beside which stood a bronze antique clock.

Lady Sara, who had been resting on a rosewood recamier, rose and smiled with such warmth that a less-determined visitor than I would have been totally disarmed. Hands extended, she moved forward, a very slender woman with grey eyes and chestnut hair. "Meredith! How delightful to see you, child. I think I must have known you anywhere."

"What's this, ma'am?" I was enfolded in a fragrant embrace. "Are you already acquainted with me?" Mephisto made a grave error in assuming I do not know chalk from cheese. It is my habit to award nothing and no one uncritical belief; and never, in my entire experience, has blind faith been so little merited as by Lady Sara Cainneach!

Lady Sara stepped back in momentary confusion, her pale cheeks flushed becomingly. "Alas, no, but Mephisto has told me so much about you that I feel we are already old friends." She guided me to a dainty rosewood chair. "Nor did he tell me half enough, for he neglected to add that you are charming as well as lovely!"

Lord Denham was far more likely to damn me with faint praise than to laud me, but I did not quibble. Instead, I crossed my dainty ankles and regarded my prospective chaperone as a cat might a foolhardy mouse. "You and my guardian are old friends?"

"Hardly that." Lady Sara's tone was wry. "Acquaintances would be more precise a word." She removed from the table beside her a handsome work-box, satinwood veneered and inlaid with a floral design, and obviously very old. From this she withdrew an exquisite piece of needlework. I watched keenly, interested neither in the feminine arts or antiques, but in Lady Sara's fingers, which trembled almost imperceptibly.

"Close enough acquaintances," I commented, "that you were willing enough to do him the favor of overseeing my come-out." Lady Sara's face was a masterpiece of sharp planes and hollows that would quicker appeal to an artist's discriminating eye than to the more common connoisseurs of feminine loveliness. She also possessed a soft musical voice and, I was soon to discover, a tongue of contrasting sharpness: The untrustworthy Sara informed Mephisto, as a result of our first interview, that I was as prickly as a porcupine.

Mephisto's displeasure was no less severe than my own, though mingled with my irritation was an exhilarating awareness that the battlelines had been clearly defined.

Her smile was slightly awry. "Not so large a favor as that, my dear!" Her nimble fingers manipulated the needle with skill as great as the most successful seamstress. "I have been buried in the wilds of Ireland so long that I leapt at the chance to return to London."

"Am I mistaken?" Ah, but I was subtle! "I was under the impression that Ireland is your home." One does not carry on a surreptitious romance for as many years as I have without developing a certain instinct for intrigue.

"You are correct," Lady Sara said, too quickly, "but I naturally visited London as a girl. My acquaintance with Christian dates from that time. We are only distantly related, you know." Abruptly, she lifted her head to study me, but I remained bland. "In truth, I imagine the relationship between you and I is closer than that between Mephisto and myself."

Though I strongly doubted this hypothetical connection, I beamed with enthusiasm. "How fascinating! Genealogy is a subject in which I am greatly interested. Dare I ask you to explain to me the intricacies of our family tree?"

"I should enjoy that immensely," Lady Sara replied, with a haunted look, "but beg that we may postpone that particular discussion until some other time." She raised a frail hand to her forehead. "Travel always fatigues me and I fear at this particular moment I could not treat the subject with the attention that it deserves."

"I perfectly understand," I said, and did. The fox, alerted, was on the run. "Forgive me for badgering you with questions so soon after your arrival. Would you prefer to be left alone?" Naturally, I had no intention of so easily abandoning my prey.

"Not at all." Lady Sara's voice lacked conviction. "Perhaps we might speak of more immediate concerns, such as your attire. Mephisto tells me Pen has taken that matter in hand?"

"Most thoroughly." I refused to be side-tracked, though most young ladies would have been enthused to the point of lunacy by the prospect of a new wardrobe. "I did not realize that you are also acquainted with Lady Penelope."

"Pen?" Lady Sara's thoughts were obviously elsewhere, a dangerous lapse under the present circumstances. I dared hope that my chaperone would damn herself with a careless word. "Oh, yes. It will be good to see her again."

"How odd!" My tone was triumphant and, I fear, smug. Lady Sara's eyes flew to my face. "You see, Lady Penelope claims no recollection of *you*."

Sara's face wore a vehemous expression, which may have borne some relation to the fact that she'd just inserted her needle squarely into her thumb. "It's not odd at all," she retorted, with only a hint of temper. "Pen knew me by my maiden name."

"And that was?" I fancied myself so hot on the scent that I forgot the need for tact.

"My dear child!" Lady Sara threw up her hands in an off-putting gesture. "I feel like you are conducting an Inquisition, with me as your target. If this is the way you mean to behave in Society, you will set the *ton* back on its heels." Having delivered this nicely-phrased snub, she set aside her needlework and applied a lace handkerchief to her wounded thumb. "Such bluntness of speech will hardly attract you a husband, I fear."

I shrugged nonchalantly, holding my own temper firmly in check. "I care not for that."

Lady Sara surveyed me in dismay. "But, my foolish girl, you must! Settling you properly is the whole purpose of your Season."

UnChristian of me, no doubt, but I hoped Lady Sara would not fail to acquaint my aunt with this viewpoint! It was Tayce's opinion that I should marry no one, contenting myself instead with the joys of financial security and a series of discrete *affaires*.

I uncrossed my ankles, folded my arms, and proceeded to demonstrate that I knew a great deal more about the matter than any young lady should. "The marriage system is essentially a property system," I observed, "and I have more than enough of *that!* I am also familiar with property settlements, including dowries, jointures, portions and trusts. Nor am I ignorant of the fact that the *nouveau riche* are eager to enhance their social standing by alliance with old aristocratic names, or that various noble families have complied in order to infuse new money into depleted treasuries."

Lady Sara's expression was horror-stricken, and she launched into a desperate discussion of *fêtes* and routs and *soirées*, musical assemblies, gala balls, and of course that holiest of holies, Almack's. Nervous as a cat on hot cobblestones, thought I, but allowed her to proceed. Lady Sara might temporarily forestall my further questions, but she was also making it glaringly clear that she had once known London remarkably well.

"You are a widow." Ruthlessly, I broke into the monologue. "I was sorry to learn that. Was the tragedy a recent one?"

Lady Sara gazed upon me with seething anger, but Bridey chose that promising moment to bustle into the room. "Dinna fash yourself, hinnie," she crooned to her mistress, placing workworn fingers on Lady Sara's brow. "I mind that day clearly, and a black time it was!"

"My husband was killed in a duel almost two years ago." Lady Sara leaned back her head and abandoned herself to her abigail's ministrations. "It was an affair of honor, concerning alleged cheating at cards." Bridey scowled at me with the utmost uncordiality. "Are there any further details you wish to know?"

Of course there were, but I hesitated to force the issue at that time. Instinct told me that, whatever tall tales Lady Sara may have spun for my benefit, the account of her husband's death was true. "Where," I persisted, "in Ireland do you live?"

"Tipperary." Bridey was inspired by our conversation to knead her mistress's brow as if it were dough. Lady Sara winced. "In a castle complete with chapel, oratory and ghost. The latter appears to be of some nobility, for she walks the battlements with scepter and crown."

I nobly ignored this tantalizing bait. "How I should love to see it! Tipperary is said to be lovely country, and excellent pasture land. I should also like to view the Rock of Cashel, where dwelt the Tuatha De Danaan, the race of sorcerers and magicians who could make themselves invisible at will." This was no idle comment; I had often mused that my endeavors would prove a hundredfold more successful could I but go about them unseen. Having impressed my audience with my powers of intellect, I rose. "You must be exhausted. I will leave you and hope to see you at dinner. May I say how much I have enjoyed our little talk?"

Lady Sara inclined her head. "It has been interesting," she agreed. "We must resume it at some not-distant time."

There was a brief silence as I gracefully took my leave. I opened and closed the anteroom door, then quickly hid myself behind a monstrous potted plant, from which vantage point I could quite clearly observe my victim. "Sure," remarked Bridey, abandoning her ministrations to drop into the newly-vacated chair, "and that one's kissed the Blarney Stone."

"Fair of word and soft of speech?" mocked Lady Sara in weary tones, apparently oblivious, or indifferent, to her maidservant's breach of decorum in addressing her with such familiarity. "Hardly that, Bridey!"

"That slip of a colleen," retorted the abigail, "could swear a hole in an iron bucket, make no doubt of it." She burrowed deeper in the chair, propped her feet on a dainty table, and pulled thoughtfully on her ear. "Sure ye've the patience of a saint to put up with her eternal questions. Had it been me in your shoes, I'd be after stranglin' her!"

"We cannot blame the lass for being suspicious." Lady Sara ran distracted fingers through her brown-gold hair, and I reflected upon the adage that the eavesdropper must not expect to hear himself praised. "Mephisto has probably handled her badly, with too heavy a hand on the reins. I should have expected it, I suppose. Time has little altered the man."

"That one!" spat Bridey. "Sure it's proper bewitched ye are." She wore a vengeful air that I could only applaud. I wondered by what unethical means Mephisto had insured Lady Sara's compliance with his schemes, for she appeared no more anxious to play goosebody to me than I was to have her do so.

Bridey reached for her knee-harp and hummed a haunting Irish tune. Lady Sara, meanwhile, gazed bemused at her maid. "You have not yet met Lord Denham, yet you dislike him so intensely?"

"By the Holy, I do that! Ah, lady, 'tis a clutch at me heart of the old foreboding that I have." Bridey got awkwardly to her feet, and I slipped quietly from the room.

Chapter 8

Wormwood and Gall

Lady Randolph sat curled up on the rug before the bedroom fire, amusing herself with those fashionable magazines for women, *La Belle Assemblée* and *The Lady's Magazine*. But her attention wandered, and she tossed aside the editorial comments on 'High Life and Fashionable Chit Chat, Continental Notes and On-dits' to gaze instead at the meagre fire. There was little need for this—if anything, the room was already too warm—but Gabrielle came from a home where even the cost of coal and kindling was reckoned dear. She thought it ironic that the only advantage of her new, exalted position was that she could appreciate the privilege of ordering as many fires laid as she pleased.

The master bedchamber was opulent, hung with crimson and gold, and it reminded Gabrielle of nothing more than a house of ill repute. This, too, was a part of her new station; only a few weeks ago, she had known nothing of either brothels or prostitutes. Now, thanks to Adam, Gabrielle knew all too much about that other side of life, the world of thieves and whores and highwaymen, of ramshackle rookeries and stinking alleys where newborn infants were left to die, of rotting corpses dangling from the black-draped gallows outside Newgate prison. She thought she would have preferred to remain ignorant.

Even the walls were hung with crimson, and draperies of that color hung at the windows and the bed. Gabrielle's eyes slid quickly away from that item, with its delicately tapered posts and gilded cornice, its domed tester and carved armorial bearings. To her it was no privilege to sleep where countless St. Erths had been born and died. She rose and moved to the corner basin stand, with its tambour shutter

58

and small cistern with tap, and splashed water on her face. She hadn't left the house since her arrival; Adam had forbidden it. Gabrielle wondered if he meant her to never set foot outside again. She eyed her satinwood toilet-table with its rosewood-banded top, and thought of the laudanum hidden in its secret door. She must conserve her meagre supply. Once it was gone, it would be difficult to obtain more.

Adam, of course, came and went as he pleased, sometimes not returning home until well into the morn. Gabrielle tucked herself into a crimson-covered chair. She didn't know where her husband went on those nocturnal visits, and was too much in awe of him to ask. Gabrielle's impressions of marriage were confused; the select young ladies' school which she'd attended had equipped her with religious knowledge, an aptitude for both the French and English languages, a familiarity with geography and the globes, music and dancing and painting on silks, but it had taught her nothing of how to deal with gentlemen. Gabrielle reminded herself once again that her younger sisters' futures depended on her. Only she, as the eldest, had received the rudiments of a formal education.

Much good it had done her, Gabrielle reflected, and dropped her forehead into her hands. She was perfectly willing, even eager, to learn to love her husband, who had first appeared to her dazzled eyes as a figure of romance, but she did not know how to go about the thing. She irritated when she wished most to please, and he aroused in her not wifely devotion but fear. Gabrielle reluctantly faced the truth. She could not esteem, regard or look up to Adam as a wife should her husband.

Yet she tried to find excuses, both for herself and for him. To be sure, he drank rather a lot; but surely that was understandable in his present circumstances. What bridegroom with a timid bride would do otherwise? It was not an incurable fault. And if he was both drinking hard and plunging deep, he had ample funds to cover his debts. Even his taste for low pursuits, like cockfighting and gaming-hells, was shared with many other Members of Parliament. Yet, despite this fine reasonableness, Gabrielle remained unconsoled. She reflected gloomily that her father would have been mad to refuse so advantageous an offer for her hand. And yet, in accepting Lord Randolph as his son-in-law, he had made

59

the most unfortunate choice possible. Familiar footsteps sounded in the hallway and Gabrielle swallowed, hard.

Adam, as he had made a point of informing her, had gone to view a prize-fight. This, too, was beyond Gabrielle's comprehension, for all that pugilism was the darling spectacle of men, so universally popular that magistrates and constables dared not break up illegal matches for fear of provoking a riot. Gentlemen of rank and fashion presided over the ceremonies, where the bruisers dealt out merciless punishment with their bare fists, to the joy of the rough and often violent mob. London boasted more than one academy for the instruction of those eager to be initiated in the mystery of boxing, where novices, Lord Randolph among them, flocked to learn all the various stops and blows, their ardor uncooled by the attendant inconveniences of black eyes, bloody noses and broken jaws.

The door flew open. Gabrielle tensed. Adam had been most explicit in describing the sport to her, dwelling in great detail upon the blood and serious injuries, and explaining the science employed by such legendary figures as Mendoza, Gully and the Chicken, Belcher and Tom Cribb; but she could summon forth no emotion but revulsion. As did so many things, violence frightened Gabrielle. She stared wide-eyed at her husband, who with an oath kicked shut the door. In one hand he held a wine decanter, and Gabrielle's heart sank to her toes. From all signs—and she had already learned to read them well—Adam was in a sulky humor, waiting for any excuse, fair or unfair, to fly into a rage.

He approached her, a dangerous gleam in his hazel eyes, and Gabrielle quailed. "The coal heaver," said Lord Randolph thickly, pouring the ruby liquid into a glass, "is master in *his* own house." The glass was thrust into her face. "Can I be less? Drink, my lady! 'Tis a very tolerable brew."

Gabrielle wished the chair might swallow her. It was quite evident that Adam had already imbibed a large quantity of some more potent brew. "I beg you, Adam, no. I do not care for the taste of spirits."

"My good, dutiful wife!" he sneered. "You do not care for many things, I think, myself among them." He grasped the back of her head and forced the glass to her lips. "Cruel and unnatural I may be, but I am your husband, and you must learn to compromise with circumstance. Drink, I say!"

Gabrielle, nauseated by the strong smell of the wine, considered flinging herself upon his mercy. Instead, she obeyed, and half-choked on the beverage's harshness. She did not like to consider the consequences were she to hang round Adam's neck in tears.

"Well done!" mocked Lord Randolph, and released her. Gabrielle had a moment's relief, but he merely refilled the glass and pressed it into her unwilling hand. "I shall not yet despair of you." He raised the decanter to his lips and drank deeply.

"Despair?" Already the wine had given Gabrielle unaccustomed courage. She remembered vaguely that she had not eaten that day. "What do you mean, Adam?"

"Why, that you may yet prove a docile and obedient wife." Abruptly, he pulled her from the chair then seated himself, drawing her into his lap. "Instead of forever lamenting the dreadful situation into which you have been placed."

Gabrielle was not so easily disarmed, though it was pleasant to be treated in this unfamiliar gentle way. "I have not complained, Adam," she said quietly.

"Have you not?" he inquired. "Drink your wine. My dear, your very looks are filled with reproach and grief. It is not necessary that you say a word."

Gabrielle spoke cautiously. "Then I must apologize. I did not mean to reproach you, my lord."

"So you do not find me unspeakably odious?" he asked softly. "Cruel in the greatest degree? It is for this reason I have kept you sequestered. I do not care to have our matrimonial difficulties published to the world, or to have you gain fame for conduct that affronts your family, friends, peers and the public in general."

Gabrielle had, due to extreme cowardice, consumed a great deal of wine in a very short period of time, and thus did not fathom his intent. Nor did she remember that Adam's tongue was as cruel an instrument of torture as the guillotine. "No, Adam," she whispered. "You are not repugnant to me."

He forced her face up so that he could look into her eyes. "So you are in love with me? Say it straight out. It is much more simple!" But there was no tenderness in his face, or in the arms that crushed her to his chest. Ineffectually, Gabrielle tried to push him away. The violence of his passion frightened her.

61

"Are you shocked by my lack of restraint?" Adam made a shambles of her gown and petticoat of fine calico. "I fear you have read too many romances, my lady wife, and thus are prey to deranged ideas. The courtship is over. You may wish me to the devil, but you remain my property—property for which I paid a high price, and which I mean to use well."

Gabrielle squirmed, but could not free herself. She gazed at him, completely blinded by tears. "Yes," mused Adam, further tightening his grasp until she could barely breathe. "I have discovered too late that my wife has a mind overheated by fanciful ideas—in short, a troubled brain. What shall I do with you, I wonder? Return you to your father and let it be known that my bride is demented, her reason overthrown?"

So terrified was Gabrielle that she forgot to struggle against his bold advances. "You wouldn't!" Her eyes were round as saucers, and filled with tears.

Lord Randolph's expression was sad. "There, you see? Further evidence of your lunacy. I can do as I please with you, Gabrielle. I can even have you locked away for the remainder of your life, and no one would question me. It is already common knowledge that you suffer uncertain health." Rigid, Gabrielle stared at him with horror. Adam smiled. "You see, I know everything about you, my dear, including the aunt who is kept so carefully locked away."

Gabrielle closed her eyes tightly, as if she could in that manner hide from him her fears. She had only seen her aunt once, and then by accident, but the occurrence had long remained to haunt her dreams. The old woman dwelt in virtual isolation, save for her burly attendant and six huge wolfhounds. She was indeed a figure of nightmare, with sparse and straggling hair, vacant eyes, and lax lips dripping spittle. Gabrielle shuddered.

"We begin to understand one another, I think." Lord Randolph was brisk. "Of course, it need not come to that, if you cooperate with me."

"What would you have me do?" Gabrielle's heart had descended to her toes. She did not even react when Adam's hand moved roughly to her breast.

"I am in need of information." There was an eerie, disquieting light in his eyes. "You will procure it for me. You will go into Society, concerning yourself with the trivialities of life—and learn all you can about Mephisto's ward, and the woman brought to be her companion and chaperone."

"You wish me to spy for you?" Without prompting, Gabrielle reached for more wine. "Why?" But what alternative was there, save to be incarcerated in a lunatic asylum as impregnable as the French Bastille, where victims of royal disfavor had been committed by *lettres de cachet*, secret orders of the king. Gabrielle knew that Adam made no idle threats, and that the price of her refusal would be painfully severe.

"You exhibit an unbecoming degree of curiosity." She gasped as he took gross liberties. "Suffice it to say that I suspect Mephisto of deep duplicity." Abruptly, he rose and carried her to the crimson bed. A scene straight from hell, thought Gabrielle muzzily, then closed her eyes as the room began to spin. She wished for nothing more than to escape him, but her leaden limbs would not obey her mind's command. Nor would she find help from anyone in that household; the servants were too in awe of their master—and too contemptuous of her. She felt his weight beside her, and stiffened.

"You will do as I say?" He leaned over her and his breath was warm on her skin. Gabrielle wondered if a madhouse might not, after all, be preferable.

"You leave me no choice." She had wished for love, and she might as well have cried for the moon. Nausea overcame her, and she retched weakly. Adam swore, flung himself off her and out of the room. Gabrielle lay as he had left her, sprawled in abject misery on the ancestral bed.

Chapter 9

In point of fact, Lady Sara did not join us for dinner that first night, and I was forced to defer my investigations for two entire days.

"There is a Japanese proverb," she remarked, as we proceeded down the dark hallway on that occasion, "that though a woman's tongue is only three inches long, it can kill a man six feet high." We entered the drawing-room. "I think, with some justification, one might say the same of Mephisto, not that he is a woman, of course, but you know what I mean."

In way of reply, I giggled. This loathesome habit is foreign to me, but my temporary aberration may perhaps be excused by the amount of wine I had taken with dinner. Whatever restrictions Mephisto meant to impose on me, he didn't insist on conformance with the dictum that young ladies might imbibe no more than three glasses of wine with their evening meal. Nor had Lady Sara intervened, for she was even less temperate than I.

I watched, with narrowed eyes, as my companion moved across the room, detecting in her careful movements ample evidence of tipsiness. It came to me, as revelations often do, like heaven-sent lightning-bolts, that both her unladylike consumption of spirits and her forced gaiety of manner were prompted by disquietude. It was very perplexing, and I strove valiantly to impose order on my muddled thoughts. Surely it was *I*, placed in an untenable situation, who should be afflicted by nerves, and not my erstwhile chaperone?

The drawing-room was furnished with a vast quantity of drab dull furniture, mahogany chairs and tables, a couple of Burjairs or half couches, one with a fall-down back, all of which would have been the better for a thorough cleaning.

Drawing her shawl—delicate cream silk bordered with woven rust—over her bare shoulders, Lady Sara moved closer to the fireplace and held out her hands to the uncertain flame. I noted that *this* grate hadn't been polished for many a long day. "Sometimes I think," she murmured absently, "that I shall never be warm again."

We dined alone together many times—Mephisto, Lady Sara and I—for even so innocent a gathering as a family dinner smacks of idle gaiety to Tayce, who preferred to take her meals alone in the library, with the result that her immortal manuscript was liberally festooned with drops of wine and crumbs. But that first occasion stands out starkly in memory, indicative as it was of so many things to come. Had I been of a less-assured disposition, Lady Sara would have totally bewildered me that night, and as it was she gave me so much food for thought that I nearly suffered a fever of the brain. Nor did we, I might confess, give credence to the popular assumption that women have delicate appetites, doing full justice to a dinner served, *à la Française*, in a grand style and consisting of turbot, lobster sauce, boiled fowl, ham, a quarter of lamb and cauliflowers, duck, green peas, a gooseberry-and-currant pie, followed by an elaborate sweet.

Dust billowed as I plumped down on an oval-backed chair. Lady Sara sneezed. "Does Ireland," I inquired politely, "possess so different a climate? Forgive me for saying so, but it sounds dreary."

"It is not the weather that chills me." Lady Sara applied a poker, with some dexterity, to the feeble fire. We had left Mephisto to enjoy his port at the horse-shoe dining table, seven feet long and more than two feet wide, which boasted a veneered rail and plain taper legs and was the focal point of the gloomy dining room. The table was adorned with a grotesque silver epergne, with convoluted tree-like branches that supported glass baskets of fruit. An equally grotesque portrait of the previous Lord Denham, whose high color hinted at a choleric temperament and a tendency to gout, hung upon the wall.

It was the custom, after the ladies left the room, for the gentlemen to lock the door and forthwith drink themselves under the table. For their convenience, the sideboard was furnished with chamberpots. At the conclusion of these festivities, valets carried their sodden masters to their coaches and saw them safely home. I considered bribing Wiggins to place my guardian, in the aforementioned condition, into the wrong coach, thus to be conveyed to some unknown destination and seen by us nevermore.

But I had been given a perfect opportunity to continue my gentle probing while Mephisto tarried over his port. "You must find London greatly altered," I ventured, "since you have not visited here in so long."

Lady Sara turned toward me, the firelight transforming her burnished hair into an undeserved halo, and subjected me to a scrutiny that left me feeling as if I'd been turned inside out, wrung and shaken briskly, then hung upon the line to dry. At that most auspicious moment, Tayce hobbled into the room. I stared at her in amazement, for this was an unprecedented conviviality and earned a severe frown. "Ring for some coffee, *petite*," demanded Tayce, seating herself on an ancient sofa supported by nude figures terminating in scaly tails, and drawing forth the knitting with which she employed herself on such occasions, "and introduce me to your chaperone."

Lady Sara was all delighted charm, a sentiment which Tayce did not appear to return. I occupied myself during this cloying sentimentality by procuring the requested refreshment.

"Don't let me interrupt," said Tayce, breaking into Lady Sara's fulsome animadversions on London-town. "Continue with your conversation, pray."

"My aunt," I explained to my bewildered chaperone, "is a trifle anti-social." I knew Tayce meant to oversee the progression of my inquiries and, had I not so dearly loved the wretch, I could cheerfully have throttled her. "We will go on much better if we pretend she isn't there. You were speaking of London, I believe?"

After a last puzzled glance at my aunt, Lady Sara, with that abrupt chameleon quality so native to her, embarked with unusual animation upon a discussion of the great changes she'd found in London, seeming startled to learn that the King's Theatre in Drury Lane had burned down and was in the process of being rebuilt. "Your circle of acquaintance must be very small," I remarked in tones as demure and missish as my pale gauze gown, "for you not to have known." Tayce swore as she dropped a stitch.

Lady Sara smiled gently. "Have I not said I lived a very quiet life? All the same, it is a great pity. I well recall the old theatre's interior, fantastic and beautiful with ceilings supported on near-Gothic columns. It was built by Henry Holland." Her strange eyes were like a mirror, reflecting what was before them, and revealing nothing of what lay within. "I particularly enjoyed the musical evenings, despite the unfortunate practice of executing an opera by embellishing it with additional numbers, or presenting an act taken willy-nilly from here and there." She was still lost in reminiscence when Lord Denham joined us. "We were speaking of Drury Lane. Do you remember, Mephisto, the evenings that you escorted me there?"

He was dressed in a black double-breasted full dress coat with covered buttons and black florentine silk breeches, and as a consequence looked even more diabolical than usual. In line with his appearance, Mephisto immediately proved himself immune to sentiment, though he did cast Tayce a startled glance. She ignored us all, seemingly intent on her knitting—which, incidentally, was atrocious; Tayce had never been known to finish anything, despairing at some half-way point and unravelling the entire misguided creation, only to begin again. She had been knitting and reknitting the same skeins of yarn for as long as I had known her, with unfelicitous results but admirable economy.

"I have a poor view of music," Mephisto said. "It often draws persons to mix with such company as they would otherwise avoid."

Lady Sara's reaction was so slight as to have gone unnoticed by a less sharp eye, but I was aware of quickly-stifled rage. "Ah, well!" She glanced at me ruefully. "What else can one expect from the gentlemen?"

In contrast with Mephisto's satanic air, Lady Sara looked positively angelic, for she'd chosen to appear in a gown of grey satin, cut in the Empire style with short puff sleeves, and veiled with Brussels net. Her hair was gathered into clouds of curls high on the back of her head, with wispy tendrils left loose to cluster in ringlets around her fragile face. Silently, I complimented Bridey's skill, and wondered how that outspoken creature fared on the servants' side of the

67

green-baize door. It was not likely she would appreciate her quarters in the attics, which were bitterly cold in winter and hot as the nether regions in summer.

But the welfare of the lower classes was not my concern at that moment, for I anticipated that Lady Sara would acquaint Mephisto with every detail of our earlier meeting, including the pointed nature of my inquiries. That she thus far had found no opportunity to speak with him privately, I had made it my business to know. In retrospect, I cursed my impatience, for I had put her on guard, but the thing was done. While I waited for Lady Sara to let the cat out of the bag, I pondered how best to cope with Mephisto's inevitable displeasure.

"I am delighted," remarked Mephisto, with a fine blend of sarcasm and indifference, "to see that you two are so quickly on the way to becoming bosom-bows." Unless I was mistaken—an unlikely event but not impossible due to the large quantity of wine I had imbibed—this development did not suit him at all. "Since much remains to be discussed, I beg you will defer any girlish confidences that remain to be exchanged."

Lady Sara's eye kindled, but her voice remained calm. "Ah, yes, Merrie and I will deal remarkably well together, I believe." She smiled at me with the utmost friendliness, and I returned the compliment, certain of her insincerity but quite willing to play her game. Lady Sara, it seemed, meant to convince Mephisto that she and I were already bosom-bows. I was not as concerned with the reasons for this inexplicable behavior as with how I might turn it to my advantage. Tayce knitted even more furiously. I wondered if this was how she had occupied herself while her lovers rode in their tumbrels to the guillotine.

Mephisto arranged himself artistically near two wine-cisterns in the form of sarcophagi—one decorated with a bunch of grapes, the other with Cupids—and I contemplated the pleasant vision of my guardian tucked away securely in a casket of his own. He observed us much as a hawk might eye its prey. I experienced a sudden chill, due no doubt to the dankness of the room. "You have no small task before you," he announced abruptly. "Merrie suffers the effects of a classical education and harbors a great number of fantastic notions in her charming little head."

So startled was I by this back-handed compliment that I

choked on my coffee. Tayce, roused, pushed her spectacles up to the bridge of her nose, and glared malevolently at Mephisto. *"Que diable!"* she spat. "You Englishmen, who think your women should be beautiful but unheard! Praise God Merrie has had the benefit of my influence, for in France we do things differently." My aunt was grimly rabid about her campaign to liberate womankind and considered that in me she had nurtured a spiritual Valkyrie. I rather tarnished this shining image by my various escapades, but as I pointed out to Tayce, one cannot logically expect to make a silk purse out of a sow's ear.

My guardian eyed Tayce askance, for she was brandishing her knitting-needles in a most threatening way. But Mephisto was no coward, and possessed a damnable fondness for provoking others to wrath. "In France," he retorted, "you had a Revolution. Need I say more?"

Lady Sara raised a delicate brow. "I have seen no sign of eccentricity," she remarked calmly, as if bloody mayhem was not about to be enacted before our very eyes. Tayce looked sufficiently venomous to have decapitated Mephisto on the spot, and without the assistance of Madame Guillotine. "Tell me, what do you think Merrie will do?"

I too was curious about the answer to this, but as usual Mephisto failed to oblige me. "I've no idea," he said, with marked disinterest, "but thought you should be warned. Her past career doesn't bear speaking of." His cold eyes rested on me. "She is an extremely devious chit, and will deceive you as far as she is able. It is better that you be on guard."

Tayce had, it seemed, abandoned me to the lions, for she offered no further word in my defense, applying herself instead to her knitting with a thin-lipped frenzy that suggested Mephisto would pay dearly for his impertinence. So many scathing retorts sprang to *my* tongue that I was momentarily speechless.

Lady Sara furthered this unprecedented condition by moving to my side and gently squeezing my hand. "Do you expect her to behave like a raw schoolgirl, alternately missish and casting out lures? Or perhaps to encourage the advances of rakeshames or fortune-hunters? Nonsense, Christian! I am sure Merrie is far too wise to do any of those things." Tayce sniffed.

I thought it very obliging of Lady Sara to rush so promptly

to my defense, even though her conclusions demonstrated a marked lack of perspicacity. "Must I remind you," Mephisto interrupted, "that a considerable sum of money is at stake? You might bear that in mind, lest you find yourself embroiled in foibles and indiscretions and shameless larks." It would have nicely suited his notions of male dominance to lock the both of us away!

Mephisto's scathing tone brought color to Lady Sara's pale face. "I assure you that I'll do everything in the world to prevent Merrie from falling into either extravagance or dissipation," she said evenly. Their eyes met and locked, driving me almost wild with the mystery of it. Even in my—I blush to admit it—inebriated condition, I was aware of the odd undercurrents that flew through the air, nay, practically bounced off the walls of the room! "After all, was not that your purpose in bringing me here?"

Mephisto did not answer, observing instead my aunt's bowed head. Again, I wondered at Lady Sara's forebearance concerning myself, and at what possible motive could lie behind her cordiality. The truth was that we were as wary of each other as two strange dogs.

Lady Sara's efforts with the fire had been almost too successful; the room grew uncomfortably warm. I tried desperately to keep my eyes open and alert, but the lids grew increasingly heavy and my thoughts muzzy and vague. "St. Erth has returned," Mephisto said suddenly, and I became aware that his attention rested on me. "One hopes that matters of state will keep him sufficiently occupied that he will refrain from interesting himself in other affairs." His thin lips twisted scornfully, a grimace no doubt perfected by long practice in front of a looking-glass.

I retained my air of sleepiness. Adam St. Erth, Lord Randolph, was of little interest to me, though as co-executor of my father's estate, I supposed I might turn to him if Mephisto's endeavors in my behalf became too much to bear. In truth, I cared even less for St. Erth than for Mephisto himself! Lord Randolph was very much the grand seigneur, as widely known—and little liked!—for the eloquence of his political oratories as for his ability in the realm of sport. He was equally famed for a tendency toward temper. Lest the reader wonder why I did not at once seek the support of this gentleman—particularly since he and Mephisto were forever at odds—I will explain that St. Erth was lamentably high in the instep, and I considered it extremely unlikely that he would countenance my attachment to a charming scapegrace with an inferior background and pockets to let. Events were, alas, to prove my assumptions correct.

This brief thought of Ninian had, as ever, distracted me, and I returned to the present to find Lady Sara staring as if she'd seen a ghost. Trained in a school of sorrow, I thought, forcibly stricken by her sad and haunted look. This brief sympathy was summarily dispelled. "Merrie," said the lady, "you are looking shockingly worn-down. I have tired you, I fear, with my incessant talking. We will understand, dear child, if you wish to retire."

"But—" I protested, all senses alert. The room was a positive whirlpool of emotion, and I meant to discover why.

"Lady Sara is correct," Tayce interrupted, in a tone that allowed no argument. She popped out of her chair with the force of a child's jumping-top. "Young women and old ladies perforce need their beauty sleep." With a senile cackle, she indicated that I was to escort her from the room.

I might have argued with this abrupt ordering of my actions had not I been wildly intrigued by Tayce's behavior. Instead, as behooved a well-brought-up young lady, I took leave of my mentors most winsomely. Once in the hallway Tayce indicated, by way of hideous grimaces and emphatic gestures, what she meant me to do. Slowly she climbed the marble stair, making in the process enough noise to have marked the passage of *all* of Wellington's troops; while I bent and applied my ear to the closed door. I positively blessed Mephisto, for his disrespect of lofty principles had goaded my vengeful aunt into action far more effectively than I could ever have done.

"Adam!" said Lady Sara, in a tone quite unlike any I had previously heard her use. "Mephisto, how could you be such a fool?"

Had *I* dared address my guardian with such insolence, I would have been sent forthwith to an early grave, but Lady Sara was to be spared this particular fate. "I had not anticipated that he would return so soon." Mephisto remained calm, perhaps because he had need of her services—whatever they might be! "It intrigues me greatly, this matter of his interrupted honeymoon."

71

"I wonder at you!" Lady Sara was brusque. Prey to the greatest curiosity, I bent and applied one eye to the keyhole. She stood before him, hands on hips, and regarded him with every evidence of impending rage. "How can you be so calm?"

"It is," Mephisto explained apologetically, "a matter of temperament." Exasperated, Lady Sara threw her arms into the air, and he caught her hand. "Understand me, Sparrow: Tantrums will not serve. You might reflect that even the walls have ears."

He spoke more truly than he knew! Complacently, I thought it would take a very clever person to throw the dust in my eyes. Alas, I would soon learn that Mephisto was prodigiously sly.

Lady Sara was looking at him with puzzlement. "Sparrow? Why do you call me that?"

Mephisto's glance was, for him, gentle, and I wondered to what end he sought to beguile her. "I recall your appearance when first you came to me." The inspection that followed would have set my blood aboil, but Lady Sara—or Sparrow, as even I came to call her, for somehow the name seemed to fit—was of a different temperament. "You have been transformed into a nightingale. No few eyes will be following you."

"I will be a subject of conjecture in any case," she retorted. I noted that he had not released her hand. "Due to this incredible situation that you have thrust me into. Dear heaven, but I must be mad!"

She may or may not have been, but their incomprehensible conversation would drive me into lunacy if it were not quickly explained! I pressed closer to the door.

"As for Adam," Mephisto remarked, turning over Sparrow's hand to gaze upon her palm, "he has recently wed a schoolroom miss. I don't think we can rely on *her* to hold his interest either long or well." Lady Sara stood very, very still. "But, then, I need not explain Adam's nature to you, need I?"

To my astonishment—and utter delight—Sparrow wrenched away from my guardian and applied her outstretched palm, with a very satisfying force, to his mocking face. Mephisto's expression turned so dark that I was forced to stifle an impulse to interfere.

Sparrow faced him defiantly. "You have brought me here," she said sourly, "to suit some purpose of your own—what, I do not know, nor do I care to, although I suspect you of grave duplicity concerning that odd child." So bemused was I by these events that, at first, I didn't realize she referred to me. It was then that she added insult to injury and referred to me as a porcupine, thereby destroying any kindly sentiments that I might have felt for her. "In that, you must do as you wish—although I warn you, Mephisto, that I will not stand idly by and see you do her harm."

His hands were on her shoulders, as if he meant to shake her senseless, but instead he frowned. "You seem to think me a monster of inhumanity."

"I know you." Sparrow's tone was flat. "And I know you do nothing to disoblige yourself. You mean to make use of both Merrie and me, and I cannot even begin to guess what, nor does it particularly matter." I could not applaud this detachment: Sparrow made a splendid martyr, but I had no intention of joining her at the stake. My head had begun to ache hideously. "But my life is my own, Mephisto, whatever mistakes I may have made, and you have no right to either comment or condemn."

"I see." Mephisto was uncommonly thoughtful.

Sparrow's laughter was hollow. "I set out upon this harebrained escapade to expiate the follies of my youth, and instead I find that this is the greatest folly of them all! Let me go back to Ireland, and find someone else to assist in your schemes."

"I am said to be of disobliging nature." Mephisto was unstirred by her obvious distress. "Alas, little Sparrow, you are firmly caught, for no one else will serve my purposes as well." She glared at him. "Console yourself with the gratifying reflection that you are indispensable to me."

"How?" I applauded this brevity, and heartily wished for more of it.

"So suspicious," mourned Mephisto. I suspected he was enjoying the exchange. He released her and turned away. "I will strike a bargain with you: My confidence in return for your own."

"So curious!" mocked Sparrow. She moved again to the fire, seeking its warmth with a desperation that made me wonder if she was, or had been, ill, for that would explain both her half-starved look and the chill that seemed to plague her frail body on even the sunniest day. "We have reached an impasse, then."

And I had reached the limits of my endurance. Wincing, for I had remained too long in that cramped position, I rose. It was the sheerest ill luck that Wiggins should have chosen that moment to enter the hall. With my most ingenuous smile, I passed by him, then fled with undignified haste to the comparative safety of my room.

Chapter 10

A Cuckoo in the Nest

Lady Penelope had suffered a trying afternoon. The entire household was abustle with preparations for her *soirée*—a battalion of maidservants scrubbed floors with white sand, whisked the window curtains, shook mats and carpets, brushed ledges and window-frames and furniture; while a steady stream of tradesmen called, laden with flowers and delicacies. In the midst of all this confusion, the young Palmerstons ran wild, wreaking more havoc than a herd of stampeding elephants, while their tearful governess swooned in the nursery and had to be revived with burnt feathers and vinaigrette.

In despair, Pen delegated the responsibility of overseeing all these activities to her trusted house steward, an awesome individual who was in sole charge of the household accounts, and retired to her sitting-room. Even there she found little respite. First, Jason's extremely expensive French chef had to be assuaged, for he was offended that so little interest was taken in the elaborate meals that he prepared and had consequently quarrelled violently with the subordinate to whom was delegated the simple task of roasting; and then, Mephisto came to call.

Pen was dismayed to learn that Lord Denham, too, had quarrelled, and with his ward. She raised anxious eyes to his face. "But, Christian," she protested, "surely you exaggerate!

Merrie is a trifle high-spirited, perhaps, but nothing to signify." She had spent several hours in the girl's lively company, hours during which they dealt with milliners and modistes and the innumerable other menials whose livings were derived from the intricacies of a fashionable lady's attire, and had found Miss Sherrington most amiable. Pen had also found Merrie most curious about the Palmerston household, offspring and rakish patriarch—and particularly about Lord Denham.

"Meredith," said Mephisto dourly, propping one gleaming boot on the coal scuttle, "suffers a morbid excess of animal spirits, and nothing can be more revolting." Ice would have been more flexible. "If we cannot contrive to curb her volatility, the chit will go headlong to her ruin! Every day she becomes more imprudent in her conduct, more heedless of consequence."

"Oh, dear." Pen recalled her own youth, and the rocky progression of her romance. Though she was sincerely attached to her older brother, Pen admitted that playing mentor to young damsels was not precisely his *metier*. "Perhaps she did not truly mean to eavesdrop on you, Christian, despite the compromising circumstances in which she was found. I am sure there must be some innocent explanation!"

Mephisto snorted. "Then why did she not present it when given the opportunity?"

Pen wrinkled her brow and plunged stubbornly on. "Perhaps she was hurt that you should accept the worst of her and take a servant's word over her own."

Lord Denham sneered. "Are you suggesting that I should not? Wiggins has been with me for years, and is incurably truthful. *He* suffers no swelled head due to the exaggerated praises that have been bestowed upon him."

Pen could not deny this; praise from Lord Denham was as rare as pearls in a pig-sty. "Merrie is, perhaps, a bit too accustomed to having her own way. Christian, consider: You cannot have the girl under your eye both night and day! Not only would such strict chaperonage give rise to unwelcome comment, it would doubtless inspire her to even worse escapades. Perhaps," she added with little hope, "if you were to be more lenient with her, she might be inclined to act more as you wish."

"On the contrary," Mephisto retorted ominously, "she already has more liberty than is prudent. Meredith must speedily set aside the idle nonsense of thinking that she has a will of her own."

"But, Christian, she obviously does," Pen pointed out reasonably. "Personally, I find her refreshing—I would much rather see a young girl in tearing spirits than one who is meek and cowed."

"*You* are not responsible for her." Mephisto was not noticeably moved by either his sister's logic or her plea. "The chit is always seeking amusement and, unfortunately, at the expense of both prudence and propriety."

Pen sighed, anticipating a dreadful battle of wills. Merrie was not one to lightly accept a restriction of her movements. "What will you do?"

"I will take adequate measures, of course." His pale eyes had all the warmth of a polar icecap. "When Meredith marries, she will do as her husband pleases. For the present, however, she will do as *I* wish." This assured pronouncement inspired his sister not with admiration, but with a presentiment that she was to see Lord Denham, for the first time in countless years, proved wrong.

"Who," asked Pen, "do you mean for her to wed?" No one could claim that Mephisto appeared to be taken with the girl, but she knew him to be extremely devious. "I cannot help but feel that you have some definite plan in mind."

"I have several." Lord Denham was sublime. "But I think I will not acquaint you with them just yet." He looked upon his sister's worried face and burst into laughter."Good God! You cannot think I mean the minx for *myself!?*"

Pen was amazed by this unusual merriment. "It would be a shocking *mésalliance*," she said cautiously.

"Unlike St. Erth," said Mephisto wryly, "I nurse no ambition to rob the cradle. Merrie is as stiff-necked, stubborn and silly a girl as I have ever seen, and she has, in addition, a regrettable tendency to raise my spleen. Were we to wed she doubtless would be widowed soon, for I should in no time go off in an apoplexy!" He seated himself by his sister, all amusement gone. "It was not about Meredith that I wished to speak with you."

"What, then?" Pen thought suddenly that Mephisto was like a wizard weaving some maleficent spell. "Is it Luke?"

"Luke?" Lord Denham paused in the act of taking snuff. His cold eyes rested on her face. "Should it be?"

Pen frowned. "I don't know. I have wondered lately if there is something on his mind."

"Quite a few things, I should imagine, but I am not in Luke's confidence." With an expert flick of his wrist, Mephisto closed the snuff-box. "No, my dear, I wished to speak with you concerning Lady Sara Cainneach."

"Oh." Pen toyed idly with a porcelain figurine. "Who is she, Christian? For I vow I do not know her."

"But you do." His expression was almost benign. "Though by another name. Cast back your mind ten years and tell me what you first recall."

"Ten years?" Pen nearly crumbled under the strain.

"You can remember very well," Lord Denham urged patiently, "if you but try. You had not yet met Jason, and were here in London with me. Luke was away at school." Still she was uncomprehending, and he sighed. "There was a scandal, and it involved someone you knew quite well."

Under this gentle prompting, Pen's dilatory memory awoke. She gasped and dropped the figurine, which shattered on the floor. "You don't mean—"

"I do." Mephisto actually smiled. "The truth is known to none but myself—and now to you. I could not take the chance that you would recognize her and with an unwitting word put an end to my little game."

If a game, thought Pen, he played with a stacked deck of cards. "But why? How did you persuade her to agree? Is she well?"

"As to her health, you must inquire of her. I have given out that you and Lady Sara are old friends." Lord Denham picked an invisible speck of lint from his sleeve. "And the reasons for my actions must, for the present, remain undefined. I must ask that you promise to reveal this to no one."

"I don't understand!" wailed Pen, afloat in a sea of confused curiosity.

"I do not expect it of you." Mephisto rose. "I require only that you give me your word."

"You have it." Pen had never seen so fixed a determination as Mephisto displayed, and she wondered to what end. "I shall not breathe a word of this to anyone."

"See that you do not." Lord Denham bent to salute her

hand. "Even the most idle remark might cause the lady great embarrassment, if not worse." He was gone before she could demand that he explain.

Sir Jason Palmerston had spent an entertaining, and profitable, few hours at Garraway's coffee-house in Exchange Alley where congregated the most prominent auctioneers and brokers in merchandise; and had witnessed the sale of a plantation on the island of Granada, complete with one hundred slaves, as well as sugar, Spanish tobacco, ivory and various salvaged goods. Having contented himself with the purchase of some Jamaica rum and a small and impish turbaned page, intended as an amusing present for his wife and doubtless destined to become another cherished pet of the younger Palmerstons—who had already amassed a sizeable menagerie, including cats, dogs, geese, innumerable rabbits, a draggle-tailed donkey and a pregnant sow—he turned toward home, where the long-suffering housekeeper expressed only token rebellion when ordered to give Sir Jason's latest acquisition a thorough scrubbing. Shrieking at this betrayal, the page was dragged away. Sir Jason turned toward his wife's sitting-room.

Thus was Mephisto met in the hallway. He did not appear the least bit delighted by this chance encounter with his brother-in-law.

"You're leaving?" inquired Sir Jason, with mock regret. "What a pity that I did not return sooner! It grieves me excessively to have missed what must have been a fascinating conversation." Mephisto snarled and stalked wrathfully away.

Lady Penelope was on her knees, gathering up the shards of her figurine. "A lamentable accident, my love," commented Sir Jason as he entered the room. "May I hope that you hurled it at Mephisto's offensive head?" Pen gave a little shriek and dropped the pieces once again.

"Jason! How long have you been here?" Realizing that this was hardly a warm greeting for a beloved spouse, she rose and nervously smoothed her hair. "I mean, I did not expect you back so soon."

"My business took less time than I expected." Sir Jason took his wife's hands and drew her down on the sofa beside him. "Sit down, my love. I particularly wish to speak with you."

"Of course." Pen wondered frantically how much he'd heard. If only she had not been sworn to silence! Prevarication was not among Lady Penelope's accomplishments.

"Darling Pen, you are quite distrait!" Sir Jason could, on occasion, be quite as devious as his brother-in-law. "If this is the effect Mephisto has, I fear I must forbid him admission to this house. What did he want, by the way?"

"I asked him to call." So tumultuous were Pen's processes of thought that her fingers trembled in his. "You see, I had thought of a masque, and wished his opinion."

"You said nothing of this to me." Jason was impressed anew by the eccentricities of his wife's mind. Such entertainments—consisting of dances in masquerade, with beautiful costumes and elaborate scenery, songs and set arrangements—had not been popular for at least a century. "What was it to be?"

"It came to me this morning, after you had gone." Pen's piquant features were unusually harassed. "I thought, 'Pleasure Reconciled to Virtue,' with Comus, the God of Cheer, riding in triumph, crowned with roses and flowers." She cast a frantic look at her husband. "We could open with wild music—cymbals, perhaps, with flutes and tabors joining in."

Jason, enjoying himself immensely, turned over her hand and traced out an intricate design on the palm. "Mephisto, of course, did not agree."

"No." Gratefully, Pen seized upon the diversion. "Jason, I was wrong. He assures me he does *not* mean to wed Merrie."

"And you are relieved." His smile was lazy and she decided that, after all, he had not heard.

"I am." Visibly, Pen relaxed. "I think I must invite Ottolie to my *soirée*."

Jason grimaced dreadfully. "Must you? I, for one, find little amusement in her determined pursuit of Mephisto—though there's little doubt they'd make a perfect pair, for she's as mercenary as he is underhanded. But, Lord! She's been pursuing him so long that no one even bothers to wager, now, on her success."

"Jason!" Pen was reproving. "That is unkind." Lady Ottolie Carlisle was a rather full-blown widow whose determination to become the Duchess of Denham was equalled only by the equanimity with which she accepted continued defeat. "Christian seems to like her well enough."

79

"Has he a choice?" inquired Jason, unrepentant. "Never have I seen a more tenacious female! I am only surprised that she has not contrived to compromise herself, so that he would be duty-bound to marry her and thus save her good name. Perhaps she has sufficient wit to know it would not serve. Mephisto would be far more likely to bid her go and be damned, and I could not blame him for it." He observed his wife's worried countenance. She looked extremely fetching in a simple blue muslin gown with long sleeves and two frills at the hem. "Tell me, my love, why are you suddenly so anxious to see Mephisto settled in matrimony?"

"It would be the making of him, wouldn't it?" Pen's blue eyes were wide and innocent. "And you yourself have said it's shocking that he has no direct heir."

Sir Jason squelched a desire to take his feather-headed wife into his arms that very moment and see to the matter of further increasing the number of his own progeny. He contented himself with merely kissing her neck. "So you think Mephisto has awakened to his responsibilities, albeit belatedly?"

"Do you not?" Pen's voice was husky and her husband was forced to stifle yet another errant impulse. "He has discarded Delilah, after all these years. What else can that mean but that he intends to embark upon a more honorable relationship?"

"My little innocent!" Jason placed an arm around her shoulders and drew her closer. "It could just as easily portend boredom—though, considering the incomparable Delilah's charms, I rather doubt that. Still, the termination of a long-standing *affaire* does not necessarily presage a plunge into matrimony."

Perhaps no woman wed to a rake, Pen reflected, her head resting comfortably on the profligate's broad chest, ever rid herself totally of fear. Though Jason had never given her cause to doubt his fidelity, still she was prey to uncertainty, to the niggling dread that he one day might grow tired of her and continue his remarkable achievements in the petticoat-line. "All the same," she murmured, "if Christian marries anyone, it will be Ottolie."

Fortunately for Jason's will-power, which had been considerably weakened by his armful of tantalizing femininity, the young Palmerstons had discovered the newest addition to the household and interrupted their parents with wholehearted approval of this purchase. Jason reluctantly released his wife, who gazed upon her offspring with a marked lack of maternal approbation. "Whatever am I to do with that wretched Maria?" she moaned. "On this, of all days, she has declared she cannot cope, and I have a thousand things yet to do!"

"Then allow me to be of assistance," said Sir Jason gallantly, if without enthusiasm. "I daresay the lot of them will be happy enough to visit the exhibition of wild beasts at Exeter 'Change, in the Strand." He was proved correct by an ecstatic din.

"Bless you!" said Pen fervently, scrabbling through cluttered desk drawers in search of her quill. "Jason, would you truly dislike it if I invited Ottolie?"

Sir Jason paused on the threshold, children clinging to his limbs as if he were a tree. "Invite whom you wish, my love. It makes little difference to me." In truth, Jason did not at all mind seeing Mephisto discomposed by the admiring attentions of Lady Carlisle, who tended to regard Lord Denham as a chicken hawk might a particularly plump fowl.

But Pen had already forgotten his presence. "Dear heaven!" she gasped. "And I invited Adam and his wife!"

"My dear?" inquired Sir Jason, being pulled, via impatient tugs on various portions of his anatomy, through the doorway.

"It's nothing." Pen nibbled absently on her quill. "I had forgotten that Adam refused the invitation. It seems the new Lady Randolph is of uncertain health. Odd! She did not strike me in that manner, but I suppose Adam must know."

Accepting this fond dismissal, Jason gathered together his juvenile horde, including the briskly-scrubbed pageboy who now grinned from ear to ear, and bore them off to view the wild animals. Although he remarked that he shuddered to think what his intimates would say were they to observe him in such grubby company, and successfully persuaded Miss Samantha Palmerston that an ancient and flea-ridden lion named Nero would *not* make an admirable addition to the household, he was noticeably preoccupied. Sir Jason struggled to make sense of the conversation that he'd overheard.

Chapter 11

Saturday 13 April 1811

It was apparent—if I may say so without appearing unduly immodest—within a half-hour of my entrance into Society that I would score a *succès fou.* Nor was it wonderful that even Royalty regarded me with a warm and avaricious eye! I had long and diligently practiced my feminine wiles, progressing from a tinker's lad, one of Papa's grooms and his librarian, through such examples of young manhood as Bath, with its octogenarian populace, could offer. (And despite my aunt's comments on the subject, I had *not* left my virtue, together with my petticoat, beneath a bramble bush!)

The Palmerston ballroom was crowded past capacity. Pen was a noted hostess and commanded the presence of the *crème de la crème*; already we had been promised vouchers for Almack's, and had received more invitations than we could possibly hope to honor. *Most* young ladies, served up with a rich spread of compliments every bit as sugary as Turkish delight—a diet sufficiently rich and glutinous as to have choked a horse!—would have made greedy-guts of themselves. *I* was heartily bored.

Even Prinny was present, and for hours he beat on his thighs the proper time for the band, while singing out loud and looking about for accompaniment. It was a curious sight to see a Regent thus employed, but he seemed in high good humor, despite the fact that his reputation had been further besmirched by his suggested reinstatement of Frederick, Duke of York, as our military commander-in-chief, a post which that gentleman forfeited when a Parliamentary enquiry disclosed that his mistress was selling commissions and promotions. Prinny, however, did not receive half the attention he deserved: I spotted a familiar manly figure across the room. Ninian turned his head and looked straight at me, then pointedly away.

There was a lull in the festivities while pages and footmen brought around iced champagne punch and lemonade and sandwiches, and my mentors plunged deep in a very animated discussion of the particular shape and make of the wig worn by George II. I mumbled an excuse of a torn skirt-flounce, and slipped quietly from the room.

Only Lord Alvanley remarked my passing, and I disarmed him with a fluttering green-eyed glance, more than sufficient cajolery for a gentleman so eccentric as to, after reading late, extinguish his candle by throwing it on the floor and hurling a pillow at it. Without a single misstep, I found my way to the master bedroom and entered, carefully leaving the door ajar. My brain was greatly exercised by Ninian's inexplicable presence in the Palmerston home.

It was very improper, and foolhardy of me to risk a *tête-à-tête* with Ninian at that moment—particularly in that house, and under Mephisto's very nose! I nourished an appetite as insatiable as that of any rapacious opium-eater. Ninian found me standing on a chair and rummaging through the uppermost drawers of a mahogany tallboy with a dignified cornice, and impudently grasped my waist to swing me to the floor.

"It took you long enough, Mr. Northcliffe!" My complaint lacked conviction, perhaps due to the fact that he still clasped me—though I was sufficiently clear-minded to note smugly that my waist measured even smaller than his hand-span.

Ninian smiled. "Discretion is the better part of valor, Merrie. It would hardly be prudent to let your guardian see me panting hard upon your heels."

"Confound my guardian!" said I, with fervor. The wretched Wiggins had been quick to inform his master of my stealthy presence outside the drawing-room door, and as a result of this talebearing I received a severe lecture on the evils of eavesdropping. Mephisto expressed strong skepticism regarding the fainting spell that had kept me languishing in the hallway; nor did he believe that I had sent Tayce on ahead to spare her the pain that must surely result from witnessing my infirmity. I accepted Mephisto's recriminations with a surface meekness appropriate for one who sat, clad in sackcloth and ashes, on the stool of repentance, but to no avail. My guardian voiced his wish that I might be flayed with a cat-o'-nine-tails. Following this ill-natured comment, the conversation deteriorated rapidly into a strident quarrel which was overheard two floors above. I graciously allowed the brute to have the last word.

Further comments on Mephisto's infamy were forestalled by Ninian, who lifted me in his arms and kissed me *most* thoroughly. It was an illuminating embrace. Though Ninian and I had explored various parts of London—including Westminster Abbey where English kings were crowned on the sacred stone of Scone, purloined by Edward I from Scotland; the Tower and its exhibitions of the king's jewels and a menagerie of wild animals collected during commercial voyages; the British Museum and the Parthenon marbles recently brought from the brigand-infested wastes of Athens—we had found few opportunities to be completely alone. I suspected prudence would fly quickly out the window if we found many more!

Either Ninian was a superb actor or he was no less affected than I. His voice was husky. "It seems I must keep a *very* sharp eye on you, poppet!" He moved away from me to absently inspect an ingenious shut-up dressing-table containing three mirrors and four drawers for toilet requisites. "It is going to be damned difficult to stand by and watch you making sheep's eyes at other men."

Since I had previously reflected that I would give half my fortune to see Ninian suffer the slightest twinge of jealousy, it was with utmost horror that I heard myself speaking words designed not to enflame a lover's ardor, but to dispel his uncertainty. "I very seriously and solemnly assure you that I have not the slightest interest in any of them." After which confession, I damned myself to perdition.

"My fears are laid to rest!" Ninian broke into laughter. "My poppet, your expression is ludicrous!"

"Enough of this nonsense." I was furious with myself, and didn't doubt it showed. One drawback to a long courtship is the difficulty of preserving any air of mystery. "How do you come to be *here?*"

Ninian shrugged. "It was easy enough to come by an invitation." My pulses quickened most pleasurably as he again stood close to me. "Had you not scurried away in that impetuous manner, I would have secured an introduction so that I might become a legitimate member of your admiring

84

retinue." He tugged one of my curls. "I said I mean to stay as close as your shadow, if you will recall."

"Would that you could." Feeling deliciously giddy, I leaned against him. "I suppose you *must* have a fortune, Ninian?" His muscles tensed—a fascinating sensation—but he firmly set me away from him.

"No more of this!" My fortune-hunter was stern. "You told me only scant days past that an elopement would forfeit you your wealth, and I am hardly able to maintain you in the manner to which you are accustomed." His grey eyes were not laughing now. "We will find a way out of this damnable coil—and if not, we will simply wait till you are of age." I opened my mouth. "*No*, Merrie! I will listen to no cork-brained schemes, or stand by while you so disgrace yourself that no one else will have you. Do you understand? You would do much better to leave this entire matter to me."

He had certainly made his position clear: He did not want my wealth if it meant loss of his place in society. Had I any degree of sensibility, I would have been cast into the depths of despondency by so unromantic a view, but, contrariwise, I was elated to learn that my beloved was not totally without principle. "Yes, Ninian," said I, with my fingers crossed, and earned an approving hug for my docility. It was clearly midsummer moon with the both of us.

This intimate conversation was doomed to a premature end, for voices sounded in the hall. "Deuce take it!" I hissed, looking frantically about me. The prospect of discovery turned me perfectly sick. If Ninian and I were found together in these extremely compromising surroundings, there would be the very devil—Mephisto!—to pay. Ninian, however, had his wits about him; he drew me behind the concealing draperies of a recessed window enclosure. I only hoped that Pen wouldn't succumb to a desire for fresh air.

"Drat that wretched girl!" said Sparrow, in irritated tones. "Where can she have gone?" So adaptable am I to circumstance that I immediately pricked up my ears. The situation—providing I could restrain the tickling in my nostrils that betokened a horrendous sneeze—was uncommonly promising.

"I'm sure you need not fret about Merrie," soothed Pen, with an obvious lack of both interest and wit. I risked a peep through the curtains. She was seated on the edge of the huge

State bed, which was embellished with a dome tester, ornaments of burnished gold, and rich fringe. "Come, forget your charge for the moment. This is the first chance we've had to speak privately! I vow, Christian is the most complete hand. I could have sunk right through the floor when he told me you were Lady Sara Cainneach!"

"That is my name, now." Sparrow perched on a graceful Hepplewhite chair of blue damask which matched the bed hangings and the lush window-draperies that cascaded from ceiling to floor, and behind which we hid. She was, of course, an adventuress, and I was to witness the horrifying result of her endeavors—but, all in all, I must consider her contrivances justified, and her crusade just. "You will not use our previous acquaintance but in the most discrete manner?"

"No human being," said Pen solemnly, "shall ever know of it as long as we live. Does that satisfy you?" The blue eyes were surprisingly alert. "My dear, you are the object of the wildest speculations! Every sentence you utter is caught and repeated with various commentaries, and the world is agog to know where Christian found you, but in too much awe of him to ask. Now, if you please, explain to me *why!*"

Sparrow clutched her exquisite fan so tightly that the delicate ivory sticks snapped. "I cannot. You must trust me, Pen. On the strength of our old friendship, if you cannot do so now."

"Goose!" Pen crossed the room to embrace my chaperone. "Was there ever anything equal to this? I am every day struck by the endless mine of Christian's intellectual resources. To have so cleverly brought you here!"

Sparrow gently disentangled herself. "He is as plausible, cunning and jesuitical as the very devil, and I don't like the appearance of things at all. Never would I have accepted the possibility of a man of his character and situation in life of being capable of such an abominable proceeding!" Poor Pen looked bewildered. Sparrow's ominous utterances alarmed *me* not a little, and I heard Ninian's sharp intake of breath. "But I confess it pleases me beyond measure to again be with you."

"I thought you *liked* Christian," Pen wailed. Never, I thought, was a man so misnamed. Sparrow's cryptic remarks were obviously beyond Pen's limited comprehension. Unfortunately, they were also beyond mine.

Sparrow was walking up and down the room in great agitation, the skin so taut across her delicate features that she looked an animated death-mask. "Once, perhaps, I did," she admitted, "but your brother is making a cat's paw of me. I am compelled to be in the practice of daily dissimulation with that wretched child, and my patience is exhausted!" To avoid voicing a scathing comment, I bit my tongue. "But I fear *that* is past praying for!" Abruptly, she halted. "I must tell you that I am very happy for you, Pen. Sir Jason is exactly the husband that you need."

Pen brightened. This topic of conversation, at least, she could understand. "He is," she agreed, and then consternation struck. "Adam! What will *he* say?"

"Your brother assures me I will go unrecognized." Grey eyes burned feverishly in her haggard face. "Pen, he *must* not know."

"Oh, my dear." Pen teetered on the brink of tears. *I* was positively atwitch with curiosity! Sparrow's story contained a gap so large that one might drive a coach and six through it.

"Hush," said Sparrow quickly. "We must forget that time." They fell into each other's arms. Extreme as was my perplexity, I had never seen a more affecting scene. Even Ninian, who is ordinarily unmoved by displays of emotion, tensed and bit back a sudden exclamation, but the ladies were so engrossed in their maudlin excesses that the sound went unremarked.

"What of Merrie?" Pen inquired, recovering first. Sparrow's features shifted like quicksand, rearranging themselves into something approaching normalcy—and indeed she was as treacherous and as deadly as any quagmire. Neither flesh, nor fowl, nor good red herring was Lady Sara Cainneach! "How can you refer to her as a wretched girl? I have found her both artless and eager to please." Ninian pinched me and I trod smartly on his foot. Pen thought of me exactly as I wished, and I waited breathlessly for Sparrow's reply.

"That urchin," sighed my chaperone, with great emotion, "may well be the death of me!" We little knew how truly she spoke. "I consider her one of the greatest curiosities I have ever seen—and would that I had been spared the sight! It would be infinitely droll to observe her efforts to learn my past, were not the matter so serious."

"Merrie?" Pen doubted the fidelity of her own ears. "Surely

you are mistaken." Ninian, fortunately, managed to stifle his amusement.

"I am not," Sparrow replied, without the slightest hesitation. "She has been quizzing me most dreadfully. Just this morning she invaded my bed-chamber bent on examining all the details of my history—or the *scant* details of the history your scheming brother has given me! She asked questions without end, until I was forced to temporarily silence her by expressing my impatience to get to my breakfast!" Sparrow's divination of my subtle purpose indicated that she was far more shrewd than she appeared, and I immediately perceived the need for a change in tactics. "I tell you, I live in terror that I may at any moment set my foot wrong."

"You've changed." Pen's tone indicated that she was uncertain whether to rejoice or mourn.

"My dear Pen, it has been ten years!" Sparrow was more than a trifle tart. "Indeed, it would be wonderful if I had not. Much has transpired since we last met."

"Water under the bridge." Pen quickly dealt with the ravages of emotion. Sparrow looked none the worse for venting her sensibilities—and no small wonder, since she had not shed as much as a single tear. "The important thing is that you are returned to us again."

"You were always determined to look on the bright side of things." Sparrow's smile was faint. "I shall humor you, even though everything is going as badly as possible!" She frowned and glanced once more around the room. "Where can that confounded chit have gone? I pray to heaven we may get her safely tied-up before she contrives to ruin herself!" I suppose it was wonderful that the marriage of a considerable, and underage, heiress should greatly exercise so many minds, but I was hardly appreciative of this universal concern.

"You fret too much." Pen took her friend's arm and guided her to the door. "Merrie has surely returned to the ballroom by this time. No young girl would willingly abandon the festivities when she is an unquestionable belle!"

"I begin to think," Sparrow said sourly, "that you don't know Merrie very well." She turned for one last survey of the chamber and her cloud-colored eyes rested briefly on the draperies behind which we stood concealed. It would be exaggeration to say I quaked in my dainty satin slippers, but I experienced a moment of definite unease.

The ladies' departure went almost unobserved, due to the fact that Ninian was nibbling gently on my ear. We emerged from behind the stifling draperies, and I heaved a sigh of relief, which turned into the long-suppressed sneeze. "A narrow escape," I said shakily, my unevenness of tone due not to fright but to Ninian, who had abandoned my tingling ear to nuzzle my neck.

"Yes," he said, reluctantly abandoning his pursuits, "and I fear our absence has been remarked. I can simply slip away, but you must concoct some tale to explain where you've been."

I shrugged and inspected a golden cage, complete with a stuffed bird that sang when wound up and a porcelain clock, an item as impractical and charming as Pen herself. "I will think of something. Ninian, what is your reaction to what we just heard? More important, what think you of Lady Sara?"

"Very baffling, my precious, but we must see what we can make of it." With unusual flippancy, he kissed my hand. "*Adieu*, sweetheart! Loath as I am to tear myself from your arms, I must depart immediately."

I did not follow him from the room, but perched on the edge of the bed. Ninian's reaction was not what I had expected—in fact, it was most odd. If it had not been so unlikely, I would have thought Mr. Northcliffe was very eager to take his leave of me.

Chapter 12

Bumblebath

Lady Randolph was, in the vulgar parlance, drunk as an owl.

"Swallow this," commanded Lord Camden, and shoved a cup of steaming coffee under Gabrielle's nose. She hiccoughed, but took it in her hands. "And try not to look like you expect the world to end at any moment! With a little courage, we'll brush through this well enough." The Palmerstons' superior butler sidled toward the door. "Jarvis! Not a word of this to anyone, do you understand?"

"Very good, my lord." A tear slipped down the young lady's cheek and Jarvis abruptly forgot his dignity. "Don't you worry, little miss! Master Luke will fix it up all right and tight, and you needn't fear that *I'll* let the cat out of the bag! Just drink your coffee and in a trice you'll be feeling more the thing."

Gabrielle stared after the butler in astonishment, her mortification briefly eased. "What a *nice* man!" Adam's servants were of a different breed. To cross Lord Randolph's path, unless he wished to see you, was little short of a crime, and his retainers conducted themselves accordingly.

"Jarvis has a benevolent disposition," Luke agreed, and came to sit by her. "Now, do you mind explaining what has driven you to this state? You must know it's little short of scandalous that you should be out unescorted! The streets of London at night are no place for a lady alone."

A singular chain of events had brought Lady Randolph to Palmerston House on the evening of Miss Sherrington's formal introduction to society. That day she had finally been permitted to step outside her prison, a longed-for event that was a great deal less felicitous than it first seemed, since her husband had taken her to view St. Luke's Hospital for the insane, with its gloomy facade and statuaries of Melancholy and Raving Madness, then revived her flagging spirits with forceful recourse to the brandy bottle. These were hardly matters that Gabrielle could explain, even to so sympathetic a gentleman.

"I didn't know." She stared into the cup. "I found Lady Penelope's invitation—Adam must have overlooked it—and I wished to meet Miss Sherrington. Since he had already left the house, I decided to come alone. I guess the servants thought it would be unseemly to hint I was behaving most improperly."

"There's no harm done, you know." The Marquis was not immune to those downcast features, or the little mouth that quivered so vulnerably. Tactfully, he avoided the matter of her inebriation. "May I presume to drop a hint or two? You

90

must not repeat this evening's folly, or you will become a subject of grave censure, and find your name on every tongue."

Gabrielle thought of her husband, who had gone through three bottles of wine at dinner, beside maraschino, punch and eau de Garuche, which he liked excessively strong and hot, before blithely departing to play faro at Brook's club. Ironic that in wishing to please him—was it not his expressed wish that she cultivate Miss Sherrington?—she had nearly done herself irreparable harm. "What must you think of me, Lord Camden? I am so ashamed."

Sensing the incipient onset of a fit of the blue-devils, Luke poured more coffee. "Nonsense!" he said cheerfully. "You are neither the first nor the last to find yourself at point nonplus, my dear. The worst result of this escapade is that you may find yourself with the devil of a head." Fortunate that he had, due to the beauty of the evening, decided to proceed to his sister's house on foot; equally fortunate that Gabrielle had taken him up in her carriage, thus allowing him an opportunity to assess her rather startling condition and to, consequently, whisk her unnoticed through a side door into Palmerston House.

Gabrielle set down the empty cup. "All the same, you have been exceedingly kind, and to a virtual stranger. I don't know how I can ever thank you." She raised large, agonized eyes to his face. "But I beg you will allow me to impose upon you for yet another favor."

"Certainly." In that ridiculously sophisticated gown, she seemed a child masquerading as an adult.

"Pray," she whispered, "don't tell Adam of this." Her chin trembled. "He would be so angry with me."

Lord Camden was discovering in himself an appalling weakness for frail and tearful femininity. "It is not my custom to interfere between husband and wife," he replied, more sternly than he wished. "However, you have my word." Gabrielle bit her lip and he cursed his clumsiness. "Are you feeling better? I will take you to my sister."

"Oh, no!" She sounded frightened. "I have already caused you too much trouble. I would much rather return home."

"That is utterly out of the question." Luke rose. "Your coachman will talk, you know, and it would be markedly irregular to arrive and depart almost immediately. Would you have it said that you and my sister had quarrelled?"

91

"No," replied Gabrielle hopelessly. She allowed him to pull her to her feet and briskly twitch her curls into place, then to retie the narrow sash of green ribbon that encircled her small waist. No more than Luke did she approve of her fashionable gown, a round frock of Italian crepe worn over a white satin slip, with Melton sleeves formed of alternate stripes of green satin and white crepe, and ornamented on the hem and low-cut bodice with green and silver ribbon. Gabrielle was complete to a shade, from her white kid gloves to the green satin slippers tied round her ankles with silver ribbon. She was also miserable and wished only to find a corner where she might hide.

Lord Camden, who guessed a good deal of what passed through her mind, wondered that Adam did not take better care of his young bride. With a flourish, he swept open the door. "Do you come with me, ma'am! We shall make so grand an entrance that every other lady will be stricken dumb with envy." With a trusting smile that wreaked absolute havoc with Luke's peace of mind, Gabrielle allowed herself to be escorted from the room.

The Palmerston house was excellently furnished in the great native traditions of Sheraton and Vile; and the ceilings contained exquisite scenes painted by Angelica Kauffman, the only woman to ever have become a member of the Royal Academy. The powdered footmen, in their plush breeches and silk stockings, were the grandest Gabrielle had ever seen. She stepped over the ballroom's threshold with a composure that was greatly strengthened by Jarvis's approving nod.

"There you behold Henry Luttrell," said Lord Camden, determined to put this very young lady at her ease, "one of our most welcome diners-out and wits. It is a well-known secret that he's the illegitimate offspring of a gardener's daughter and an Irish peer. And beside him is Prince Paul Esterhazy, Austrian Ambassador to the Court of St. James's." Gabrielle gazed upon a lushly apparelled gentleman. "He has a taste for oriental splendor, as you see."

In this manner they made their way across the crowded ballroom. Gabrielle was introduced to the popular Lord Alvanley, famed for his wit and humor and willingness to bet on anything; to Lady Melbourne, one of the most successful hostesses in Society; and to Lady Holland, who ran away from her first husband with the third Baron Holland and later married him. Lord Petersham, who carefully chose his snuff-boxes to match the weather, not risking a cold by using a light snuff-box in an East wind, spoke to her most kindly; the Countess Lieven, wife of the Russian Ambassador, issued an imperious command that the new Lady Randolph present herself at Almack's; and the incomparable Beau Brummel, grandson of a valet and intimate of the Regent, gazed into Gabrielle's bedazzled eyes and pronounced himself charmed.

"There," said Luke, having nicely succeeded in distracting his companion from whatever fears were preying on her mind. "That was not so terrible."

"It's wonderful!" Gabrielle breathed. "Never have I seen anything half so magnificent, and everyone is so kind." Luke hoped that Lady Randolph would not soon discover that she and her short-lived bridal journey were matters of spiteful conjecture among these same members of the *beau monde*.

Though Gabrielle might be too naïve to understand why she was so well-received by persons of rank—Adam was of disposition that made many of his acquaintances wish fervently to reveal him as a mountebank with feet of clay—she could not help remarking the difference between her husband and Lord Camden. The Marquis afforded her every remark a flattering interest; and though she had involved him in unwitting folly, he had neither raged nor called her a fool. Adam might say that Luke was as dull as ditch-water, but Gabrielle was fast learning that there were few matters on which she and her husband agreed.

Lady Penelope stood beside her elder brother, which caused several people to make the obvious comparison between virtue and depravity. Her bronze curls came barely to Mephisto's chin. A few feet away Sir Jason was engaged in what appeared to be reluctant conversation with Lady Ottolie Carlisle.

Not by so much as an eyelid's blink did Pen reveal her astonishment at Lady Randolph's presence. "Dear Gabrielle, how good to see you again." Deftly, Pen drew the girl into the group, leaving Lord Camden to amuse an unattractive damsel who was doubtless destined for spinsterhood. Luke cast a speaking glance at his sister but politely solicited the young lady's hand for the set of country dances that was, just then, forming.

"What a crush!" said Pen. "All of London must be here! Come, child, let me make you known to Lady Sara Cainneach."

The center of an admiring circle, Lady Sara presented an enchanting picture in a round robe of green velvet with an antique bodice. Her short full sleeves were ornamented *à l'Espagnole*, and a shade of gold-edged Paris net was fastened to her shoulders with an emerald brooch. The brown-gold hair was confined in a gold caul. In her slender hands was a fan of carved ivory, and she reminded Gabrielle strongly of a medieval portrait, perhaps one of the infamous Borgias. So this was Miss Sherrington's chaperone, in whom Adam had expressed so marked an interest. Gabrielle watched intently, for what she didn't know.

"The Irish are incurably superstitious!" Lady Sara's expression was droll. "My maid vows she saw fairies, little men in green tunics and scarlet breeches, riding down the mountain on their white horses, one summer morning while milking cows." So diverting was her narrative that no one appeared to notice that the lady was on pins and needles, as if the nerve-wracking debut into Society was her own, or took leave to question why an abigail should occupy herself with a milkmaid's task. Gabrielle wondered just who this woman was, and why Pen regarded Lady Sara much as she might a corpse newly risen from the dead.

Among the countless others who had noted the arrival of Lord Randolph's child bride was Miss Fanny Allingham, a young lady who possessed incredible wealth and no manners at all. By the expedient of applying her elbow to a few notable ribs, Fanny managed to secure a position near this Countess about whom everyone was talking; then gained Gabrielle's attention by smartly pinching her arm.

"I'm Fanny Allingham." The heiress openly inspected Gabrielle from head to toe. "We might as well introduce ourselves and save a great deal of time! I know who *you* are of course—I don't think to make as splendid a match as you did, and without a farthing to your name! But we needn't marvel at it. No other of these ladies could hold a candle to you!"

Lady Randolph murmured an incoherent response, and Fanny grinned. She was a plump, sallow-skinned young woman, talkative and sometimes coarse. She was also notorious for the immodest manner in which she climbed in and out of carriages, exhibiting to fascinated onlookers a glimpse of lace and stocky legs. That she possessed neither feminine grace nor dignity, and displayed taste neither in her manner nor in her dress, Fanny was aware, but she also knew that the hint of a vast fortune is a powerful aphrodisiac, quickening the pulses of even the most fastidious gentleman."You mustn't mind my way. They say I lounge and loll about without any self-control, and I daresay they're right, though it's no skin off *my* teeth, I'm sure!"

Gabrielle recovered sufficiently to politely protest. "Moonshine!" boomed Fanny, with a vigor that caused several heads to turn. "The truth with no bark on it, that's *my* way! And wasn't my da' so determined I should form an eligible connection, you can bet your bootlaces I wouldn't be here, for this *ton* isn't what's to my taste!" Gabrielle followed these disclosures with wonder, and Fanny winked. "It seems I must pick a husband, and that I've done—a frippery fellow, to be sure, but we'll rub on well enough together with my da's blunt to grease the way."

Gabrielle pondered this revelation and concluded that congratulations were, perhaps, in order. "I hope you'll be very happy," she ventured. "Who is this fortunate gentleman?"

"Ah! Now *that* I can't tell you." Fanny smirked. "Since he doesn't yet know himself. Even so, I'll point him out to you, if you'll vow to keep a still tongue in your head." She craned her neck to survey the room. "Odd, he doesn't seem to be here." A scowl creased her shiny forehead. "And neither does Miss Sherrington!"

Gabrielle, by now in desperate wish of escape, met Lady Sara's eye. Miss Sherrington's chaperone frowned but said nothing, and no one else seemed to remark the coincidence.

Perhaps sensing Gabrielle's dilemma, Lord Camden intervened. With a polite apology to the unhappy Miss Allingham, Gabrielle allowed him to draw her away. "You seem to be always rescuing me," she said, with a shy smile. If only her father had seen fit to marry her to as understanding a man.

"It is my pleasure," he replied, so kindly that Lady Randolph very nearly burst into tears. "I beg that if you have need of further assistance, you will not hesitate to come to me."

Lady Penelope, perhaps as a result of marriage with a rakehell, knew that London was a hotbed of gossip, and that these well-born lords and ladies were energetic muck-rakers.

She placed herself between Lord Camden and Lady Randolph, who were enjoying each other's company a trifle too well, cast her twin a reproachful glance, and inexorably bore the girl away. "My dear," she said, "isn't my brother the most delightful person! He has been the despair of match-making mamas for years. But there's Merrie! I must speak with her." Gabrielle watched her hostess glide skillfully through the crowd in the direction of a dark-haired young lady clad in a demure gown of white gauze.

"Pen's efforts at match-making," said Lord Denham, suddenly beside her, "are far from subtle. The whole world knows she means *this* heiress for Luke, and many think it most poor-spirited of her to deny the other contestants a sporting chance." He handed Gabrielle a glass. "You will not think me presumptuous if I say you look in need of refreshment? Good. Since your husband refused Pen's invitation, your presence here is a doubly delightful surprise."

Gabrielle's hand shook so badly that Mephisto was forced to rescue the glass. "My dear Lady Randolph, you are trembling like a leaf!" Again the glass was pressed on her. "Drink! A hair of the dog that bit you, as it were, though you may be assured that your secret is safe with me."

It was as well, perhaps, that Gabrielle had not time in which to ponder this remark. For Lord Randolph stood in the doorway, his face an emotionless mask that betokened murderous rage.

"Drink," said Lord Denham again, quietly, and she obeyed. He set the empty glass aside, then drew her nerveless hand through his arm. "He has a damned unpleasant temper, does he not! It may yet bring down on him some less-than-pleasant consequences." Gabrielle's fingers clenched convulsively on his sleeve, and his hand covered hers. "*Doucement, ma chère, doucement.* You are quite safe, I promise you."

Lord Randolph stood before them, his eyes fixed on his wife, an expression in them that left her faint. That her defiance had been innocent would not weigh in her defense. "St. Erth! So you found that you could join us, after all." Only the pressure of Mephisto's hand kept Gabrielle erect. "I must scold you for keeping your enchanting bride hidden away."

Since the *ton* knew well that Lord Randolph and the Duke of Denham shared a long-standing, if civilized, dislike, no one thought it particularly remarkable that the conversation between them was either one-sided or unamused. Indeed, Lord Randolph's eloquence was most often reserved for the House of Lords and the cock-pit, while Lord Denham's smiles were as scarce as hen's teeth. "In fact," continued Mephisto, "I positively demand that you permit us to see a great deal more of Lady Randolph. She will make an ideal friend for my young ward." Though pleasantly said, it was a command.

A muscle twitched in Adam's dark cheek, and Gabrielle barely dared to breathe. Would he entomb her forever in the great mausoleum that was his home, or would he acquiesce? Adam bowed stiffly. "Naturally, it will be as you wish."

"Yes." The Duke was bland. "It usually is."

The word might accord Lord Denham a heartless monster, call him devil and agree him capable of any villainy, but at least one of Lady Penelope's guests could not agree. Gabrielle looked up gratefully at her stern-faced guardian angel.

Chapter 13

Monday 15 April 1811

The library was a mammoth chamber, pleasant and well-lit; and the bookshelves were an integral part of the room's design. On those shelves were such treasures as the autobiographical *Life and Adventures and Opinions of Colonel Hangar*, containing not only an amusing frontispiece that depicted the gentleman swinging from a gibbet, but such fascinating tidbits as a prediction of war between the Northern and Southern powers of America, and a suggestion that preachers employ trumpet calls and drums to keep drowsy congregations awake during long sermons. "*Que diable!*" swore Tayce, who had temporarily set aside her literary masterpiece to deal with an equally voluminous correspondence.

It was the chaotic state of Denham House that led to my unusual regard for the proprieties and my subsequent invasion of my aunt's solitude with callers in tow; my chaperone was otherwise engaged. Sparrow's scathing tongue had at last prompted Mephisto's housekeeper to depart the premises in a huff, taking with her any small and portable item that came to hand, including various pieces of the gold plate. Since my guardian, as might have been expected, did not look kindly upon these domestic difficulties, and Sparrow's lack of repentance added fuel to the flame, *his* departure had followed shortly after.

To my boundless delight, Mephisto's sinister valet was not spared involvement in this contretemps: Sparrow lined up all the servants, including Wiggins, and induced them by various dire threats to utilize an excellent tooth-powder comprised of bole amoniac, bark, camphor and powdered myrrh. As a result, Wiggins threatened to accept an offer of employment recently received from a gentleman named Akers, whose greatest aspiration was to expectorate in the manner of Hell Fire Dick, driver of the Cambridge Telegraph coach. I wished him godspeed! Nor had *I* made any effort to remedy the morning's difficulties, finding it more to my advantage to have my guardian and my chaperone on less-than-cordial terms.

To a man, we overlooked Tayce's ungraciousness. *"Eh bien!"* said she, and plucked at her straggling grey hair. "So you have come *ventre à terre* to see how my niece survives her excesses? Believe me, *mes amis*, if your concern is for her health, it is misplaced. Merrie is as robust as a pig, though happily less malodorous!" Her smile was beautiful. I, too, smiled and controlled my rage. I still sought to inveigle Tayce to act in my behalf. Like Napoleon, she never allowed morality to hinder victory, and trusted to success to whitewash her sins.

"Isn't this a nice surprise?" I inquired, and turned my attention to our callers. "Mephisto promised that Lady Randolph would call, but didn't tell me that Lord Camden would bear her company." Had I not been occupied with other matters—primarily the possibility that I might be out-jockeyed by my guardian—I should surely have seen what was smack under my nose! Lady Randolph seemed to be exceedingly timid and quiet, and I covertly examined her modish carriage dress, of an amber shade that matched her eyes. How I longed for the day when, as a married lady, I could dress as daringly as I pleased, perhaps adapting the mode of the French ladies after Robespierre's fall, who discarded petticoats and chemise for simple flowing gowns of shocking transparency, though I could not admire the predilection of those same ladies for wigs made from the cut tresses of young women who died on the guillotine.

"Oh, delightful!" spat my aunt. "We shall be *so* comfortable." She adjusted her spectacles, leaned back in her chair, and prepared to be entertained.

"I believe Lord Denham truly meant to bring me," ventured Lady Randolph shyly, "but he sent word with Luke—Lord Camden—that he had been detained." Although she lacked animation, not even Gabrielle's sternest detractor could deny her loveliness. Still, I thought it strange that Adam should choose a Countess almost thirty years younger than he.

Luke proceeded to prove himself the soul of tact, and engaged my aunt in a discussion of Napoleon's long career. His efforts were not entirely successful; Tayce displayed a ghoulish tendency to linger in contemplation of Nelson's corpse. This was carried, immersed upright in a brandy cast to delay decomposition, from Trafalgar to England where it was given the most splendid funeral in living memory. The sailors who conducted the precious cargo home drank Nelson's embalming fluid when the *Victory* ran dry. They called this "broaching the Admiral," and said their hero would have wished it so.

Yet even I was interested to learn that the weary and defeated French troops had at last recrossed the Spanish frontier, returning to their base at Salamanca; although it was a pity our British soldiers, moving far ahead of their supplies, could pursue the enemy no further.

Tayce, as usual, was even more well-informed. "Will you tell us, too, of what the French left behind them in Santarem? Streets strewn with rotting bodies, mutilated peasants with gouged-out eyes?" Gabrielle blanched at her additional description of raped women found bleeding in charred buildings, children with bones protruding through their flesh who clung to the corpses of their parents. Though long acquainted with my aunt's blood-lust, I could not but share Gabrielle's malaise. Even Lord Camden looked grim. "An English victory, perhaps, but paid for with peasants' lives."

"An English victory, definitely." Luke was firm. "Massena's attempt to drive the British leopards into the sea has failed disastrously. The French troops must be exhausted and utterly demoralized. They lost thirty-five thousand men and most of their baggage, and left Portugal still unsubdued."

Meanwhile, I reflected, Wellington's career progressed by leaps and bounds. Three years ago an unknown Sepoy general, now British Commander-in-chief and a major European figure, Wellington's proclamation to the people of Portugal, announcing their country cleared of the enemy, had been read by the whole world.

"You English!" Tayce hoisted her cane. "As shocked by our Revolution, and the fact that royalty went to the guillotine, as if your ancestors hadn't taken the axe to your own Charles I, as if you haven't left as much carnage in your wake as ever have the French! *Perfide Albion!*"

As a conversation-killer, this was unsurpassed. I promptly stepped into the breach. "You must not mind Mme. Dore," I remarked to our flabbergasted guests. "She prides herself on being outspoken. Nor must you argue with her, unless you wish to hear of her personal experiences during the Terror."

Whether or not Lady Randolph and the Marquis wished to be stimulated by this stirring first-hand account remains unknown. I adjusted my skirts, allowing the visitors a tantalizing glimpse of a well-turned ankle, and adroitly turned the conversation to the subject of my chaperone. Tayce glared balefully but did not interfere. She had as much at stake as I.

"Lady Sara will be sorry to have missed your visit, but she is otherwise engaged." I sighed, with near-sickening sentimentality. "It is a great pity that she was widowed so young, and in a duel! A shocking thing, to be sure."

Tayce muttered to herself, and dragged out her knitting. "*Très bien!*" My aunt shoved her spectacles up to the bridge of her nose, took the needles in her slender ink-stained hands, and adopted a listening attitude. Faced with so attentive an audience, the Sphinx itself would speak.

"Such a tragedy," I continued, with an annoyed glance at my French albatross. I projected an image of sensitive girlishness, a deception greatly aided by a finely stitched and gathered plain white muslin dress, and it was most unfair of Tayce to compare me with a wolf in sheep's clothing. She must have suspected that I meant to attempt the Herculean

100

task of bringing Mephisto to heel; but Mme. Dore professed a preference for wallowing in ignorance, preserving a conscience unburdened by the precise knowledge of what I planned. "I cannot understand why gentlemen persist in such perplexing pastimes as gambling away their fortunes and killing one another in duels."

The Marquis smiled kindly upon Gabrielle, who was following both the conversation and my aunt's attempt at knitting with wide-eyed interest. Surely there was more to her than at first appeared! Despite her surface sophistication, Lady Randolph struck me as singularly innocent and uninformed. "It was an affair of honor," Luke replied, as if that explained everything. Perhaps to him it did.

I wrinkled my nose in apparent perplexity, a gesture that for some fathomless reason never failed to bring a sparkle into an observant gentleman's eye. Lord Camden was no exception. "I fear I do not follow your reasoning."

"Ah, but you're not expected to. A gentleman's notion of honor is not something to worry a young lady's pretty head." Behind Luke's back, Tayce growled and eyed her cane.

Ignoring my aunt's rising ire, I pouted prettily. "I *do* wish you'd explain," I said in plaintive tones. "How could Lady Sara's husband risk his life in a duel with no thought of his poor wife? It seems positively inhuman to me."

"It was unavoidable." Luke condescended to share with us his vast knowledge of the masculine world. "There was an accusation concerning marked cards; to let such an insinuation go unchallenged would be practically an admission of guilt." Lady Randolph gasped.

"Mad dogs," murmured Tayce dourly, "and Englishmen!" My aunt nourished loyalty for no country! She could have regained her old privileged standing in Napoleon's New Order—and possibly, like many of her compatriots, a great deal of her property—for the Emperor welcomed with open arms those of the old aristocracy who embraced his regime. But the Neighboring Monster had little favor with my aunt, due primarily to his opinion of women, who he believed were by nature intended to be man's slaves. Furthermore, the Corsican had been sufficiently short-sighted to celebrate the advent of the Regency, believing that Prinny would recall Wellington's troops. My aunt had scant tolerance for such stupidity.

"*Who* was accused?" Gabrielle asked hastily, perhaps in hope of forestalling further outrageous observations from my aunt. "Lady Sara's husband? What a shocking thing!"

Lord Camden was proving almost too persuadable. "He was a notable swordsman, and it was thought he would easily vanquish his foe—but you will not wish to hear the sordid details. It is hardly a subject fit for young ladies' ears." Lady Randolph looked as though she heartily agreed.

Tayce smirked, as well she might, having for numerous years filled *my* young ears with tales of blood and gore. "*Allons! I* am extremely interested, young man." I clasped my hands and leaned forward eagerly, and received a wicked look. "You needn't fear my niece will have an attack of the vapors. She has no more sensibility than that chair. Tell us more of Lady Sara's husband, please!"

Piqued, I contemplated the article in question, a utilitarian piece fashioned of sturdy oak. "His sword broke," said the Marquis, with every indication of reluctance, "in a point-blank thrust into the opponent's chest. Upon this he closed, and they both fell." He stopped, as if this were the entire tale.

"That," snapped Tayce, with the callousness of a woman who has kept her skin almost intact while sleeping in the broken doorways of foul refuse-strewn streets, "is hardly sufficient." I often suspected her of *nostalgie de la boue*, a homesickness for the gutter, a nostalgia for the mud.

Luke seemed loath to continue, but he could not gracefully extricate himself. "Lady Sara's husband was stabbed countless times, in the face and body. There was little doubt that he would die." Gabrielle clasped her hands and looked ready to swoon.

"*Diabolique!*" remarked Mme. Dore, with relish. Her knitting-needles clicked rhythmically.

"Surely at least the seconds and a medical man must have been present!" I had a poor notion of honor if it meant those gentlemen stood idly by while gross butchery was enacted before their very eyes! "Just who *was* this other man?"

"I don't know." In the face of my gentle queries, Lord Camden had grown distrait. "I had the story from my sister, who had it from Lady Sara."

"Such fast friends they've become," I commented blandly. "The vision of Lady Sara unburdening herself to your sister positively warms my heart. I can almost see them weeping on

102

one another's breasts, exchanging the confidences of these past many years." I was downright dreamy-eyed with excess sentiment.

Tayce shot me a suspicious glance. "*Allez!* It is most odd that a sword should break in that manner." Among Mme. Dore's other accomplishments, learned only she and God knew where, was a masterful grasp of the art of fencing. Her movements were hardly graceful, due to her crippled leg, but I had more than once seen her, with a deft flick of the wrist, lop off a frantic chicken's head. Her victims invariably turned up, suitably garnished and stewed, on the supper table.

"There was a rumor," Luke admitted reluctantly, "that the other man wore some sort of armor."

"How dreadful!" gasped Lady Randolph, inspired by horror to state the obvious.

"Heavens!" Thrilled, I sat still further forward, and nearly tumbled from the sofa. The Marquis was playing his audience as skillfully as he might a fish on his line. "Were no inquiries made?" In the distance came a persistent hammering.

"There might have been, had the man not disappeared." Lord Camden had turned balky. "You understand this was told me in confidence. I can say no more."

"*Aide-toi,*" remarked Tayce, in tones of approval, "*le ciel t'aidera.* Help yourself and heaven will help you." So this, I mused, was Luke's purpose, and most intriguing it was. Why should he wish us to think that Sparrow's husband had been murdered, and in a most arrogantly cold-blooded way?

The wretched noise persisted and I, roused from my frenzied speculations, went impatiently to investigate. The noise led me to the front door. Bridey, less careful of her status in the household than any other lady's maid I'd ever known, was before me in the hallway.

"Sure and the grand look of ye is a fine sight to see," she said, and I slid back into the shadows, all senses alert. " 'Tis long enough it took ye to arrive! Herself has been all afret. Now follow me and mind what ye're about."

My fancy nicely tickled, I peered at the woman who, on those words, stepped through Mephisto's front door. She was a tall and placid-looking creature, perhaps in her late thirties, with greying auburn hair. As stealthy as a master cracksman, I followed Bridey and the newcomer into the nether regions of Denham House, where Sparrow had established command. On last sight—when, to be precise, she had exiled me from her domain—my chaperone had been enshrouded in a voluminous white apron which looked most incongruous with her stylish muslin morning gown, and immersed in Elizabeth Raffald's *The Experienced English Housekeeper*, an excellent reference work for the use and ease of ladies, housekeepers and cooks.

Sparrow was giving voice to fulsome Gaelic curses that speeded the sullen housemaids in their various tasks of mixing silver sand and vinegar to scour the kitchen's copper pots; polishing the floors with melted beeswax and turpentine; and shining the furniture with ivory-black, treacle, oil, small beer and sulphuric acid. " 'Tis Mrs. Selkirk, my lady," announced Bridey with uncharacteristic subservience, doubtless employed for the benefit of her audience, "come to inquire about the position of housekeeper." Heavens, thought I, news certainly travels quickly among the Great Unwashed!

"Mrs. Selkirk?" Sparrow repeated thoughtfully, and wiped her hands on her apron. "I assume, Mrs. Selkirk, that you have references?"

"Aye, my lady," the woman replied in a soft and melodious voice that made me fair leap out of my skin. She, too, was Irish! No believer in coincidence, particularly not so mind-boggling a coincidence as that an Irish housekeeper should just happen to inquire for work on the very day that the previous holder of the position had been induced to leave by my Irish chaperone, I studied the woman again.

"Come with me," said Sparrow. I ducked into the china closet, fortunately untenanted, as she led Mrs. Selkirk into the housekeeper's room; then slipped from my hiding-place and proceeded on by a circuitous route. The door stood ajar and I flattened myself against the wall.

"I am proficient," Mrs. Selkirk offered, "in the running of a large household, and can concoct simple medicaments like liquorice lozenges or scurvy-grass wine for invalids. I am also familiar with the making of confectionary, preserves, wines and pickles; I can distil rose water from damask roses, prepare lavender to keep the linen cupboard sweet, make jam, candy peel, and prepare morello cherries in brandy."

"Commendable," responded Sparrow, sounding very much like she wanted to laugh. What an odd conversation! I was as curious as the proverbial ill-fated cat—a comparison that it would have behooved me to closer note—and edged nearer to the door. There was much more to a housekeeper's duties than Mrs. Selkirk had remarked—such worthies oversaw all that went on in the house, including the servants' performance and moral character.

Sparrow continued: "Your references appear to be in order. You understand, of course, that Lord Denham will make the final decision?" Mrs. Selkirk murmured an affirmative. "If his lordship agrees that the position is yours, you will be granted a fortnight's holiday each year, plus a half day every Sunday, one day off per month, and an evening out weekly. Is this satisfactory?"

"Very generous, my lady." Now Mrs. Selkirk's voice was amused. Intrigued beyond bearing, I carefully peered through the crack afforded by the half-open door. Mrs. Selkirk certainly looked the ideal housekeeper, steady and middle-aged and exemplary in conduct, and would doubtless apply herself assiduously to all matters necessary to the harmony, comfort and economy of the family. Why, then, had I this feeling that she was not what she seemed, that in fact I witnessed nothing more than a well-rehearsed scene?

Mephisto's new housekeeper—I had no doubt that Sparrow would see Mrs. Selkirk played this role—and my chaperone gazed upon each other with the utmost cordiality, while Bridey looked on with a face-splitting grin. *"Sláinte mhór!"* said the maidservant wryly. I have enough of the Gaelic to know that Sparrow's abigail wished the newcomer luck—but why?

It struck me that Mrs. Selkirk might well be a female of gentle birth fallen upon hard times. Her bearing was remarkably ladylike, so much so that my interest was further aroused. I heartily regretted that convention made it impossible for me to take my meals in the servants' hall, and immediately determined to press my imbecilic maid into service as a second set of ears and eyes. If the instrument was faulty, no matter. *Au pays des aveugles les borgnes sont rois*, as Tayce was fond of saying: In the country of the blind the one-eyed men are kings.

Further deductions were, alas, forestalled. One would think that, in view of my daily conversations with the Deity, I might have been granted some warning, but Gabriel did not sound his golden trumpet on my account. Mephisto clapped one hand over my mouth; and with the other grasped my ear and led me ungently away.

Chapter 14

On the Horns of a Dilemma

Sir Jason Palmerston was not only the most noted of sportsmen and the most polished of seducers, he was an astute businessman. Not for him was the tacit rule that the fashionable gentleman of Mayfair never ventured into the City! Already that day he had visited Lloyd's, principal center for all concerned with traffic on the high seas, and contributed to the subscription for relief of widows and orphans of the seamen who fought Napoleon; then proceeded to inspect warehouses filled with valuable goods that could find no sale due to Napoleon's land blockade against British commerce. England was in the midst of a financial crisis, vast stocks of manufactured goods piling up in industrial regions which could find no outlet. Yet Napoleon's clever strategy had also worked against him, mused Jason. Paris financial houses were failing, sixty-one in January alone.

Hyde Park at 5 P.M. was the promenade of London, the rendezvous of fashion and beauty, and Sir Jason guided his mount onto Rotton Row, once *route du roi*, the pathway of kings from Westminster to the hunting forests. He was not at all happy about his wife, who was suffering fits of great abstraction, jumping half out of her skin each time he entered a room, and putting off his concerned queries with taradiddles that wouldn't deceive even Miss Samantha Palmerston, aged six years old. In fact, that precocious young lady had inquired of her father just what maggot had got into mama's head. It was a question that Sir Jason echoed, though he suspected the answer might involve Lady Sara Cainneach. There was something smoky there, or Sir Jason was no judge of human nature, particularly the nature of his brother-in-law. Sir Jason cared little what devilish intrigues Mephisto was embarked upon, but he cared very much that Pen should be involved.

The ladies drove out in superbly appointed carriages, attended by powdered footmen in gorgeous livery and be-wigged coachmen with three-cornered hats and French gloves; and the gentlemen vied with one another in the excellence of their steeds. Sir Jason, an acclaimed favorite despite his lamentable tendency to confine his amorous exploits within the hallowed bounds of matrimony, nodded and bowed. When he glimpsed his Regent—the most conspicuous horseman of them all, due not to expertise but to the astounding royal girth—Jason turned abruptly aside and into a leafy glade. This simple duplicity was to bring an illuminating reward.

Hyde Park was not only the meeting place of fashion and wealth, but also the hunting-ground of professional courtesans. Hariette Wilson was queen among these Fashionably Impures, and so alluring that the Marquis of Worcester, heir to the Duke of Beaufort, had recently caused a frightful rumpus in his family by wanting to marry her before he came of age. Alas for the lady's hopes! Young Worcester was torn from her ample bosom by his irate family and whisked off to the Peninsula.

But it was not Harry's satin-lined carriage that Jason espied, or her bright auburn curls; it was a *vis à vis*, a smart carriage designed to hold only two, and in it sat the same Delilah whose charms had long been Lord Denham's exclusive province. Pulled up beside the carriage, mounted on a superb bay mare, was Lady Sara Cainneach. The woman obviously wished to be private. Sir Jason dismounted and approached on foot.

"It sits in a heathered valley," said Lady Sara, "with giant boulders, yellow-flowered gorse bushes and rowan trees." Her words were rapid and high-pitched. "I wish you might see the castle, surrounded by sun-kissed mist. It is truly a vision so delicious as to be food for the old gods."

"Very interesting, I'm sure," retorted Delilah, "and very inconvenient too! Surely you cannot think I contrived so mightily to speak with you so that you might describe to me the weather and your Irish home! Better you had stayed there, where you were safe from harm."

"What then?" Jason could not see their faces, but tension was evident in even the angle of Lady Sara's head. "Perhaps you have discovered that you were not sufficiently well-paid for your efforts in my behalf?"

Delilah laughed, a pleasant husky sound. "My, but you're the leery one! No, Mephisto is no pinch-purse, I'll say that for him, devil though he may be." She grew serious. "But I *have* made a discovery, and one that is of utmost importance to you."

"What?" Lady Sara's voice was as strained as if strangling hands were clasped around her throat.

Delilah turned to scrutinize her companion, affording Sir Jason a glimpse of exotic features and an astonishingly low-cut *décolletage*. "Very well! I know, dear Sparrow, precisely who you are."

So rigid was the lady that she might have been carved of stone. "How?"

Delilah shrugged. "I was very curious, both about you and why Mephisto brought you to me. Shortly after your departure, a man came asking questions—a shockingly shabby little fellow, not at all the sort I am accustomed to finding on my doorstep, I assure you!" Her smile flashed. "He spun me a yarn about his reasons for seeking you—and no doubt a person less astute than I would have been satisfied, but I already knew his identity." She leaned forward in the seat. "I also know whose creature he is. Sparrow, I do not wish to know more of this matter, but I must earnestly implore you to refrain from rushing into certain trouble and possible danger!"

Lady Sara looked penetrated with grief and said not a word. Delilah sighed and settled back again. "It's on your head then, and none of my concern. I wonder that I should have interfered so far, for I told him nothing. You might thank me! Your pursuer is not one whose wrath *I* should wish to inspire."

"I do thank you," Sara said softly, "very much. But I beg you will ask me no more questions. The subject is very painful to me."

"I don't wonder at it! To be frank, your case is desperate. I hope you do not look to Mephisto for protection, for he serves

108

only his own interests, as you must surely realize." Despite her professed lack of curiosity, Delilah's eyes narrowed speculatively. "Just what part did he play in that *débâcle* of so many years ago? And what hold has it given him over you?"

As if summoned by some dark incantation, Lord Denham chose that moment to appear. Seated on a huge black gelding, he looked every inch the Prince of Darkness, risen straight from the depths of hell. Lady Sara winced, no doubt thunderstruck at seeing so diabolic a vision, and Delilah smiled. Sir Jason retreated and swung into his saddle. It was apparent that, however Delilah had arranged this odd meeting, Mephisto had not been informed. A slight movement caught his attention. Jason had not been the only one privileged to witness that strange confrontation.

It was not the first time that day that Sir Jason had encountered the Northcliffe lad. Only a few hours previous they had met at a certain jeweller's in Cranbourn Alley, where Jason had gone to retrieve a sapphire necklace that belonged to his wife. This was a long-standing arrangement between Sir Jason and Hamlet, the accommodating jeweller: Lady Penelope, having overspent her more-than-generous allowance, would pawn one of her baubles; Sir Jason would then redeem the gems and stealthily replace them in her jewellery box. It was an admirable arrangement for all parties—Hamlet received a handsome profit and Sir Jason's gratitude; Lady Penelope was spared the embarrassment of requesting additional funds; and Sir Jason avoided the necessity of scolding his wife for her lack of economy—but sometimes Jason wondered if his paper-skulled spouse was aware of his efforts, or whether, confronted with her overflowing jewel-box, she lacked the wit to remember precisely what she'd pawned.

Ninian Northcliffe was not unknown to Sir Jason, who considered him an amusing rattle, and Jason had not been particularly surprised to find the young man in those particular surroundings. It was common knowledge that Ninian was far from being plump in the pocket. But Jason was very surprised indeed to find young Northcliffe lingering in Hyde Park and staring at Lady Sara with such fixed intensity. The lady glanced up, caught that gaze, and shook her head slightly. Then she touched her heel to her horse's flank and followed Mephisto out of the glade. Young Northcliffe departed also, in a different direction. Sir Jason urged his steed forward, mulling over what he'd just seen. Only Delilah remained.

She, too, was lost in thought, but her frown fled with Sir Jason's approach. The gentleman's appreciative expression led her to abruptly wonder if he had at last grown so weary of domestic life that he meant to resume philandering. Mephisto would not be pleased if his sister was forced to play second fiddle to a Cyprian! Delilah smiled, a frank invitation in her slanted eyes.

Not for nothing did Jason have behind him a long and reprehensible career; he could easily imagine what schemes passed through Delilah's mind. Nonetheless, he returned her warm regard. "Well met, madam, and most fortunately, for I have grown heartily bored with my own company."

"And for *me*, my lord, as well." She leaned slightly forward, the better to display her gown's daring neckline. "You see me positively abandoned! Isn't it the most dreadful thing?"

"Grievous." On Jason's features was the beguiling look that had caused many a straw damsel to throw her hat over the windmill for nothing more rewarding than love. "Shall we console one another, then?"

"Pray, how, my lord?" Past mistress of the come-hither look, Delilah cast her admirer a glance so sizzling that it scorched the very air. "I have my reputation to consider! What would the world think if it saw me in such intimate conversation with you?"

"Since no one has observed us, we shall never know." Sir Jason employed his rare smile to such good effect that Delilah's knees grew weak. "Will you bid the world go and be damned, lovely Delilah, and laugh away an hour with me?" There was, of course, no question but that she would agree.

Chapter 15

It was no doubt fortunate that mystery is the breath of life to me, else I would have positively suffocated under my ever-heavier blanket of intrigue! Not only had I yet to learn Mephisto's precise plans—which no one acquainted with the man could doubt were sinister in the extreme—and to flesh out the skeleton of Sparrow's all-too-meagre history, but now I must discover the truth of Maeve Selkirk's identity. She was no more a housekeeper than I was a candidate for sainthood! Yet Mephisto employed her, as I predicted, without as much as a glance at her references, and she was quickly installed in her quarters at Denham House.

My guardian, as a result of my investigative endeavors, awarded me a lecture that lasted quite two hours. I shall spare the reader the more unpleasant details of that interview, though I must confess that Mephisto was not filled with admiration for my daring and talented attempt to bamboozle him, nor was he (alas!) struck dumb and lifeless by my audacity. It is no wonder that I was perpetually vowing vengeance against the fiend! It seemed I was to have no say in my own future, but must leave the matter entirely to him. The result of rebellion—though he vowed to keep me on a tight rein!—would be that he should exercise the control that he legally held, and in a manner that promised to be monstrous unpleasant. Must I add that I was neither daunted by these ominous threats, nor swayed from my intent?

These cogitations were interrupted by Miss Fanny Allingham. This Wednesday evening found Sparrow and me at Almack's, the assembly rooms in King Street that had been founded in the preceding century by a Scottish valet. Mephisto had declined to join us—a pity, since I would have derived a

111

great and perverse enjoyment from watching my epicurian guardian refreshing himself with lemonade and tea, bread and butter and stale cake!—and instead passed the evening playing cards at White's Club, thereby causing several unhappy acquaintances the deepest chagrin as he divested them of the larger portion of their fortunes. White's was famous for the strange wagers recorded in its betting book, one of the most notable being whether a pedestrian run down outside would live or die.

I had previously been introduced to Miss Allingham, and it was an acquaintance that I did not wish to pursue. Since *she* was rich as Solomon, and *I* was born with the proverbial silver spoon in my mouth, our encounter attracted a great deal of notice, particularly from those gentlemen who were less blessed with this world's goods! "I've a bone to pick with you," Fanny said, in her frankly vulgar way.

"Oh?" I inquired. "What might that be?" With little hope that Miss Allingham would recognize a set-down, let alone be silenced, I gazed about me at aristocratic ladies in flimsy muslin, with bared shoulders and jewels in their hair, and gentlemen in knee-breeches, excellently fitting coats of superfine, and pristine white cravats. More than three quarters of the nobility were excluded from the Assembly Rooms, and the intrigue and subterfuge that went on to gain the *entrée* to this exclusive temple of the *ton*, a greater distinction than being presented at Court and more difficult to obtain, would have done credit even to Napoleon.

"The *on-dit* is that your guardian has already received several eligible offers for your hand." Startled, I turned my attention to her, then as quickly away. Fanny was a squat little squab of a girl with dishwater hair and protuberant eyes. The gown she wore beggared description, so I will content myself with remarking only that it was unflattering to an astonishing degree. My own was only slightly less repellant, being a disgustingly girlish creation of white muslin embroidered with a tiny flower motif.

"I'm afraid I do not take your meaning." I smiled at Lady Jersey, one of the committee of seven high-born ladies who ruled Almack's—known to the impious as the Marriage Mart—with absolute authority. They alone had the privilege of granting vouchers of admission to the subscription balls, and no one was allowed to enter these hallowed walls without

112

their approval. No more than two hundred people were present, and admission after eleven o'clock was granted to none.

"I mean," said Fanny, with a smile that was singularly unpleasant, perhaps due to the uneven and slightly discolored teeth thus displayed, "that I've seen you casting eyes at the particular gentleman that I mean for my own, and I warn you that I don't intend to gracefully bow out of the lists."

This could not be doubted. It was inconceivable that Miss Allingham should perform any act with even a modicum of grace. But I had no notion whom she meant, and thus wasn't particularly concerned that the wench's nose had been put out of joint. Instead, I surveyed my surroundings. I confess to no small perplexity as to why Almack's was so much the rage! Among those fair well-tended young damsels, the choicest blooms to be plucked from this year's crop, I felt as misplaced as a weed.

Determined to shatter my good spirits, Miss Allingham clutched my arm. "I fancy I've the advantage," she hissed, with that same obnoxious smile. "You see, *I* don't stand to be cut off without a farthing for marrying without consent. Does the gentleman in question know *that*, I wonder? And you know quite well who I mean! Perhaps I should make it a point to acquaint him with the precise terms of your late father's will."

She had certainly secured my interest, but I would not let her know that her words acted as a cold hand clutched around my heart. How in heaven's name had she secured access to such confidential information? Had it been noised around the town? "This," I said sternly, "is the height of absurdity!"

Still she wore that damned knowing face. "You may say what you choose, but I don't have windmills in my head! Be warned: I mean to have Northcliffe, and there's an end to it."

"I beg to differ," I replied sweetly, leaving her to wonder if I referred to Ninian or to the condition of her skull. "I do not consider this conversation to be at all the thing. You will excuse me now?"

It took me an entire moment to regain my composure. My worst fear had been realized: Not only did London possess an heiress even wealthier than I, but she had chosen *my* Ninian as her prey! What was I to do, my hands tied as it were by my

113

father's accursed will? But the sour chimera of uncertainty perched only briefly on my shoulders before being irritably shrugged away. I had, at my aunt's insistence, studied the careers of both Machiavelli and Napoleon, and was surely sufficiently sharp-witted to out-maneuver the stodgy Miss Allingham. I recalled the Corsican's belief that man is motivated only by interest or fear. If I could not circumvent her by more ordinary means, I would find some way to strike terror in her unlovely breast.

Then, with Luke, I trod the stately measures of a quadrille. Briefly, I envied my saturnine guardian, dining at White's on boiled fowl, oyster sauce and apple tart, and doubtless without a thought of his browbeaten ward ever in his head.

"A penny for your thoughts," offered the generous Marquis.

"Ah." I smiled pensively, imparting an air of mysterious sorrow. "They are not worth so much." I could hardly tell him I puzzled over my guardian's treacherous conduct: Mephisto had made no mention of ardent hearts, eligible or otherwise, laid on my behalf at his feet, there to be employed as a doormat. Suddenly, I succumbed to a sudden impulse to discover if Luke was truly as dull as he seemed. "If you must know, I find this campaign to marry me off distasteful in the extreme! I feel like the goose who laid the golden egg being trussed up for the cooking-pot!" It was not an inept observation: Upon my marriage, my entire property would become my husband's, to dispose of as he pleased. He would have absolute control over any money I earned, any gift I received; he could sell or give away my clothes and jewels, even dispose of my property at will. Is it necessary to add that, for Ninian, I would have whistled any number of fortunes down the wind?

Luke grinned. To my surprise, in this rare moment of amusement he was as delightful as was Pen. "My dear Meredith, you are full of surprises."

"For heaven's sake," I said, pleased to have whetted his interest, "don't repeat that to your sister, or I shall sink myself beyond reproach! I should not have admitted to such freakishness."

"Nonsense." Luke escorted me from the floor. "You may say anything you wish to me! Marriages of convenience are most often arranged for the convenience of others and with precious little consideration for the parties most closely con-

114

cerned." He recalled himself, his surroundings, and the extreme impropriety of speaking in this manner to me. "Forgive me! You should not encourage me to ride my hobby-horse. I hope I have not offended you."

"On the contrary," I replied, with an admiring glance. Never had I thought to hear the staid and sober Marquis give vent to such a diatribe. "I like a man who speaks his mind, and find your opinions of the greatest interest. But there is Lady Sara, beckoning to me." It was not Sparrow who inspired me to a feverish frenzy of fluttering fidgets, but the godlike young gentleman who stood by her side. I half-dragged Luke across the floor toward my chaperone, in conversation with Lady Jersey. Ninian, standing slightly behind them, winked, a signal which may have been, for some unfathomable reason, directed at Lord Camden, but which I preferred to think was meant for me.

Sparrow was recounting a tale of Grania O'Malley, Queen of the West and of the Isles, a legendarily fierce, flamboyant and ruthless lady who refused to bow to Tudor rule. "Trailed by a semi-circular bodyguard of gallowglasses," said my chaperone, with faint envy, "Grania arrived at Whitehall to see Queen Elizabeth. She wore a gown of tawny satin with a train three ells long, and her famous knee-length hair was bound in a snood of gold threads and topped by a huge black beret. Instead of rendering the proper obsequence, Grania casually unbuttoned her bodice to reveal full plate armor from head to toe." Sparrow related the story with great animation, Ninian listened with enthusiastic interest, and all the while Lady Jersey watched me.

"Meredith." With every evidence of affection, Lady Sara clasped my hand. "I would like to make you known to Sir Ninian Northcliffe." Wistfully, I eyed him, suffering anew cupid's sting. The wretch knew it; his lips twitched. Perhaps I have not previously mentioned that Ninian is a baronet, a hereditary title that brought with it singularly small reward.

Ninian made an elegant bow and I smiled demurely. Sparrow had obviously been charmed by my enterprising beau. I wondered how long it would be before she learned his residence was Queer Street, his consort Lady Poverty. Perhaps she already knew, and her seeming benevolence was truly fellow-feeling for one who was as impecunious—and as enterprising—as herself.

115

"May I recommend Sir Ninian to you," suggested Lady Jersey, "as a partner for the next set? I believe you'll find in him no small expertise." Shyly, I acquiesced.

I really believed that I had played my cards, thus far, excellently well with these people, and truly thought, in that extremely misguided moment, that there were no dragons I could not slay. (Some of this asininity may be excused by the tingling sensations roused by the touch of Ninian's hand on my arm—palpitations which must have gone right to my brain!) I meant to learn Mephisto's weaknesses—surely even so calloused a creature must possess an Achilles heel!—and to compel him to eat out of my hand. That this was a preposterous piece of nonsense, I freely admit, and can only say in my defense that I did not mean to play the fool.

But this rare moment of sanctioned intimacy with my beloved was not to be squandered in idle reflection. "Ninian," I murmured softly, "are you angry with me? You took your leave so abruptly when last we met that I feared I had said something to offend."

"I adore you, my poppet." The roguish gleam in Ninian's grey eyes made me determine to experiment with a Wash of the Ladies of Denmark, a beautifying concoction of bean flower, pumpkin, melon, cucumber and gourd seeds. "If my departure seemed abrupt, it was only because I feared the consequences were I to remain longer in your enchanting company. 'Twill hardly serve our purposes for you to find yourself compromised."

"It is much too dreadful to contemplate," I lied, and batted my eye-lashes. He was a superb dancer, and our steps fitted together perfectly. "Ninian, the most terrible thing has happened. I am near-desperate." I was also prone to exaggeration, when it suited my ends. "Tell me when we may meet and speak privately."

Ninian's hand tightened on mine, but his expression remained affable. Anyone observing us—and many were—would see only a handsome young couple engaging in a decorous conversation. How appearances deceive! "Friday," replied Ninian, in a fine spirit of romance, love and the world well lost. "Surely *you* have not reached wit's end! Would it relieve you to learn that I have undertaken inquiries of my own?"

I was not so great a simpleton as to tell him it did not. Nor

116

did I inform him of my confrontation with Miss Allingham, or point out that she was glowering at us most malevolently. "Dear Ninian," I whispered, and the rest of our remarks, though more than slightly *risqué*, have little bearing here.

All too soon, Ninian returned me to my chaperone, who had been joined in my absence by Adam St. Erth and his young wife. Adam, for some strange reason, was observing me with a black scowl, while Sparrow looked as though ice water ran in her veins. Never have I seen so severe a state of perturbation! Fortunately, a pallid off-white complexion was in fashion, and no one noted her bizarre nervousness but me. "Lord Randolph," I said, and dropped a curtsey. "It is good to see you again. Have you been presented to my *dame de compaigne*?" I would have introduced Ninian also, but he had unobtrusively slipped away.

"I have." Adam was polite but unimpressed, and I recalled Sparrow's earlier conversation with Pen. If Lord Randolph had once known my chaperone, he did not seem to recognize her now, and Sparrow made no effort to recall the acquaintance to mind. I wondered if a shameful secret lurked in Lady Sara's past, one so dreadful that she lived in terror of momentary exposure. Or perhaps it was Adam that she feared, but if so, why? I wondered, too, if Adam was involved in Mephisto's unspecified but doubtlessly diabolic schemes concerning myself. Ah, my wretched curiosity! The truth was a lesson bitterly learned.

Timid as a churchmouse, Lady Randolph complimented me on my dark curls, dressed that evening in an Apollo knot. "You are too kind," I murmured, and she was. Beside Gabrielle's stunning beauty, I must have appeared a dowd. Nor did Sparrow show to advantage, being if not precisely stricken in years, beyond her first youth—and I conjectured spitefully that this disadvantage partially accounted for my chaperone's discomfort. Immensely cheered by this ignoble deduction, I promptly agreed that I should be delighted to accompany Lady Randolph on a shopping expedition.

So constrained was the conversation among the four of us—though Gabrielle and I firmly cemented our friendship, even beneath Adam's jaundiced eye—that I was relieved when Lord Camden appeared to claim yet another dance. The reader must not think, because I mention no other admirers, that I was not sought-after. Though my popularity was

117

flattering, it was not unexpected, and it is no more my purpose to relate the evening's duller moments than to gust enthusiastic over assemblies and balls and suppers where every imaginable delicacy was served under Grecian lamps and exotic festoons. Ninian had bewitched me! In his absence, all else was tiresome as a twice-told tale.

I smiled at Luke as we glided smoothly around the floor. The Marquis did not return the salute, but looked uncomfortable. "I should say nothing," he ventured, gazing right at Ninian. "It is none of my concern, but I feel I must drop a word of warning. I hope you will not take it amiss."

"Oh?" I, too, glanced at the apple of my eye, and my wits promptly went bird-nesting. I felt in my bones that I knew what Luke would say.

So must France's *ancien noblesse* have looked when they rode bravely to the guillotine. "To be blunt," Lord Camden announced, "people are not always precisely what they seem."

As if I didn't know! I interrupted him in mid-speech—even now I cringe at being such a Johnny-head-in-the-air! But my self-control was severely strained by Ninian's animated conversation with Miss Allingham. "I suppose you mean to tell me that young Northcliffe is dangling after a rich heiress, and that you don't wish to see me encourage the attentions of a fortune-hunter!"

"I do?" Luke was stunned, I thought by my perspicacity.

"I don't know where you learned your fantastic notions!" I continued furiously. "I have never seen a greater appearance of worth and honor in any young man in my life." Having dug my own grave, I proceeded to bury myself in it. "Although I appreciate your apprehensions, I think them unfounded. Sir Ninian is very much relished by those who know him well and is the most popular person possible with all parties."

"I cannot deny that." Luke's expression was odd. Once more he stared at Ninian, who returned our interest with a polite little bow. "Strangely, Meredith, it never entered my head to warn you off young Northcliffe."

"Heigh ho!" I muttered, from the utter depths of gloom. Like Don Quixote, I had gone tilting at windmills, and had come to no less grief. "Now you *will* tell me that Ninian hasn't a feather to fly with, and that Mephisto would hardly approve."

"Not if you don't wish me to." Lord Camden's blue eyes

were alight with amusement, and I began to think I'd misjudged the man. "Take that mulish expression off your face! It matters not to *me*, and I vow I shan't say a word."

This forebearance was encouraging! It might yet work to my advantage that I had let the cat out of the bag. "How *kind* you are!" I whispered, meaning to cajole Luke into an appreciation of my odious situation, but at that moment the movement of the dance afforded us a clear view of Lord and Lady Randolph. Adam toyed with a gold-handled quizzing-glass, looking immeasurably bored; but Gabrielle's face was as easily read as a well-written book. She was looking straight at Luke.

"Humph!" said I. "Nor would Mephisto approve of *that*, I fear!"

I smiled, optimism restored, while my escort blushed several interesting shades of red. The Marquis had just become my fellow conspirator, like it or no, and I saw that my most immediate endeavor must be to show him how to go about the thing. Alas, I was so elated at this unexpected development that it did not occur to me to ask what warning he'd meant to issue.

Chapter 16

A Household on Its Ear

Palmerston House had already, that day, been the scene of considerable chaos, most of which could be laid at the door of fond, if misguided, Uncle Luke, who had treated the siblings to an acrobatic display. Thus inspired, Miss Samantha undertook some gymnastics of her own, and suffered a rather severe tumble while attempting a triple somersault on the back-yard swing. The damsel's main injury, it was quickly ascertained, was primarily to her pride; as Sir Jason remarked, nobody suffering severe physical damage could so strenuously exercise her lungs. Miss Samantha's outraged shrieks penetrated the neighborhood, leading several of the less courageous dwellers there to believe that London had been invaded by Napoleon during the night, that the French troops at that very moment wreaked havoc and mayhem on Queen Anne Street, summarily murdering peace-loving citizens in their beds.

At length the neighbors were assuaged, and the doctor summoned. Though Miss Samantha, it turned out, had little need of his services, the governess was found shrieking and drumming her heels on the nursery floor, and had to be doused with a bucket of water, so his trip was not in vain. At length Maria, revived with burnt feathers stuck under her nose, was packed off to bed with a liberal dose of tincture of opium; and Miss Samantha, a bandage wrapped rakishly around her brow, was enthroned in her own bedroom, attended by Nanny, the nursery maid, and three of the household canines—as the young lady pointed out, Wellington took an entire *pack* of dogs with him to the Peninsula. Sir Jason, after surveying his wife's harassed features, nobly swept the remaining young Palmerstons off to Astley's Royal Amphitheatre, there to behold splendid equestrian feats. Next, Lady Penelope supposed, she would be privileged to see one of her children attempt a similar feat of horsemanship. She smiled as she thought of Sir Jason's reaction when one of his thoroughbreds was appropriated for trick-riding.

Pen was a lovely vision in a frothy blue confection that exactly matched her eyes. The sunlight gleamed in her golden hair. Lady Ottolie Carlisle returned the smile, smug in the knowledge that she would soon cause her hostess to wear an expression of an entirely different sort. "I believe," said Lady Carlisle, "that you may expect an interesting announcement soon."

Pen regarded Ottolie, who wore a simpering expression, without enthusiasm. "Oh?" Lady Carlisle was not only pursuing Mephisto with the grimmest determination, she was with equal fervor cultivating a future sister-in-law.

"My dear!" Ottolie was arch. "I wasn't born yesterday."

Pen nobly refrained from comment; the lady was forty if she was a year. Lady Carlisle's dark hair owed more to art than to nature, her highly-colored complexion spoke of surreptitious dips into the rouge-pot, and her plump figure was

120

tightly laced into an improbable hour-glass shape. Pen had a naughty vision of Lady Carlisle climbing onto the great scales at Berry Brothers, there—along with the huge bags of coffee—to be weighed.

"I refer," continued Ottolie, undeterred by Pen's silence, "to your brother and Denham's ward. I am not the only one to remark the extraordinary attention that Luke is paying Miss Sherrington!"

"I see." Pen had no more desire to discuss this particular matter than she had wished to answer her guest's previous questions about Lady Sara Cainneach. "I thought perhaps you referred to my *other* brother, and yourself!" It was not the kindest of remarks. To joust with Mephisto was to splinter one's lance against his unbreakable heart. Even Lady Carlisle could not but admit she had won no favors in the tournament of love.

No whit discomposed, Ottolie raised an eyebrow and smiled in a manner that made Pen wish uncharitably that the lady might be seized by a white slavery ring and shipped to Buenos Aires. "As to *that*," Ottolie said, "you understand that I can announce nothing yet, but I can safely tell you that I believe his affections to have become fixed!"

Though she wished very much to see Lord Denham settle in matrimony, Pen was depressed by this broad hint. Of late she had begun to wonder—but it was apparently not meant to be. "Oh?" she asked bluntly. "Christian has made you an offer then?"

Lady Carlisle cocked her head, which made the plumes on her black satin bonnet sway. "Shall I say I am in momentary expectation of more news?" She poked Pen's knee. "There's no need to beat around the bush, dear Lady Penelope! I know your brother has severed his connection with that Paphian girl, and high time, though the gentlemen *will* have their bits o' muslin, and their passion without delight." She laughed, rather crudely. "Do you know that the fair Delilah was once supported by a syndicate of seven ardent admirers? They pooled their money to keep her, and each was given a separate night of the week to visit. They symbolized their collective devotion by combining to present her with a magnificent dressing-table containing seven drawers!"

Pen did not like this conversation. She toyed with the fringe of her Norwich silk shawl. "You're very tolerant."

"It is merely that I understand the ways of gentlemen."
Ottolie preened. "We have *our* interests, too, do we not? So we
must grant them their *amours* and their pretty wenches, and
not begrudge them their forays among the flesh-pots."

"It is to be a marriage of convenience, then?" Pen asked
drily. Ottolie prided herself on an ability to tread unscathed
upon sacred ground.

"Lady Penelope! I hope I am too wise to engage in a love-
match! Denham and I shall suit well enough together, but
speaking of *him* was not my purpose in coming here." Had
Ottolie been endowed with more than a catty tongue—and
visage—she would have lashed her tail. "You must be prepared to hear very bad news."

"What?" It was said, rather spitefully, that the Heavenly
Vansittart Twins possessed two minds with but a single
thought, and that in Luke's head, but Pen was sufficiently
acute to know that she was being tossed about by an ill-wind
of hurricane proportions. A notorious scandalmonger, Ottolie
was big with news.

Smirking, Lady Carlisle leaned forward. "I regret that I
must be the one to tell you this, but I consider myself one of
the family! I hastened immediately to your side as soon as I
learned of Sir Jason's deceit and duplicity." It was commonly
believed that the acidity, and ceaseless activity, of Lady
Carlisle's tongue had driven *her* husband into an early grave.
"My poor Lady Penelope, you must not do violence to your
feelings! I hope I am not one to say I told you so, but you
should have expected it! Particularly from a rough diamond
like your rogue of a husband, who is incapable of resisting
any woman who wants him."

"Just *what* are you talking about?" demanded Pen. "Be
more explicit, I beg!"

Ottolie was delighted to do so. Lady Penelope looked ready
to gnash her teeth. Obviously the moment was ripe. "Then
you do not know! I feared as much, and saw my duty clear. In
short, it seems your husband is desirous of mounting a
mistress. He is often in Delilah's company." She paused to
fan herself vigorously with a highly-scented handkerchief.
"It is not at all wonderful, you know! Not even *you*, Lady
Penelope, can turn a noted profligate into a pattern-card of
respectability."

Though Pen nearly gagged on this bitter draught, she

managed to speak calmly. "What a foolish tale! Who told it to you?"

"Poor child," Ottolie murmured, with considerable malice and no small disappointment. At the very least, Lady Penelope should have swooned. "You do not wish to believe your own ears. It is true enough, I vow! I saw them myself. She was hanging on him in the most disgusting manner, which of course he doted on. He goes frequently to her dinner parties, I hear, and lingers long after the other guests have gone."

Pen silently vowed that she would *not* succumb to hysterics. The situation might not be as dire as Ottolie hinted—probably it was not—but there had to be a kernel of truth in the story. Though Lady Carlisle had a positive genius for dragging the dirty linen out of one's closet and airing it in public, even she would not make up such disclosures out of whole cloth. At the very least Jason had been seen enjoying Delilah's company, and that alone was enough to make Pen throw fits.

"Lady Penelope!" Ottolie was pitiless. "You seem in a sad way. It is very hard, of course, but console yourself with the fact that your husband is enamored of the most dazzling high-flyer in all of the town, one of such perfection that even Denham was ensnared." Her bonnet-plumes twitched and fluttered as she shook her head. "Why, one might almost say that they had conspired between them to keep the lady's favors in the family!"

Pen's laughter, though faint, was genuine. "And Luke will be next, I suppose! Forgive me, Ottolie, but you are being remarkably foolish."

"You must not stand on ceremony with me!" Lady Carlisle pursed her lips, rather like a prune. "Go ahead and cry, my dear! When your spirits are in this state it is much better to give vent to tears than to choke yourself by swallowing them."

But Pen, though undeniably a feather-brain, had a good deal of the Vansittart iron in her backbone. She drew herself up and awarded Ottolie a look so haughty—and so reminiscent of Lord Denham in the process of delivering a set-down—that her visitor's mouth fell open. "Tears?" inquired Lady Penelope. "You mistake the matter, Ottolie! Do you think me cast into the dumps by your silly *on-dits*? On the contrary, I am very much obliged to you for such an amusing tale!"

Lady Carlisle's cheeks were bright with more than rouge.

123

Pen, one arm draped gracefully along the back of the gilt sofa, was a picture of composure. "You needn't put a bold face on it for *my* benefit," Ottolie snapped. "It is perfectly evident that you are quite overset."

A liveried footman threw open the door. "Lady Sara Cainneach." Sparrow was not alone; she leaned heavily on her maid.

But Pen was in the grip of what Sir Jason fondly called a fit of bloody-mindedness and failed to notice that Sara was even paler than usual, and walked as if in pain. "Dear Ottolie," she murmured, "you are all about in your head." Serenely, she contemplated her wedding-ring. "Since we are speaking so frankly, I will tell you that I have as little reason to doubt Jason's devotion as his virility." Lady Carlisle goggled, but Pen had by no means exhausted her rage. She dropped her hand to her belly in a manner so suggestive that it would have made even her rakeshame husband stare.

This was too much for even Lady Carlisle. She was shocked to the very depths of her soul by such vulgarity. She rose majestically to her feet and drew in a deep breath, the better to discharge her last word, which she meant to carry the impact of a cannonball.

"Arragh!" snapped Bridey, for Lady Carlisle blocked the entrance. "Herself is taken faint and ye must stand there blatherin'! Get your carcase out of my way, ye great bloody cow!"

Ottolie stared dumbfounded, then pushed past them and stalked out of the room. Already she had set in effect certain inquiries concerning Lady Sara Cainneach; now she added to her black-list Lady Sara's maid.

Pen moved quickly to the window and inhaled deeply of the fresh air. She didn't know whether to laugh or cry. "Thank heaven you came when you did!" she said. "I fear I was about to engage in a brangle with that terrible woman right in the middle of my own drawing-room!"

"By all the blessed saints!" spat Bridey, and Pen quickly spun around. Sara, white as death and doubled over with pain, clung to her maid's arm. Her breath came in shallow gasps, her frail body writhed in the grip of violent convulsions.

"Mustard water!" cried Bridey, herself so ashen that her

124

freckles stood out like dabs of lamp-black. "Quickly, as ye value her life!"

Pen fled, pausing only to threaten the startled footman with his own imminent demise if he dared allow anyone else into the room. Upon her return, she and Bridey poured the nauseous mixture down Sparrow's throat, then bathed her convulsed limbs and burning brow with cool water.

At last Lady Sara grew quieter and her pulse diminished noticeably. Pen sank back on her heels and wiped a hand across her own flushed brow. "Poor Pen," murmured Sparrow. "That's the worst of it, I think." She allowed herself to be half-carried to the couch, obediently swallowed the mixture of bicarbonate of potash and chloroform that was meant to ease her retching, and with a sigh closed her eyes.

"Yerra!" muttered Bridey, and flopped gracelessly into a chair. " 'Tis dry as the bones of St. Kevin I am." The subtle hint was ignored.

Pen's own shocked stupor was wearing off; she dropped to her knees and grasped her friend's hands. "My dear!" she cried. "You must tell me what has driven you to this terrible thing."

Sparrow stared at Pen's horrified face, then burst into weak laughter that quickly became a coughing spell. "The devil!" she gasped, when the spasm was done. "What a clever beast he is. If even *you* think I meant to put a period to my existence, the world would hardly conclude otherwise."

Now Pen turned ashen, her blue eyes huge in her face. Her hands tightened and Sparrow winced with pain. "No!" breathed Pen. "You cannot mean that you have been *poisoned!*"

"She canna'?" inquired Bridey, fanning herself with the hem of her skirt. "Go away with ye, do!"

Sparrow's voice rasped in her throat. "You must tell no one, Pen, no one! Not even Mephisto."

Pen tried hard to withstand that pitiful urgency. "But you are in danger!" It was all she could think to say.

Lady Sara, however, was in no condition to argue. "Promise!" Reluctantly, Pen complied. Almost immediately Sparrow slept, but it was nothing more ominous than the deep natural slumber of exhaustion. Occasionally her thin body twitched, as if she ran from danger even in her dreams.

Pen, too, was worn to the bone, but nothing in the world could have prevented her from standing guard over her friend. It was a silent vigil shared with Bridey, whose lips were clamped as tightly shut as Lady Sara's eyes, and whose homely features were no more revealing than a rag doll.

Wearily, Pen moved to the window and leaned her forehead against the cool glass, staring blindly at the sunlit day. Who could want Sparrow dead? And why? Never had Pen felt so useless, or so alone.

Chapter 17

Friday 19 April 1811

Tayce shoved her spectacles into place and shrewdly inspected me. I wore a frock of fine cambric with muslin flounces, richly embroidered with Clarence blue, and a silk spencer with wide cuffs and lapels. The matching bonnet was finished at the edge with a double row of white-and-blue larkspur blossoms and surmounted by a full bouquet of roses. My hands and feet respectively were sheathed in yellow limerick gloves and white kid boots, and a light cashmere shawl was draped artistically around my shoulders.

"A trifle grand," observed my aunt waspishly, "for an expedition to the Royal Institute!" This was more the *ton* than anything, although I fail to understand why ladies of all ages should submit to a dreadful squeeze just to hear lectures on Human Understanding and Geology.

I met her basilisk stare—rendered even more effective by her sliding spectacles and the knitting-needles that were inexplicably stuck in her untidy hair—with girlish ingenuity. "What if I should meet with a mishap?" I inquired. "Would you want me to go to meet my Maker in any less than my best finery?"

Her expression was definitely ribald. "So you have prepared to be clasped to *Abraham's* bosom?" For some reason which my clam-like aunt refrained from telling me, she had temporarily abandoned her pothoods and hangers—which dealt currently with Paris during the Terror, when six hundred muskets were produced each day from shops set up in the gardens of the Tuileries and the Luxemborg—to install herself in Sparrow's sitting-room. "Unlikely, *petite!* Nor do I anticipate that danger awaits you in the streets. You are your own worst enemy." My aunt steadfastly refused to be convinced that I was the target of a cloak-and-dagger conspiracy. I amused myself with picturing the red-white-and-blue cockade of the Revolution affixed to her greying head.

My chaperone gave every indication of having got up on the wrong side of the bed. Her gloomy gaze lifted from some forty invitations, five or six for each day, which included such rare treats as a *soirée* at Lady Cowper's, another at Prince Polignac's and a private concert in Grosvenor Square. "You look very nice, Merrie," she said absently. "I hope you have a good time."

I thanked her. Sparrow was haggard, listless, lackluster and could only be unfavorably compared with a skeleton at the feast. But Tayce's eyes glittered wickedly, an infallible indication of mischief a-brew, and I callously abandoned my poor chaperone to the inexplicable ministrations of that Job's comforter.

It was a lovely morning, the air itself was fresh and exhilarating, and I felt as though I stood on the threshold of a new world. With soaring spirits I executed a neat and unladylike little jig on the pavement—much to the astonishment of the passers-by!—then sent my paper-skulled maid about her own business. The simpering little dunce had a face to stop a clock, but she nourished a violent *tendre* for Ninian, and would happily have accompanied me to the moon for the chance to gawk at him. She was reluctant to leave me, and argued with me in a most forward manner for the better part of three minutes, until at last going on her way very sulkily. Mephisto and I were not totally inimicable, it seemed; we shared a positive genius for making enemies!

Ninian was waiting in his tilbury. "What a happy accident!" I half-sang, and hopped up by his side. There was little danger of being observed at so unfashionably early an hour, and it would signify little if we were. Ninian's groom, a well-trained individual subject to convenient attacks of deafness, was a perfectly adequate chaperone.

"Miss Sherrington!" said Ninian, a twinkle in his grey eyes, "luck is with me today! How fortunate that we should meet in this manner, and that I am able to be of service to you."

"The luck," I retorted complacently, "is mine, sir. Already I had discovered that walking is not a pursuit for which these shoes were designed." I revealed one of those items, affording my companion an opportunity to observe its shapely contents.

The matched greys were fresh, and eager to be off, so we indulged them in a brisk trot through Hyde Park. Yet, though Ninian's conversation was as easy as ever, and his appearance so dashing that any maiden young or old must be thrilled to enjoy his company, I was not happy about him. Ninian followed with precision the pursuits of a leisured gentleman: He lounged in Bond Street and loitered in Pall Mall; he was at home in Holland House, Covent Garden and Tom Cribb's; he was a devotee of prize-fights and a follower of the Turf. Such activities took money, and I was only too aware that my feckless friend's accounts were of the most desponding cast. Nor was *I* in any position to tow him out of the River Tick!

"Where to, Miss Sherrington?" he said. "My horses, and I myself, are entirely at your service. Had you a particular destination in mind, or shall I show you some of London's less common sights?"

"The sights, by all means," I replied. "I can improve my mind some other day."

That Ninian was the very pink of perfection did not at all slake my unease. His curly-brimmed beaver could have come only from Lock's, the famous hatters in St. James's Street; his gleaming top boots had been designed by Hoby, favorite bootmaker to the *ton*. The superbly-fitting blue coat with its brass buttons, buff-colored waistcoat, buckskin breeches and drab Benjamin lined with silk bore the unmistakable stamp of Weston, Brummel's own tailor. I wondered, with sinking heart, how Ninian had come by the wherewithal to pay for his fine plumage—or if, in fact, he *had* paid for it. It would hardly advance our situation if my favored suitor was hauled into Newgate for debt!

"Ninian," I said, then stopped. No matter how great my tact, remonstration would be ill-advised. He regarded me quizzically. "We must talk." How I wish I had dared tell him of my fears! But perhaps it would have made no difference. We must all pay the piper, in the end. "I have incurred my guardian's displeasure."

"Again?" inquired Ninian. I ignored his untimely levity.

"He has threatened to exercise his authority over me, though I will spare you the details of that afflictive interview. It was cruel in the greatest degree." I gazed at my companion beseechingly. Perhaps I might involve him so completely in my own affairs that he might forego his daily dissipations. "Ninian, what are we to do?"

"Don't tease yourself." Ninian executed a sharp turn with consummate skill. "He cannot force you to marry against your wishes." We passed by a wonder-working mountebank selling packet-cures.

"No?" A sideways glance revealed faint shadows beneath those fine eyes, which roused in me an immediate desire to take that flaxen head upon my breast and soothe away all care. I considered the probable consequences—Ninian's horses would doubtless, while their master was thus happily engaged, take the opportunity to run amok among the scandalized pedestrians—and refrained. "I wish I were so sure. How progress your inquiries? Have you learned anything?"

"Nothing to any purpose." Ninian smiled at me. "Do you know, poppet, I think you have an exaggerated idea of your guardian's capabilities?"

It was a blow between the eyes. "*How* can you be so stupid?" I hissed, tempted to box his ears. "Mephisto has made it obvious that he will give no quarter! *You* were not privileged to hear his threats!" I paused to catch my breath, and Ninian eyed me with unimpaired good humor. Belatedly, I put a bridle on my tongue. "All the same, it would be a great deal easier if we could find some means to bring the wretch to heel. I doubt that even Mephisto would care to have his misdeeds published to the world."

"An astute deduction," Ninian commented reasonably, "but I have just pointed out that there is no hint of infamy in Lord Denham's past."

"Then we must find one." I was altogether displeased by this uncooperativeness. "There is always Lady Sara." At least *I* had not been altogether idle, having inveigled Lord Camden into a mock courtship with the aim of deluding both

129

Mephisto and Pen. Surely Luke was a suitor that even my guardian could not disprove! I pointedly refrained from acquainting Ninian with the reasons behind this latest stratagem.

He stopped the tilbury so that I might witness a performing bear, lately arrived from abroad, that shuffled through comic country dances and hornpipes to the accompaniment of an ill-tuned violin. I did so glumly. "You are devilish out of humor," observed my beau.

"Can you wonder at it?" I snapped, then discretely lowered my tone. "I am sick to death of the way I am told to curb my imagination when it is apparent that something havey-cavey is afoot!" I glowered at him. "Nor has it escaped my attention that you clam up like an oyster whenever I mention Sparrow's name."

But Ninian was not to be provoked into explanations. "Is that all?"

"No, it is not!" I was as imprudent as a maddened bull. "I have further noted your disinclination to discuss the matters which so concern me, and suspect a vast disinterest. Were I to hazard a conjecture, I would say that you have played fast and loose with me and now regret the commitment!"

"Are you wishful," inquired Ninian pleasantly, "of enacting me a Cheltenham tragedy? Because, my poppet, you are doing precisely that!"

I gazed upon my gloves as Ninian lifted the reins. Despite the fact that we were attracting a certain amount of public notice, I remained unsubdued. "I am *not* your poppet," I announced, with unabated wrath. "Nor am I a pigeon for anyone's plucking! If you are wishful of it, Sir Ninian, you may consider yourself relieved of any obligation to further associate with me!"

Ninian said nothing but directed his efforts to guiding us safely through the traffic around Berkeley Square. I, too, fell silent, fearing I had gone too far. Even as I consoled myself that a gazetted fortune-hunter would hardly let a plum so ripe as myself go by unplucked, I recalled Miss Allingham's avowed intentions, and battled a most vexatious urge to dissolve into tears.

We stopped outside Gunther's, the celebrated pastry-cook, and the groom sprang to hold the horses while Ninian helped me to alight. "I don't know," he said ruefully, "what gooseish notion has got into your pretty head, but I would guess it is my fault." With bated breath, I awaited further disclosures. "The truth is, Merrie, I have a great many things on my mind, not least of them this huggermugger fashion in which I must meet you, and your certainty that Mephisto will look upon me as a person unfit for association with respectable ladies, let alone eligible to seek your hand!"

"I suppose," I said meekly, as I allowed him to guide me through the crowd, "that I have behaved badly."

"Abominably." Ninian could have charmed the birds out of their trees! "You are doubtless bound for perdition, my little termagent, and I shall follow faithfully on your heels. Indeed, my devotion to you is the only virtue I can claim!" His roguish, pleading glance was expertly done. "Can you not trust me, Merrie?"

"Of course I can. I do. I will." Apparently my fervor was sufficient; Ninian grinned.

Stricken with remorse, I valiantly refrained from further questioning. In an irresistible, clownish mood, Ninian entertained me with the latest gossip concerning Prinny, reportedly engaged with religion and reading a chapter of the Bible daily in Lady Hertford's devoutly Protestant company. As I was debating whether to choose a biscuit, cake, fine or common sugar plum, or a cream or fruit ice, I felt a gentle tug on my sleeve.

Lady Randolph was a fetching vision in jaconet muslin embroidered up the front, and a cottage mantle of brown cloth lined with gold silk. Her high-crowned bonnet had long broad ribbons that crossed beneath her dainty chin. Though I was far from pleased to, in the midst of an assignation, come smack upon Adam's wife, I smiled. "A difficult choice, is it not?"

"Yes." Gabrielle glanced nervously at Ninian, who observed *her* with marked approval. Were I not granted the opportunity to reform him, this handsome rascal was doubtless destined for a strikingly successful rake's career! "Forgive me for interrupting you so rudely, but I felt you should be warned."

"Warned?" I repeated, with remarkable stupidity. "Is there something wrong with these ices?" These were fashioned from blocks of ice brought from the Greenland Sea and buried in the ground under the cellars of Berkeley Square.

131

"No, no!" Lady Randolph was justifiably exasperated by my slowness of intellect. "Not the ice, but Adam!"

"The deuce!" said Ninian. "We are indeed undone." He looked about us and began to softly whistle a jolly tune.

"I don't understand." I observed Gabrielle's anxious face with no small perplexity. "What has your husband to do with anything?"

Gabrielle flushed beet-red, but she was determined to assist in what she considered grand romance. "Adam does not hold Sir Ninian in very high esteem. I fear he will be greatly incensed if he sees you in intimate conversation with someone who he considers not quite the thing."

"Fiddlestick!" My tone was withering. "I am surprised, Lady Randolph, to hear you talking such skimble-skamble stuff!" Ninian, the toad, accorded my defense of himself a marked joviality.

"It's not *me*," Gabrielle protested. I feared sobs were imminent. "I vow I will help you all I can. But my husband's temper is terrible—you cannot know!" Finding me an unsympathetic auditor, she turned to Ninian. "Quickly, you must flee!" Clearly she expected him to leap head-first through the window and take quickly to his heels!

"Don't put yourself in a taking. Since I have done nothing exceptionable, I see no need to avoid his lordship." Ninian treated our benefactress to a dazzling smile. Abruptly that smile faded as he gazed over my head. "Anyway, it is too late."

Chapter 18

A Pretty Kettle of Fish

Mme. Dore scolded her niece up hill and down dale, concluding with a particularly vituperative malediction to the effect that the hell-born brat should be returned to the nether regions straightaway. Tayce's self-imposed task as chronicler to the archives of history was not being fulfilled apace with her intention, due entirely to the exasperating Miss Sherrington. Mme. Dore had no objection to fighting her own battles over again for the edification of posterity, but that particular war for independence was ended, the spilled blood long since soaked into the ground. Now Merrie had contrived that Mme. Dore must once more unsheathe her sword and leap headlong into the thick of the fray.

Miss Sherrington had taken to revolution with as much fervor as the most avid *sans-culotte*. Upon being requested by Lord Randolph to defend her conduct, Merrie had uttered several vehemous oaths, struck in a most agitated manner upon the Holy Book, and vowed that she had done all in her power to please everyone concerned. With her opponent temporarily rendered speechless, Miss Sherrington further announced that, since her exemplary efforts had met with so little appreciation, she intended to withdraw altogether from Society. Having, in this daring manner, thoroughly trounced the foe, she retired, crowned with victorious laurels, from the battlefield. But Tayce was better versed in the subtleties of warfare. She knew that only a minor skirmish had been won, and not the entire campaign.

She sighed and rose, leaning heavily on her cane. Even Mme. Dore could not ignore a summons from her host. She cast a last regretful glance at her current unfinished chapter—a caustic vilification of Joseph Fouché, Napoleon's dreaded minister of police, who had ridden full gallop to one celebrated massacre with a pair of human ears stuck one on each side of his hat—and limped slowly to the door.

"And *furthermore,*" announced Miss Sherrington, who in the privacy of her chambers was unburdening herself to, of all people, Lady Sara Cainneach, "it may be gratifying to be so sought after by the *gens du monde,* but I can summon up no joy at the prospect of attending yet another ludicrous rout! One can hardly find standing room on the staircase, and is pushed and shoved and kept for hours in a hothouse temperature! Thank you, but I prefer to remain at home, and let the world think what they will—and what they'll probably think is that Mephisto has murdered me, which is no more than he deserves!"

"Oh, dear," said Sparrow, weakly.

Tayce adroitly avoided that particular doorway and proceeded down the stair. In the hallway she surprised the new housekeeper, who flushed and went quickly on her way. Truly a *ménage extraordinaire*, thought Tayce, with all of them spying on one another, and only *le bon Dieu* knew where it would end. As Maeve had before her, Mme. Dore applied her ear to the drawing-room door.

"A fine vulgar miss!" said Lord Randolph grimly, and Tayce frowned. It could only be he. "She needs to be taught a good lesson, by God! And I'm tempted to administer it myself."

"Must I remind you," inquired Mephisto in silky tones, "that Miss Sherrington was left in my sole care? Over her fortune you may exercise some control; over her person you exercise none." And as well, added Tayce silently, though she didn't trust the Duke even a fraction of an inch. There was pleasure, however dangerous, in honing one's wits against a foe as cunning as Mephisto; but Adam had already committed a cardinal error of strategy.

Lord Randolph voiced an obscenity. "You would be better advised," added Mephisto, "to confine your attention to Parliament. Think how ingenious the French chemists have proven, meeting the British exclusions by transforming beetroot into sugar, woad into dyes and potatoes into brandy! Surely my ward isn't a more interesting prospect than the complexities of government?" This kindly advice was met by a snarl. Tayce held her breath, hoping Lord Randolph would take umbrage and return post-haste to Westminster, thus sparing her a confrontation with the man.

"I suppose," snapped Adam, "that you think you are playing some deep game! You may find yourself incapable of extricating yourself without the most serious injury."

"Adam!" Lord Denham sounded amused. "That sounded suspiciously like a threat—but of course I know you cannot have intended such." What wizardry is this? mused Mme. Dore. He reads men's minds, as well as the rest? "I cannot tolerate further interference in my affairs. Already you may have done considerable harm."

"I hope I have!" Lord Randolph retorted. "Your Miss Sherrington has proven such an unsuitable influence on my wife that I have had to remonstrate with Gabrielle."

"Ah, yes. I will concede that Meredith is a trifle lacking in the ladylike arts, but her upbringing has been unconventional." Ladylike arts! Tayce fumed. A singular waste of time, this British preoccupation with entering rooms gracefully, exchanging nougats of conversation and pouring tea!

"Too," added Mephisto, "the girl possesses a great number of half-baked ideas." In the hallway, the oven in which those notions had cooked threatened to explode. "Your wife, however, has proven an excellent companion for my ward. I believe we shall not interfere with their friendship. Or do you mean Gabrielle to have no acquaintances near her own age, to content herself with your sole company?"

Adam veered off on another tack. "You have made an odd choice of chaperone. It seems that Lady Sara's understanding is not great—or perhaps you had a reason for choosing a light-minded female, one who would encourage your ward to make a by-word of herself?"

There was no doubt of it; Mephisto was enjoying the exchange. "Fustian, Adam! Next you will accuse Meredith of being an atheist and an immoral woman." Mme. Dore, who was one and had in her time been the other, considered exposing to Lord Denham the rough side of her tongue.

Lord Randolph's voice was cold. "The girl's religious convictions do not particularly interest me. As to the other, you have permitted her to behave in a manner that is most reprehensible. We shall be fortunate if her husband-to-be does not find himself in the unpalatable position of bargaining for spoiled goods." What a prig he sounded, with his strict adherence to *les convenances*, his jealous concern with the irreproachable conduct of his innocent child bride.

"As I have said before," Mephisto replied indifferently, "Meredith's comportment is none of your concern. I assure you the matter may be safely left in my hands."

"Nevertheless," Adam's frustration was evident, "I do not mean to do so." More fool you, thought Mme. Dore. Better men have danced to Mephisto's tune. "*Damned* if I can fathom your purpose!"

Seizing the moment, Tayce threw open the door. Both men turned as, greying hair wildly astraggle, she limped heavily into the room. She settled on the ancient sofa, adjusted her spectacles, and took up her knitting.

"Adam," said Mephisto, in the tones of one who expects to be well-entertained, "let me make you known to Meredith's aunt, Mme. Dore."

"Enchanté!" lied Tayce, concentrating on her needles, which were disastrously entangled in the yarn. Lord Randolph was precisely as she had expected him to be, a cold and cruel-looking man whose exalted position in the world would not hinder him from going to any lengths to have his own way.

Adam stared. Tayce fancied she didn't fit his preconceived notions of Miss Sherrington's scholarly reclusive aunt. She smiled to herself as she grasped the needles. Mme. Dore had in her lifetime played many *rôles;* and it was ironic in the extreme that this, of them all, should prove the most challenging, the most difficult to sustain. How Merrie would stare to learn that her spinsterish aunt longed sometimes to cast aside her spectacles and take down her hair and leave Denham House behind for the unspeakable excitements of London's teeming underworld! But Tayce was a realist. The face that looked out of her mirror was not the same face that once held royalty in thrall. Time's harsh passage was the price of her misdeeds. No matter. Tayce gazed upon her ink-stained hands, inelegant, unlovely now—but those hands had once been kissed by a king of France. Mme. Dore might take only memory to share her cold bed, but the years that had stolen her beauty had left her aspirations, and her wit.

Lord Randolph's eyes narrowed, and his nostrils flared as if filled with an unpleasant scent. "I regret, madam," he retorted rudely, "that the occasion prevents me from returning the sentiment."

Tayce had always enjoyed a challenge. She removed her spectacles, polished them on the hem of her gown, replaced them, and peered at Adam intently. "Could you have visited France during the Terror, *monsieur?* I see in you something very familiar."

"Never, madam." His outrage, at least, was sincere.

"A pity," murmured Tayce, at her most provocative. "You would have enjoyed it vastly, I conjecture. The Revolutionary Tribunal issued death sentences at a rate of seven per day." She shrugged, and turned business-like. *"Enfin!* It does not signify. A clever rascal, *that* one was, with the curious facility of exhibiting himself as a perfect gentleman or a perfect blackguard." There! she thought. Another small victory. "Now explain to me, if you please, the reason for this contretemps."

Lord Randolph looked ready to breathe fire. "You ask that,

madam?" His tone was sulfurous. "It should be obvious. A lady's reputation resides not in what she does, but in what she may be considered to have done, and the most trifling indiscretion may be sufficient to bring total ruin."

This one dared lecture *her?* Tayce leaned forward, intent. "*What* indiscretion, pray? Is my niece to be surrounded by duennas each time she speaks to a young man?" Mephisto casually inhaled a pinch of snuff, a glint in his cold eye.

"One can only assume," Adam retorted, "that you are not familiar with the extents to which a fortune-hunter may go. Would you wish to see your niece abducted, forced into marriage? It is not an unlikely contingency." No one could doubt that he found this entire matter—and his interrogator—extremely distasteful.

Mme. Dore had always liked a rogue, and had known more than her share. "I would prefer," she was blunt, "not to see my niece wed at all. But you will not care to hear *those* views!" Mephisto's eyes narrowed. "Your interest in Merrie seems excessive, Lord Randolph. Why should my family be of such concern to you?"

Adam flushed. "Young Northcliffe is the last person in the world to be a suitable companion for a young lady of Miss Sherrington's lineage and wealth. His prospects are practically non-existent. No one with proper feeling could help but be concerned."

"And no one but a proper fool would dare to interfere." Tayce didn't believe for an instant that he practiced what he preached, this upright gentleman. "You are making mountains out of molehills. In what way did you expect the boy to harm her? To ravish her in the midst of Gunther's Confectionary?" She shook her head in emphatic disgust and neatly caught her spectacles as they tumbled off the end of her nose. "Pah! *Had* you been in Paris during the Terror, you would know that preventing people from meeting in public only encourages them to do so secretly."

A number of emotions crossed Lord Randolph's face, none of which could be clearly described. Tayce saw anger, frustration, even a faint and grudging admiration. "You are overwrought," she said. "Perhaps we should postpone this discussion until some more propitious time."

"Further discussion is pointless." Lord Randolph prepared

to leave. "Do not think, either of you, that you have heard the last of me."

As the door slammed behind him, Tayce settled back on the sofa with the air of one who does not mean to be easily evicted. "Excessive concern, *n'est-ce pas?*" she observed to Lord Denham, "for a girl whom he apparently holds in such poor esteem?"

Mephisto returned her regard, but retaliated with a question of his own. "Tell me, Mme. Dore, just what is your opinion of this?"

Tayce leaned her head to one side, the better to study him. Despite those eyes that were as chill as if he had once glimpsed heaven and would no more, Lord Denham was not without a certain charm. "A tempest in a teapot," she retorted. "My niece is no fool."

"And young Northcliffe?" Mephisto settled opposite her in an oval-backed chair, prepared to journey through the dim labyrinth of Tayce's mind. He would not, decided the lady, have an easy time of it.

"I am not in Merrie's confidence." Mme. Dore was not one to suffer guilt over a slight equivocation. She tapped a foot upon the floor. "I can tell you that the surest way to insure my niece desires something is to forbid it to her. Her feelings are already so agitated upon this subject that to forbid her to see Sir Ninian again would be worse than a crime, it would be a colossal blunder." She paused, but Mephisto remained silent. "Come, *mon ami*, I have been frank with you! In turn, you will acquaint me with the reason for Lord Randolph's dark mutterings."

The cold eyes assessed her shrewdly, but Tayce did not flinch. She had survived worse inquisitions, including the one that left her lame. Mephisto inclined his head slightly, as if he had expected no less. "It is true that he seemed familiar to you?"

Still she held his gaze. "A chance resemblance, nothing more." Cathedral bells could have chimed with no more profound sincerity.

Lord Denham did not persevere, but instead regarded his enamelled snuff-box. He was expert in the art of moistening, mixing and blending snuff, and as noted a connoisseur as the Regent, whose snuff-cellar, worth thousands of pounds, was superintended by his Chief Page, assisted by periodic visits of inspection by Messrs. Fribourg and Treyer. "I understand that you are a student of history, Mme. Dore?"

Tayce sniffed. A student? Mme. Dore had seen history made! She had known them all: the pock-marked Robespierre, once loved by the people of Paris but still fated for the guillotine; Louis-Antoine Saint-Just, *enfant terrible* of the Revolution, who wrote an erotic poem in twenty cantos celebrating rape, especially of nuns, and followed Robespierre to death; Danton, popular with the Parisians, who lost his life when he dared suggest the Terror had gone too far; Charlotte Corday, who killed Marat with a kitchen knife because she considered him responsible for the September Massacres, when hearts were torn from corpses and eaten by fervent republicans. "You know I am."

"So I heard." Considering that ever since Tayce's arrival the Duke's library was declared off-limits even to him, it is little wonder that his tone was wry. "Then you are aware that history has an odd tendency to repeat itself."

"I am aware," snapped Tayce, who had no patience with this sort of parrying, and furthermore had appearances to maintain, "as so many of you English are not, that conditions here are little better than they were prior to the Revolution in France. You have a starving population, an overwhelming debt, impoverished landholders, bankrupt traders—and fine balls at the Regent's." She thought of the French monarch who had not only taken seven years to consummate his marriage, but allowed his gay queen to meddle in matters of state; and of the mobs who stormed through Paris armed with swords and knives, clubs and pikes. "You British were ever fools!"

Mephisto gave voice to his rare laughter. "Do you predict that we, too, will have a Revolution? If so, I trust you are mistaken, Mme Dore."

"I predict nothing." Tayce was again in a ravaged France, watching the triumphant *sans-culottes* parading past her window, bearing aloft severed heads on bloody poles. "Surely you do not mean to recount to me the lessons learned from the past."

"No," Mephisto replied. "I mean to relate to you a particular history—that of Adam St. Erth."

"Eh bien!" Had he drunk from some sorcerer's cup, this Duke with a dead-man's stare? How much could those pale

139

eyes see? No stranger to illusion, Tayce wove a counter-spell. She adjusted her spectacles and took up her knitting once again, a comfortable and innocuous grandmotherly figure of indeterminable years. "Proceed."

"Adam was a younger son, with few prospects and even less fortune of his own, and as is customary in this country was set for a military career." Mephisto's sole purpose might have been her enlightenment, so congenial was his manner, but Tayce was not so easily deceived. "Then came the death of his elder brother, in a freak carriage accident. Since the Earl, though recently wed, remained childless, Adam inherited the title. He resigned from his regiment and returned to England to take up the duties of a peer of the realm."

Mme. Dore muttered an uncomplimentary comment concerning lordly responsibilities, and the Duke raised a quizzical brow. "That was in seventeen ninety-four." Industriously knitting, Tayce felt his sharp gaze. "A few years later, Adam in turn chose a bride, slightly older and a great deal more worldly than Gabrielle."

"Each to his own taste," commented Tayce, with a Gallic shrug. "What happened to the girl?"

"Astute of you," Mephisto murmured, "to have realized he did not marry her. The betrothal was announced, and all was on the way to being settled, with the prospective Lady Randolph seemingly quite content with her future lot." He waited.

"And?" Impatient, Tayce brandished the knitting-needles in a threatening way.

"And she left him at the altar, so to speak, to run off with a penniless ne'er-do-well." Lord Denham took snuff.

Tayce was strongly tempted to stab her tormentor. The devil certainly knew how to spin out a tale! "Why?"

"Ah, *that* no one knows." Deftly, he flicked closed the snuff-box. "The young lady was promptly disowned by her family, and no word of her reached London again. You can understand that it was a bitter experience for a man of Adam's pride."

"I still do not see," growled Mme. Dore, "what this has to say to the present case. Do you deliberately pose me a conundrum?" Already she had reached a number of conclusions, and damnably inconvenient ones. "Is it that Lord Randolph expects Merrie to behave like that other young woman

140

and elope? Utter foolishness! Believe me, my niece harbors no thought of such a thing."

"It is not your niece's thoughts that concern us, but Adam's." It was as if he urged her towards some particular conclusion, and found her progress tediously slow.

So he expected her to be frustrated? Tayce obligingly ground her teeth. "I have already told you that they will not elope. What then? Does Lord Randolph expect that Sir Ninian will demand a sum of money to relinquish all claim to Merrie's hand? This grows more and more absurd! Why should Lord Randolph so distrust this young man, of whom it seems the *worst* that can be said is that he is not wealthy? It is most unreasonable!"

"I have not said," Lord Denham pointed out gently, "that Adam is a reasonable man. His distrust is not so much of Sir Ninian as it is of the Northcliffe way of doing things. Even now he has not forgiven Daphne for making him an object of ridicule."

It was a moment that called forth consummate skill. Mme. Dore closed her mouth, which she had allowed to fall open, and once more adjusted her spectacles. *"Mon Dieu!"* she said, no more dismally than she felt. "A relation, I comprehend?"

"Yes." Mephisto savored some immense private amusement. "Of particularly close degree."

Chapter 19

Saturday 20 April 1811

Even now it amazes me that one's life can be turned upside-down, and almost abruptly terminated, within the space of a few short weeks. Never did I think that I would be forced to such expedients and shifts, surrounded as it were by madmen and villains and very nearly doomed to perish in my own intrigues! But the voice of conscience prompts me to cease playing on the heart-strings of my reader—even if it be a veritable symphony of tantalizing point and counterpoint worthy of the great Beethoven!—so let the tale proceed.

"Your *what?*" I cried, with more astonishment than tact. It must have been years since the dingy drawing-room had seen such frequent use.

Ninian sat beside me on the hideous old sofa. He might have been seated on a pincushion, so acute was his unease. "My sister," he repeated patiently. "Daphne. She was several years older than I."

"Was?" Enthroned in an oval-backed chair, Lady Sara played the role of chaperone with excessive benevolence. Due to the combined efforts of Sparrow and my aunt, Mephisto had conceded that association with Ninian would do me little harm—and that any of them were concerned with either my wishes or my hopes, I took leave to doubt!

"You didn't tell me you had a sister." I fear I sounded sulky, for Sparrow shot me an admonishing glance and Ninian made a quickly-checked movement. Soothed by a conviction that he had meant to take me in his arms, I added with considerably more grace, "Will you tell us about her?"

"Yes," agreed Sparrow, eyeing her needlework as critically as an artist with an embryonic masterpiece, "please do. I confess myself positively fascinated by what Mephisto told Mme. Dore."

While Sparrow kept her diligent vigil, Tayce was once again barricaded in the library, making verbal mincemeat of the fearsome Fouché. Only Mephisto was absent: His Satanic Majesty had gone with Sir Jason to the Mansion House, official residence of the Lord Mayor. Mephisto's easy capitulation had increased both my mistrust of him and my conviction that he and Sparrow shared some perilous secret. How I would have loved to learn that she was his *chère amie*, some low-born bit o' muslin masquerading as a Ladyship, for with so dangerous a weapon I might have held them both at bay.

"There is not a great deal to tell." Ninian stretched out his long muscular legs in their skin-tight breeches, and my pulse rattled into rat-a-tat-tattoo percussion, while my heart thumped like a big bass drum. "Daphne was betrothed to St. Erth before she was even officially out. It was thought no small triumph."

"To so quickly snare one of London's most eligible bache-lors?" Idly I pleated my white muslin dress. "I should think. How did it come about?" Sparrow's quick sharp needle flickered in and out of her sampler, trailing strands of colored silk.

"Are you imagining Randolph with a broken heart?" Ninian's grey eyes twinkled at me. "You must be disappointed, then. St. Erth and my father arranged the thing between them and then informed Daphne. She balked a bit at first, but then seemed to come around."

I pondered upon the perfidy of fathers and their lamentable inclination to meddle in the lives of their offspring. "It is not unusual," Sparrow said quietly. "No doubt your father thought he was doing the best possible thing. As Lady Randolph, your sister would have both position and wealth—the very things, in fact, to which most young women aspire." She looked at me and smiled, I thought with genuine affection. Had my loathing of Adam's high-handed manner disposed her kindly towards me? It made me wonder at her even more.

"When did she change her mind?" I asked. Ninian still watched Sparrow, apparently mesmerized by her flashing needle and deft hands. My beloved had an eye for the ladies—first Gabrielle and now my chaperone!—and a potential for profligacy rivalled only by Sir Jason. I contemplated embarking upon a bloody series of *crimes passionel.*

"No one knew she had." Ninian toyed with his curly-brimmed hat. "Even I suspected nothing amiss, though Daphne was in the habit of confiding in me, despite our difference in age. One day she was peacocking it over the other young ladies—all of them were green with envy—and the next she was gone." His somber expression wrenched my heart. "We were frantic. My father ordered the countryside searched, and then we had a letter saying she'd eloped."

"But *why?*" I demanded. 'Twas the crux of the matter, it seemed. Even Sparrow seemed affected by this sad tale; her slender fingers paused in their work.

"She did not explain." Ninian's tone was bitter. "Nor can I explain her behavior, though an accounting of her reasons would have made all the difference. My father was not unjust, he would not have forced her to wed St. Erth if the man was so repugnant to her. Yet Daphne voiced no objections. She simply ran away."

"Perhaps," said Sparrow gently, "there were reasons she

could not explain. Sometimes, when one is very young, one finds oneself in situations so overwhelming that it seems simplest just to flee." I liked her better in that moment than I ever had, for she obviously sought to ease the pain of an old tragedy, and I wished I might wring the young Daphne's neck for behaving so inconsiderately. It occurred to me that I was not normally motivated by thoughtfulness for others and probably was no less selfish than Ninian's sister had been—a *most* lowering reflection!

"And is it," inquired Ninian, still with that sober air, "easier to flee?"

"Of course not." Sparrow bent once more over her work. "But that realization comes only with time."

Here I was, a diamond of the first water, and for all the attention Ninian paid me I might as well have been an antidote! "What was she like, this sister of yours?" I asked, and at last he turned to me.

"As much of a minx as you yourself." He tweaked one of my dark curls. "And every bit as beautiful, though taller and with hair as light as mine. The gentlemen flocked around Daphne from the day she first smiled, and she accepted it as her just due—yet she was never unkind to anyone. That made her behavior towards St. Erth even the odder, for there is no denying she treated him very badly. I cannot fault Lord Randolph for bearing a grudge against the Northcliffe name."

"Perhaps not, but *I* can." I plumped a pillow viciously. "She may have behaved badly, but *you* are not to blame!"

Sparrow frowned at us. "Perhaps there were also reasons for her behavior towards St. Erth. Have you considered that? It sounds uncommonly like she was afraid of the man." I wondered what, in Sparrow's past, led to this odd championship of someone unknown. Had she, too, eloped? I was so close to the truth then, and still so very far away!

"She should have told us." Ninian was not to be chastised. "We would have understood."

"Who was this man she ran off with?" I asked quickly. Sparrow at best was an uncertain ally, and it was hardly advantageous that she should quarrel with Ninian.

Ninian shrugged. "A penniless wastrel. He was among her admirers, but I never paid much heed. Nor, I thought, did Daphne, but of course she must have been meeting him secretly for some time."

144

Sparrow's lips tightened, and I plunged hastily ahead. "And your father disowned her. What happened to your sister, Ninian? Do you know?"

"How could I? My father not only disowned Daphne, he forbade any mention of her name. I have for years thought of my sister as dead." Never had I seen him look so grave. "I can only suppose it is what she wishes, since she has never sent me word."

"But, Ninian!" I cried, clutching his sleeve. "Perhaps she truly *is* dead, and has been all along. And you think so ill of her! How terrible."

He looked at me and blinked, as if slowly returning to the here and now. "No, my poppet." His warm gaze caressed my face. "I am certain she is not. But Daphne is a thing of the past. Can we not speak of more important matters?"

"Of course," I whispered, tingling from head to toe, then discovered Sparrow had sympathetically slipped from the room. "Oh, Ninian, I have been so worried!"

He, too, realized we were alone and drew me closer. "Why, Merrie? Surely you did not think I would allow anyone to separate me from you."

"I didn't know what to think." My head rested most comfortably against his chest. "Perhaps the shifts we are put to may become tiresome, may lower me in your esteem." I cannot explain my gooseishness, unless the uncertainty I was in had deranged my ideas.

"Merrie!" Ninian hugged me to him tightly. Vulnerability brings its own reward! "As if I care a groat for any inconvenience, save that it has cut up your peace." He released me and applied his handkerchief to my damp cheeks. "Tell me, have you been so very unhappy? Shall I speak to Mephisto?"

I shook my head violently and took hold of my emotions, which were of late seething in a most turbulent and capricious way. "I was catechised and sermonized for quite an hour by St. Erth—he even sent Gabrielle home alone so that he might bully me without restraint!—but Mephisto seems to think it all a hum." More likely my infernal guardian thought it a fine opportunity to annoy St. Erth! I wadded the handkerchief into a crumpled ball, but Ninian intervened before I could hurl it into a corner. "He has no notion of the true state of things, of course. Despite his forebearance in this instance, Mephisto is hardly likely to bestow upon you my hand."

145

Ninian rose and pulled me to my feet. "Nor will he be pleased if he walks in to find us alone like this." All too briefly, he clasped me in his arms. "I must go, poppet, but don't fear. We are closer to success than you may think."

Ninian clearly possessed an optimistic soul! I conquered an urge to throw my arms around his neck with the fervor of a drowning man. My beloved was already over head and ears in debt and I did not mean to be a fatal encumbrance. In subdued silence, I accompanied him to the door.

With a residue of the new-found—and short-lived—humility inspired by Ninian's account of his sister's sins, I made my way to Sparrow's chambers. All I sought was distraction from the persistent vision of my beloved languishing in debtors' prison. It was *not*, at least on this occasion, my intention to eavesdrop, and I had already entered the ante-room before I realized that my chaperone was not alone. I hesitated—unusual behavior, perhaps, but whatever her reasons Sparrow had been kind to me, and I was loath to abuse her confidence.

"Oh, Maeve! If only we could go home." Conscience bid a quick *adieu* as I moved closed to the bedroom door.

Mrs. Selkirk's arm was around Sparrow's shoulders—no small liberty for a housekeeper! "Hush, my honey, do!" she crooned, and smoothed Sparrow's hair. "Would *you* turn tail and run? Whist, now, what would Paddy say to that!" I hoped she might elucidate; I was agog to know! "Your conscience has been plaguing you sorely all this time. Do what you must, and see an end to it! Paddy would wish it so."

Stunned by sudden realization, I sank plump into a chair. Mephisto's housekeeper had known Sparrow's husband?

"Paddy's death was my fault, Maeve." Sparrow's voice was husky. "You know it as well as I." Luke's tale was true, then? How could Sparrow blame herself? But Maeve was speaking again.

"Welladay! Will you be taking on your shoulders the evil of all men? Was Paddy one to die of old age in his bed?" Her tone was brisk. "Faith, no! Paddy was a rascal and a rogue, and he would've doubtless swung from the hang-man's rope had he not met up with you. Instead, he gained a greater fortune than he ever dreamed of, and died a gentleman. Is it for making him wealthy that you would blame yourself?"

146

These disclosures were coming at all too rapid a rate! Sparrow wasn't poor? Had she deliberately deceived Mephisto?

"I blame myself," my chaperone repeated, "for his death." *How,* I thought frantically. "Do not seek to deny it, Maeve, for you know you cannot. Dublin was entirely my idea."

Dublin? And *who,* I almost shouted, was this Maeve? Why was she here, in Denham House, serving in a menial capacity? "Now," added Sparrow glumly, "I've involved both Bridey and you."

"Paddy knew," Maeve retorted, with a hint of exasperation, "the risks he took. He was a gambler, *acushla!* The curse was in his blood." Sparrow sniffled, and Mrs. Selkirk continued in gentler tones. "You must know that Bridey would follow you to the end of the earth, no matter how sternly you ordered her to remain at home. And should *I* sit snugly by while you rush into danger? 'Twould haunt me till the end of my days."

"Oh, Maeve." Sparrow had grown more composed. *I* certainly had not! "I fear I've made a grave error. It would have been much better, perhaps, to let sleeping dogs lie."

"Dogs, perhaps," Maeve retorted, "but murder? 'Tis too late now to flee. Even in Ireland you would not be safe. You must stay and see justice done."

"It's more likely," Sparrow murmured, "that I'll see my grave." High melodrama, I thought, and in so doing misjudged the lady yet once again. But one with her secretive nature cannot expect not to be misunderstood!

Maeve, however, took Sparrow more seriously. "I fear for your safety, little one. Why will you not seek Lord Denham's protection? You came here at his bidding—why can you not trust the man?"

"If I laid the truth before him, do you think he would believe it? Could anyone?" Sparrow's laughter was bitter. "You have it backwards, Maeve. I have known Mephisto all my life, and it is he who cannot trust me."

I was to learn no more. Tayce stood in the hallway glowering at me.

Chapter 20

A Spanner in the Works

"So Lord Randolph doesn't care for you, Sir Ninian!" Fanny smirked. Unlike Miss Sherrington, no one would haul *her* over the coals for riding in Sir Ninian Northcliffe's snug and sporting curricle! Fanny knew a great deal about Miss Sherrington's affairs—Merrie's blockish maid could talk the hindquarters off a donkey when her tongue was loosened by a draught of gin—and Miss Allingham fancied she'd flattened her opponent as effectively as with a battering-ram. "Well, never mind! Play your cards right and you may yet make a recovery, Sir Ninian."

"Lord Randolph's opinion," Ninian replied repressively, "is of little consequence." He still didn't understand how he had been maneuvered into squiring Miss Allingham about the town. It was as if the young lady meant to overpower him and take possession of him quite by force, much as Lady Hamilton had conquered Lord Nelson.

Fanny was impossible to snub. "In *your* position, my lad, everyone's opinion matters! Don't think I don't know you're under the hatches, down to your last cent."

Ninian had, several times during the past hour, had recourse to his pocket handkerchief, and now once again applied it to his damp brow. This platter-faced female had the most peculiar manners, never sitting quiet, from time to time stamping her foot, laughing a great deal and talking still more. To set the seal to his discomfort, her intentions regarding himself were becoming appallingly clear.

Despite her countless shortcomings, Fanny did not lack understanding. "I believe in the word with no bark on it! You'll get used to my little ways." Like it or no, she added silently. Sir Ninian would soon be as neatly trussed up as a

148

bullock at branding-time, and she meant to lead him to the altar by the ring in his nose. With the intention of thwarting a stampede for freedom, she soothed him with the familiar tittle-tattle so dear to young gentlemen of the town: to wit, an account of a recent party at the Military Academy which ended with the Regent, the Duke of York and the Sovereign Prince of Orange collapsing drunkenly under the dining-room table.

The London streets were crowded with people and vehicles of every description, low-slung landaus with varnished, polished sides; coaches and tilburies; dowagers' laudalets. There were butchers in high dogcarts, milkmen in pony-drawn carts laden with big churns. Bakers carried bread in large covered baskets. Muffin men, with trays on their heads, rang handbells as they plied their wares from door to door. Street cries mingled with a barrel organ's tinkling tunes. A gypsy sitting on the kerb, recaning the seat of a chair, laughed raucously as a mail coach narrowly avoided collision with the Regent's state carriage, and liberally splattered a footman's magnificent scarlet livery with mud. Fanny craned her head, the better to see it all, never staunching her geyser of words.

Ninian's civility, if not his pocketbook, was sufficient proof of his breeding: He maintained his courteous manner even under not-inconsiderable duress. Ninian had not yet recovered from the previous evening's debauch when, flown with insolence and wine, he had engaged himself in a phaeton race which unfortunately became metamorphosed into a competition for repeating by heart the longest possible ode of Homer. Alas, Ninian handled the classics with far less skill than he did the reins! There was nothing for so severe a disappointment but to drown one's sorrows in further drink, and nothing more pleasant when thus in one's cups than to stake bold wagers on the board of green cloth. Again, alas. Somehow, during the course of the long night, what had begun as libations to Bacchus turned into ceremonial slaughter, with Ninian the victim. Merrie had not been far off the mark when she accused him of burning the candle at both ends.

"Do you like the city?" Fanny turned on him with clumsy playfulness. Lord, but she was a cock-a-hoop, and Ninian didn't dare think why. She was full of compliments—laying them on with a trowel, in fact, with none of his blushes spared.

149

"It is well enough," Ninian replied cautiously. "As is the country. I have no real preference." He was in the very odd and unenviable position of having a young lady pay him court, smothering him with arch affection, clinging to his arm, and fluttering her eyelashes at him constantly. Under *different* circumstances—if the damsel beside him had been small and mischievous and green-eyed, for example—such attentions might have sent Ninian to cloud-cuckoo land.

Fanny smiled, a monstrous exercise in coyness which inspired her companion with a grave foreboding that any moment Miss Allingham would offer—nay, demand!—to bestow her favors on him. "My da' has considerable property in Kent, Shropshire and Cornwall. He also owns four mansions here in London alone." There was no other word for it: She swaggered, even sitting down. "A regular nabob he is, and as knaggy an old gager as you might ever wish to see."

"How nice for you," replied Ninian politely. He had no desire whatsoever to make the acquaintance of the elder Allingham, a gentleman by birth who was so careless of his position that he had set out to make a fortune in trade and had succeeded beyond all decency. Now Allingham meant to marry his daughter into the aristocracy that he had scorned; and, thought Ninian, in spite of Fanny's dowdy looks and atrocious manners, the old man would probably succeed.

"Yes, it is." Fanny displayed what was for her a remarkable subtlety. "I am always plump in the pocket, you know, and can waste the ready as I please. My da' is very openfisted," she chortled. "A far cry from Miss Sherrington, I'll wager! Denham will keep her short of funds, no matter how wealthy she may be, or I'm no judge of character!"

In truth, Fanny had a good head on her shoulders, for all it was not especially pleasant to look upon; and was quick to turn the subject when a frown appeared on Sir Ninian's noble brow. High in the instep, was he, and mighty touchy on the subject of Miss Sherrington? Fanny rather admired Merrie, and certainly meant her no harm. However, she also wished to add Ninian to her collection of exotic playthings. Miss Allingham no more doubted that this request would be granted than she thought the moon was made of green cheese.

"Look!" she said, pointing in an underbred manner to a group of half-starved, shabby men who stood on a street corner arguing angrily. "Do you know who they are? Merchants'

150

clerks, I'll vow, who've lost their places because their masters have gone bankrupt. For this you can thank that curst Napoleon! He's almost destroyed our foreign trade, and the Custom House duties are reduced upwards of one-half." Ninian turned a startled face towards her and she chuckled. "Didn't I say my da' was a damned knowing one? *He*'ll take no harm from the blockade, no matter if an entire army of customs men keep watch on the coasts, and the ports swarm with spies!" For once, her voice dropped to a reasonable volume. "Nor are any of *his* goods publicly seized and burnt to the accompaniment of martial music and in the presence of local magistrates!"

Sir Ninian's eye bore a glazed expression, and he barely avoided running smack over a vehemently-protesting pedestrian. Smuggling, was it? It was not particularly surprising that the elder Allingham was engaged in such a profitable side-line—by all accounts, the old man was thoroughly unscrupulous in any matter regarding finance—but Ninian was surprised that Fanny should so boldly gloat about these nefarious activities. He wondered if it was just Lyons silk and Valenciennes lace that Allingham smuggled into England, or whether his illegal endeavors included the transportation of French spies.

Having cleverly engaged her intended's interest, Fanny was in high gig. "I shall tell you a secret," she confided, "my da' is to be knighted for his services to the crown." There was little need to add that these services had been financial, a temporary easing of the difficulties engendered by the Regent's extravagant tastes and empty treasuries. "It will have to wait till next year, but that's time enough! He may even enter public life and begin his own collection of blue and scarlet ribbons, glittering orders and strawberry leaves." She wondered if she need further dwell upon the obvious rewards of an alliance with herself.

"What are your father's politics?" This seemed a fairly innocuous topic. Ninian's vision of the elder Allingham wreaking havoc in government circles was staggering.

Fanny's grasp of the political world was considerable for a female, and she was not at all loath to elucidate. "Tory, of course. Did you think him a Whig, his brain aswim with ideals of emancipating Roman Catholics and slaves and reforming Parliament? Not he!" Her protuberant eyes gleamed.

151

"I think him admirably equipped to government. He would be excellent at raising levies and forcing through the penal taxation necessary to continue the war."

The amusing side of the conversation struck Ninian, the ironic ambiguity of a man who with one hand raised money and provisions for Wellington to wage war against the French, and with the other smuggled in enemy contraband. Misinterpreting his sudden smile, Miss Allingham snuggled up to him.

From a certain other heiress, Ninian would have welcomed this familiarity; from Fanny he did not. Thus it was with barely-suppressed relief that he drew up in front of The Temple of the Muses, John Lackington's bookshop in Finsbury Square, so that Miss Allingham might procure a copy of *Udolpho;* and with a face of perfect horror that he observed the approach of a familiar carriage.

Fanny surveyed the barouche—a vehicle in the first stare of fashion, with space for four passengers within and two outside—with no similar dismay. Instead, an expression of sublime vindication settled on her plain features, and she nodded grandly at Lord Camden, Lady Penelope and Lady Randolph. Now Miss Sherrington was sure to hear of this outing, and with no notion that Sir Ninian had been cleverly manipulated to provide his escort. "I have changed my mind," she announced, after the barouche had passed them by. "I wish to drive by Newgate, if you please!"

"Newgate?" repeated Ninian. He did *not* please, since the prison raised unpleasant reminders of his outstanding debts. How these had reached such vast proportions, Ninian could not begin to guess; but he had added them up that very morning, and the total was astonishing. "As you wish."

Aye, my lad, thought Fanny, soon enough it *will* be as I please! This handsome scalawag might contrive to outrun the constable, but he'd have to be quick as the wind itself to outdistance Papa Allingham! "Think of Marie Louise," she said and batted her sparse lashes coquettishly. "She barely knew Napoleon when they were wed, yet he sent her an incredible amount of gifts when they wed by proxy. Can you imagine! Clothes that cost over four hundred thousand francs, including forty-eight pairs of shoes, and jewelled fans and Kashmir shawls and even painted enamel chamber-pots!

Yet, from all accounts, they enjoyed their honeymoon well enough."

Her words fell on deaf ears. Ninian gazed up at the towering prison and his face was as grim as the shadow it cast. He was at the mercy of his creditors, and it was not likely they would handle him with velvet gloves.

" 'Tis said," murmured Miss Allingham, edging even closer, "that Napoleon's conduct, when they met, more resembled a ravishment than a wooing, but I doubt she cared for that." Her glance spoke volumes, none of them printable. "*I* should expect to be treated with more delicacy."

Ninian's eyes brushed past her, and he flicked a horsefly neatly in mid-air with his practiced whip. "Perhaps you may," he said, with calculated indifference.

Fanny knew herself to be both plump and homely, but she had dressed with special care for this occasion in a white carriage dress and pearl-gray bonnet and pelisse. Her gorge rose. So this frippery gentleman thought her beneath his notice? He'd learn a sharp lesson when she laid her yoke on him!

"Newgate," mused Miss Allingham, "where even gentlemen are confined when they fail to pay their debts." Savoring the glory of the moment, she brought forth a snuff-box, dug pudgy fingers into it, and inhaled. "Violet Strasburg, made from Rappee and bitter almonds, ambergris and attargul: Queen Charlotte's sort," she explained, having mistaken Sir Ninian's abhorrence for admiration. A fit of sneezing overtook her. Quickly, she closed the box. "What do *your* debts amount to, Sir Ninian? Quite seven thousand pounds, which you have no hope of paying. Perhaps you should consider what you mean to do."

Ninian whipped up his horses and moved hastily away from the prison. The way matters stood, he was likely to return there all too soon. "I do not see that such matters need concern you, ma'am." What he *did* see was the immediate necessity of removing himself from this repellant female's vicinity. He turned his steeds towards the Allingham town mansion, a structure remarkable only for its ostentatious vulgarity.

"No?" said Fanny softly, and gripped his knee. "Already you are in the hands of the cent-per-cents, and have borrowed so heavily against your expectations that you are unlikely to

153

be loaned more. In short, Sir Ninian, you are unable to raise the wind!"

Had not Ninian's hands been engaged with the reins, he would have fetched Miss Allingham a blow that landed her in the cobbled street, plump on her ample backside. In moments of such gruelling indignity, gentlemanly principles be damned! "I repeat," he said stiffly, "it is none of your concern."

Starched-up, was he? Fanny grinned. "How do you mean to extricate yourself from your difficulties? Flee the country as others have done before you? Or will you join the army as a common foot-soldier, despite the poor pay and savage discipline?" Boldly she moved her plump little fingers further up his thigh.

"Miss Allingham," said Ninian, through gritted teeth, "if you do not unhand me this very moment I will not be responsible for the consequences!"

"Oh, fie!" cried Fanny, striking a dramatic pose. "And me an unmarried lass! What will you say next, Sir Ninian? You've made me blush, I swear."

It was Ninian who wished to swear, and he only refrained from doing so through heroic effort. At least those greedy hands had moved from his lap to her own! Lest he say something unforgivable—though why he should consider the sensibilities of a young lady who had clearly shown herself capable of tying her garter in public, he couldn't imagine— Ninian said nothing at all.

Fanny preened. She may have roused his temper instead of his ardor, but Miss Allingham liked to see modesty in a man. "Seven thousand pounds," she gloated. Tomorrow she would begin to choose her bride-clothes! "I knew as soon as I clapped eyes on you, Sir Ninian, that you'd suit me right down to the ground, though I was mortal afraid to put it to the touch till I learned of that seven thousand pounds. In truth, my da' wasn't best pleased to learn that I'd set my cap at you, thinking I could do better than a mere baronet, but I've managed to bring him around." Her laughter rumbled ominous as a thunder-cloud, and Ninian received a dig in the ribs from a surprisingly bony elbow. "Well, sir, what do you say?"

Ninian was so dismayed that he dropped the reins. "Miss Allingham," he replied with commendable honesty, "I don't know *what* to say!"

Almost, as she reached in front of him and pulled the

horses to a halt, Fanny felt sorry for her feckless groom-to-be. "You have a couple minutes to think about it," she said kindly. "My da' said particularly that I was to bring you in so that he might have a private word with you."

Chapter 21

Tuesday 23 April 1811

"Reconciliation?" I shrieked. "You must be mad!" Gabrielle cringed back in her chair just as if she'd been struck. "Forgive me," I begged, more quietly. "You must see that there is little possibility of such a thing."

For all the privacy I found in my chamber this day, I might as well have sought solitude in the middle of Hyde Park. So much for my well-kept secret! No sooner did the morning papers arrive, and with them the announcement of Miss Fanny Allingham's betrothal to Sir Ninian Northcliffe, than I was positively besieged with sympathy. Sparrow appeared, wringing her hands as if *she* had been cast aside, babbling inanities about blue skies and silver linings and rays of hope; and behind her came Maeve, bearing a tisane which mixed most headily with the port I'd already consumed. Even Bridey invaded my bedchamber, and offered to put the curse of the Wild Women of Gonn on my faithless lover from this day out. I most cordially thanked her and requested that her maledictions be directed towards the treacherous Miss Allingham.

"I beg you," whispered Gabrielle, looking the merest child in that baroque carved and gilded chair, "not to do anything desperate. Surely there has been some error. It is inconceivable that Sir Ninian should treat you in this cavalier fashion."

"The wretch!" I growled and flopped gracelessly upon my bed. My pen is almost too feeble to express my emotions. "I promise you I do not mean to wear the willow for him." The

155

mortification of it all! When I considered the length and faithfulness of my attachment to Ninian, and the struggles I had been compelled to make for his sake, I could have screamed with pure rage. The grossest inequity of all was that I had lost him to a squat dab of a female without a single asset, save money, to her name! Not only all of the Denham household but all of London must know that Fanny Allingham had stolen a march on me. The ignominy of it, to be tumbled off my perch, knocked over with a feather, to be brought so low! I ground my teeth, rather to their detriment. Was I now to slink away with my tail between my legs like a whipped cur? The intelligent reader may have already guessed that the answer was emphatically, *No!*

"You do not," Gabrielle ventured, "mean to do anything as inconsidered as entering a nunnery?"

My jaw dropped open, but I reminded myself sternly that Lady Randolph meant well, for all her lamentable tendency to talk through her beribboned hat. "No. Nor do I mean to put a period to my existence." I clutched my satin bedspread—yellow, to match the window draperies—and wrung it as if it were Ninian's perfidious neck. "I shall have my revenge, I promise you."

Even Tayce had seen fit to offer her condolences, though since these had consisted of such provoking remarks as *à bon chat, bon rat*—to a good cat, a good rat—I, by way of a well-aimed pillow, speeded her departure from my room. Why did I ever think I would benefit from my aunt's involvement in my affairs? She would only remark, enigmatic as the Sphinx, that the pieces of the puzzle were fitting together nicely, and then would say no more.

"What will you do?" It occurred to me that Gabrielle was behaving oddly, and I took a closer look at her. She seemed almost unnaturally calm. Would that *I* could achieve that state and forget that Ninian, only three days past, had avowed his devotion to *me!* So over-heated was my mind that I vacillated between wishing to see my beloved drawn and quartered and longing once more to be clasped in his arms, preferably while they were still attached to the rest of him. "Adam is most concerned," she added, almost as an after-thought. "He asked me to give you his regards."

I bit back the various sarcastic rejoinders that sprang to my lips. It was no more than I deserved for having been fool enough to wear my heart on my sleeve and allow Fanny to fling darts at it. "How kind of him." And how relieved he must be that I was, however unwillingly, freed of the Northcliffe curse! "As for my course of action, I have not yet determined that."

What I wished to do more than anything was to seek out Ninian and demand that he explain. It did not seem possible, after all this time, that he should turn his back on me—but was it not what I had so long feared? I dared not call at his lodgings, and it was useless to write. Ninian never got two-penny post letters because he had no money to pay for them, and the postman wouldn't leave them otherwise. I toyed with the thought of sending a note by hand, but my maid had lately begun to act in the strangest manner, and I suspected her of having gone over to the enemy. *Which* enemy, I could not say; it seemed I was surrounded by them! This enforced inaction only added to my frustrated anger, which—as the reader may have already noted—was not inconsiderable.

"Merrie." Gabrielle clasped her hands and leaned forward earnestly. "I know that Sir Ninian has treated you abominably—and, indeed, I still think there must be some error. He did not seem that sort of man." If error, I thought grimly, then mine; but refrained from pointing out that Gabrielle's experience of men was, at best, limited. She stared at me with an odd intensity, as if she meant more than she said. "It is only natural that you would wish to be revenged. But you must not do anything rash! Your whole life is ahead of you."

"Dear Lady Randolph," I urged, briefly forgetting my own problems in her struggle with coherence, "what is it you're trying to say?"

"Do not rush into marriage with someone else because of this." Gabrielle refused to meet my gaze. "It is forever, after all." Then she did look at me, and I would much rather she had not. Those soft brown eyes were as world-weary as Mephisto's, and infinitely more resigned. Ho! thought I, here's no bed of roses. In case I had failed to take her point, Gabrielle added: It is not a pleasant thing to discover yourself wed to a man you cannot love."

"Oh, dear!" I said, rather helplessly, and promptly abandoned all notions of, with poor Luke in tow, beating Ninian to the altar. I mused upon the tendency of our dreams to

157

crumble to dust before we ourselves do. The Almighty, in His infinite whimsey, arranged matters in this mortal sphere with considerable inequity.

"Lady Randolph." Mephisto stood in the doorway. He paid my scowl no heed, but bent upon Gabrielle a look of incredible gentleness. "Your carriage waits." With that same unusual courtesy, he drew her to her feet and escorted her out the door. Though I said all that was proper, I was not at all sorry to see Lady Randolph leave. Ninian's betrayal weighed heavy on me. At least, I reflected gloomily, if my heart broke I could hardly eat it out.

When they had gone, I rose and wandered idly about the room. It was a pleasant chamber, with its floral-patterned carpet and papered walls and the delicate arabesques painted on ceiling and doorway. So great was my abstraction that I walked smack into a small table piled high with albums and books. When Mephisto returned, as I had known he would, he found me righting the damage that I'd caused. He dropped into the chair that Gabrielle had vacated and regarded me. Deliberately, I said nothing. Let him make the first move.

"Well, Merrie." From the look of him, Mephisto meant to make a prolonged stay. "I am relieved to see that you do not mean to sink into a decline, to waste away as it were, from unrequited love."

Never have I met one who could so easily provoke me to rage. "It is not," I snapped, "unrequited! No matter how it may seem, Ninian has for years been devoted to me."

"Oh?" inquired Mephisto. "He chooses a strange way to show it." My guardian had just come from riding and still wore his leather breeches and top-boots, and the blue coat that, in contrast, made his eyes even more pale. Like pieces of ice, I thought. Would that his horse had thrown and trampled him! "It is time you faced facts, Meredith. You have engaged in conduct that is altogether displeasing, have made and kept countless assignations, and only barely, through no effort of your own, avoided ruin." Was the man omniscient? I was dumbfounded, for the second time that day. "It would seem that you have been quite soundly taken-in, and by a young scapegrace who played you false at the first opportunity."

"Not the *first*, surely." I still struggled with the revelation that Mephisto had seen through my clever ploys. "And Ninian is not a scapegrace."

158

Mephisto shrugged. "A fashionable fribble, then. I will not quibble over terms. I suppose it was with Sir Ninian that you absented yourself from my sister's *soirée?*"

I dropped my eyes and summoned forth a blush, wondering what fell purpose prompted my guardian's unprecedented amicability. Heaven knows he made both Wellington and Napoleon appear rank amateurs in matters of deceit and strategy! "You misjudge me greatly, sir."

"The shoe," sighed Mephisto, "is on the other foot. Very well, I shall not pursue the matter. I do not mean to question your conduct, but merely to put you on guard." So sincere must Satan have sounded when he tempted Our Lord! "You will, however, behave with more prudence in the future. I trust I make myself clear?"

So we were to do battle, after all. I welcomed it, for only rage could hold at bay the sense of bereavement that threatened to send me plummeting my fists against the wall.

"Perfectly," I snarled. "It is all your doing, is it not? You think you have driven Ninian away from me. You think that now I will fall in meekly with your schemes." Arms akimbo I glared at him and proceeded to burn all my bridges with a single touch of the torch. "Well, my lord, you err! I not only assure you of a present attachment between Ninian and myself, but I promise you that I shall do everything within my power to insure a future connection between us, either legal *or* illegal!" If only I might have convinced myself.

"My dear child, you are coming it rather too strong." His tone was decidedly unfond, and his long fingers twitched as if he wished to forcibly silence me. "It seems I must remind you again of your position. Much as we may dislike it, Meredith, you are my ward. To be blunt, you are completely in my power, and it grows increasingly apparent that you are in sore need of discipline."

"Discipline?" I echoed, thinking frantically. I was, all too truly, in the devil's clutches. What would he do, clap me in irons, keep me under lock and key?

"Precisely." My *âme damnée* was enjoying himself. "As in punishment. In the future, you will do as I say."

"Oh?" I was to be put to the torture, thumbscrew and rack, broken on the wheel! Or perhaps, were Mephisto in a benign mood, he might merely lay open my back with his horsewhip!

159

It was not difficult to don the air of one unjustly condemned. "You do not temper your judgments with mercy, I see."

I have said Mephisto was a man of little mirth. My surprise, therefore, was by no means small when he threw back his head and roared with genuine amusement. "An incurable humbugger," announced my guardian, with total disregard of the fact that he was every bit as great a prevaricator as I. "However, you waste time playing off your airs for me. I do not mean to deal hardly with you, Meredith, but I will brook no further nonsense. Your father wished to see you established, and established you will be."

Both furious and desolate, I kicked at the chimney-piece. "You will have to drag me screaming to the altar! I have done with men." Mephisto made a sound indicative of stark disbelief. "You have not answered my questions," I persevered. "Did you or did you not scheme to part me from Ninian? I did not think that even *you* would behave so shabbily."

"You are determined to have a poor opinion of me." Not even accusations of arrant treachery could disturb that man's sublime indifference! "Tell me, are you truly so fond of young Northcliffe?"

I whirled to stare at him, astonished. *"Fond?"* I gasped. "My God, you are insupportable! For years Ninian and I have planned to wed, and then you spoil it all with this damned May-game you must play! Is it not enough that you have ruined my life? Must you come now to gloat and moralize over me?"

"You are fast," said Mephisto grimly, rising from the chair, "putting me out of patience with you."

"I wish I might!" I cried, truly in a frenzy of rage. "Then you would leave me alone. You do not care whose lives you disrupt, only that you may pursue your accursed schemes!" My hands were clenched so tightly that my fingernails bit into the palms. "I tell you now, *I* won't serve as your cat's-paw!"

"Insolent baggage." Mephisto strode purposefully toward me. "Do you flatter yourself against all evidence into a belief that you may outmaneuver me?" Roughly, he grasped my arms. I must admit that the action was not without provocation, since I had made a frenzied attempt to scratch out his eyes. "Let us return to the matter of your infatuation with Sir Ninian."

"It is not infatuation!" Aware that I had gone too far, and equally aware that Mephisto truly *could* do as he wished with me, I discarded a notion of securing my release by kicking him. "And I don't wish to discuss it any more."

"Nevertheless, you will." Ruthlessly, Mephisto propelled me towards the chair. "Lay all these bristles, you absurd child! I had nothing to do with the lad's betrothal to Miss Allingham."

I stared at him, stunned, then—I blush to confess—howled like an infant.

"Sweet heaven!" said Mephisto in disgust as I wept all over his lapels. "What other trials does this day hold in store?" Firmly he pushed me into the chair.

I clutched the handkerchief that he had been so considerate as to place in my hand. "You don't understand!" I wailed. "If you did not force Ninian into an alliance with Fanny, then all truly *is* at an end!"

"I had thought you possessed of a superior understanding." Mephisto's gaze fell upon the port decanter, which I had failed to hide, and he promptly appropriated it for his own use. So overset was I that I failed to appreciate my vast achievement in finally discomposing him. "I have yet to see any evidence of it."

Cautiously, I lowered the handkerchief and regarded him with one eye. "What do you mean?"

"Much better," approved my fiendish guardian. "I would much rather see that familiar look of mistrust than witness any further lachrymose displays. It seems very odd, dear Meredith, that your mistrust extends to a gentleman for whom you swear such undying passion."

Much refreshed by my bout of tears, I uncovered my other eye and applied the handkerchief to my nose. "Ninian?"

"Ninian." Mephisto was saturnine. "There may be many a slip 'twixt the cup and the lip, my girl, but a lad who has been remarkably faithful to you for five years"—I gulped and choked, and he politely paused until I caught my breath again—"is not likely to strike the cup from your hand."

"You mean—" I was quite sure he wouldn't tell me how he knew so much about me and Ninian.

Mephisto's expression was positively benign, but I did not pause, then, to wonder at this unexpected *volte-face*. "I mean," he said softly, "that I am not the only one with a stake in this game."

Chapter 22

Crocodile Tears

Lord Camden and Lady Penelope sat in a private parlor of the Bull and Mouth Inn in St. Martins-le-Grand. Watching the coaches arrive and depart was a pastime that had once rated almost as high with them as putting frogs in their elder brother's bed. As a harried waiter removed the remnants of their breakfast—cold pigeon pie, grilled kidneys and bacon, hot buttered muffins and coffee—the Marquis silently regarded his twin. Pen was looking shockingly worn-down. Luke, who had heard rumors of Sir Jason's entanglement with a notorious courtesan, thought it understandable that she lacked appetite.

"Poor puss," he murmured, and touched her cheek. "Won't you tell me what's troubling you?"

Since she could no longer occupy herself by building neat landscapes on her plate, Pen drew damp abstracts with her glass on the table-top. "Dear Luke, you are very good." The dark circles around her fine eyes prompted Lord Camden with a violent desire to apply his polished boot to the seat of his brother-in-law's breeches. "Pay no mind to my foolish megrims. It is just that Mephisto's habit of meddling in other people's lives sometimes frightens me. He is a singularly selfish man."

Luke, with an eye to potential breakage, removed the glass from her hand. "You're just discovering this? Our half-brother serves no one but himself."

"I never minded that." Luke looked skeptical, and she frowned at him. "Truly I did not, even when he was such a brute about Jason." Quickly she shied away from this unhappy train of thought. "I never felt that he meant me harm. Now, I do not know."

162

Luke leaned forward, his elbows on the table. He was very concerned about Pen, whose moods skittered from the heights of nervous agitation to the depths of despondency. "What are you saying, puss? You cannot think Mephisto would harm you, or allow anyone else to do so? My dear, you are being singularly foolish!"

"Don't be absurd!" Pen was cross. It was little short of miraculous that word of Jason's infatuation with Delilah had not yet reached Lord Denham's ears, and she shuddered to think what Mephisto's reaction would be. "I do not refer to myself. I can say no more, Luke. Do not press me, I have given my word."

"My honorable sister." Lord Camden's tone was devoid of any sarcasm. "If you should change your mind, Pen, you know you may trust me."

"Yes. More than anyone." Pen's voice was choked, and Luke deemed it a prudent time to leave. He bundled her into her satin-lined, fur-trimmed velvet pelisse, adjusted her elegant bonnet, and led her into the courtyard.

Here was none of the frantic bustle that had prevailed earlier when the day coaches took on bleary-eyed passengers who tumbled out of bed in scant time for a fortifying nip of brandy, and the night coaches spilled forth cold and touseled travellers who untangled aching limbs to stagger into the coffee-room. The inn-yard, then, seethed with excitement and activity, as not only the passengers but the inn's huge staff—coachmen and guards, stable-boys and ostlers, housekeepers, chambermaids, porters and cooks—scurried to and fro.

Pen stepped into Lord Camden's barouche, her mind on Sir Richard Croft, London's leading and most fashionable *accoucher,* whom she'd visited earlier that day, and who had prescribed a weak and unappetizing diet composed mainly of liquids. It had not been difficult to secure the doctor's promise of silence, though what he made of her request was best not dwelt upon. The perfidy of man, thought Pen. At least Jason, whatever his countless sins, had never arranged that she give birth in the midst of a social gathering, as Napoleon's poor Empress had done. The guests had been shepherded into the billiards-room, where they sipped wine and chocolate while listening to Marie Louise's screams.

"Does Jason know?" asked Luke abruptly, as he closed the carriage door.

"No!" Lord Camden's well-sprung barouche swayed solemnly from side to side like a stately ship afloat, and Pen's stomach tried to leap overboard. "He must not, Luke. Promise me."

Since the Marquis had no intention of making such an outrageous vow, it was with relief that he spied his sister's friend. "There's Lady Sara. What can she be doing here?"

"And who's that with her?" Pen poked her head through the window. "Luke, that coach! She'll be killed!" But already he had shouted to his driver and leaped to the ground.

It was only due to Lord Camden's quick action that Lady Sara escaped serious injury, for the other carriage streaked down the street at break-neck speed. Had Luke not reached Sparrow's side the precise instant that he did, and shoved her out of harm's way, she must have surely been crushed beneath the wicked wheels.

The runaway coach pelted past, scattering astonished pedestrians. Lord Camden's mettlesome steeds, perhaps in sympathy with their renegade brothers, bugled and attempted to kick over the traces, and poor Pen was pitched about like a bucket in a well. Luke lifted Lady Sara in his arms and forced a pathway through the rapidly-gathering crowd. Since his footman was otherwise occupied, hanging onto the wild-eyed horses' bridles and shouting obscenities, Lord Camden wrenched open the barouche door.

"Is she all right?" gasped Pen, picking herself up from the floor.

"I think so." Luke carefully placed Sparrow on the seat. Pen knelt to grimly, gently, wipe the blood and dirt from that pallid face. "She's had a nasty knock on the head. We must get her home without delay."

The trip to Denham House was accomplished in record time. It was Wiggins who admitted them, with Bridey close on his heels. "By the living Holy and all his wounds!" cried that damsel. Uttering dire Gaelic curses, she soon had her mistress ensconced comfortably on the drawing-room sofa. Maeve appeared as if by magic to apply cold compresses to Lady Sara's brow, while Wiggins held a basin of water, gulped and looked as though he might at any moment faint dead away.

"Sure and ye've the glamourie upon ye!" Bridey uselessly patted her mistress's limp hand. "Gramercy! 'Tis daft the way ye must be skelterin' abroad at all times." Maeve cast the girl a reprimanding look and sent her in search of vinaigrette.

"Surely," said Luke quietly to his twin, "you do not mean to suggest that I keep this secret as well?"

"Please," whispered Pen. She refused to meet his eyes. Lord Camden clamped his lips together, lest he give unwise voice to thought. Luke had remarked the identity of Lady Sara's companion, and the quickness with which Delilah had melted back into the crowd.

Turmoil swept like a whirlwind through Denham House, crashing through the wine-cellar where Lord Denham was overseeing the laying-down of some priceless old port, reeling into the library where Mme. Dore was engaged in an analysis of Rousseau. Exasperated, Tayce threw down her quill. As is the way of noble ideals, particularly when adapted for revolutionary purposes, Rousseau's touted sovereignty of the people had rapidly deteriorated into the sovereignty of one man, Napoleon, who was bitten by his wife's pet dog, Fortune, on his wedding night. Mme. Dore considered this a moral lesson of an elevating degree.

Mephisto stood in the doorway of the drawing-room. "May I inquire," he said ironically, "what is going on here?" His arctic gaze fell on Sparrow's prostrate form, and Tayce thought he flinched.

Briefly, Luke explained. "Of all the cork-brained—" A muscle in Mephisto's cheek twitched furiously. "What possessed the little fool?"

Tayce itched for a closer view, but Mephisto blocked her path. *"Que diable!"* She disposed of the obstacle to her vision with a vicious jab of her silver-topped cane. "Is one to be allowed no peace in this household?"

Bridey skittered sideways into the room, a vinaigrette clutched in her hand, then stopped short. A superstitious soul, Bridey could not be persuaded that Mme. Dore was anything but a witch; and at that particular moment, with grey hair wildly disheveled, and wire-rimmed spectacles perched precariously on the very tip of her nose, Tayce looked exceptionally malevolent. "I demand," announced Mephisto, gingerly inspecting his ribs, "an explanation!"

Tayce appropriated the vinaigrette. *"Dieu vous garde!"* she snapped. "And so do we all! But this one is in no condition to render it." She pushed the silent Maeve aside and stuck the vinaigrette under Sparrow's nose.

Lord Denham seethed like a volcano on the verge of eruption, but Lady Sara groaned and weakly sneezed. "Welcome back, *chérie!*" Mme. Dore put her arm around the invalid's thin shoulders and propelled her into a sitting position. So! Sparrow's bones were as sharp and as fragile as those of the bird whose name she bore.

Lady Sara stared wildly about her. "A family deputation?" she inquired. "Why are you all so dour?"

"Lady Sara," said Luke gently, as he took her hands, "are you feeling better now?" A singularly foolish question, thought Tayce. Sparrow's eyes were sunken and feverish.

And her laughter was manic. "Mr. Facing-both-ways!" Sara cried, but it was to Mephisto that she spoke. So shrill was her tone that even Luke recoiled, and Pen froze in the act of rising from her chair. "You said I would be safe. *Safe?* Better you had bid me go and be damned!"

"Sparrow," said Lord Denham grimly, "you are speaking nonsense!" Ignoring his housekeeper's protest, and Mme. Dore's avid interest, he moved forward.

Sparrow was not the least intimidated by the harsh-visaged spectre who loomed over her. "I dislike your manners, sir!" she announced pertly. "It quite decides me not to marry you." Tayce cackled—one who once wagered on how many heads would be severed from their bodies in a single day would hardly be horrified by a simple attack of lunacy—but the others were aghast.

"I do not recall," Mephisto retorted, though in softer tones, "asking you to do so." Intent, Mme. Dore leaned forward, balancing her weight on her cane, and Bridey skuttled to the farthest corner of the room.

"No, you wouldn't, would you?" Sparrow wrenched away from Luke and hugged herself as if against a chill. "Damaged goods, you'd say, and toss me out the window with the other trash. Very unsanitary of you, my lord! Think of the poor people passing below."

" 'Tis a fever of the brain, your grace." Maeve touched Mephisto's arm. "I am familiar with such things. We must take her to her chamber."

But Lady Sara might have been Medusa, with snaking writhing hair, for Mephisto had been turned to stone. Mme.

166

Dore considered it a pity that his condition was not permanent.

" 'Twas a long room," Sparrow whispered, "the air blue with candle-smoke and heavy fog drifting in the open door. And in the middle of the room was a large table, and on that lay Paddy, with a sheet drawn up to his chin." She smiled brightly at Tayce, inspiring that worthy with a sudden conviction that there were worse fates than laying one's head on the block. From Bridey came a keening sound. "I did not wish him to be cold, you see. His coffin was of new-planed ash-wood. It lay open beside the bier."

"Come, *acushla*," murmured Maeve, taking Lady Sara's arm. "Don't fret yourself, my honey. Come along with me."

"No!" Sparrow scowled and shook off the helpful hand. "I must tell them so they'll know what they must do."

"There is no need." Mephisto drew her to her feet. "You are not going to die." She swayed slightly and clutched his arm. "You must trust me."

"Trust you?" she echoed weakly and crumpled into his arms.

Scowling ferociously, Tayce watched the sad little procession leave the room. Was it sudden indigestion, this crippling cramping pain—or did advancing age bring with its myriad other afflictions an onslaught of conscience? Slowly, she hobbled back to her sanctuary, so deep in thought that she even overlooked an opportunity to frighten the credulous Bridey out of her remaining wits. Even in the midst of a delirium, Sparrow had grasped the truth. Her death was as inevitable as if she rode in a tumbrel to a *tête-à-tête* with Madame Guillotine.

Chapter 23

Thursday 25 April 1811

"I make you my compliments," I said, eyes downcast in
maidenly woe. A carrot dangled before the nose provokes a
peppier gait than a whiplash to the hindquarters—*not* that I
mean to compare Ninian to a jackass! "You are to form the
extremely profitable connection that you wished, and I shall
resign myself to the will of God and strive to forget that you
have dealt me a crushing blow."

"I can see," Tayce cackled, "that I am *de trop!*" I scowled;
she was much too farcical an element for my melodramatic
scene. Ah, but Mme. Dore had made the world her stage, she
was a virtuoso, a prima donna of burlesque—and a librettist
of crafty scenarios. It was not so that I might speak privately
with Ninian that my aunt had arranged this surreptitious
expedition to Vauxhall!

My aunt snickered. *"Allons!* I shall take myself away. We
will meet in an hour at the entrance to the Dark Walk."
Mme. Dore was looking remarkably like a tart in a violet
satin dress trimmed with black lace, a dark-colored satin
pelisse with gold clasps, and a cap of violet-and-green satin
adorned with green feathers. She adjusted her spectacles and
cast me one last admonishing look. "Pray conduct yourself
with a modicum of decorum, *petite!*"

Fine advice from one who force-fed me from the cradle with
a nigh-indigestible diet of revolutionary psychology and the
tenets of Mary Wollstonecraft, spiced with the inexpedience
of truth and sweetened with free love! But Ninian was beside
me, looking so delicious that I fair watered at the mouth. I
fear I did not do him credit, having disguised myself in drab
clothing pilfered from my maid. Even my sharp-sighted papa

wouldn't have recognized me! How ironic was life. Now it was Ninian who would suffer were *this* meeting to be known.

"Well?" I inquired sharply. "Have you nothing to say to me? No word of explanation to extend? Never did I think that *you* would serve me so ill!"

Ninian cast a watchful eye upon our fellow-revellers. "Now, Merrie," he soothed, "don't go into high fidgets! I admit that my behavior has been abominable."

"You," I retorted, determined to have my pound of flesh, "are a great deal too easy on yourself! First you declare your lasting passion for me, then turn promptly around and engage yourself to that pudding-faced female. If that were not bad enough, *then* you publish your betrothal to the world, without even warning me!"

"True." Ninian wore no more expression than a block of wood. He drew me out of the way of a drunken lady-bird, old and ugly beyond even the lax standards of Hyde Park. I answered the hag's vulgar suggestion with one of my own. Ninian ignored us both. "Believe me, Merrie, I did not know that announcement was to appear. I cannot tell you how deeply I have regretted it."

"I hope," I said snidely, and twitched my ugly skirts, "that you may not also come to regret your choice. It is what I should have expected, I suppose, of a fortune-hunter—a basket-scrambler, in fact! Your interest is in a fortune, and Miss Allingham's is far handier than mine." I laughed hollowly. "When one nourishes a serpent in one's bosom, one cannot expect not to be stung!"

Ninian's lips twitched. May his words stick in his throat like a chicken bone, I thought viciously, and choke him! But he gave no indication of an imminent seizure, so I debated whether I preferred to wring his neck, roast him alive or put him to the sword. Oblivious to this murderous intent, Ninian took my arm—and the way in which he did so was far from lover-like—and escorted me through the noisy crowd.

Vauxhall, the pleasure gardens, were no longer the province of the *ton*. The walks were crowded with people of all ranks; women of the town boldly accosted strangers and asked for wine. Had I not been stricken to the soul by Ninian's treachery, I should have greatly enjoyed this vast and diverse parade of humanity; as it was, I accorded scant interest in either the visitors or the entertainment. My eyes were swimming in hot tears; Indian jugglers and sword-swallowers might have made mincemeat of each other, the entire orchestra might have performed in a state of nature, and I would not have seen.

"I would explain if I could," Ninian said abruptly. "I swear that, Merrie; there is much you do not understand."

I did not appreciate this slur upon my powers of intellect. "Your hands are tied?" I asked sweetly. "I hope Miss Allingham may not find you an uncomfortable bedfellow! You can provide no reasons for your iniquitous act that would satisfy me—save that you are both a jackanapes and a ninnyhammer!"

The wrath that blazed in his grey eyes sent a delightful shudder down my spine. With a wrench that practically pulled my arm from its socket, Ninian dragged me from the rotunda—a magnificent curved building with beautiful chandeliers and large mirrors, illuminated paintings and statues—and down a path lined with tall trees. He didn't pause until we entered a sylvan grotto where, with little ceremony, he pushed me onto a marble bench.

I adjusted my dreadful black bonnet and stared up at him. Scant light from the thousands of little colored lamps that decked trees and triumphal arches penetrated here, and I was glad of it. Not only was my face blotched with temper, Ninian's masterful conduct took my breath away.

"You have formed an unfavorable opinion of me," he said, "and I do not wonder at it, although I should have thought you clever enough to see beyond the end of your nose." His foot was propped on the bench beside me, effectively preventing the escape that I had no wish to make. With difficulty I averted my gaze from his muscular thigh. "There are circumstances that forced me to act as I did."

"*What* circumstances?" I clasped my hands together, pressed them to my cheek, and looked soulful. "Is it debt, Ninian? If so, why did you not tell *me?* I would have gotten the money for you somewhere."

So somber was my beloved that he might have been shoveling dirt onto a casket in its open grave. His funereal expression struck a chord of memory—and, by not pursuing that off-key thought, I nearly sounded my own death-knell! "I could not let you do that, Merrie," he said, "no matter how loathesome your opinion of me."

It did not seem the moment to quibble about my sentiments regarding himself. "You will allow Fanny Allingham to do so! What difference does it make? You would have had my fortune when we wed, why are you unwilling to broach it now?"

"Talking won't pay toll! I am bound by my decision, though I know such decision must inevitably mean the ruin of all my hopes." When I heard these sober words, I spouted tears as fulsomely as any watering-pot. Though I had opened my mouth, Ninian allowed me no time for comment. "How do you come to be here, Merrie? Where is your chaperone?"

"It was Tayce's doing," I said mournfully, "and I'm sure I don't know why. As for Sparrow, I trust she's safely in her bed, having driven the entire family to wit's end."

"What do you mean?" It did not elevate my spirits to note that Ninian was more concerned with my chaperone's fate than with my own. I explained, although I felt more like gnashing my teeth, beating my breast and tearing out my hair!

"She'll be right as a trivet," I concluded. "The brain-storm has passed. While in its grip, I'm told, Sparrow said the strangest things, among them that someone wishes to murder her." Surely Ninian's horror was an extreme reaction to the mishap of a woman whom he barely knew? "Who, I wonder?" I mused. "I think I should place my money on Mephisto. He brought her here, after all. Perhaps he thought it easier to dispose of her in London than at her home. Perhaps"—and I didn't like this notion at all—"he means for someone else to take the blame."

"Fustian, Merrie." Ninian certainly didn't mean to flatter me! "You are a great deal too imaginative."

"And *you*," I retorted, briefly forgetting my pain, "are a stiff-necked whopstraw! Do you mean to champion *Mephisto?* I tell you now, I will never have confidence in him, or in anyone who forces him upon me." Ninian was as expressionless as a tombstone. "At least tell me if Mephisto is responsible for your betrothal to Miss Allingham."

"No." It was the death-rattle of my dreams. "I think you have misjudged your guardian."

"Perhaps." I withdrew my gaze from his granite face and regarded the toe of his gleaming boot. It was an error; that homely article inspired me with another attack of overwhelm-

171

ing sadness, placed as it would soon be under another young lady's bed. "I have certainly misjudged *you*."

Almost unwillingly, I thought, Ninian placed his hand beneath my chin and tilted up my face. "I can only apologize to you, poppet. This is not what I had envisioned for either of us."

I blinked, rapidly. "Cry off," I whispered, succumbing to one of the feminine weaknesses that Tayce so abhorred. "You do not truly wish to marry her."

"How can I?" Bemused, Ninian twitched the atrocious bonnet from my head. "It would be scandalous. I do not care for Miss Allingham, but I would not make her an object of ridicule."

Hope leaped like a frog into my throat as his fingers wound in my curls. "If you cannot, then she must. Perhaps if you explained—"

Ninian laughed, mirthlessly. "It's easy to see that you are not well-acquainted with Miss Allingham! No, Merrie. She will not release me from an alliance that she has schemed so mightily to secure."

From somewhere, I drew enough will-power to push his hands away. "What, then?" I cried. "Do you mean to wait until her death dissolves your connection with her? And what am I to do in the interim, dwindle into an old maid? Or do you mean to set me up in a neat little establishment where you may visit me at will, or when Miss Allingham lets you off your leading-strings?"

Granted, I had meant to provoke Ninian to a display of emotion, but I had hardly expected him to slap me. How Tayce would have mourned!—this unprecedented act of violence only heightened my affection for the brute. I placed a hand to my flaming cheek, determined to slit my own throat before I told him so. "At last I believe you," I whispered. "This truly *is* the end."

Ninian, however, was every bit as perverse a creature as I. Hot on the heels of violence trailed passion of a different sort—and to the devil goes the hindmost, as Tayce often said, to which I was sufficiently depraved to add, damn the consequence. In a trice I was sniffling happily into Ninian's cravat.

"Forgive me," he murmured, into my disheveled curls. "I am a beast."

"Yes," I agreed, and snuggled closer. "It is one of the things

I like most in you." A *most* indecorous interval followed. At length, I drew back to peer up at him. "But I must know, Ninian. Do you still mean to cast me aside?"

"I can do nothing else." Again he wore that withdrawn, brooding look. Then I *did* gnash my teeth. But I was not going to stand by helpless and watch my cherished hopes shuffle off this mortal coil, snuffed out like a candle, numbered with the dead! As true a daughter of Eve as ever lived, I hiccoughed dolefully. The look vanished and so did his scruples: his lips travelled over my forehead, my cheeks, down to my neck, and halted only at the accursedly modest neckline of my shabby gown. "And yet it seems I cannot."

"Dear Ninian," I whispered, over the wild singing in my blood, "I am *so* glad you feel that way."

"Love," remarked Tayce, interrupting us in what may justly be considered the very nick of time. "The more it changes, the more it remains the same thing." Beside her, his arm gripped tight in her claw-like hand, with a shabby seedy little man.

Chapter 24

A Parthian Shot

"**Y**ou must tell my friends," said Lady Carlisle, *"exactly* what you have told me. They will be agog with interest, I promise you." An eye for an eye, she thought, and nudged her newest acquaintance into the corridor. The Good Book notwithstanding, Lady Carlisle claimed vengeance for her own.

"But is it quite the thing," protested Miss de la Torre, "to insinuate oneself so abruptly into a private theatre-party? Whatever will they think?"

"They will think your presence positively providential, my dear!" Even if the creature *did* look more like a refugee from

173

the devil's sweatship than an emissary from the higher latitudes! "I am quite one of the family, Miss de la Torre! We do not stand on ceremony." A slight exaggeration of the truth, perhaps, but Ottolie had revelations to impart, so awesomely illuminating that they would cast even the burning bush into the shade! The damnable Lord Denham would at last be brought to his knees, not to propose, not even to pray, but to eat of the crop he had sown—in a word: crow.

It was a relatively uneventful night at the King's Theatre, also known as the Royal Italian Opera House. The great horseshoe auditorium—its five tiers of boxes, the gallery and the pit—capacious enough to hold three thousand and more—was filled to capacity. Fops and dandies strolled about, the chatter of their voices even louder than the rattle of their snuff-boxes and canes. The boxes, sold on a subscription basis for as much as £2,500 the season, were filled with bejewelled bare-shouldered women and men in glittering orders and evening-dress. Ladies of the evening peddled their wares in the corridors; servants and tradesmen and sailors whistled and cracked nuts.

Tonight, however, and to the disappointment of many, there had been no unexpected diversions, unlike the evening during a benefit performance when Madame Rose Didelot, the Parisian *danseuse*, threw up her fine muscular arms, into a graceful attitude and inadvertently levelled three spectators. Never mind that! Lady Carlisle's tongue flickered over dry lips. It would be a great deal more uplifting to watch Denham cut down.

Miss de la Torre, with little notion that she was cast as the terrible swift sword which was to bring the mighty low, gazed about her with interest. It was not yet time for the grand opera, which was to begin at eight o'clock. The theatre was abuzz with conversation, some of it concerning George III, now convinced he was an animal in Noah's Ark; some concerning the progress of the Peninsular War. But the name most frequently on people's lips, Duke and demi-rep alike, was not that of Wellington, or the Farmer King, but that of a hitherto-untried horse that had broken all records at Newmarket that day, thus winning fortunes for a few far-sighted souls, and losing ruinous sums for a great many more. "Don't dwaddle!" snapped Lady Carlisle, then smiled placatingly. Heaven forbid this pudding-faced creature should take a pet!

174

"Here we are! Remember, repeat to Lord Denham exactly what you have told me."

"Of course," replied Miss de la Torre.

Thus it was that Lady Carlisle marched into Lord Denham's box like a conquering army on the tramp. One could almost hear the rattle of platoon fire, the clash of sabres, the cannon's salute; so may Wellington have looked at Vimeiro, Talvera, Bussaco, standing triumphant on the battlefield, whiffing the heady scent of grapeshot and scorched flesh. That none of them—Sir Jason, Lady Penelope, Lord Randolph, even Denham himself—neither threw up their hands nor down their arms detracted not in the slightest from her victorious air.

In point of fact, thought Pen, Ottolie even resembled Wellington, particularly in the shape and size of her nose—Old Douro's troops said the sight of that magnificent appendage in a fight was worth a reinforcement of 10,000 men. Pen was familiar not only with the Iron Duke's physiognomy but countless particulars of his life and career. Master Jeremiah Palmerston, eldest of her progeny, daily announced his intention to join in the battle against the Frogs, and refused to be put off by such logical considerations as that the Peninsular War was not likely to drag on quite so many years as it would take Master Jeremiah to come of age.

"Lady Carlisle!" said Gabrielle, when no one else spoke. She greeted the invasion with ill-concealed relief, perhaps because Lord Randolph had been amusing himself by relating tales of the fires that raged through London theatres with fair regularity, conflagrations that leapt swiftly into disaster, fed by flimsy costumes and scenery. Gabrielle glanced nervously at the flame-colored dome, the ladies in red-curtained boxes, their jewels sparkling brilliantly in the blaze of countless candles. So tightly was the audience packed in that escape was nigh impossible. She shivered and hoped that the scene-shifters were neither careless nor drunk.

Ottolie's bright and malicious eyes swept around the box. "Oh!" she cried, in mock disappointment. "Lady Sara is not with you? I was sure she would be."

"Make yourself comfortable, Ottolie, since you're here." Mephisto, in a black evening coat with flat gilt buttons and a velvet collar, looked even more unregenerate than usual. As if the offer had been extended with the utmost politeness,

175

Lady Ottolie complied, carefully arranging her primrose gown, beneath which she wore only the thinnest chemise and waist-petticoat, and stockings gathered to the knee.

"Let me make known to you Miss de la Torre," she said, and performed the introductions. Credulous Gabrielle sympathized with Miss de la Torre's sallow-skinned and over-dressed unworldliness; while Pen, with a suspicious sideways glance at her spouse, thought her a would-be Jezebel. "Miss de la Torre is visiting friends, but makes her home in Dublin, and knows Lady Sara well."

"Indeed," tittered Miss de la Torre, "I do."

Lady Ottolie was reproving. "All in good time, my dear." She wore a guise so saintly that a halo might have hovered above her head. "But where *is* Lady Sara? She will be sorry to have missed Miss de la Torre! I hope she is not ill?" In the opposite box Delilah laughed and flirted brazenly with the gentlemen who crowded around her. No wonder Lady Penelope was looking so cross!

"Not ill," replied Mephisto. "Merely worn down with the exigencies of a London season." Arch-fiend! thought Ottolie. And hellish, the way he had toyed with her.

Even Gabrielle, benumbed by the laudanum she had taken to fortify herself for the evening, sensed strange undercurrents. Since Adam's attention was centred on the newcomers, she dared touch Lady Penelope's hand. "Look," she whispered, "there's Miss Allingham. She does not look to be in spirits, despite her recent betrothal." Distracted, both by Lady Ottolie's strange behavior and Delilah's infuriating presence, Pen only nodded absently.

Sir Jason, who had a great deal less preying on his mind, cast Gabrielle a speculative glance: "Sir Ninian, however, is remarkably cheerful." Poor Merrie, thought Gabrielle, to give her heart to so false a man. Miss Sherrington was so distrait that she refused to appear in public, staying at home instead with her chaperone. "He has good reason," added Sir Jason, "having put three thousand pounds on a horse that fortunately won."

"Where are your manners, my darling?" inquired Adam of his wife. "If you cannot contribute to a conversation, you must remain silent and not interrupt." Gabrielle bit back the rebellious words that trembled on the tip of her tongue. In spite of Adam she meant to enjoy this evening, for there was

176

no knowing when she'd be allowed a similar treat. If her husband made good his threats, her next excursion would be to Bedlam, where curious visitors might come to gape and jeer as if she were a beast in a cage.

Having put his wife in her place, Lord Randolph turned to Jason with elaborate unconcern. "What's this? How came Northcliffe to make such a wager?"

"My dear Adam, how should I know?" Miss Allingham, mused Sir Jason, wore a face of unbecoming sullenness. "If you are so curious, you must ask the young man."

Lady Ottolie deemed it time to whet the sword. "It is the most extraordinary and most delightful coincidence!" she exclaimed, patting Miss de la Torre's plump arm. "You must know that we are all wild with curiosity about Lady Sara! She is the most secretive thing."

"We are?" inquired Lord Denham, leaning his broad shoulders against the wall. "Speak for yourself, Ottolie."

Miss de la Torre's moment had come. "The lady was quite a figure in Dublin Society," she volunteered. Lord Randolph frowned. "Her parties were the talk of the town, lasting as they did till dawn with the most brazen gambling and goings-on."

"My dear, what are you saying?" prodded Ottolie, nicely scandalized. Lord Denham's expression could only be called blasphemous. "Surely you don't mean to tell us that Lady Sara ran a gaming-hell!"

"I don't know what else you'd call it!" Miss de la Torre was nettled, and justifiably; Lady Carlisle knew perfectly well what she meant to say. What Lady Carlisle did *not* know was that her new acquaintance had suddenly guessed the reason for this confrontation, and considered it highly amusing. Lord Denham had opened his arms to a female who was no better than she should be, leaving Ottolie to hold only a passionate grudge. "The establishment was quite notorious, decorated in the richest manner with lustre chandeliers, marble chimney pieces and parquet floors. The furniture was painted white and gold, the banquettes and sofas upholstered in crimson damask."

"An eyewitness account?" inquired Denham, in blighting tones. Miss de la Torre bridled.

Sir Jason felt it behooved him to intervene. "Where," he asked quickly, "was this opulent establishment located?"

"In Smock Alley," Miss de la Torre replied haughtily. The Duke was certainly ill-bred! "Just next to the Playhouse. There is no question of the house's nature, sir! Play was deep, with wagers running high, and the rooms were sometimes darkened and the chandeliers lit in full daylight to heighten the excitement." She made a moue. "There were often quarrels, and even duels fought on the spot."

Gabrielle recalled her husband's interest in Lady Sara. Perhaps he'd suspected her past was not quite acceptable. But his face—how had she ever thought him handsome?— revealed nothing of his thoughts.

"Duels?" repeated Pen faintly. "Not the duel in which her husband was killed?"

"Right in the middle of the gaming-rooms!" Ottolie sat silently seraphic as Miss de la Torre slashed Lady Sara's reputation into tatters and shreds. "It was the *most* dreadful scandal! And over an accusation of card-sharping! I'm surprised, Lady Penelope, that you knew of *that*."

"We might all be surprised," murmured Sir Jason, touching his wife's cheek, "at the things Pen knows." Lady Penelope dropped her eyes to her lap, and Lord Denham watched them thoughtfully. Even Gabrielle remarked the coolness in Sir Jason's tone. Marriages made in heaven! she thought ruefully. In Gabrielle's experience, matrimony was less sacred than profane.

"I trust," said Mephisto calmly, "that you are sure of your information?" Not for the first time, Sir Jason marvelled at his brother-in-law's *savoir-faire*.

"Of course!" Miss de la Torre was arch. "Your Lady Sara, if you must know, presided over the place—and while I might not have recognized her, so greatly has she changed, I could hardly mistake Bridey O'Toole!"

"Bridey?" echoed Pen. The threads of her thoughts were as tangled as Tayce's ravelled yarn. "Sara's maid?"

"Maid!" A less genteel lady might have been said to huff. "Hardly, my dear! She's a girl from the streets who the McDougals hired to preside over the faro table. And I suspect she wasn't above tampering with the cards!"

"McDougals?" echoed Sir Jason, almost as befuddled as his wife. "I thought we were discussing Lady Sara Cainneach."

"I still don't understand." Gabrielle, fascinated, forgot her husband's strictures until he glanced at her impatiently.

178

Even so, her curiosity outweighed her fear. "What was Lady Sara doing in a gaming-hell?"

"Such vulgar expressions," growled Lord Randolph, "are unfitting to you, ma'am."

"Cut line, Adam!" said Lord Denham. "Pray continue, Miss de la Torre." His cold eyes were hooded, and the long fingers of one hand drummed on the back of the chair.

Miss de la Torre, feeling suddenly like she had fallen into the hands of the Spanish inquisition, swallowed hard. "They were once very poor, I believe. Not that you'd know it from the way they behaved!" If only she could squander the ready with equal profligacy! "That gambling-house brought them a fortune, and little wonder, for Paddy McDougal was one to grasp the main chance, and completely conscienceless." Her smile bordered on the grotesque. "It is even rumored that he once rode with highwaymen."

Lady Ottolie, little concerned with deceased Irish gamblers, adroitly turned the conversation. "Pretty companions for a man of honor!" she sneered. "And what did Lady Sara do while her husband was engaging in these boyish pranks?"

Miss de la Torre shrugged again, an ungraceful gesture that made her head appear to rest flat on her shoulders. "One can only assume she accompanied him—if, indeed, she was at that time his wife! The rumor is that they ran off together and before the knot was tied."

"An elopement!" whispered Gabrielle. Here was true romance! "Did they go to Gretna Green?" Adam gripped her arm, so tightly that he may have wished to crush the fragile bones.

"Who can say?" Miss de la Torre seemed disappointed that she lacked further, and more titillating, details.

"Fascinating," remarked Sir Jason. Pen supposed she should take some consolation from the fact that he did not acknowledge Delilah's nods and bows. "But, if I may be blunt, to what purpose?"

"Sir Jason!" Lady Carlisle was indignant. "Is *that* the sort of woman with whom you wish to associate?" The gentleman raised a quizzical brow and, belatedly, she recalled to whom she spoke. "Well, I do not, and I consider it little short of scandalous that she should be pushed upon the *ton!* My God, next we shall be hob-nobbing with the bourgeoise, encouraging commoners to take all sorts of encroaching fancies!"

179

"She disappeared, you say?" Lord Randolph was unusually genial. "I wonder why, and where."

"I'm sure I couldn't say." Miss de la Torre tittered. "I'll warrant she thought no one would recognize her here! She has trusted to fortune once too often, then."

"No wonder she has been so secretive!" Lady Carlisle was clearly on the side of the angels. To give the devil his due—and she did so in a most miserly manner—Mephisto had suffered these disclosures with little evidence of pain. In truth, Lord Denham looked more derisive than distressed, and Ottolie experienced a twinge of doubt. "Shockingly irregular conduct, to be sure!"

"More to the point than Lady Sara's social position," interrupted Adam, his gaze fixed upon Lord Denham, "is that she has been given the charge of a young girl. I doubt you could search the entire monarchy and find one less suitable to play chaperone."

"Adam!" The laudanum had made Gabrielle sleepy and less than wise. "Surely you exaggerate." Fortunately for Lady Randolph's continued well-being—her husband turned upon her a look sufficiently vehemous to shrivel a far more hardy soul—Catalini, the famed and temperamental virago who commanded huge sums for her performances, and whose fits of rage and jealousy behind the scenes were notorious, stepped onto the stage.

Briefly, everyone's attention was on her. Even Lord Denham deigned to observe this woman, whose voice was so rich and powerful, with such great range and flexibility, that even her detractors—who complained that Catalini sang with a constant smile on her face, even when acting scenes of sorrow and misplaced love—could not deny her virtuosity.

But *Semiramide*, even when performed with proper attention to the composer's requirements, could not long silence Lady Carlisle. "Well?" she inquired of Lord Denham. "What have you to say for yourself, you shameless man?"

"To you?" retorted Mephisto. "Nothing at all."

It was, perhaps, an inauspicious moment to enter the box, but Lord Camden gave his companions only the slightest of puzzled glances before going to Sir Jason's side. "Did you see the race this morning? Splendid, was it not! A more magnificent creature I have yet to see."

"I am afraid," Sir Jason welcomed a change of subject,

"that I was unable to attend. Perhaps luckily, since I was bound to wager on the wrong horse."

Lady Penelope already had been regaled with several versions of the race in question, and had no great interest in yet another account, even if the animal was generally accorded a remarkable specimen, a dapple grey of particularly noticeable appearance that moved with wonderful coordination and ease. She had not failed to see, during her surreptitious scrutiny of the opposite box, that Luke had been among the gentlemen to seek out Delilah's company. Like a plague, thought Pen, and wondered why the Almighty should single out the males of her family. On the stage, the performance went on, the artists long inured to the disrespect of their audience.

"Men!" Lady Carlisle swelled with frustration, her cheeks so puffed-out they threatened to burst. "They have little notion of what is *truly* important! Come, Denham, I think you must explain to us why you have foisted a straw damsel on the *ton!*"

"I must?" inquired Mephisto, with interest. "Why?"

Lord Camden looked in puzzlement at his twin. "A straw damsel?"

"Sara," Pen sighed, and ceased to try and understand.

"A woman out of a gambling-house!" Ottolie looked very much like a mottled balloon. "So much for your Lady Sara Cainneach!"

"Then there's no castle?" said Gabrielle suddenly. "The stories she told weren't true?" Was no one what he seemed?

"Truth!" Ottolie sputtered. "I doubt the creature knows the meaning of the word!"

"There's a castle, certainly." Miss de la Torre wondered if Lady Carlisle was going to fly apart at the seams. "And a grand show-place it is. But no Cainneachs have lived there for at least a hundred years."

"The Cainneach stables!" said Luke, pleased to realize that he had not been totally deprived of his wits. "The finest stud-farm in all of Ireland."

Lord Denham carelessly flicked open his snuff-box. "Lady Sara," he murmured, "has rather a penchant for anonymity."

Though the King's Theatre was extremely noisy that evening, Lord Denham's box was—despite an energetic exchange of speaking glances—quiet as a tomb. Lady Penelope and

181

Lady Randolph shared a bewilderment no less keen than that of Sir Jason and Lord Camden, Lady Carlisle made a hissing sound, and Lord Randolph was extraordinarily alert.

"Keep us in suspense no longer, Miss de la Torre!" Adam was jubilant, as befit a gentleman whose suspicions had been proven correct. "Give us the lady's name." Gabrielle winced as his fingers bit deeper into her arm.

"She's no more a lady than I am!" Miss de la Torre found it singularly unpleasant to serve as target for Lord Denham's piercing, icy eyes. "In Dublin she called herself Daphne McDougal, though I couldn't swear that even that was her true name."

Chapter 25

Saturday 27 April 1811

"Seven thousand pounds!" I was struck all of a heap. "*How* did you contrive to get so deeply in debt?"

Ninian sheepishly toyed with the brim of his hat. "It was not so difficult." How good it was to see the laughter in his eyes again! "Not half so difficult as seeing my way clear again."

"But to place three thousand on a horse!" I was horrified, not at the size of the wager, but at what must have happened if the horse had failed to win. Ninian would have been torn to pieces by the wolves that slavered at his door! "How were you able to raise such a prodigious sum?"

"It was all in the world I could beg or borrow." With one finger, he traced the line of my chin, effectively distracting me. "How could I by-pass such an opportunity? The horse was sure to win."

I perked up my ears. "How could you know that?"

Ninian appeared fascinated by the movement of my lips. "Have you forgotten my interest in the Turf? Lady Sara was kind enough to drop me a hint. She has no small knowledge of such things. It seems her husband was horse-mad."

Lady Sara! Faro's daughter, Sparrow was, trusting only to the spin of a coin and the luck of the draw, cheating nearly all of us with her poker-face and sleight of hand—and Ninian had gambled on *her* advice, even knowing that she must have at least one more card in her sleeve! But a reconciliation scene is not the best time to quibble over minor details. I sighed blissfully, gazing with near-affection upon the naked fish-tailed females who supported the sofa. It was not a contentment that would long last.

"Merrie." Ninian cleared his throat. "I'm afraid that this is not quite the solution to our problems that it may seem."

The door swung open. I glowered at Sparrow—I could never think of her otherwise, no matter what name she used—and she eyed me quizzically, but proceeded into the room. My chaperone had made a quick recovery from her illness, and I silently wished upon her a quick relapse so that Ninian and I might resume our *tête-à-tête*. I had an uncomfortable feeling that my bed of roses was about to sprout thorns.

Ninian, the coward, greeted Sparrow with obvious relief. "Lady Sara, I am very glad to see you up and around again." My chaperone replied in a gracious manner, smiling as if from a private amusement, and soon they were deep in a discussion of horseflesh. While Sparrow described, in great detail, the kelp treatment upon which all her horses thrived, and which supposedly strengthened their hocks and quarter muscles, I struggled with a strong impulse to gnaw my nails down to the bone.

Up she may have been, but Sparrow was certainly not about, avoiding with great cunning the steady stream of visitors that besieged Denham House. The news had speard through London like wildfire but—and doubtless to Lady Carlisle's chagrin!—I was not the only one who found it difficult to envision Sparrow at home in a gaming-hell. Since I, too, followed the evasive policy, cards were piled in large quantities on the silver tray in the hallway, and persistent callers were conducted to Mme. Dore who, in a sudden excess of garrulous amiability, had emerged from the library to deal most effectively with these scandal-seekers, a process which she referred to as "sending them off with a flea in their ear."

Mephisto had left the house early, in pursuit of his nefarious activities. If it took my last breath, I meant to discover what these were! The world believed that Lord Denham had known all along of Lady Sara's wealth and somewhat scurrilous history. *I* knew better, having been privileged—and *quite* by accident—to overhear a resounding argument between them on that very subject. Mephisto's rather violent protest that Sparrow had failed to lay her cards on the table was countered by *her* opinion of his devious and deceitful character, and thus they reached another impasse.

Save for Sparrow's close association with Lord Denham, however, matters might not have gone so well with her. The *ton*, confronted with startling facts and even more scandalous rumors concerning my chaperone, hemmed and hawed but recalled in time Mephisto's ways of dealing with those who displeased him, and prudently decided to be amused. Yet, though these recent disclosures answered some of my questions about the lady, I could not help but feel I still did not have the entire truth.

She was watching me narrowly, as if she could read my mind. "Your eyes are as large and bright as Deidre of the Sorrows," she remarked. "Her eyes too were green—and, as Bridey would tell you, bright as stars continual with weepin' and wailin'. I hope, Merrie, that your reasons are not the same."

Well they might be, I thought, and briefly pondered the advantages of spinsterhood, as espoused by my aunt. "Why did you let Mephisto persuade you to play chaperone to me?" I asked abruptly. Ninian frowned.

Sparrow grimaced ruefully. "I did not wish to disoblige him." Here was a guilelessness unmatched by any I might assume! Needless to say, I didn't believe a word. "And, too, I wished to see London again. Ireland is beautiful, but I grew desperate for more exciting amusements than taking cross-country walks, and watching the rooks fight at twilight for resting-places in the rowan-trees, and predicting how frequently the weather might change from soft to raw and back again." Nevertheless, she sounded wistful. "Nor did I care to return to Dublin, despite the elegant living and witty conversation and countless foreign visitors of which Miss de la Torre is so fond. The cream of the jest is that the lady was a

184

frequent visitor to our home there. She had little skill with the cards, and even less luck."

"No doubt," I said absently, "that is why she dumped you into the scandal-broth and stirred it so vigorously." At that moment even the Witch of Endor could not have fascinated me. What impediment—aside from Mephisto—did Ninian *now* mean to tell me stood in our way? "And Bridey became your maid?"

"Of course." Such wide-eyed innocence. "Why should you think anything else?"

"I didn't." Perhaps I was a trifle abrupt. "Who is Maeve?"

"Maeve," replied Sparrow, as if to a slow-witted child, "is your guardian's housekeeper. What are you getting at, Merrie?"

"Nothing at all." I presented her with my own imitation of guilelessness. It was not terribly convincing, I suspect, since her amusement grew. "Sir Ninian and I were discussing matters of honor just before you arrived. Perhaps you can settle a point of contention for us."

"I shall try," offered Sparrow cautiously, "if that is what you wish."

Sweetly, I smiled at Ninian, who did not appear best-pleased at this turn of events. "Will you explain? I'm sure you will do a much better job of it than I."

"Perhaps," murmured Sparrow, when he remained stubbornly silent, "I might venture a guess. It concerns your betrothal, does it not, to Miss Allingham?"

"It does," I replied, since Ninian would not. "Sir Ninian claims he is not anxious to marry the lady, and now that he has won enough money to pay off all his debts, he does not need to do so. Yet he will not break the engagement."

Sparrow pushed the hair off her forehead. Odd that the lifting of her burden of deception had brought so little ease. If anything, Sparrow looked even more heavy-laden than usual, and I wondered what crippling mill-stone still hung around her neck. "Is this true?" she demanded. "Forgive me for being so frank, Sir Ninian, but were your debts the sole reason that you offered for Miss Allingham?"

"They were." I was relieved to learn that he hadn't lost all power of speech. "Though not in the manner in which you may think."

185

"I see." Sparrow frowned. "You were, in short, compelled to offer for her."

"I suppose I must tell you the whole," Ninian said reluctantly, "unflattering as it is to me." I gazed rapt upon his beguiling face and wished down upon Miss Allingham's unlovely head all the ills to which flesh is heir. "Papa Allingham has not made so spectacular a success in the world of business without learning the uses of blackmail. He bought up all my vowels, and thus made himself my chief creditor."

"And," remarked Sparrow, with a brief flash of anger that puzzled me, "you were given a choice of betrothing yourself to Miss Allingham, or being clapped into debtors' prison without further ado."

"Precisely." Ninian was remorseful, and Sparrow looked fatigued. *My* temperature soared to such fever-pitch that it nearly turned my brain.

"I suppose," Sparrow glanced cautiously at me, "that the Allinghams are not best-pleased that you have made a comeabout."

Ninian grinned. "No. The old man actually declared he would not let me buy back my vowels! Of course, he changed his mind. Allingham is not one to turn aside money, no matter how it irks him to be out-maneuvered."

"But, in truth, it is you who have been backed into a corner"—Sparrow sighed. I could barely breathe, so scalding was my rage. The Allinghams' treachery had already sent me seething like a boiling pot, and Ninian's willingness to confide in Sparrow only added fuel to the flame—"since it is clear that, in turn, you are not to be released from the marriage-contract."

"Quite clear." Almost absently, Ninian took my hand. "It is as much as my life is worth to try to renege, according to Allingham."

I could remain silent no longer. "This," I cried, "has gone entirely too far! Will you allow yourself to be brow-beaten and bullied into a course of action that is repugnant to you? Ninian, where is your backbone?"

"Where it belongs, I trust." He pressed my hand, as if in warning. "Don't get onto your high ropes, Merrie! Something may be contrived."

"Something," I retorted snappily, "had dashed well better be!"

186

"Tsk!" Leaning heavily on her cane, Tayce hobbled into the room. "I do not know where you learned this vulgarity, *petite*. Certainly not from me." She settled in an oval-backed chair and drew forth her knitting.

"Have all the callers gone?" Sparrow could never watch my aunt's ill-advised efforts with anything but awe.

"They have," replied Tayce, with such utmost cordiality that I immediately grew alert. "A mealy-mouthed lot, to be sure! You might thank me for rescuing you from their infernal prose."

"I do." There was no doubt of Sparrow's sincerity.

Tayce was off on some scent of her own. "Brummel called, and Lady Jersey. Even Lord Randolph came to extend his regards."

Sparrow sat up straighter, a spot of color in each cheek. "Did you inquire after Gabrielle?" she asked quickly. "Such a charming child, though a trifle lacking in animation."

Tayce shrugged, totally unconcerned. "I doubt there's little wrong with the girl that a discrete *affaire* would not cure."

"Did you," Ninian inquired with interest, "make known your opinion to Lord Randolph?"

With a cackle, my aunt adjusted her spectacles. "I was mighty tempted, young man! It is entirely Randolph's own fault that the girl is terrified of him. One does not treat a child like a woman off the streets, after all." She surveyed Sparrow over the rim of her glasses, again on the end of her nose. "Am I not correct? *You* do not sanction May/December marriages, surely?"

"I am certain," Sparrow replied evasively, "that you are correct." From the intensity with which she surveyed her knuckles, they might have been hitherto-unexplored territory.

"Some men are not meant for marriage at all," observed Tayce, knitting-needles clicking busily and with disastrous results. "Look at Jean Larousse! That one was the most impudent rascal that ever existed. A regular devil with the ladies—as I can personally attest!—and yet I pity the woman he would have as a bride."

"Jean Larousse?" repeated Ninian, justifiably tantalized by this glimpse of my aunt's past career. She was only too delighted to explain.

"He went too far," said Tayce serenely, "when he became

involved in a foreign p' >t to assassinate the revolutionary leaders. *Eh bien!* We fled."

No one asked the obvious question—the reason for Tayce's bland assertion that she, too, must flee at the same time—but I'm sure it was uppermost in every mind. "What happened to him?" asked Sparrow. My interest was at least as great; it was at this point that Tayce invariably ended the tale.

I had long nourished a lively curiosity about the legendary Jean Larousse. He remained almost wraith-like, so little of him was known. Like Saint-Just, he was one of the members of the Great Committee of Public Safety in 1792; but where Saint-Just was both chosen president of the Convention and beheaded during the following year, Jean Larousse proved more far-sighted. Despite intensive inquiries, I was able to learn nothing more of him, save that he was approximately twenty-eight years old in 1793, when he and my aunt so abruptly departed France. Tayce was then thirty-three.

My aunt shrugged. "Who knows? They have never been able to trace him."

Who? I wondered, but blinding illumination struck just then. Ninian and Sparrow were staring at my aunt with identical expressions of disappointed curiosity. I gasped.

Sparrow's eyes were the cold, dead ashes of a fire that burned out long ago. "I wondered," she said, "how long it would take you to realize."

"Too long," commented Tayce. "Such is the blindness of love." It was obviously an illness of which she had particular experience.

Stung by this censure, I turned on Ninian, wrenching my hand away. "Why didn't you *tell* me?" Not an original remark, perhaps, but I resented having been made to look the fool.

Ninian laughed, not the least affected by my wrath. "How could I, poppet? It was not my secret to tell." His eyes met Sparrow's identical grey eyes. "In truth, I did not realize myself, at first. It had been a very long time."

" 'Twas better so," Sparrow said softly. The resemblance grew even stronger as they both smiled at me. "Now you understand another of the reasons I was eager to return. Mephisto told me Ninian had taken up residence in town."

My head positively swam. "*Mephisto* knew?" Lest the reader fall victim to the same error I did, I add a word of caution:

leaping to conclusions can be quite as dangerous as leaping off the sheerest precipice. I, to my sorrow, know.

"Of course. He and I *are* distantly related, and spent much time together when we both were young." It did not seem a particularly pleasant memory. "You and I, however, are not. Had I known then of your, ah, association with Ninian, I would not have told that particular fib."

A polite word, I mused, for outright prevarication. How many other so-called fibs must she have told? The sum must truly have been staggering! "But for what purpose did Mephisto bring you here?"

"My dear, you might as well inquire of me why the Almighty causes the sun to shine!" The merriment had left her thin features, almost as if that same sun had retreated behind a cloud. "Mephisto keeps his own counsel—sometimes, I think, too well."

The ramifications were slow to appear to me, an event that may be partially related to the fact that Ninian's arm was stretched out along the back of the sofa, his hand so close to the nape of my neck that the skin burned. Conversation ceased, briefly, while Wiggins bowed himself into the room and extended to Lady Sara a folded note on a tray. She took it in puzzlement, scanned the few lines, and her face turned that shade of dead-white that laundry-maids aspired to for the linens and so seldom achieved. With a mumbled excuse, my chaperone fairly ran from the room.

"Poor Lady Sara! This has been hard for her." Tayce radiated Christian charity. I eyed her shrewdly. Even the milk of human kindness in *that* container would quickly sour!

"I wish," I said plaintively, firmly removing Ninian's hand, which now trespassed among my curls, "you would inform me of what is going on!"

"Are you never content, *petite?* Too many explanations will only overtax your mind." My aunt looked like an emaciated Buddha, so bland and serene was her smile.

Ninian chuckled and I glowered at the both of them. "I still think," I snapped, "that I might have been told that Sparrow is Ninian's sister." Before I could indulge myself with further outpourings, the previously-mentioned ramifications hit me in full force. "Dear God!" I cried, cheeks atingle. "Does *Adam* realize?"

189

Chapter 26

The Mark of Cain

Once again Lady Randolph was curled up on the bedroom rug, her back propped against a chair, staring into the cold fireplace. She made a lovely picture, her plain dark dress accentuating her lovely skin and fiery hair. A key turned in the lock.

"My dear," said Lord Randolph, stepping into the room, "will you never learn to comport yourself in a manner suitable to your rank and station?"

Gabrielle sprang to her feet in a flurry of dark skirts and petticoats. "I think," she said, with all the firmness she could muster, which was not considerable, "that there are some things we should discuss, Adam."

"Oh?" He grasped her throat and forced back her head so that he might look deep into her eyes. "What might those be?"

He was like an occultist, drawing her will from her body to replace it with his own. Gabrielle's voice, when she spoke, was faint. "You are very interested in Lady Sara Cainneach, or whatever her name is. I would like to know why."

"Poor demented Gabrielle!" As if she were repellant, disfigured, he pushed her away. "Your sick fancies, these delusions that can spring only from a troubled brain, grow steadily worse. I fear you will soon live entirely in a dream world."

Lady Randolph's next action indicated that she truly *had* been deprived of her wits. She persevered. "Lady Sara, my lord?"

Adam's smile turned his wife's bones to the consistency of pudding. "You are such a perfect angel, with those innocent brown eyes that positively tug at one's heart-strings." Heart?

thought Gabrielle. In Lord Randolph's chest that organ must lay as black and mute and cold as a lump of coal.

He moved to the dressing-table and placed an idle hand on the delicate satinwood. "A pity, my dear, but there is a nothingness in you that is in the last degree fatiguing, to say nothing of your odd humors. It is why I must insist that you do not go into public, lest our entire acquaintance becomes aware of your lunacy."

It would never be any different between them. He was the turnkey, and she was as effectively imprisoned as any lawless felon awaiting execution in the condemned cell. Life in a lunatic asylum might be preferable. "I think, my lord," Gabrielle said quietly, "that it is you who are mad."

He spun around and struck her with a force that lifted her completely off her feet. She lay where she had fallen, too stunned and terrified to move. Adam nudged her with the toe of his boot and then walked away.

"You might as well get up," he said contemptuously. "I hardly imagine it's comfortable for you to be sprawling on the floor."

He didn't sound as if he intended further violence and Gabrielle cautiously opened her eyes. Immediately, she wished she had not. Adam held the bottle of laudanum in one strong, tanned hand.

"Lady Sara Cainneach?" he mused. "Do you think I have nourished an excessive interest in her, a *tendre* perhaps? Paugh!" He hurled the bottle into the fireplace, where it shattered. "Better the wench was dead." It was a thought that occupied him all the way down the stairs.

But Lord Randolph was not to leave his house just then, despite the crucial engagement that he dared not fail to keep. His butler hovered in the hallway. "A caller, my lord," said that worthy, with marked reluctance. "In the book-room."

With a curse that sent the terrified servant scurrying for shelter, Adam strode swiftly to the small study where he drafted the terse, pithy and pungent speeches for which he was famous—or infamous. His opponents complained that Lord Randolph turned Parliament into a Roman arena, with themselves serving as dinner for the lions—in the House of Lords. A quick glance at his desk, strewn with official-looking papers and dog-eared books, assured him that nothing of an incriminating nature lay in view.

191

Mephisto had made himself comfortable in a worn leather chair. "I've heard the oddest things about that will of Sherrington's," Adam said abruptly. His uninvited, and unwelcome, visitor looked as endurable and immovable as a mountain cliff. "I recall no codicil to the effect that Miss Sherrington loses all if she weds without consent."

"Ah." Lord Denham's glacial eyes had left even Brummel complaining of a frost-bitten nose and chilblains. "But then, you have not particularly concerned yourself with the Sherrington estate, have you, Adam? Shocking negligence in an executor."

"I assumed you preferred to deal with the matter yourself." It was not awe but prudence that dictated Lord Randolph's reply. Mephisto crushed men as easily as lesser beings swatted flies.

"You were quick enough to interfere in the instance of young Northcliffe." Lord Denham contemplated his glass. "It was singularly ill-advised of you."

"Was it?" Adam paced irritably. Mephisto was an uncanny devil, but even he was not omniscient. "That problem, at least, is solved. Young Northcliffe won't get his hands on the Sherrington fortune now. Allingham will see to that."

"How much of that, I wonder, was your doing?" Lord Randolph reached for the brandy decanter, and Mephisto's thin lips twisted mirthlessly. "It would behoove you greatly, Adam, to refrain from further meddling in my plans for Miss Sherrington!"

Docility did not come easily to Lord Randolph, but he had no time, then, for quarrels. White-lipped, he bowed. "As you wish, of course. I still think it's damned odd I didn't know about that rider to the old man's will."

"It seems I have not made myself clear." Mephisto's fingers on the rim of the brandy glass brought forth a melancholy chime. "You are not to further exercise your mind, Adam, in that affair. You do understand?"

Irritably, Adam shuffled through his papers—an acerbic dissertation on the controversial Corn Laws—and arranged them in a neat stack. "Perfectly." How much easier life would go on without the Duke of Denham's continual interference! "You arrange all to suit yourself, and always have."

"Yes." Lord Denham projected an aura of considerable malevolence. "It is a way of life which suits me admirably.

Tell me, how does your charming wife? We have not been privileged to see her since the Opera."

Lord Randolph's pained mien expressed husbandly concern and distress. "I tell you this in strictest confidence, but my wife is far from well. I am considering removing her to the country, since it grows increasingly apparent that town-life does not agree with her." Gabrielle would quick enough be changed from a stubborn filly into a docile brood mare. If she balked, all the better. Adam was not adverse to the use of whip and spur.

But if there was a woman who concerned both these men, it was not Lady Randolph. Mephisto rose and approached the desk. "Another speech?" he inquired. "More vehement opposition to treating with Napoleon?"

"Not precisely." This game they played was for hazardously high stakes. Adam glanced impatiently at the wall-clock and called his opponent's hand. "What's on your mind, Denham? You did not come here to exchange gossip with me, or even, unless I miss my guess, to inquire into Gabrielle's welfare."

"How perceptive!" Mephisto's heavy lids half-hooded his pale eyes. "An odd rumor has come to my attention. I thought you might find it of some interest, being so actively opposed to all things French." He flicked open his snuff-box. "Odd, isn't it, that Mme. Dore should find you familiar?"

So now they came down to it! Adam frowned. "A simple error, as she explained. I pity you, Denham, having that hellhag residing in your house! Go on. What is this rumor?"

"No new suspicion, certainly, but one that bears consideration." Lord Denham's harsh features were grim. "In short, the notion has occurred to various concerned parties that certain privileged information has a strange way of falling into French hands."

"Spies!" Adam grimaced as if he'd bitten into something sour. Yet the disclosure came as little surprise. "In Westminster, I suppose! Poppycock!"

"Is it? I wonder." Lord Denham lifted a pinch of snuff to one arched nostril. "Consider: Wellington's plan to recapture Badajoz has been foiled; he found the fortress not only provisioned for several months but strong enough to withstand anything short of full-scale attack by experienced sappers and battering-guns. He himself was almost captured during the reconnaissance, by a sudden sortie. If the troops at Alameida can be reprovisioned, and with Badajoz also in French hands, Napoleon will remain free to renew the invasion of Portugal."

"Are you reciting for me a history of the French progress?" Adam inquired testily. "I assure you it is unnecessary." Only moments more and he would be too late.

"Patience, Adam." Lord Denham was at his most genial when treading on someone's corns. "I am well aware that you are vigorous in your prosecution of the war. To continue, despite repeated warnings, Spain has allowed the only regular bridge of boats in the allies' possession to fall into enemy hands. Plans have gone astray, the most secret information has been ferreted out and sold to the French." He raised a dark brow. "Need I say more?"

"No." Perhaps a tolerant amusement was the best attitude to take. "Be reasonable, Denham! There are always rumors of such things. We have been for twenty years at war with France, and now the first faint signs of victory are showing themselves. Wellington is more than holding his own in the Peninsula."

"My sentiments precisely. You reassure me greatly, Adam, since you are in a position to know." Lord Randolph's eyes narrowed, but Mephisto's stern features gave nothing away. With a murmured apology for keeping his host from more important pursuits, Lord Denham departed, leaving Adam wondering at his purpose, and if it had been achieved. Carefully, Adam closed the book-room door behind him as he stepped into the hall.

Powerful as Mephisto was, he could not hold off destiny any more than Napoleon could prevent Wellington's inevitable march through the Peninsula, over the Pyrenees and into France. Adam opened the front door. Once the Northcliffe imbroglio was resolved, he might concentrate on Gabrielle, locked safely in her room like a bird in a golden cage—a cage to which only he had the key.

But Lord Randolph erred in his judgement of his wife, who was at that moment also exiting the house, by way of a huge gnarled tree. It was not an exercise that she performed with any noteworthy skill, and there was one terror-filled moment when she thought she would fall straight to her death, but she gained the ground without serious mishap. Gabrielle

194

looked at the house one last time, and shuddered. She did not know where she would go, but she vowed to never return.

Lady Randolph's progress through London's labyrinth of dark alleys and elegant squares only proved once more that the Almighty is kindly disposed towards innocents and fools. Despite the countless horrors that lurked in wait for young women who ventured alone and penniless into those ill-lit streets, she was molested by neither footpads or bosky gentlemen. Her most anxious moment was caused by the sound of her husband's voice.

She had not meant to follow him, and shrank back into one of those black alleyways. The street was deserted except for Adam and his companion, a shabby seedy little man, and an old-fashioned coach. "She stepped into the rattler as sweetly as you please," said the stranger, "and we had her trussed up as neat as can be in near-record time."

"I trust," murmured Adam, "that the coach was not distinguishable." Gabrielle held her breath against the sickly-sweet stench of rotting drains.

"O' course not, guv'nor." Indignantly, the little man gestured. "As you can see. We took her to Madame Eugenie's as instructed, and left her stretched out as stiff as a corpse." He chuckled. " 'Tis a long way from Ireland, when all's said!"

"You're paid," growled Lord Randolph, "to keep your mouth shut. Must I remind you of that?"

"No, guv'nor." The hireling was abashed. "But murder's what I don't hold with, not being wishful of ending up on the Nubbing Cheat."

"Do you mean to tell me my business?" The mere sound of Adam's voice made Gabrielle's blood run cold.

"Not at all, guv'nor, not at all!" The little man seemed to share her malady. "You know your business best, I'm sure." Without another word, he melted into the night.

Gabrielle stood still as a statue as Adam stepped into the waiting carriage, passing within mere feet of her, then lifted her skirts and fled. Several times she tripped and fell on the uneven cobblestones.

It was a breathless and disheveled Countess who at last came to Denham House. Gabrielle's gown was torn, her hands lacerated and filthy, and a hideous bruise was forming on her jaw. Without a word to the horrified Wiggins, she stumbled directly into the drawing-room.

195

Miss Sherrington and Mme. Dore were within. *"Merde!"* said Tayce, and dropped her knitting. Making soothing noises, Merrie guided Lady Randolph to the couch.

"Adam!" gasped Gabrielle, through her tears. "He's taken Lady Sara to someone called Eugenie."

Chapter 27

Monday 29 April 1811

My aunt should have known that I would follow her, and what a wild chase it was, with Tayce careening *ventre à terre* through London's dark deserted streets. Among my aunt's myriad other accomplishments was no small expertise in handling the reins. Mephisto's head groom had not been eager to harness his master's favorite blacks to the light and sporty little gig, but my aunt overcame this reluctance with a few well-aimed jabs of her cane.

I followed, astride Mephisto's huge roan gelding, at a discreet distance. Folly, to have disobeyed my aunt's stern injunction to remain in Denham House and apprise Mephisto, upon his return, of what had transpired; but I could not wait quietly while Tayce went to rendezvous with danger, unescorted and unarmed. Instead, I had scrawled a note to my guardian, consigned the half-hysterical Gabrielle to Maeve's astonished care, and set out upon my own mission of rescue.

Madame Eugenie was a third-rate milliner, with an establishment in the Haymarket. She was also a shrewd businesswoman, renting out her ill-kept rooms to lovers and other fools, then blackmailing them. Reflecting how my reputation must suffer from this discreditable excursion, I slipped from the horse's broad warm back and thrust the reins into the hands of a goggling links-boy.

Effecting an entrance to the shabby little shop presented no great difficulty: Tayce, in her haste, had left the door ajar.

There were a number of questions I might have asked, had not Tayce's peril and Sparrow's plight been uppermost in my mind, such as how my aunt had learned so much about the nature of this shop. But the implications escaped me and I moved gingerly into the dark interior, past counters piled high with clothes and merchandise, through cramped workrooms, up a narrow flight of stairs. What a trusting, stupid little fool! I hoped that Tayce had found Sparrow before Adam caused her harm. It was a puzzle to me that he should nourish such rancor after so many years, and for so little cause. Pride, as Tayce often said, is a great weakness in a man.

Moving quietly as a ghost, I gained the upper hallway, then stood motionless. Voices came to me faintly and I moved towards their source, keeping close to the wall lest the old floorboards creak. A faint glimmer of light escaped through the cracks in a warped door. I sank to my knees before it and gazed through the keyhole.

Tayce was seated primly on a straight wooden chair, her hands folded on her silver-knobbed cane, looking for all the world as if she was waiting for her tea. "I believe," she said thoughtfully, "I preferred you as Jean Larousse." My mouth dropped open; *Adam* had been an adventurer, a revolutionary, an anarchist? It was only the first in a series of disclosures that struck me like hammerblows.

Lord Randolph stood before my aunt. Whatever he once may have felt for Tayce, he did not love her now. "You," and I flinched at the anger in his voice, "are a damned interfering woman."

"*Vraiment!*" retorted Tayce, admirably composed. Sparrow lay on a mean cot, but I had no way of telling if she was merely unconscious, or dead. "It is what you should have expected. Fortunate, that I arrived in time! Of course you will allow her to regain her senses so that you may describe to her in detail just how she will die. It is your usual manner, is it not?"

In Adam's eyes flared the dehumanized blood-lust of a tiger crouched to spring. "How the *devil* do you come to be here?" Even the rough timbre in his voice was feral, virulent. He would devour my aunt in one gulp, then spit out her scrawny bones.

"Your wife." Tayce's composure would have done credit to a

lion-tamer. "We waste time, *mon ami*. This love of death is a weakness in you, it makes you vulnerable."

"Vulnerable!" I shared Adam's astonishment. It was Tayce who was defenseless—or so it seemed. "I do not think you have considered your own position, Mme. Dore."

Perhaps she had not, but *I* had and I was half-sick with fear for her. "It is you who have not considered," she replied. "It is another of your flaws. Had you planned better the matter of your brother's death, Sparrow would not have learned of it. Had you not then let her escape you, and failed to track her down, you would not be in this predicament now. Nor were you quick to realize who she was."

Lord Randolph did not deny responsibility for his brother's murder. I wondered how many other men's blood stained his hands, and if he meant to add both Sparrow and Tayce to his death-roll. "You are," he said softly, "too astute for your own good."

My aunt's nose twitched as she drew her cane into her lap. "And *you* are in a quandary!" There was mingled sarcasm and satisfaction in her tone. "Do you think that if you kill Sparrow, Mephisto will allow you to go free? *Au contraire.* Yet if you do not kill her, she will expose you. Then there is your wife, whose behavior cannot be predicted. A pretty dilemma!"

"It is kind of you," replied Lord Randolph, with equal sarcasm, "to concern yourself with my affairs." There was barely-suppressed violence in his every movement, even the way he crossed his arms, and a brutal hatred in the gaze he bent on her.

"Pah!" My aunt rose, leaning heavily on her cane. "You have left me no choice. I cannot afford investigation into the activities of the one-time Jean Larousse."

It was only due to the stunning nature of the drama being played out before my eyes that I failed to see what Tayce might wish to hide. Lord Randolph understood, however. He swore an oath of unhuman savagery.

"Did you think I would not recognize you after so many years, and without your disguise?" Tayce frowned at him, over the top of her spectacles, much like a disapproving schoolmistress. "Cretin! All along I was aware of your identity. And I knew when we came to London that I would eventually have to deal with you."

"Lest it be discovered that Mme. Dore now serves France as she once did England." I almost moaned aloud. Adam stepped towards her.

My aunt only laughed. "You Englishmen!" she jeered. "So virtuously loyal to your country, yet capable of the most barbaric butchery! Me, I am loyal only to myself."

"It was you who betrayed me to the Committee." Barbaric was the word for Adam at that moment, and I feared that butchery would follow apace.

Tayce didn't bat an eyelid. "Of course! Do not take it so personally, *mon chou!* I admit it was an error, but you had grown careless, and I could not take the chance that your bungling would also bring me down. And as matters were, it nearly did."

I had my hand on the doorknob, ready to hurl myself into the room, but Adam didn't touch her. Perhaps he dared not. "How many lives have you been responsible for? Robespierre, Saint-Just—you even betrayed your precious Marie Antoinette, and made possible her capture at Varennes. How many others, Mme. Dore?"

Never had my aunt appeared more decorously sedate, and I prayed that Lord Randolph was mistaken, that Tayce couldn't have done these things. But the Almighty turned a deaf ear to my entreaties that day. "I did not count them, *chéri.* France breeds idealists and takes great delight in killing them. I merely contrived to remain alive."

"Contrived! Yes, you contrived." It was almost as if he admired her unemotional triumph over impossible odds. Suddenly I realized how this confrontation must end. Too late, then, to run for help, and I had taken only one step forward when Adam spoke again. "As you contrived to deceive your niece about her father's will."

Tayce threw back her head to look him straight in the face, but said nothing. "I am very familiar with that document." Adam's smile was vicious. "Your niece is free to wed as she wishes, and will suffer no loss of her fortune if she does so without consent. A sad come-down for the brilliant Mme. Dore! To be dependant on a mere girl for the very bread you eat."

I suppose I was a ridiculous sight, doubled over in the hallway, but Fate, that bloody pugilist, had dealt me a body blow. "I am not so dependant on my niece's good graces as you

199

assume." Tayce limped towards him with an admirable aplomb. "I will admit to you that Merrie has not been one of my successes. I had hoped to persuade her against matrimony and thus enable us both to live out our days comfortably, but I have failed. Soon enough she will marry and control of her fortune will pass into other hands." She shrugged. "One cannot expect always to win."

Sparrow moaned faintly and stirred, an act that sent Lord Randolph to bend over her, scowling, and brought a similar frown to my aunt's face. Adam turned back to her, his eyes narrowed to rabid slits. "I do not think you understand that you have presented me with an excellent opportunity, Mme. Dore!"

"To catch—or kill—a spy?" Calmly, Tayce glanced at Sparrow, quiet once more. "I think I prefer to remain a reclusive maiden aunt."

And *I* swallowed bile. How easy it must have been for Tayce to delude my father, to caress him with one hand while with the other she pilfered from his pockets secrets of state. Oh, God, it explained so much!

"Do you think," Adam hissed, "that I offer you a choice?"

"No." Tayce held up her cane as if with that puny weapon she might stave him off. "But I did not come here to die."

It was the moment for a dramatic entrance—but I caught my heel in the flounce of my skirt, fell against the door, and tumbled ignominiously into the room.

"Petite!" My aunt looked as she always did, a gaunt black-clad figure with straggling grey hair, her spectacles perched on the tip of her nose, and in her hand the ebony cane; but she was a total, terrible stranger to me. "You heard?"

I cautiously picked myself up from the floor, and nodded. "All of it."

Adam moved towards me, as swift and grim as the Angel of Death. I darted away from him as best I could on an ankle that was newly-sprained; then stopped short in my tracks as Tayce withdrew a wicked rapier from the sheath of her cane. My eyes widened. With an oath, Adam swung around.

I would like to say that a battle royal ensued, with Adam armed and bent on slaughter, and my aunt fighting desperately for all our lives; but it would not be true. Adam had no weapon—a startling omission for a villain, perhaps, but the fact remains—and some vestige of honor prevented him from dealing with a crippled woman as harshly as he would a man. He merely meant to disarm her, I think, but he did not succeed. Tayce dispatched him with her usual brisk efficiency, and I stood rooted to the floor and watched murder done.

"You've overreached yourself this time," Adam gasped. "M—" And then he fell.

Tayce was muttering beneath her breath, a mixture of Gallic curses and what sounded like a lament for *le Chevalier* and *l'amour*. She jerked the sword from Adam's body and turned towards me.

"*Le Chevalier?*" I asked faintly, overwhelmed by warring emotions. This was my aunt, astringent perhaps, certainly conscienceless, but part of my memory for as far back as I could recall, and I could not reconcile what I knew of her with what I had just learned.

"Did I not tell you that tale, *petite?* A pity for now there is no time. Sparrow will awaken soon." Inscrutable, she wiped the bloody sword on a ragged window-drapery.

"We must get help." I was thinking frantically, and not too well. The fate of murderers was all-too-clearly in my mind, and I thought we must contrive mightily to see that my aunt did not hang. "A doctor! Perhaps Adam is not dead. I will swear to Mephisto that it was Adam who was a spy."

"No, *petite.*" Tayce's voice was very, very kind. "I shall say something of the sort, *naturellement,* but *you* will say nothing at all." She hobbled within a rapier's length of me and, had she then raised the *épée*, might have decapitated me with a single thrust. Instead she moved closer, and for the first time that I can recall, bent to brush her dry lips against my cheek. It seemed an odd time for such demonstrativeness, with Sparrow sprawled, barely breathing, on the cot, and blood from Adam's body soaking into the floor. "Tayce," I protested, "we must make plans!"

"I already have, Merrie. That is what I am trying to tell you." She raised the sword. Behind her spectacles, the faded eyes were sad. "You should have listened to me, and stayed safely at home. *Ma pauvre petite!* I regret, but the best secrets are kept by only one."

But I was no longer held immobile. As she lunged, I leaped towards the window. The rapier caught my arm and, in agony, I clutched the curtains. The building was old and rotting; with a groan, the rod came loose, and Tayce was

201

caught in the fabric's filthy folds. She fell back, coughing and gasping, and I stumbled across the room.

Where I would have gone, what Tayce would have done, I do not know. Mephisto stood in the doorway, a pistol in his hand. With the other arm, he caught me and drew me against his chest, where I sobbed bitterly. "You have indeed over-reached yourself," he said calmly, "this time, Mme. Dore."

Chapter 28

Across the Rubicon

Pen was as round-eyed as a golden owl caught napping. "I simply can't believe it!" she cried, not for the first time. "Mme. Dore! Thank heaven that you arrived in time."

"In point of fact," said Lord Denham, who had a slightly raffish air, perhaps because he had not seen his bed the preceding night, "I was there all along. I was aware that Adam had Sparrow in, er, custody, and expected that Tayce would make an appearance." He sat down on the mermaid sofa and stretched out his long legs. "I did *not* anticipate Meredith's arrival—which, considering my past experience with the chit, was singularly remiss of me. The curst brat and her eternal eavesdropping!"

Pen cast her elder brother a perplexed glance. Despite the severity of his words, she suspected he was amused. Never would she understand the man! "I shudder to think what might have happened to her. Poor child!"

"Yes." Mephisto passed her his tea-cup and Pen refilled it, finding solace in the familiar activity. "I fear I haven't handled this affair with my usual efficiency! I never thought that even Meredith would be sufficiently cork-brained to interfere, and thus failed to intervene in time."

"She isn't seriously wounded?" Sir Jason, who'd been gazing out the window, glanced back at them.

202

"No. Her arm will heal faster, I suspect, than her disillusionment. She had no idea of her aunt's activities. However, Meredith's main reaction seems to be not horror or dismay, but pique that she failed to see what went on right under her nose." Mephisto elevated a sardonic brow. "Meredith is prodigiously like her aunt! I suppose we should be grateful that Mme. Dore did not involve the child in espionage."

Pen addressed her husband, who wore a wry expression, with a certain acerbity. "I fail to see, Jason, how you can consider this a source of amusement!"

"Not this, but that!" Jason flicked the window-curtain. He had an excellent view of the gardens below. "I'll wager our grieving widow will not go unsolaced long."

"Gabrielle!" Lord Camden had undertaken to escort the young lady, now considerably calmer than she had been the previous evening, on a gentle constitutional. Lady Randolph had accepted Adam's death stoically, but adamantly refused to return to her husband's house.

"You will soon have your wish." Mephisto drained his teacup. "At least one of your brothers will be happily established."

"Christian!" Pen scolding her elder brother was rather like a lamb chastising a lion, and had about as much effect. "Gabrielle has only been widowed a matter of hours! There must be a decent period of mourning before she can even consider marrying again. Remember, none but ourselves know what really occurred." To the world Gabrielle must appear grief-stricken, for Mephisto had employed considerable finesse in hushing up the more scandalous aspects of Adam's demise. Lord Randolph would be remembered by many as a discerning, if irascible, politician; by some, as the superior British agent who had caused such useful dissent among the leaders of Revolutionary France; and by a very few as an executioner more bloody, more inhuman, than the guillotine.

Jason cast one last, amused glance out the window, then moved away. "My dear," he said to his wife, "rest assured that the proprieties will be observed. Gabrielle will withdraw to the bosom of her family, and Luke will soon find reason to travel frequently into that part of the country. I doubt that before long he will be considered a part of the family! But he will not press his suit, thus allowing Gabrielle sufficient time

203

to forget her unhappy experience with the marital state, and at the same time, to become dependant on his company. At the year's end"—he snapped his fingers—"wedding bells!"

Lord Denham's matrimonial prospects did not appear similarly optimistic, since Lady Carlisle was directing her not-inconsiderable energies towards the defamation of his character. Pen regarded her husband, that veteran survivor of mud-slinging campaigns. "You seem very sure," her tone was uncomplimentary, "of how it will be."

"Of course." Sir Jason was bland. "I have had considerable experience in such matters, you know."

"Speaking of Mme. Dore," interrupted Mephisto firmly, and startling both of them. "We were, you know. She maintained an incredible correspondence, and in that way passed on her information without ever leaving the house. It had not escaped the attention of certain interested parties that Tayce possessed highly questionable politics, but nothing could be done while Sherrington remained so adamant in her defense."

"I still cannot credit!" Pen repeated once again. "Mme. Dore a French spy!"

"Not only French." Mephisto sounded rueful. "Tayce sold information to whomever seemed expeditious. While in England, she dealt with the French; while in France, with the English." His smile was genuine. "And God alone knows who else!"

"What will happen now?" Pen still could not believe that limping bespectacled figure was England's dangerous foe. "What have you done with her?"

"She is in Newgate for the moment." Mephisto answered the last question first. His sister gasped. "In a private cell, Pen. She is quite comfortable. She has also confessed everything, complete to such details as names, in the hope that she may now get on with her manuscript."

Jason laughed and leaned indolently against his wife's chair. "Truly an indomitable female!"

"Yes," agreed Mephisto. "I confess to a sneaking affection for the wretch, for all she led me a merry dance. As to her fate, that I cannot predict, but Meredith has extracted my oath that her aunt will not hang, an oath prompted by my own distaste for the scandal *that* would mean." He made no

204

effort to suppress a yawn. "It is a pity Tayce possesses none of her niece's loyalty."

"Hang!" Pen was aghast. "Oh no, Christian! Surely she did nothing so terrible that she must hang!"

Lord Denham was afflicted by a sudden choking fit, and Sir Jason dropped a hand to his wife's shoulder. "It is the customary punishment," he murmured, "for treason."

"Then it is injust." Many might call Lady Penelope empty-headed, but none could deny her heart was in the right place.

"Is it?" Again Mephisto demonstrated his affection for his frivolous half-sister; his tone was gentle. "Consider the state of the British economy. Mills and factories have closed down, the cost of bread has risen to almost famine point, large numbers of workers are unemployed, and wages have dropped to starvation level. Soon we shall have labor troubles and rioting again."

"What has that to do with Mme. Dore?" Pen, a vigorous champion of the oppressed, immediately took Mme. Dore under her wing, there to shelter with an ill-assorted company which included orphans, fallen women and stray dogs. Sir Jason amused himself by imagining what Tayce would say to such philanthropy.

"It has a great deal to do with Napoleon's Continental Blockade." Mephisto exhibited great patience. "Where do you think he got the idea? Yet, despite her helpfulness, Tayce is not a fan of Napoleon and doesn't believe that he will remain in power long. With an eye to the future, she has also established contact with the exiled Bourbons."

So much for the addle-pated notion of Mme. Dore as an unfortunate plaything of the gods! Sir Jason smiled upon his crusading wife, who had been stricken dumb. "Consider, too," Lord Denham continued, "the French privateers who terrorize our coasts. Last year they captured over six hundred British ships; and grew so daring that they dashed by dozens into every fleet, taking prizes in plain sight of English farmers. They knew the English coast-lines and routes of trade, the tactics of the British cruisers, the time of arrival and departure of convoys. Need I remind you that Sherrington held a high position in the Admiralty?"

As Pen sat shaking her head in disbelief, Sparrow quietly entered the room. "Merrie's fine," she said in answer to Mephisto's questioning look. "Her spirits have been consid-

205

erably elevated by the arrival of a huge floral offering from a certain young gentleman." She bent to press her cheek to Pen's. "You were speaking of Tayce? I never suspected she was anything but what she seemed. I suppose Adam became acquainted with her in France, when they were both English agents?" She sank into a chair. "I did not know of *that*, either, although that Adam should have been involved in a revolution comes as no great surprise!"

Pen begged to differ. The whole thing, spies and counterspies and espionage, was far-fetched to the point of farce—except that Merrie lay upstairs with a wounded arm, and Mme. Dore was in Newgate Prison, and Lord Randolph was dead.

"No." Mephisto became aware of his empty tea-cup, and set it down. "In his capacity as an agent, Adam was a considerable asset to England. Unfortunately, during the Terror, he also found innumerable opportunities to indulge his less-pleasant tendencies." Pen thought she'd never seen him look so tired. "Adam was an intimate of the infamous Comte de Sade. There was an unfortunate occasion when a young girl died, and other occasions even more unspeakable. Nevertheless, Adam was loyal to his country, and was sincere in his efforts for social reform." His stern features were rueful. "Ironically, Tayce also rendered considerable service to England at one time. It will weigh in her favor."

"Tayce," remarked Sparrow tartly, "seems to have been remarkably adept at keeping one foot in both camps!"

"Agreed." Mephisto's voice was amused. "In truth, she has unwittingly provided us with another advantage, which may help us to end this accursed war. I provided her false information, with the result that Napoleon has been grossly misled concerning the British abilities and the condition of our troops and plans to withdraw his forces from Portugal and Spain. It is the opportunity that Wellington has been awaiting so long."

"But what," persisted poor, befuddled Pen, "did Tayce mean to do with Sara—I mean, Daphne?"

"Nothing." Mephisto ceded Sparrow the floor. "She meant me to waken in a corpse-strewn room, nothing more. There would naturally, have been no way to link the murders to her."

"But—" wailed Pen.

"But she had taken my horses," Mephisto interrupted, "and Gabrielle knew where she'd gone. I doubt Mme. Dore meant to ever return to Denham House." He smiled. "That accurst brat truly upset the apple-cart."

"By killing Adam and Merrie," Sparrow mused, "Tayce would have disposed of the only people who might expose her activities." She glanced at Mephisto. "Or so she thought."

Pen's efforts at comprehension had thus far resulted in only a monstrous headache. "Wait!" she wailed. "Who tried to poison you? Who was responsible for that runaway coach? If it was Mme. Dore why did she change her mind at the end? And if it was Adam—but why should it be Adam?—I think I shall go mad!"

"Twaddle!" retorted Sparrow bracingly. "Mme. Dore was behind both those early attempts; she wanted to frighten me away. She must have suspected early on that Ninian and I were kin—remember, it was not to Mme. Dore's advantage that Merrie should wed, and in me Ninian would have an ally. Then she learned the rest of the story, from Mephisto, and realized that because of my involvement with Adam the situation would not be resolved so easily."

"But why did Adam wish to kill *you?*" Pen persevered doggedly. "Why did you run away from him all those years ago? You said you didn't know what he had done in France!"

"I knew he'd arranged his brother's death." Perhaps out of consideration for her friend's limited powers of intellect, Sparrow refrained from detail. "I found out quite by accident. It was foolish, perhaps, but I didn't think anyone would believe me. Adam learned of my discovery, and Paddy wished to marry me, so the simplest thing seemed to be to elope."

"*Very* foolish," said Mephisto, without even a trace of sympathy.

Sparrow looked at her hands. "I have felt guilty ever since. That is why I grasped the opportunity to return, though I had little notion of what I should do." Her thin face was sombre. "I thought I would be safe under your protection—erroneously, it seems. Adam recognized me quickly enough, even though I took the precaution of changing my name."

"What you *should* have done was to inform me at the time." Mephisto's disdainful tone indicated strong doubt that she would ever do anything so reasonable. "That you did not nearly caused your premature demise, my girl! I had no idea of why anyone should wish to murder you—other than myself, of course."

Pen shuddered, but Sparrow sat pugnaciously erect. "Fancy that!" she said rudely. "The great Lord Denham admits himself not awake on all suits!"

"Luke almost let the cat out of the bag," intervened Pen, with some hope of making peace, "and told Merrie who you were, but she assumed he was speaking of something else."

"Thank God for that!" said Mephisto, fervently.

Wiggins appeared in the doorway, his squint even more pronounced than usual. His audience watched with fascination as he opened and closed his mouth wordlessly several times, shrugged in defeat, and stepped aside. With a rustle of crimson taffeta, Delilah swept into the room. She noted the varying degrees of astonishment, and beamed.

"I cannot stay but a moment!" she announced, though an invitation to do otherwise was noticeably absent. "Mephisto, what have you done to Lady Ottolie? She is saying the most remarkable things about you!" Sir Jason received an arch look, which prompted his wife to clench her jaw, and Sparrow a warm smile. "So you have emerged with skin intact? I am glad of it! I did not think you would."

"Now that the amenities have been observed," Lord Denham accepted the presence of a fallen woman in his drawing-room with remarkable tranquillity, "what have you come to report?"

An odd choice of words, thought Pen, who had noted that Jason greeted Delilah's arrival with faint amusement and even less interest. "The bird," Delilah replied cheerfully, "has flown. Back into the sewer from which he came, I would suppose. He will cause no more trouble, now that his master's dead."

"Who?" asked Sparrow. Pen puzzled mightily over the easy familiarity between these two.

"No one of importance, now. A shabby seedy little man." Delilah looked at Mephisto. "I assume that this concludes your need of my services? Believe me, I have other more pleasurable ways in which to pass my time!"

Lord Denham rose. "Your help has been invaluable. I am in your debt."

"Gratitude!" Delilah curled her lip. "I would prefer the deed to my house." A document changed hands. She clutched

208

it triumphantly. "Farewell, little Sparrow, and this time I think for good! Mephisto has used you grievously. I hope you too intend to be adequately repaid." With this practical advice, she drifted out of the room.

"I hate to repeat myself," Pen ventured, with wrinkled brow, "but—"

"You don't understand," Jason concluded. "This part, I think, I can explain." Pen bit back a sharp comment and waited. "When your brother brought Lady Sara—excuse me, Daphne—to London, he sent her to Delilah to be refurbished." His eye lit, appreciatively, on the brown-gold hair. "Mephisto labored under the delusion that Daphne was in straitened circumstances."

"Reprehensible of me," said Sparrow, with no evident remorse, "but I could not resist."

"I retained a certain interest in you," Jason continued, "and when I observed you meeting with Delilah in Hyde Park, I grew even more curious." He smiled down at his wife. "Pen was telling no secrets, and I could fathom no reasonable connection between Lady Sara Cainneach and a notorious Paphian."

"She tried to warn me." Sparrow neatly crossed her ankles, and looked very, very prim. "Adam's man was asking pointed questions. Our acquaintance was no secret, it seems. The rendezvous I set out to keep last night was with Delilah, and the note I received was signed with her name."

"Delilah kept an eye on you, and when she chanced to see Tayce at Vauxhall, in conference with Adam's henchman, she scented mischief and came to me." Mephisto regarded Sparrow. "Her efforts in your behalf were not entirely altruistic. She received no small recompense for the information she provided."

"In short," concluded Sir Jason, who still stood behind Pen's chair, "Delilah quite effectively followed Daphne every time she set foot out of Denham House, It interfered grievously with her private life, I understand! And that is how Luke came to see Delilah in the crowd when Daphne encountered the runaway coach."

"He did?" asked Pen, somewhat querulously.

"You understand," observed Lord Denham, pale eyes hooded, "a great deal. I did not think Delilah quite so great a blabbermouth."

209

"Ah," replied Sir Jason, at his most suave. "You forget my legendary persuasiveness."

The others might find this an amusing sally, but Pen could not agree. She clenched her hands so tightly that one glove split its seam. "My love," said her husband, "you are a peagoose." She looked up at him, startled. "My interest in Delilah was prompted solely by my concern for you. I did not care to see you involved in Mephisto's damnable stratagems, and I knew Mephisto had been approached by certain officials regarding Mme. Dore."

Pen made what was for her a brilliant deduction. "So *that's* why Christian made such efforts regarding Miss Sherrington! So that he might have Mme. Dore under his roof and his eye!" She wrinkled her nose. "And to think I once believed he meant to marry the girl himself."

"The devil!" For once, Mephisto exhibited emotion. "I can think of no worse fate."

But Lady Penelope was too bemused to lament his lack of charity. She blinked rapidly at her husband. "Oh, Jason!"

"Precisely, my love!" Sir Jason seemed to consider it a great privilege to have his hand clasped and wept upon.

"I think," murmured Lord Denham, offering Sparrow his arm, "that we are about to witness a reconciliation scene." Sparrow smiled. "I furthermore think it is a treat which I may happily forego."

"Wait!" cried Pen. "Why should *Christian* be asked to apprehend a spy?"

Sir Jason and Lord Denham exchanged a glance that, if not precisely congenial, contained a large amount of masculine complicity. "My love," said Jason plaintively, "*must* we discuss your brother's convoluted affairs at this particular time? I would much rather discuss the impending addition to our own nursery."

Pen froze in the act of raising the handkerchief to her eyes. "You *knew?*"

"My darling nitwit," retorted Sir Jason, in doting tones, "of course I knew. Not only has Luke been most concerned about you, but I have no reason to doubt the evidence of my own eyes."

"Having had," murmured Pen, with a delightful, if watery, chuckle, "a great deal of experience in such matters!" With marked consideration, Lord Denham closed the door.

"Well!" remarked Sparrow, as Mephisto escorted her down the hallway, "I am glad to see *that* problem solved. Between us, we have caused all sorts of misunderstandings."

"And I am glad to see you accept a share of the responsibility." Lord Denham was cordial. "While we are doling out blame, we must not forget Miss Sherrington."

"Ah, yes." Sparrow's thin face lit with mischief. "Miss Sherrington. I believe I will take Delilah's advice and demand of you full payment for the beastly way you have misused me."

"So you think I have made use of you?" murmured the Duke. "I will admit my intentions were along that line."

The provocation was ignored. "I mean to settle a considerable sum on Ninian," continued Sparrow, "as well as my partial interest in a breeding-stable. He always had a great interest in horseflesh, and overseeing the operation will provide him the responsibility he needs." She chuckled. "Furthermore, Merrie has assured me she would find Ireland greatly to her taste."

"I begin to see," Mephisto displayed considerable acumen, "the thrust of this conversation." Their progress halted as he gripped her arm.

"I thought you might." Sparrow was firm. "In short, dear Mephisto, the price you must pay me—and in return for which I pledge my silence on certain matters which you will not wish made known—is your agreement to Ninian's marriage to Miss Sherrington!"

"I cannot imagine," said Lord Denham, with some warmth, "why you should think so ill of me!" Sparrow looked astonished and his mouth twisted viciously. "*I* am not the obstacle in the path of love's young—and in this case, singularly foolish!—dream."

"Then you agree?" Sparrow's gasp was partially prompted by the pressure of his hand.

"I would pay your price, whatever it was." His eyes were as cold as the depths of winter. "But may I remind you of your brother's betrothal to Miss Allingham?"

Chapter 29

Tuesday 30 April 1811

What atrocious situations and ferocious circumstances—theft and murder and treason—like a chapter out of Newgate Calendar! But life continued on as always in that town of sophisticated passions and revels constantly coming round. On this particularly lovely day, the King had already run a race with a horse (I cannot say which won); the Regent had commissioned a bronze lamp to illustrate the Royal Academy's Great Room; Wellington continued his endeavors in the Peninsula, now unhampered by the machinations of my aunt; and Ninian sat on the edge of my bed.

Lest the reader fear for my well-being, I will admit to a certain degree of duplicity, for I was perfectly able to be up and about. But it did not suit my purpose to appear *quite* that resilient and robust, so instead I lounged upon my pillows, clad in a nightgown and wrapper that were *most* unsuitable for one of my tender years, and played the part of the delicately nurtured English lady to the hilt. Ah, but I was an artfully baited trap! With the bed-hangings partially drawn, Ninian and I might have lolled alone in an Eastern tent—and, indeed, my thought had a marked tendency to stray to harems and sultans and desert sheiks. Ninian bestowed upon me a smile of bewitching tenderness, and I upon him a look of dewy innocence, and at the most inopportune of all moments Mephisto burst in upon us, quite effectively thwarting the most brilliant move of my entire campaign.

"Wretched brat!" he said to me, and drew the gilded chair closer to the bed. "Are you quite determined to cast propriety to the winds?" If I had not known him incapable of good humor, I might have thought he was laughing at me.

"Alas!" I mourned, languidly dropping back onto my pillows. "I am totally misunderstood." Ninian chuckled, but did not move from his extremely compromising place on my bed.

"No, you aggravating child," Mephisto retorted, arranging himself comfortably in the chair, "you are all too well understood." He raised a hand. "Spare me any further whoppers! I have just come from a conference concerning your aunt."

My mellow mood abruptly fled, as did my invalidism. Abandoning my languishing attitude, I sat up straight. Ninian's gaze rested, with interest, on my *décolletage*, and Mephisto's lips twitched. "That," he commented, "is an extremely vulgar gown."

"Yes," I agreed cordially. "It suits me, I believe. But I have no intention of engaging in a brangle with you, Lord Denham. Please tell me what's been decided about my aunt."

Mephisto quirked a sardonic brow. "You do not mean to argue with me? How refreshing!" I fear I scowled at the provoking creature. "As for Mme. Dore, there is a special circle of hell reserved for traitoresses. The English government will be happy to speed her entrance there."

"No!" I shrieked, and thought: Lucifer, guard well your fiery throne! "You gave your word! Is this the damnable honor that I hear so much about?" Poor Ninian was included in my wrath. "You are a *beast*, Lord Denham! And however much it may suit your purpose, I will not let Tayce be hung!"

He looked even more saturnine. "You are determined to make me the villain of this piece! Consider your aunt's crimes."

I was trying my best *not* to consider those very things. "She didn't truly *wish* to kill me," I insisted. "I left her no choice. I perfectly understand that, and in her position would probably have done the same."

"Probably," agreed Mephisto. "It does not excuse either of you. Think, girl! Tayce betrayed everyone in turn. She murdered Adam as well."

"Not murder," I argued. "He would have killed me. And he deserved to die, anyway. He was *canaille*."

"Perhaps." Now both Mephisto and Ninian looked grim. "But what would you call your aunt? We cannot begin to guess how many people she deliberately sent to the guillotine."

"I don't care what she's done." It is true that, on occasion, I can be stubborn as a mule.

"Not that she had your father twisted around her little

213

finger, and betrayed him? Or that she lied to you about his will?"

"No." In truth, this last was the hardest for me to accept, that Tayce had deliberately set me to chasing will-o'-the-wisps when instead I might have been marrying Ninian. I observed Mephisto with acute dislike. "You knew she lied, why didn't you tell me? Or was it too perfect a set-up to spoil, since it kept me under your thumb?"

"Sparrow was right. You *are* a porcupine." Mephisto's pale eyes gleamed. "I do not expect you to believe this, Meredith, but I considered you far safer as it was. I didn't know to what lengths Tayce might go to prevent you from turning your fortune over to a husband."

"You're right!" I snapped. "I *don't* believe you. You've had your own plans all along."

"Gently, poppet." Ninian took my hand.

"Beside," I continued, "by rights Tayce should have had some of that money! Heaven knows my father should have married her, or at least seen her provided for." I frowned. "I have never understood why he did not."

"Probably," said Mephisto, betraying no surprise that I was aware Tayce had once been my father's paramour, "because he was aware of her true nature, despite his protestations of her innocence, and had a healthy respect for his own skin." He surveyed me as if I was a particularly repellant species of worm. "And yours. If your aunt had stood to inherit, I fear neither of you would have lived long." I looked down my nose at my lower lip, and Mephisto made an exasperated noise. "Why do you think your father made me your guardian, if not to provide me an opportunity to expose Tayce?"

"Any number of people," and Ninian squeezed my hand, "were intrigued by your unusual interest in Merrie. We might have guessed that it was not what it seemed."

"You might." My devious guardian took snuff. "I doubt we ever learn what hold Tayce had over Sherrington. Affection alone would not have bought his silence."

Briefly, I reviewed my knowledge of secret vice—lore obtained, of course, from my informative aunt—but could not guess which degenerate practice poor Papa had enjoyed. "I don't care," I said once again. "Tayce must not hang. I will

214

pledge my entire fortune to see that she does not, if you will not help me."

"This loyalty of yours is a curst nuisance!" said Mephisto. "Though it is like you to possess but one virtue, and then to overdo that." He regarded Ninian.

"Ninian has no need of my fortune!" It was not difficult to interpret that look. "He has just amassed a couple of his own. Beside," and the joy went further out of the morning, "he is betrothed to Miss Allingham."

"You will at last concede," persisted Mephisto, "that Mme. Dore cannot go free. A pledge of good faith is useless in this case; she would immediately resume her career."

I started to protest, then recalled that dreadful moment when Tayce's rapier had nearly skewered me, and conceded. "She must have every comfort. She must not be mistreated in any way." I had already forgive her, of course, as she must have known I would.

"There will be a great deal of talk, a certain amount of scandal." As if there had not already been! Mephisto was certainly one for harping on unpleasantness. "The newspapers have loaded their pages with fact and rumor and are speculating about certain events during the nonsense of 1792. We can play that matter down, but to keep it entirely secret is impossible. Your name cannot help but be involved."

"My name!" Only Ninian's restraining hand kept me from flying at the brute. "What can my name signify in comparison with my aunt's well-being? I care not if my reputation is torn to shreds."

"So I have concluded," said Mephisto drily, "from your past behavior. Perhaps we should strike a bargain: Your aunt's life in return for your promise to conduct yourself with propriety." I stared, then swore, and he laughed. "Silly child! Your aunt is perfectly safe. Contrary to your opinion, I do not break my word."

Nor did he. Even Newgate Prison can be rendered comfortable, when one has sufficient money to buy private quarters and decent food. Perhaps it will come as little surprise that Tayce quickly became the focus of what passed in Newgate as "Society," the delight of murderers and paupers and prostitutes. She told me once that the prison reminded her of Louis XVI's court, but in Newgate she was queen. Only once did she step outside those grim walls, on the occasion of my eldest daughter's marriage to the Honorable Jeremiah Palmerston—the children considered it no small privilege to claim a great-aunt who resided in prison!—and professed herself happy enough to return.

Tayce died at seventy-eight years of age, the recognized authority on the French Revolution. Her history became an immediate success, and has gone through so many printings that I have quite lost count. Ah, the incomparable Mme. Dore! Forever she remains fixed in my memory, a gaunt and indomitable figure, hair wildly askew, brandishing her ebony cane. I learned, upon her death, that Tayce had made me her heir.

But at this particular moment, on that long-past April day, I came close to sharing Tayce's cell—for the crime of murdering Mephisto. Ninian intervened. "You are suffering from a misapprehension, poppet, regarding Miss Allingham." I eyed him warily, being in no mood to trust any gentleman. He smiled. "The engagement is at an end."

"I thought you might contrive that," murmured Mephisto, "having in common with your sister a fair amount of ingenuity. Do you mind telling me how?"

The smile broadened into an outright grin. "Miss Allingham boasted to me about certain of her father's activities, and investigation bore her stories out. Allingham was not pleased to have the tables turned, but since he would have been even less pleased to have any information laid against him for smuggling, Miss Allingham has been persuaded to cry off."

"Ninian!" I was breathless with admiration. "How brilliant of you!"

"Reprehensible chit!" Mephisto frowned at me. I wrenched my gaze away from Ninian's handsome face to glower in turn at him.

"I," I announced, "am going to marry Ninian, no matter what you say."

"Oh?" inquired Lord Denham politely. "Has he asked you?" I stared horrified at Ninian, for of course he never had.

Wiggins, staggering under the weight of a heavily-laden tray, interrupted us. My opinion of this sinister-looking individual had changed; since my dire experiences, he had come to look upon me as a heroine. (So, in point of fact, had I.) But for Mephisto's valet to play maidservant to me was taking things a bit far.

Mephisto apparently agreed. "Wiggins!" His face was as dark as a thundercloud. "What the deuce does this mean?"

Wiggins set down the tray with hands that trembled noticeably. "The household is at sixes and sevens, my lord," he said, gaze prudently directed heavenward.

"Do you mind," inquired Mephisto ominously, "telling me why?"

"Well, my lord, I do." Wiggins was positively ashen. Mephisto cursed and he gulped. "It's Lady Sara, sir."

"What about Lady Sara?" For a man reputed to seldom lose his temper, Lord Denham—in my experience—succumbed rather frequently to rage.

Wiggins backed cautiously towards the door. "This morning, while you were at Whitehall—" Words seemed to fail him. I wondered why Ninian tried so hard to restrain merriment. Wiggins clutched the doorhandle. "Well, sir, she's gone."

"What!" roared Mephisto, with such force that the tea-cups rattled. "Where?"

"Back to Ireland, my lord." I thought Wiggins might swoon. "She and her maid and Mrs. Selkirk."

"Maeve?" I gasped, but my inquiry went unnoticed. Mephisto slammed down his fist with such fury that the tea-tray was upended on my bed. I leaped aside with an alacrity unprecedented in an invalid, and Wiggins wisely fled. Mephisto turned on Ninian, who was quite pink with emotion. "What do *you* know of this, young man?"

"Nothing, I swear," gasped Ninian, picking pieces of china off my quilt. "Perhaps she felt she had completed her mission here."

"And perhaps," retorted Mephisto sharply, "she is playing the concave suit." Though his expression was still severe, I thought him oddly exhilarated by the event. He turned those cold eyes on me. "You are very eager to give up your freedom."

"No less eager," interrupted Ninian, before I could protest, "than was once another girl." His expression was slightly malicious. "Do you suggest, Lord Denham, that we should repeat your mistakes?"

Perhaps it was advancing age that so exacerbated my guardian's temper, but it was certain he looked ready to explode. "There's one thing I don't understand," I said;

ignoring their foolishness. "If Adam didn't know where Sparrow was, who was responsible for her husband's death?"

"Responsible?" queried Mephisto. "I suspect, Meredith, that you have been listening at keyholes again."

"Unjust!" I cried, neatly skirting the issue. "It was Luke who told us of the duel, and that Paddy's opponent wore some type of armor. A neat way of committing murder, it would seem."

"Or of protecting oneself." Mephisto folded his arms and regarded me severely. "You have entirely too lively an imagination, Miss Sherrington! McDougal was a master of his profession, but he'd lived too long on his wits. He grew careless, and was caught, and died in a duel. There's nothing more."

"Then why," I demanded, silently cursing Luke, "did Sparrow blame herself for his death?"

"Because," and his voice was ice cracking, "the gaming-house was her idea."

"Oh." How disappointing! I plucked at the coverlet. "Now I *must* be married. I cannot reside in Denham House unchaperoned."

Mephisto reached into a pocket and I thought for a horrified moment that he meant to abruptly terminate his guardianship via a bullet in my breast. Instead, he dropped a document on the bed. "A special license," he explained kindly. "Conjecture cannot be avoided, but you will be safely on your honeymoon." He looked at Ninian who, hands full of china, appeared to be deriving an inordinate enjoyment from the exchange. "I rather think, after this vile contretemps, that a change of climate might also prove of benefit to me."

I cannot claim to have greeted this development with any great aplomb, being torn between sheer ecstacy and a nasty suspicion that I had come close to making a rare mull of it. Even when Mephisto's pale eyes turned to me, I uttered not a word. "What can I be thinking of?" Ruefully, he shook his head. "To allow you to marry into my family! I fear I have just deprived myself of a peaceful old age."

"Never fear, Lord Denham!" My power of speech returned as abruptly as it had fled. "Considering your capacity for making enemies, it is, in any event, doubtful that you will be allowed to live so long." With what I swear was a genuine smile, and a shocking disregard for the proprieties, he left us alone.

But Ninian did not take immediate advantage of this heaven-sent opportunity. Instead, he fell back on my pillows, convulsed with mirth. "Oh, poppet!" He reached out for me. "If only you could have seen your face!"

I eluded him, being no giddy fool. "You should not be here," I said severely. "It would be most improper even if we were betrothed, and we are not."

"What's this?" Ninian propped himself up on one elbow. "Did you not tell me many years ago that you meant to marry me?"

I winced at this reminder of my brazenness. "Circumstances have changed." I pleated the silk—tea-stained—coverlet. "Now you have a fortune of your own. Not so large as mine, granted, but more than sufficient for your needs."

"I do," Ninian agreed pleasantly, toying in a most forward manner with the lace of my robe. "What has that to do with it?"

I scowled. "Ninnyhammer!" Nobility of action is not natural to me. "Now you can marry whomever you please."

"But that is just what I mean to do." He took a firmer grip on the lace, and me with it. "It wasn't your fortune that I coveted, poppet, but I knew perfectly well that you wouldn't believe I never meant to touch a penny of it."

"You're *not* a fortune-hunter?" My eyes must have threatened to pop right out of my head.

"Not a bit of it!" Ninian's voice was muffled in my neck. "You are an atrocious judge of character, my love."

But another thought occurred to me. With reluctance, I pushed him away. "I mean to have some answers, my lad! When Mephisto said I might marry you, you weren't the least surprised!"

"That's true." He was busy unpinning my hair.

"Family!" I fairly shrieked and sat bolt upright, nearly tumbling my beloved right off the bed. "Dear God, if Sparrow is distantly related to Mephisto, so must you be!" He made no answer, having succumbed once more to mirth. "Why didn't you *tell* me?"

"Because, sweet Merrie," and Ninian drew me firmly down beside him, "you were having so much fun." It was a most comfortable position, despite such inconveniences as broken

china, tea-stained sheets, tangled bedclothes and my voluminous nightware. What followed then—and it was surely as
delightful as Papa's secret sins!—is none of the reader's
business.

"But, Ninian!" I cried, springing upright once again, at a
most ill-considered moment, and banging my elbow against
his chin. "Who was Maeve?"

Epilogue

He found her leaning against the fence of a spacious schooling field, nibbling on a piece of straw. When he called her name, she turned and blinked at him, then smiled. "You have seen Maeve, I suppose, and Bridey. I wished them both to blazes for following me to London, but they are in the habit of protecting me."

Yes, he had seen them both, and the interview rankled. Lady Maeve Selkirk was very much the chatelaine of Castle Cainneach, that museum of marble and precious porphry, rose and green and violet quartz. Freckle-faced Bridey had been more sympathetic, perhaps due to an over-indulgence in poteen from the glens, speeding him on his way to the stables with a jaunty *Slainte mhor!* "They underestimate you, then."

She cast him a sideways glance, but brushed the comment aside. "I thought I'd conjured you up with my thoughts. What do you think of Maeve's home? Paddy may have been the black sheep of the family, but we were always welcome at the castle." The merciless sunlight laid bare the grey threads in his dark hair and struck splinters from those pale cold eyes. "After Dublin, Bridey and I came here."

Gently, he took her arm. "You were thinking of me?"

She was still much too thin, and her hair was beginning to again show white. He raised long fingers to lift it from her brow. "I was remembering," she said. "What a dreadful pest I must have been! Forever at your heels and in your way."

"Did I ever say so?" His face was softer, its harsh outlines blurred, like ice that has begun to thaw.

"You did not need to." She lifted her head, but only his own small image looked back at him out of her bruised eyes. "Yet it was strange of you to be so patient with a child."

221

"Sparrow." He looked searchingly down into her face. "I am considerably older than you. It was only natural that your affections should become engaged by a younger man."

"Is that what you expected?" She was startled. "How surprised you must have been, then, to hear of my betrothal to Adam." Her smile was rueful. "I thought *that* would make you take notice, but of course it did not. What a little fool I was."

Lord Denham's expression was once again remote. "You did not love him?"

"Love Adam?" Sparrow's laughter was wild. "My God, Mephisto! Of course not. But it was no small triumph, or so I thought. I always meant to break it off before the wedding day. And then," it was almost a gasp, "I found out about his brother. Oh, pray, let me go!"

The Duke, not being noted for amiability, did nothing of the sort. "Why," he demanded, "did you not come to me then? God knows I would have believed you, having reason to suspect Adam of that very thing!"

"And how," demanded Sparrow, with marked uncordiality, "was I to know that? You had made it plain that you no longer had time for me!" Lord Denham winced, perhaps because she stamped her little foot right down on his toe. "What a brute you are, Mephisto! At least you must be satisfied that I have at last atoned for my sins, and nearly with my life."

He released her as abruptly as if she were a hot brick. "Atone?" he repeated, with an odd inflection. "You thought that?"

"What else?" Her grey eyes were not empty now, but filled with angry tears. "It is quite like you to repay me in that manner for running away! Isn't that why you're here now? Because I failed to ask your permission to leave?"

Mephisto, confronted with this piece of hardly-flattering logic, might have been expected to erupt with rage. Instead he burst into laughter and collapsed against the fence. "*What,*" demanded Sparrow, ablaze with temper, "do you find so humorous?"

"You!" The Duke, in this ignoble posture, looked at least a decade younger and infinitely more approachable. "Apropos of ignoble motives, what was yours for humoring me?"

222

"There were several," she replied, turning away. "I wished to see Ninian again."

"What else?" Lord Denham had achieved a degree of composure. "Lady Selkirk believes you suffer guilt over Adam's death."

"And well I should." Her back was still to him, and her fists clenched. "Tayce may have killed him, but I must hold myself responsible."

"I see I must further enlighten you," Mephisto remarked wryly, "concerning Mme. Dore. She'd have disposed of Adam in any event. He was a threat to her." He paused and searched for words. "Sparrow, my intentions in bringing you back to London had nothing to do with Adam, and damned little to do with my abominable ward."

She spun around, arms crossed, and eyed him thoughtfully. "You have agreed to her marriage with Ninian?"

"I have, and I was present at the ceremony. Precious glad I am to be rid of the brat!" He had recovered sufficiently to move away from the fence. "Wouldn't you care to know precisely why I *did* bring you to London?"

"Well, yes." She found his cravat of remarkable interest. "I rather think I would."

"Because," and he grasped her shoulders, "I had only then discovered your whereabouts, and I wished to see for myself how things were with you." His eyes remained pale, but they were far from cold. "It was not long after our reacquaintance that I determined to ask you a certain question, one that I would have asked you long ago had not I feared to take advantage of your youth and inexperience. And I warn you that I shall not accept a negative reply for we have already wasted too many years."

"You would ask that question of a woman from a gaming-house?" She spoke so softly that he barely caught the words. "Or perhaps you have not considered *that*."

"Sparrow." The fire that sparked from his black opal ring was no less than the warmth in his voice. "I would make you my Duchess even if, like your faithful Bridey, you were a creature from the streets."

"Ah." But the flush that stained her cheeks did not betoken indifference. "You mean to browbeat me."

"Precisely." There was a faint, and most unusual, anxiety on his forbidding features. "At least once a day."

His uncertainty might have broken Sparrow's heart, had she not already given that article away. "Upon due consideration," she murmured breathlessly, "I rather think I should also like that, my lord!"

He swept her into his arms and laughed again, exultantly. "You must explain that to your cousin-in-law. She seems convinced that I will drive you distracted with my bullying ways."

"Maeve is a gentle soul." Sparrow caressed his cheek, and her eyes were brilliant and gay. "She will never understand that I like almost nothing better than to quarrel with you."

"Then you shall, my darling." Lord Denham's arms tightened around her frail body. "But I hope you may also be persuaded to occasionally indulge in somewhat less violent pursuits."

A lady of action, Sparrow wound slender fingers through Mephisto's thick hair and tugged until his startled face was on level with her own. "Devil!" she whispered, against his lips. "On *that* wager, I'll lay you *most* favorable odds!"